THE KIRKLAND ACRES

Also by Nigel Colborn

Non Fiction

The Classic Horticulturist
This Gardening Business
Leisurely Gardening
Exposed Gardens
The Container Garden
Family Piles
The Good Old-fashioned Gardener
Short Cuts to Great Gardens

The
Kirkland
Acres

NIGEL COLBORN

ORION

The right of Nigel Colborn to be identified
as the author of this work has been
asserted by him in accordance with the
Copyright, Designs and Patents Act 1988.

First published in Great Britain in 1994 by
Orion
An imprint of Orion Books Ltd
Orion House, 5 Upper St Martin's Lane,
London WC2H 9EA

A CIP catalogue record for this book
is available from the British Library

ISBN 1 85797 244 9

Printed and bound in Great Britain by
Butler & Tanner Ltd, Frome and London

For Juliet Burton

PART ONE

Spring

Chapter One

Somewhere between London and rescue, on an up-ended concrete block, a boy sat and shivered in the rain. Although he would have passed for twenty, he had yet to celebrate his eighteenth birthday. Fatigue and rough travel had scored dark lines under each of his blue-grey eyes and hollowed his cheeks, but had done nothing to quench his natural good looks. He had fair colouring and regular features; his body was slight, unmasculine, and his mien unaggressive. Round his neck, on a leather thong, hung a gold signet ring. It was too big to wear on his hand but he had hooked his right index finger through it now, resting the weight of his arm on the thong like a sling. His faded jeans and worn trainers were saturated and the cheap nylon anorak, though it kept out some of the rain, failed to keep him warm. He was hungry but had no money in his pockets.

The boy had walked many miles, gesturing with the thumbs-up sign of the hitch hiker, but without persuading many drivers to stop. There had been a baker's van which took him a couple of miles, and a loquacious plumber on an errand to fetch a central-heating pump from somewhere near Hatfield, but no useful long-haul rides, so he had walked until he felt he could hardly take another step. Then, near this roundabout he had spotted the building block, obviously dropped from a lorry cornering too fast. He had stopped and sat down for a rest, hunching his body to keep out the cold while the rain closed in to isolate him from the busy traffic a few yards away.

After an interval – minutes, hours, he didn't know or care –

a hiss of air brakes woke him from a cold-induced doze. A lorry had stopped. He tried to get up but he was so stiff he could barely move. The lorry revved and was about to pull away but with a surge of effort, the boy managed to stagger to his feet and shout. The driver reached across and opened the door, letting out a waft of heated air, and beckoned. The boy had just enough strength left to climb the difficult step over the wheel arch into the warm, sweat-smelling cab.

Seventy-seven miles northeast, where the flat lands of Lincolnshire pucker and fold into the gently rolling limestone hills of middle England, Betty Rose was walking from Cartwright Farm to Wyckhamby Manor and trying not to worry. The first day of spring usually turned out to be a sick joke but this one was the nastiest yet! Pity the poor new lambs, she thought. All round the village, the landscape was hidden by curtains of rain cold enough to contain a flake or two of snow, swirling on a sharp northwesterly breeze. Streams of muddy water with crisscrossed ripples ran down the main road towards the River Venn, which was brown and swollen beyond normal, even for a wet year. In the pastures, newly turned-out cattle huddled under leafless trees, heads inward, steaming backs arched with discomfort and, on the arable land, rain was pounding some of the young seedlings right out of the ground.

  In spite of being rugged up in hooded oilskin jacket and waterproof trousers which swished and rustled irritatingly with every step, the cold and wet were beginning to chill Betty to the core. When her foot slipped on the muddy path, making her stumble, a trickle of icy water dribbled down the back of her neck and she shuddered. On top of everything else the weather really was the last straw. First there'd been that cold spell at early lambing time, and now this endless March rain which delayed essential farmwork. The optimum date for sowing cereals had already passed and now, every day lost, with the seed corn still waiting in its sacks in the barn, meant lower yields, lower income and increased doubt about her family's future at Cartwright Farm. To plant barley you need bright, breezy weather to dry the soil so that the seed drill can run. What a change from last year's equinox, she thought, when early gales had subsided to gentle breezes with clean skies, and bright yellow celandines had bloomed on the roadsides.

Daylight was beginning to fail as she completed the last 200 yards of her walk. As the river had risen so threateningly, she left the footpath along its banks and crossed the meadow, skirting the spinney in front of the Manor House. An overhanging branch snagged her hood, pulling it half off and, as she reached up to free herself, she staggered a little and almost fell. The incident was trifling but nearly made her cry. With numb fingers she clutched at the hood to straighten it and then stood still. She needed a moment in which to compose herself, to put on a cheerful, positive face before reporting to the Manor. She watched rainwater running down the bare twigs until they could hold no more and the drops fell. Among the winter-browned grasses and fallen leaf litter of the woodland margin, she spotted a tiny, pale disc standing out in the dying light: a primrose – the first of the year – emerging ahead of its foliage and braving the foul weather. At the sight of the flower her spirits rose a little. Now there's pluck, she thought, bending to the flower and taking off a wet glove to stroke the frail petals with the back of her forefinger. Then she said, aloud and almost with conviction, 'We will survive. I *know* we will.'

The truck driver looked at the boy again. 'Where did you say?'

'Wyckhamby.' The heat of the cab had made him drowsy. His jeans were still steaming but his shirt was almost dry and the sodden anorak was spread out in the little cabin where the driver slept, behind the seats.

'Never 'eard of it. Why there, anyway?'

'See someone.'

'What for – a job?' The boy stared ahead without answering. 'Only you don't strike me as a country boy.' Getting no response the driver lost interest, then, a mile or so later, 'You sure you know where it is exactly?'

'On the B4315.' The road number was remembered without effort, but the voice was still sleepy. 'I seen it on a map.'

'There's a road map there.' The driver gestured to a heap of documents on the floor of the cab. 'Have a look.'

'I know where. You turn off at Kendale – then it's about five miles.'

'You mean *you* get out at Kendale. I'm going on to Lincoln. Eventually.'

They cruised on, rain and spray blotting out the landscape. The regular movements of the windscreen wipers and hot air blowing through the heater vents made the boy's eyelids droop. Out of politeness, he fought sleep but couldn't think of anything to say. After another mile or two, the driver said, 'That'll be a quiet road, out of Kendale. I can't see you getting much joy with a lift.'

'I'll be OK.'

With her head held a little higher, Betty approached the house. The original manor had been destroyed by fire in 1783 and rebuilt with gracious curved walls, large windows to east and west and a fine central portico. The mansard roof, clad with heavy Cornish slates, had arched windows set into it at regular intervals, but the feature Betty loved most about the building was its colour. Instead of the red brick more usual for the period and district, the walls of Wyckhamby Manor were built with bricks the colour of honey.

She let herself into the back entrance and went straight to the bootroom to take off her wet clothes and hang them near the boiler – a monster which devoured logs the size of tree trunks, drove the central-heating system of the large household and provided unlimited hot water. In the event of a timber shortage – seldom a problem on the Wyckhamby estate, where the woodland ran to hundreds of acres – it could be appeased with kerosene which it drank by the gallon, changing the smell in the boiler room from woodsy to airport.

The warmth was almost unbearable after her chilly walk, making Betty's fingers and toes ache, and when she looked into the mirror to adjust her hair – mouse, people would say of anyone else but on Betty it was light brown – she was surprised at how crimson her cheeks had gone. The grey eyes looked directly into their reflection. 'Thirty-nine next birthday and not enough sense to come in out of the rain,' the image told her without losing eye contact. She straightened her blouse, an expensive number in cream silk from 'Second Hand Roz' in Kendale High Street and only slightly worn, adjusted the blue and beige foulard round her neck and fished in her bag for an apron. She was about to leave when she heard brisk footsteps approaching and in a moment Ashley Kirkland, owner of Wyckhamby Manor, Wyckhamby Farms and a lot more besides, erupted into the bootroom. He, too, was ruddy from exposure to the weather.

'Betty – what are you doing here?' He began to remove his outdoor clothes, shaking the water off them and stamping his booted feet. 'I say, I do like your hair short. It really suits you.' He paused, staring at her, smiling slightly, and she felt her cheeks beginning to burn again.

'I'm helping out with the dinner party, Mr Kirkland.' At forty-two, Ashley had boyish vigour, a fresh face with a fair complexion, dark hair and hazel eyes which twinkled and had crinkled corners. His beauty – virile enough but beauty all the same – was the kind that turned heads, of either sex, and was matched by a natural grace and charm. 'Comely' was the word that usually sprang to Betty's mind when she saw him, but behind that comeliness was something else, something almost fey. Whatever it was, she was sure there was more to Ashley Kirkland than met the eye – not that what met the eye wasn't considerable.

'Helping? How?'

'Oh, you know, cooking and waiting and so on.'

'What on earth for?'

'Mrs Kirkland asked me to come and give Annabel a hand.' She put on her apron, tying it deftly behind her before he had a chance to help. He held the door open for her. 'I'm rather late, I'm afraid. Annabel will be waiting.'

'Tut tut. Miss Annabel expects! Don't let her treat you like a servant, Betty.' He watched her walk along the corridor to the kitchen.

'Hooray! Guards of Honour,' whooped Sally two hours later. 'My absolute favourite. Annabel, you're a genius.'

'The butcher's the genius, Mrs Doncaster. I just roasted it.' Ashley's daughter carved the lamb into individual cutlets, adding a paper frill to each and a spoonful of thyme stuffing, and distributed vegetables, mint sauce and redcurrant jelly. It was a routine Kirkland dinner party and Annabel, as usual, had come up from London to help out. Elaine Kirkland sat at one end of the table, unable to see Ashley at the other because of the candelabras. On her right, Dr Leonard Bates was trying not to slip into the familiar groove of his favourite topics: wine and food. His fondness for the epicurean had endowed him with an ample paunch, a nose florid with erupted blood vessels and, on those rare occasions of physical exertion, shortness of breath. His bedside manner, a combination of brusqueness and sympathy, was adored by his patients, many of whom found such an unhealthy example comforting when they failed in their own attempts to diet and exercise. At his side, the Kirklands' son Andrew made no attempt to listen to him but gazed instead across the table at the skinny girl he'd brought home – all eyeliner and wispy hair.

Next to Ashley sat Sally Doncaster. What to make of her, Elaine wondered. It was hard to tell after only three weeks, but everyone knew nasty things had been done to the Old Rectory before they moved in. Her voice was louder than anyone else's and she seemed – no, surely not! – to be having the upper hand with Ashley. She certainly had the upper hand with her husband Jules, a near-perfect example of the weedy accountant, with specs, grey worsted and probably wearing St Michael underpants, Elaine decided. Within days of moving in, Sally had made sure everyone knew her income was two and a half times Jules's, and that it was she who'd bought the Rectory, not 'they' and certainly not 'he'.

'Andrew, the wine.' Elaine had noticed Maggie Bates drain her glass yet again. Her son pulled himself out of his trance and went to the William IV sideboard, where three bottles of Gevrey Chambertin stood, uncorked. Nearby was a heavy crystal decanter of vintage port, a whole stilton – its sides wrapped in a white linen napkin – and a fruit bowl piled with huge black grapes. He poured for Maggie and then moved round the table topping up the other glasses.

Leonard smiled up at him. 'This really is excellent. May I see the label?' Andrew twisted the bottle. 'Good lord, 1969! An elegant wine – your father's a generous host!' Leonard lifted the glass and buried his nose in the wine's fragrance. He watched the light from the candles sparkling in the cut crystal and thought, What a pity it's so thick. Plain glass makes it so much easier to see the true colour of the wine . . .

'Elaine, your flowers are divine.' Sally was actually shouting now from the bottom of the table. 'Such *huge* snowdrops.' She pulled one out of the vase and twirled the stem between finger and thumb. 'Ours are finished at the Rectory. And those darling little iris things.' She shook her head, making the thick honey-blonde hair swirl, and did a little pout with vermilion lips. 'Ours are gone. Gone, gone!'

'Not snowdrops, snowflakes,' Maggie, sitting opposite, informed her. 'Leucojum. They're quite different really.'

Sally ignored her and continued stridently: 'You really must come and tell us what to do with the Rectory garden. I'm so busy and Jules hasn't a clue.'

Ashley intervened, 'You should ask Maggie, really. She's the expert.'

'Oh?' Sally barely glanced across at Maggie. 'I mean, when should we start, darling?'

'Spring, I should think.' Elaine tried to think of a way to shut her up. 'Darling' was a touch familiar, she thought, for someone she hardly knew.

'Well, it's spring today, darling. Twenty-first of March.'

By now the rest of the diners had stopped talking to each other and an embarrassing tension was developing. Elaine peered round the candelabras to catch Ashley's eye but he was already at the point of intervening.

'You really should talk to Maggie,' he repeated, his voice quiet but authoritative, one hand resting for the briefest instant on her forearm. 'She's designed lots of good gardens. Maggie, do tell!' Then to Sally again, 'Maggie worked with Lanning Roper, and Percy Cane. She really is very knowledgeable.'

'I'm sure, but I love Elaine's sense of style. I mean, those gorgeous red curtains in her drawing room – so *un*-gloomy!'

The Thai silk dress, trendy hairdo and huge chunks of jewelry on Sally's ears, round her neck and on most of her fingers made Maggie feel frumpy. She glanced at her own hands, calloused and grimy even after vigorous scrubbing. She'd been planting shrubs all morning, trying to get them in before the rain turned the soil into mud. This, she thought, eyeing Sally covertly, is not a worthwhile addition to the village. Not worthwhile at all. She consoled herself with another swig of Chambertin and waited for Ashley to speak to her again. She knew he would because he was so considerate – a proper gentleman, one would have said, except that the term seemed almost derisory in the 1980s.

'Maggie, how should I treat my lawns now?' His smile was as comforting as sunshine.

'Oh Ashley, you don't really want to know. Why don't you tell me about the farm?'

'Nothing to tell, really.'

'Three thousand acres, the wettest spring on record and nothing to tell?'

'We'll manage, in spite of the weather. We always do. It's the small farmers who suffer – economies of scale and all that. But you'd be bored stiff if I talked farming.'

'I wouldn't, honestly. Tell me about your sugar beet.' She loved the way his hair grew, curling behind his ears and then ending in a point at the nape.

'Absolutely not. But I'll tell you what *is* intersting. I'm going to see that new gallery at the Tate next week, where they keep all the Turners.'

'Oh, how wonderful! I adore Turner – especially the late stuff. All misty, and those incredible sunsets!' and, having found a common interest, the pair chatted while Sally looked on, became bored and turned her attention to Andrew.

'What part of the farm do you look after, Andrew? Or are you still at university?'

'I was at Cirencester but . . . .' His Adam's apple bobbed at her frank gaze. 'I packed it in.' He shrugged and glanced over her shoulder to avoid eye contact. 'So boring!'

'Thank God! That should keep them quiet for a bit.' Annabel Kirkland, back from delivering the main course to the diners, sat on one of the kitchen chairs and took off her left shoe. 'God, but my foot hurts! Betty, be a love and fetch a ciggy for me. They're in the drawing room.'

'D'you think you should? Smoke in here, I mean?'

'Who's to know? They'll all be chugging away in there, yah? They wouldn't taste the difference between *crème brûlée* and Polyfilla anyway. Philistine pillocks.'

'Annabel, really! You shouldn't talk about your parents' guests like that. It isn't nice.'

'Isn't nice!' She imitated the older woman's tone. 'Look what happens to nice people. Look at you, Betty, how they take advantage of you.'

'They?'

'The village, everyone.' Annabel ran through a range of village voices: 'Betty, could you be an angel and do the church flowers? Betty, would you do the school run again today? Betty, I've got such a cold, might you be sweet enough to do my share of the village hall clean-up? You ought to be tougher – you'll wear yourself out.' She stretched her legs, feeling the full weight of twenty-one years' experience of Life, and waggled her toes. 'Be a sport and fetch me a fag, Betty. My foot is agony.'

Betty laughed and went to the door of the kitchen. 'Sitting room, you said?'

'No, silly, drawing room. Not the one on the left – all reds and whites with that hideous statue thing of Father's in the corner. The wishy-washy blues – that's the drawing room.'

Betty had a chance to admire the hall for a few moments. She almost managed to suppress a surge of envy as she looked at a large painting hanging above a Sheraton table. Nineteenth century, must be a Sidney Cooper, she thought, scanning the bosky landscape with its angry sky and shaggy sheep. 'Arcady it may be,' she muttered to herself, 'but it certainly isn't like real life.'

She opened the drawing-room door. All the lamps were on and the fire was burning slowly – smoking slightly, she thought. A log had slipped forward and was puffing tiny breaths of woodsmoke into the air. This room, decorated in cool pastel colours, had a twin on the opposite side of the oval hall, where Elaine had selected warm hues with red curtains and carpet. Opulence was all around: two large chesterfields, both with loose covers bearing the same floral pattern but on different background colours – one pale ultramarine, the other pearl – a group of wing chairs, a wine cooler filled with pots of growing orchids and at one end, a harpsichord. The walls were furnished with a mix of landscapes in oils or watercolour, and every surface held at least one piece of porcelain or silver. Upon the mantelshelf stood a huge clock with Meissen figures and porcelain flowers: forget-me-nots, tiny roses and gillyflowers. Betty located a cigarette box and as she was trying to unfasten it, the door opened and Ashley Kirkland came in. She started, guiltily, as if her few moments' enjoyment of the Kirklands' objets d'art had amounted to attempted theft. She wondered what he thought she was doing in there by herself.

'Ah, Betty again.' His smile was amiable, not patronising at all, but he seemed a little surprised to find her there. She couldn't think of anything to say and felt an embarrassing silence developing. He did too, and broke the ice. 'It *was* good of you to come and help but really, you should have been with us at the table, not slaving away behind the scenes,' he said, adding, 'and Jack too, of course. How is he?'

'I like helping Annabel, Mr Kirkland.' She didn't want to admit that the money was useful too. 'And Jack's fine.'

'Please call me Ashley. It's very good of you but I'm sure there's no need. Annabel's used to coping with parties twice this big.'

'She's hurt her foot.'

'Oh, *that*. She dropped a pan on it last week and has been getting mileage out of it ever since. It's just a bruise – nothing more! You ought to be at home, helping Jack. Is all your seed drilled by now?' It was a landlord's question, but asked with grace.

'Nearly, Mr – Ashley. Just a few more acres of sugar beet.'

'Well, time's marching on. We got all ours in last week. I like to be drilled up by Easter.'

'Yes?' Betty thought of the great resources of the Kirklands' estate – the team of farmworkers, the fleet of modern, reliable tractors and all the latest equipment. Then she pictured Jack, at this very moment in the workshop repairing the obsolete sugar-beet drill – an implement that could plant five rows at a time to Kirkland's eighteen – and she wondered if Ashley really knew what struggling on a couple of hundred acres was like. Wind drummed in the drawing room chimney and rain was still beating on the windows behind the closed shutters. When would it stop?

'Betty? You were miles away.'

'Sorry. What did you say?'

'What were you looking for?'

'Oh yes, cigarettes. Annabel wanted one.'

'Lazy little baggage. Don't let her take advantage, Betty.' He pushed the smoking log deeper into the fire with his foot, marking the black leather of his thin brogue with a smudge of grey ash. 'And if you want a cigarette, you're wasting your time with that box. Look.' He took it from her and pressed a lever at its base, whereupon a section of the chased silver lid popped open and out sprang a tiny bird made of coloured feathers. While she watched, it performed a complicated little song and turned its head from side to side, beak opening and shutting in coordination with the tweeting.

'Oh Ashley,' breathed Betty. 'It's enchanting!'

'Isn't it, though? A hundred and fifty years old.' The trilling song ended and the bird disappeared as the lid snapped shut. 'Heavens! I must get back. I only slipped out to check the fire. I think you'll find fags in this one.' He opened a larger, wooden box and held it out to her. 'They're probably a bit stale. Serve my daughter right for not buying her own.' Betty took two and hurried back to the kitchen.

'God, you've been absolute ages!' Annabel lit one of the cigarettes from the gas cooker, coughed and retched dramatically. 'Ugh, stale!' She took a couple more puffs then stubbed it out on one of the dirty Royal Worcester plates Betty had brought in earlier from the dining room.

'Annabel, you'll spoil the glaze!'

'Sod the glaze. Let's see if they're ready for pudding.' She began to load the serving trolley with *crème brûlée*, fruit salad and a sickly concoction of chestnut paste, chocolate and meringue. 'And, by the way, when we're in the dining room, I'll manage so you can pop back to the kitchen. You deserve a sit-down, yah?'

'Right.' They wheeled the trolley into the dining room and Betty started to collect the main-course plates.

'I told you I'd manage,' muttered Annabel. 'Just pop off, Betty.' Betty went out while Annabel picked up the rest of the plates. As she leaned over her brother's shoulder he squeezed her bottom.

'Serving wench,' he whispered.

'Pig!' she returned under her breath. She cleared the other plates and began to serve the puddings, remembering, most of the time, to limp. Sally refused what she called a dessert, saying that she'd play with a grape or two when the time came.

'So noble of you, Annabel, to do all this for your Mama. With your bad foot and all.'

'It's my job, Mrs Doncaster. I organise lunches for directors.'

'Really? I'm surprised we haven't come across each other before.'

'I only work for a small and rather select number of clients. Merchant bankers, mostly.' Andrew snorted at this but no one else noticed. Everyone chose *crème brûlée*, Andrew's favourite confection and, by giving out large helpings, Annabel managed to finish it, scraping the last of the crispy caramel crust off the sides of the dish before his turn came.

'Oh hard luck, Bro, we're fresh out of your favourite baby food.' Instead, she cut a large slice of the chestnut meringue – which she knew he loathed – and banged the plate down in front of him. 'Cream?' she asked brightly, knowing that he detested that too, and poured a couple of fluid ounces over his plate before he had time to react. Finally, she put the decanter of port, the stilton and the fruit bowl onto the table and left the room.

In the kitchen Betty was trying to peer out of the window into the dark. 'It's still pouring,' she said.

'Don't I know it,' grimaced Annabel.

'What worries me is when we'll get our spring work finished. We're weeks behind. Weeks.' Betty sighed, thinking of the stress lines on Jack's face when he railed about their misfortunes. They began to organise the dirty plates and cutlery and washed up quickly, two professionals in harmony, not having to speak much as they shared the work. At last, Betty felt she could leave.

'Can you and your mother cope with the rest?'

''Course. You pop off home.'

Betty went to the bootroom to put her outdoor clothes back on, ready for the mile walk home. She was relieved to find they had dried but outside, rain was still falling and she knew the journey would be an ordeal. She pulled her hood up, securing it under her chin with a double bow, braced herself and pulled open the back door.

'Oh!' she gasped. The wind nearly blew it out of her hand and rain stung her face but that was to be expected. The surprise was the figure standing on the doorstep. 'What do you want?' He had looked menacing at first, with his shoulders hunched and hands in pockets. Then, when the first shock had subsided, she could see that he was only a boy. About eighteen, twenty at the most, she thought.

'Is this where Mr Wilson lives?' A London accent, Betty guessed. He pulled his right hand out of his pocket and hooked the index finger through something hung round his neck, a pendant, she thought, or possibly a ring. She opened the door a little wider and in the increased light, saw that it was a signet ring – quite large, chunky.

'No. I don't know anyone called Wilson.'

'This *is* Wyckhamby Manor?' The boy was so rigid with cold he could barely speak.

'It is.' She felt she shouldn't invite him in but couldn't bear to leave him out in the rain. He seemed anything but threatening. After a pause, she said, 'You're soaking. You'd better come in.' She held the door open for him. 'Would you like to take your wet things off?'

'No. No, thank you.' He stood just inside the door, still shivering, a little pool of water growing at his feet. 'Is there a . . . you aren't Mrs Wilson?'

'No. I've been working here. I'm just off home, as a matter of fact.'

'Oh.'

'Have you come far?'

'Brixton. I hitched.' He pulled his anorak hood back. Lovely eyes, thought Betty. 'I must see Mr Wil— the boss. What's his name?'

'Mr Kirkland.'

'Kirkland?'

'I'll fetch him for you.' She took off her waterproofs again and went through to the dining room, deciding on instinct not to speak to Annabel. However, by now the party had left the table and were all in the drawing room having coffee. She tapped at the door. It was Ashley who came: seeing Betty, his face lit up.

'Not home yet, Betty? You *are* a glutton for punishment!'

'There's a visitor here who wants to see you.'

'A visitor? It's almost midnight.'

'A young man, and he's soaked to the skin.'

'I'll come.' Ashley closed the door softly behind him and moved swiftly down the hall to the back door. There was no one there. 'Betty, what are you playing at?'

'He was rather shy. I think he may have gone outside again.'

Ashley opened the door. Sure enough the boy was on the step with his back to the entrance.

'Yes?' he said, rather curtly. The boy turned round. 'Good God!' Ashley glanced behind him to where Betty was standing and quickly went out, pushing the boy down the step in front of him and closing the door behind him. Betty put her rain gear back on and waited. She wanted to go home but she knew she mustn't open the door just yet. She heard voices but the rain was falling too hard to be able to make anything of the conversation. After a couple of minutes, Ashley opened the door and came back in, panting slightly. His head and shoulders were wet and he was wiping his face with a handkerchief. Of the boy there was no sign.

'Case of mistaken identity,' he said. 'Charity thing.'

'Charity?'

'Yes. Look, Betty, I'd be awfully grateful if you didn't mention this little incident. I can't tell you why but I'd appreciate your confidence.' He opened the door for her. 'You're off now, then?'

'Yes.'

'Where's your car?'

'At home. I'm on foot.'

'In this? Oh Betty, really! The rain's turning to snow. You'll freeze.'

'I'm well rugged up. I'll be fine.'

'I won't hear of it. I'm going to run you home and that's that!' She felt unable to protest. He went to collect his car keys and within a minute, she was riding in his Daimler. They arrived at Cartwright Farm before the car had had time to warm up. Ashley reached across and opened the passenger door. 'Well, thanks so much for all your help. Elaine is more than grateful.'

'I know.'

'And I expect the pin money comes in handy.'

'I think you know it does.'

'And I can rely on your discretion on this other matter, of the . . . er, visitor?'

'Of course. I've already said you can.'

'Betty, you're a brick. I'll explain all as soon as I can. G'night.'

'Good night, Ashley.'

Chapter Two

Ten days later, Betty awoke with a start. She couldn't work out what had disturbed her and felt in the bed for Jack. Not there. She switched on the lamp and looked at her clock: 5.19. He must have gone to check up on the late lambing ewes and slammed the back door on the way out. She was tired but knew it would be impossible to go back to sleep now that her brain was getting into action, and she began to think about everything she had to do that day. If I get up now, I could put a load of clothes into the washing machine before the cheap electricity stops, she thought. I could iron the children's games clothes too, before Gill and Mandy get up. But she lay for another hour, unable to sleep but unwilling to face the morning chill and the pile of chores.

Eventually, just as *Farming Today* ended on BBC Radio 4, she forced herself out of bed and went to the window to see what the weather was like. There had been a dry spell over the last few days, with good winds to blow the surface moisture out of the land, but showers were forecast and with so much water in the soil already, even the shortest wet spell could turn it soggy again and hold up work. The morning was bright with a clear sky and slanting sunlight already sparkling on the morning dew. However, the breeze stirring the shrubs in the garden foretold rough weather and that was usually accompanied by rain at this time of year. 'Too bright too early,' Betty told the man on the radio.

When she had finished her laundry it was time to see to the children. They were always difficult to rouse on school-days, unlike at weekends, when they would be up long before the lark, playing computer games or cleaning out their guinea pigs before Sunday breakfast. Mondays were impossible. Jim, the youngest, usually developed a chest complaint. He was genuinely asthmatic but many of his attacks seemed to be deliberately timed, so that Betty had to decide whether to give her son the benefit of the doubt or tell him to pull himself together.

The girls got up sluggishly after several reminders, locking themselves in the bathroom. There was still no sign of Jim. She went to his room, fighting back the urge to shout with rage at the squalor there. His school uniform, pressed and folded by her the night before, was piled in a muddled heap on the floor. Plastic space monsters lay in pieces on the windowsill. A microscope, also dismantled, shared the desk-top with his bedside lamp, on its side, and several books, all open, spines uppermost. She opened the window before prodding the shape in the bed.

'Why are you in your sleeping bag?' As if she didn't know. Too idle to make his bed, he lay on top of crumpled sheets and blankets.

'Because it's so cold.' His voice came through clenched teeth, a fine wheeze developing.

'You sound like a flock of starlings in Leicester Square.'

'I can't help it, Mum, I feel terrible.'

'Of course. It's Monday morning.'

'I can't help it if I feel ill.' The wheezing worsened. 'I've got a terrible headache.'

'I don't believe you.'

'It's true, Mum.' The boy began to cry. 'You never believe me.' Betty put her hand on his brow. Quite hot. His eyes had a nasty look too, but that might be because he was weeping.

'What lessons have you got today?'

'Oh, nothing important.'

'Isn't it Art on Mondays?'

'No, Tuesday. I'm sure I'll be fine for tomorrow.'

'Just tell me exactly what lessons you've got today.'

'Maths.'

'Ah! Double period, isn't it?'

'With Mr Vickery. He hates me.' The asthma is getting a grip. She can see his ribcage moving convulsively and his colour is going.

'I'll go and get your Ventolin.' She ran to the bathroom and banged on the door. 'How long are you girls going to be? For heaven's sake hurry up and open the door, Jim's having an attack.' She heard the bolt slide back. 'Quick – give me his puffer.'

'Don't panic, Mum,' said Gill. 'He's only faking.'

Mandy was brushing her long, brown hair from the back, bending forward so it fell over her face. Her voice sounded funny from upside down: 'Double maths again, I suppose. Still, you never know.' She's the middle child, always seems the wisest. Betty trusts her judgement.

'I may have to keep him at home,' she said, knowing how much he would add to her workload. 'Don't say a word, though. I'll see how he is once he's up.'

She battled her way through breakfast, trying not to allow the children's squabbling to wear her down. Jack was still out with the sheep but, pleasant surprise, Jim came into the kitchen looking better. The Ventolin had worked well and he was plainly hungry, resigned now to a day at school. His blazer had a button missing so she picked up her workbasket and found a needle and thread. 'Give,' she said, reaching for the blazer. His shoes were filthy but she decided not to mention this in case it brought on a relapse.

'Christ!' Gill leapt to her feet. 'Look at the time!'

'No need to use language like that. There's plenty of time. Get your things together and we'll leave when I've got the car out.'

Betty walked through the garden to the farm buildings where the car was kept. They had no garage. The lawn was beginning to grow and she remembered she had promised to take the mower into Kendale for an overhaul. A few sweet violets were showing under the high wall and she made a mental note to pick a little bunch later, for Jack's bedside table. They both loved the scent of them and he always gave

her a box of violet creams on St Valentine's Day. The rest of
the border was weedy but she looked away quickly, trying
not to think of the work. The Escort started easily, a sure
sign of spring weather, and apart from a guilty glance at the
balding tyre, front offside, which she was supposed to have
changed last week, she managed to feel almost serene. Jack
should be able to get the seed drilling finished this week, if
the dry weather held.

She drove round to the farmhouse front door and found
the children waiting for her. Jim was to be dropped at the
bus stop a mile down the road. As he had a scholarship at the
Kendale Endowed School, the county paid his bus fare and
school fees – a remnant of the old Eleven Plus and Grammar
School system which added a ten per cent premium to house
prices in the catchment area. Capelstowe House, a private
academy for girls, was four miles further on, over the county
border where the only alternative to independent schools was
comprehensive education. Here, every private privilege was
paid for and the fees were not reasonable. It was Betty's wish
that, whatever the state of the family economy, the children's
schooling was not to be compromised. However good the
state schools might purport to be in this middle-class region,
comprehensive education was not for her children. It was a
bone of contention between her and Jack.

She was relieved to see that a couple of Jim's classmates
were already at the bus stop when they arrived, for she hated
leaving him alone in that isolated spot. He scrambled out of
the car and went off to greet them with mock punches and
boyish back-slapping. She drove on to Capelstowe House,
dropped the girls off and left as quickly as possible. She felt
shy of talking to the other mothers. They were all so well-
groomed and there were an awful lot of BMWs and Volvos
which made her want to get her shabby Escort out of the
way as quickly as she could. She drove to the exit a little too
fast and when she put her foot on the brakes, the front wheels
locked and the car's nose was well out into the main road
before it stopped. Out of the corner of her eye she saw a
movement and then felt the car thumped hard from the right.

There was silence for a moment before the driver of the Range Rover that had hit her leapt out and ran to the Escort as she too, opened the door and got out. It was Andrew Kirkland.

'What the bloody hell do you think you were doing, you stupid, stupid woman!' he shouted. Then, recognising her he deflated. 'Oh . . . Mrs Rose. What made you do a thing like that?'

'Andrew. I'm so terribly sorry.' She was shaking so hard she could barely speak. 'I must sit down.'

'You can't wait here, you're blocking the entrance.' A Volvo driven by a richly painted mother had drawn up behind her and a big Ford – Granada, possibly – was waiting on the road. 'You'd better let me drive your car out.' He jumped in and tried to turn the steering wheel but the front wing was so badly dented it obstructed the turn. He got out, ran to his Range Rover and rummaged in the back, returning with a short crowbar which he forced between wheel and wing, levering upwards until an inch or two of movement was possible. Betty sat in the passenger seat of the Escort while this was going on, waiting for the trembling to subside. She could feel her pulse drumming in her throat. Andrew got back in and managed to get the car out of the way so that other mothers could move in and out of the car park, children in incoming cars glued to the windows and pointing, eyes full of glee. He switched her engine off. 'You able to drive, d'you think?'

'I feel so ashamed.' Her pulse was returning to normal and the peripheral vision seemed to be getting less blurred. 'I really am very sorry, Andrew.' She was getting control of herself by now. 'I admit liability, of course.'

'Never mind that. What am I to tell Father?'

'I'm sure he'll understand. It wasn't your fault,' she said, but thought that if he'd been travelling at a reasonable speed he could have avoided the accident.

'You don't understand. I'm not supposed to drive his Range Rover. He doesn't know I've got it. He'll kill me when he finds out.'

'Oh, I see.' A short silence followed while this sank in. 'What are you going to do?' Betty asked.

'How the hell do I know? Perhaps you ought to tell him.'

'Me?' The thought was daunting. 'Are you sure that would be a good idea?'

'You've caused hundreds of pounds' worth of damage.'

'Hundreds? Are you sure, Andrew?'

'Come and look.' He jumped out of the Escort, slamming the door far too hard. Betty followed him to the Range Rover. There didn't seem to be all that much damage. The front light was broken and pushed in, but nothing was pouring out of the engine, no water or oil or anything.

'Are you sure it's hundreds?'

'Look at this.' He began to catalogue the bits that would need replacing, reeling off prices per part that seemed exorbitant. 'The entire light unit is smashed, this panel needs replacing – they're over a hundred each, to say nothing of labour – this tyre is cut, which will mean buying a new pair to balance the vehicle and then there's all this beating out to do. There won't be much change from five hundred, I'll be bound – about what your Escort's worth all together, I'd say.'

'All right, Andrew, I'll talk to your father.' His arrogance nettled her. 'Since you're afraid to face him on your own.' She walked back to her car.

'You can't see him today,' he called after her. 'He's in London until Thursday. Come at seven, Thursday evening.'

She turned to face him. 'Thursday evening is not convenient. I'm doing something else. I'll come on Friday morning.'

Andrew looked alarmed and then modified his tone. 'Couldn't you make a special effort?'

'You want to be absolutely sure that I'm the one to break the news?'

'Well, it *was* your fault.' He smiled the Kirkland smile, just like his father's. The arrogance had vanished. 'Please?'

'All right.'

'Thanks, Mrs Rose. Cheers then.' He leapt into his father's

vehicle and roared away, revving the engine to maximum in each gear. Betty's Escort was less mobile. The steering felt very stiff but she managed to creep back into town and left the car at Norman's Garage. She telephoned Jack from Mr Norman's office.

'Jack, I'm stuck in Kendale. Could you collect me in the Landrover?'

An hour later they were sitting with mugs of instant coffee in a kitchen that needed cleaning. He was querulous. 'How do you expect us to survive if you don't look after the equipment properly? You know what the situation is.'

'What equipment?'

'The car is as essential a piece of equipment to us as a tractor or a plough. We can't afford to replace it. We can barely afford to run it.'

'I know, Jack, but I've got so much to see to. Don't go on about it, please.' She put her mug down and moved to his side of the kitchen table to stroke the back of his head. If only she could make him relax a little. The tension lines round his dark eyes were deepening into permanence these days.

'I mean, it's only a fortnight since you let the engine overheat. You didn't even notice the radiator hose had gone that time.' His voice had an edge of desperation. She noticed the light from the kitchen window shining through his greying hair, tousled from neurotic head-scratching. He looked so tired and unhappy.

'Anything good in the post?' She wanted to get his mind off the car incident.

'Bank statement.'

'Oh Jack, is that what's making you look so cross? It's bad, isn't it?'

'Forty-one.'

'Oh Jack!' She felt the pulse in her neck returning.

'Well, forty thousand five hundred and something. Here, read it yourself.' He riffled through the pile of post in front of him on the kitchen table and pulled it out. She felt pangs of anxiety whenever she saw the printed form of the bank statements with their orange backs. There was the figure at the bottom: £40,567.49D. She skimmed through the list of cheques paid out: sundries £367.45, sundries £291.22, and one bigger than all the rest – sundries £1447.36.

'What's this fourteen hundred pounds, fertilizer?'

'No, that was all paid for last year.'

'Oh, of course. School fees.'

'Exactly, Capelstowe.'

'It is the most important thing, the kids' schooling.'

'Look, Betty, I know we've been through this time and again, but I don't think you realise our predicament.'

'Oh, but I do. Of course I do.'

'We've got nearly twenty thousand pounds' worth of wheat in the store. I have to buy materials for this year's cropping; I have to pay casual wages—'

'Jack, I know!'

'—which means that the wheat is already half used up and our overdraft limit is forty-five thousand.'

'I don't want to hear it all again – I can't stand it! I know we'll manage. Somehow.'

'Look. The interest alone is going to be more than four thousand this year.'

'Jack, stop! You'll make yourself ill. We've always managed to stay within the limit before. Mr Woods isn't concerned.'

'Only because we've always increased the limit – every year. Mr Woods doesn't mind as long as our assets exceed our borrowing. The fact is, we can't really afford these school fees.'

'You think we should send the girls to that horrible secondary modern in Kendale? Let them learn to smoke cigarettes and walk with their arms folded?'

'You make it sound like a school for sluts.'

'Have you seen the teachers? Remember that begging letter they sent asking for money for extra books? We counted five spelling mistakes and they didn't even put the date on it.'

'It can't be that bad.'

'It is. And the boys! Some of those louts are like animals. We can't possibly deprive the girls at this stage.'

'Well, what about going over the border? If we could get them into St George's Community College . . .'

'No chance at this stage, as well you know. All the county parents whose kids fail the Eleven Plus fight for places there months before the academic year begins. Besides, it would still be bad for the girls to move.'

'We shouldn't live beyond our means.'

'We'll just have to cut down on something else.'

'We're cut to the bone on everything. When did we last eat beef, or go out for a meal? We can't even afford to buy you a new dress unless it's from that "Second Hand Roz".'

'I don't mind. I'd probably still buy from her, even if we made millions.'

'Besides, are the manners at Capelstowe any better? I've seen how the other parents look down their noses. Not only that, how come our girls never star in any of the plays or read lessons at the carol service?'

'They're not natural performers.'

'Crap! They haven't got titled parents or a Rolls Royce, that's why.' Betty had to admit that the Principal was rather keen on the wealthier parents and that she and Jack always felt decidedly second class at the annual cocktail party for parents. A frozen smile with the thimble of Cyprus sherry was all they had ever received from her. The telephone shrilled, making her start. Jack answered it.

'Sally Doncaster,' he said, handed her the phone and walked out slamming the back door. The Roses' dog, a middle-aged black labrador, got up from under the table and scratched at the door.

'Hullo.'

'Betty, my dear. How *are* you?'

'Very well, thanks.' She watched the labrador run nervously round the kitchen and then back to scratch at the door.

'Would you be an absolute angel and do me a teeny favour?'

'I expect so.' She realised too late that the dog was about to be sick. 'What kind of favour?' She watched the dog's stomach heave.

'Could you be a lamb and collect Camilla from school for me and deliver her to Kendale for her dancing lesson?' It was quickly over. The dog stood looking at the three piles of vomit with surprise. Betty wondered how best to clear up the mess and why the dog had been sick – probably raided the dustbins again. Jack never bothered to stop him.

'Sorry, I didn't hear you. The dog's thrown up all over the kitchen.'

'Darling, what a bore! I said I've a terribly important tea engagement. Could you be a love and deal with Camilla?'

'All right. See you later, then.'

'You won't see me, love, I'll be out to tea. You're taking Cam to dancing – OK?'

'Of course. Glad to. Bye.'

'Bye, lovey.' Sally's voice had softened to a purr before she hung up. As soon as Betty had replaced the receiver, she remembered that she had no car. She'd have to borrow Jack's ancient Landrover which would dirty the children's uniforms and anyway, could hardly carry three passengers unless one travelled among the old sacks, spare tyres and other junk in the back. She decided to clear up the dog's mess before getting back to Sally to say she couldn't transport Camilla after all. It took a lot of newspaper, disinfectant and hot water. She resisted the impulse to gag half a dozen times and afterwards, washed and scrubbed her hands but still felt unclean. She dialled the Old Rectory. Sally's honeydew voice answered. '*This is Wyckhamby two four two—*'

'Oh Sally, Betty here again,' but the voice continued and she realised it was an answering machine. She hung up without leaving a message; she could never think what to say just like that, without a chance to prepare. I'll just have to manage, she thought. The little baggage can lower herself for once to ride in an old farm truck. She can sit on Mandy's knee. With a shock, Betty noticed the time. She still had the pigs and poultry to feed and all the housework to do. The children's sheets needed changing. Well, they'd have to wait but the livestock's needs were urgent. She collected her egg basket and bucket of kitchen slops and headed for the yard.

The Roses' pig enterprise, an important contributor to their income, was housed in old, adapted farm buildings. All the equipment had either been installed second-hand or had been made on the farm by Jack and an apprentice who was now at Agricultural College. He had proven to be adept at welding, after a couple of lessons from Jack, and had been quick to understand complex instructions. Ramshackle and quaint the buildings may have been, but the pigs were supremely healthy. Hygiene was all, Jack had explained when they began pig production – hygiene, breeding and nutrition. Those were the key words, coupled with good stockmanship. That was where Betty came in. She was the stockman, looking after the pregnant sows, taking care of the tiny pink babies from birth, injecting them with iron tonic, dipping their navels in antiseptic and clipping their eye teeth. At weaning time, she would move the mothers away from their seven-week-old children, carrying out the tricky operation gently and calmly so as not to upset them too much. On average, a sow had a litter of ten piglets twice a year. With the progeny going off to market at maturity, this meant she had charge of twenty mothers, two boars and nearly two hundred young pigs from newborn to market weight. She knew every sow intimately and, though it was bad policy to allow any emotional attachments to develop, was fond of most of them. The older boar, nearly at the end of his useful life, was a particular friend. Playful in youth, but always gentle, she had enjoyed working with him and was dreading the day when they had to decide to ship him off to market, to end up in a series of pork pies or to become meat and bone meal.

Entering the first pig house, she heard the boar's greeting, 'Huff huff huff,' and picked up an old hazel stick which stood just inside the door ready for their daily ritual. The boar would bite the stick playfully and then allow her to stroke the only area of soft skin on his body, just behind his ears. The person who made up the proverb had never experienced the silkiness of a pig's ear, Betty thought, as her fingers gently bunched and kneaded the skin at the base, feeling it move to and fro over the firm cartilage while the boar grunted softly with pleasure. In these few moments, she could sense that all was well in the piggery today. That was really the secret of good husbandry – just watching and listening and smelling. You had to find a rapport with the beasts, to get onto their wavelength so that you could sense trouble before it manifested itself as disease or distress.

She checked over the feeding and watering equipment, making sure the hoppers were full of meal, and set about feeding the sows. The noise of pigs rose to a crescendo as she worked through her charges, but quietened as they settled to their feed. It was important not to let any of them become overweight, so every animal was strictly rationed with a diet formulated to provide its optimum nutritional needs. She worked with her pigs for nearly two hours and by the time she got back to the house, Jack was in the kitchen again, about to grab a hasty lunch.

'Everything all right?'

'Fine. Just one piglet lost, squashed by its mother. No disease, touch wood.'

'Good. I'll take twenty across to Melton Mowbray on Wednesday. The prices seem to have been a little better there lately than Kendale market.' He seemed calmer now, after a couple of hours work in the field. Although it was clouding over after so bright a start, the threatened showers had not yet come.

'I don't think it'll rain before dusk. Have you started drilling yet?'

'Got another acre done. The ground's near perfect now.'

'Good. You might be finished by tomorrow, then.'

'If it stays dry. If only it would stay dry.' The harrowed look returned and his eyes darkened with worry. 'God knows what I'll do if the weath—'

'Jack, stop it!' She took him by the shoulders – he was not very much taller – and shook him gently. 'Jack, my love, you must learn not to fret. You'll make yourself ill.' She hugged his rigid frame and nuzzled his ear, whispering, 'You've got to be like the song, *Accen-tuate the Positive*,' and she nipped his ear lobe.

'Ouch!' He kissed her briefly on the mouth. 'What makes you so strong?'

'Not strong, just stupid.'

'Stupid? No way! Stubborn, though. Anyway, enough of this. I've got to eat and run if I'm going to get the drilling finished. Cheese sandwich all right for you too?' He cut two thickish slabs of cheddar and pressed them between slices of brown bread.

'Stubborn because I'm determined to hang on here?' She opened the cupboard to take out two small plates. 'And why not? This is our home, Jack. We risked everything to get this tenancy and now we're here, I want to stay. It's so *right* for us. I couldn't think of living anywhere else, not now.'

'Like I said, stubborn. Onion?'

'No, thanks. By the way, can I have the Landrover this afternoon? I've got to collect the girls and drive Camilla Doncaster to Kendale.'

'You're being taken advantage of again. That woman didn't take long to mark you down for a sucker.'

'Oh, I don't mind helping out, but heaven knows when I'm going to get the housework done. I haven't even made the beds.'

'Why couldn't La Doncaster do the ferrying?'

'"Terribly important tea engagement."' She did a passable imitation of the honeyed tones. 'Camilla's being delivered into the clutches of Miss Pickles.'

'Dancing and deportment for young ladies!'

'Mmm. I wonder if La Doncaster has found out about Miss Pickles'girlfriend yet? By the way, take the dog with you this afternoon. He was sick all over the kitchen.'

In the Old Rectory, sitting at her stripped pine kitchen table under a suspended rack festooned with assorted dried flowers, Sally Doncaster dunked her last strip of smoked salmon into a little pool of lemon juice that had run to one side of the Royal Doulton plate. She held the pepper grinder, a gargantuan model nearly two feet tall and made from polished hardwood, over it and twisted the top an eighth of a turn so that a dozen kibbles of black pepper speckled the pink surface of the fish. Then, having swapped grinder for fork she popped the morsel into her mouth. She took a tiny sip of Sancerre and dabbed her lips with the linen napkin.

'Done,' she muttered. She lit a cigarette, relaxed for three minutes and then rinsed her plate and glass before setting them aside to drain. She glanced round the kitchen, satisfying herself that it was clean enough, and went to her office in the basement. Her company's head office was in London and had the full complement of secretaries and electronic gadgetry, but the true heart of Raylon Tropicals was right here in the Old Rectory, Wyckhamby. Here, with fax, telephone, computer link to her London Office and a daily courier, Sally ran her business.

This afternoon she had a mountain of phoning to do but decided to have a bath first and change into a dressing gown. She enjoyed working like that. It was more comfortable and relaxed – one of the joys of working from home. After several false dawns, the builders had completed her private bathroom to her grudging satisfaction, less than a week ago. There had been acrimonious exchanges with the Small Works Manager, a cretinous little man who seemed unable to comprehend her carefully-worded instructions about where the pipework and everything should go. Eventually she had had to withhold payment until most of the work was redone. Even then, she had imposed a £500 discount for late completion – something the Managing Director had informed her was quite illegal but to whom she had retorted, 'Sue me, then!' But now all the work was finished and it would be quite a while before the novelty of the expensive fittings wore off. The taps and lavatory handle in matching gold plate and simulated lapis lazuli gleamed in an envy-generating way, but her favourite toy was the jacuzzi – an enlarged teak tub which frothed and bubbled round human bodies, making them look and feel like boiling potatoes. It was supposed to be sexy but she hadn't quite found out which positon to sit in yet for maximum thrills. Jules, after one trial, had avoided it like the plague and looked startled when she suggested they should both sit in it together.

I've just got time before Simon brings the mail, she thought, and turned on the bath-taps. Water gushed into the midnight-blue tub, the steam condensing on the fake gilt mirror frames and clouding the glass. Soon she was luxuriating in the water, thinking out the next round of tactics. Nigeria was getting more and more difficult at present but there were signs that new opportunities might crop up in East Africa. This new problem in Kenya, where the old Colonial dams were silting up and spoiling their hydroelectric schemes presented all kinds of openings. Wherever the British government was involved, there was bound to be incompetence and that created opportunities. She lay submerged, but for her nose and mouth, and planned.

The doorbell jarred her composure. 'Shit! He's early.' She sprang out of the bath, dried hastily and put on her towelling dressing gown. But it was Camilla ringing the bell. She pushed in past her step-mother as soon as the door was open. Betty Rose remained on the step, reluctant to stay for more than a brief moment, her mind on her next chore. 'Betty! I thought you were Simon.'

'Simon?'

'Our courier. He brings my bits and pieces from London every afternoon. He's not due until four-thirty.'

'I've brought Camilla home early. The dancing classes are off. Miss Pickles is on jury service, apparently. Camilla said she wanted to come home and that you'd be here.' Betty was puzzled. 'What about your tea appointment?'

'Oh . . . cancelled. Infuriating!'

'I wish I'd known. I've got so much to see to this week.'

'My dear, I should have told you. I only knew a little while ago. You've been *such* a help.'

'Oh, I don't mind. It's just that I have so much to do.'

'Farmer's wife chores? Women's institute, feeding the hungry man, that sort of thing?'

'Actually the pigs take up a lot of my time.'

'Pigs? Oh, how sweet! I adore their curly tails. Do they have babies? I'd love to see them some time.'

'And I'd love to let you, but we try not to allow any visitors into the piggery. It increases disease risk.'

'How on earth could I spread disease to a pig?'

'Well, on your shoes or clothes, for instance.'

'I see.' Sally's voice hardened.

'It's no reflection on you. It's the same for everyone.'

'Really?'

'And you go to Africa, don't you?'

'Yes, but I'm not sure quite what disease you think I might pick up in Africa.'

'African swine fever is the biggest threat. It's notifiable.'

'In that case, I'll try not to consort with too many pigs when I go back to Mudando.'

'Please don't be offended. It's the same for everybody.'

'What a lot there is to learn about the country. Well, thank you for bringing Camilla back – but I must let you get back to your delightful hobby. How I envy you having the time!'

'Actually, about ferrying the children – do you think it might be sensible if we shared the travelling, especially the school run?'

'But we do.'

'Shared it on a slightly more formal arrangement, I mean. That way we could both plan our days.'

'Lovely idea, Betty, but my work is rather unpredictable, and I thought, as you go to school anyway, you might just squeeze Camilla in too. I mean, going to Kendale today was a bit exceptional, but—'

'And a wasted journey, it turns out.'

'I know, you poor thing. Look, I think I'd better get dressed. I must be in my office before Simon comes.'

'I'm sorry, you must be getting cold.' She took her leave and walked back to the Landrover.

The next days fed Betty's optimism. The showers held off, the weather was warm and Jack was happy with progress on the farm. The first of the spring barley came up, making emerald stripes on the brown landscape and trees in the woods and along the lanes began to change in hue from the greys and duns of winter to the lime greens and acid yellows of the early growing season. Primroses, sweet violets and windflowers bloomed in the rich leafmould of the hedgerows and Jim found a long-tailed tit's nest in the garden. 'Look, Mummy, it's nearly round. The hole is tiny – that's where the mother bird goes in and out.' Remembering to keep an eye on that section of garden hedge, Betty was rewarded with glimpses of the little birds. Like their nest, they were rounded and had ridiculously long tails, out of proportion with their tiny bodies. The way they worked through the hedge intrigued her and she loved their colours: black eye-stripe, pinkish-grey breasts and darker backs. Local people called them Bum Barrels, presumably on account of the shape of the nest, because in some areas they also called wrens Bum Barrels. Both birds built similarly shaped nests, but the longtailed tit's was a work of art, every inch decorated with lichen and cobweb making it look pearly grey.

By Thursday, Betty had almost forgotten about Monday's incident with the car. The sun and the lengthening days, the children breaking up from school, meaning a rest from time-wasting chauffeusing, and Jack's calmer mood all helped to lift her spirits.

Seeing the words *Visit A. K. re crash* on the space marked *Thursday* in her kitchen calendar gave her a few moments of anxiety, but surely Ashley would be reasonable? He was a decent, just man. She wished she could stop feeling so uneasy in his presence, though, and furthermore, wished she knew *why* she felt uneasy. It wasn't because he was their landlord, but something about him made her uncomfortable. He seemed direct and open, and when he smiled, his eyes smiled too, narrowing but twinkling with mischief . . . and yet, whenever they were together, a fine cord of tension was strung between them.

Chapter Three

Walking with a light step to the Marble Arch underground car park, Ashley felt decidedly pleased with himself. The lunch meeting he had just come from at Grosvenor House had been a triumph, but apart from that, things were going well on almost all fronts. The wheat price was much higher than all the experts had predicted and most of his crop of 3,600 tonnes was still in store, unsold. He should be able to make £135 per tonne and that would fetch in a tidy profit. Oilseed rape had been a useful crop this year, too, thanks to the taxpayer who coughed up a large subsidy on every tonne grown. What a marvellous system it was! You were paid incentives to produce more; prices were held artificially high to allow inefficient growers to survive and then, when the European Community became embarrassed with surpluses, you were paid not to grow some crops at all. If you had enough acreage you couldn't lose.

He paid to get out of the car park and negotiated the traffic in Park Lane, driving skilfully and quite fast but without taking any risks. This was his third Daimler and by now he felt more at home at its controls than with any other car he had driven. The music system was superb – you could even play compact discs if you wanted to. He tuned to BBC Radio 3 and Mozart filled the car. One of the later piano concertos, what luck! But Ashley was quite accustomed to good luck. The interesting thing about him was that it didn't seem to spoil him.

He had been born with a silver spoon wedged between his gums and had spent most of his adult life gilding it. At school he had performed well at games and quite brilliantly in class, winning an open scholarship to Cambridge. His first major disappointment had been about that. His father, Oliver Kirkland, worried about what he saw as effeteness or worse, an artistic streak developing in his son, persuaded him to abandon the idea of Cambridge and go instead to the Royal Agricultural College at Circencester. Out of loyalty he had obeyed, but from then on his academic career was undistinguished.

Oliver Kirkland died suddenly, three years after Ashley had finished at Cirencester, leaving the young man with the Lordship of the Manor and 1200 acres of productive land. There were death duties to pay but, by working hard and living frugally, he managed to settle them and even expanded his acreage, with the help of the bank, to 1600.

The other 1000 acres arrived with Elaine. Their union was hardly unexpected but the marriage settlement, in the form of a large portion of the neighbouring estate, came as a complete surprise to both of them. Elaine was the only daughter of a wealthy farmer in North Lincolnshire. The vision of her bright brown hair, dark eyes and full, sensuous lips tugged at the groins of every farmer's son in the county but her intelligence and vivacity also won the hearts of the brighter ones. She and Ashley made a dazzling pair, setting up their home at Wyckhamby Manor, not with the air of newlyweds but giving the impression of a squire and his lady taking up their inheritance. Elaine's father, notorious for his miserly attitude, gave the young couple nothing, but his brother, to whom he never spoke, was so taken with his niece's wise choice of partner that he purchased, in secret, part of the neighbouring estate and presented it to the couple.

Ashley occupied all of the Kirkland acres except for the small farm which the Roses rented. He had never seen any sense in buying tenanted land but this small parcel had been included in the original legacy. The economics of tenanted land were so heavily weighted against the landlord, after postwar legislation, that it was usually valued at about half the vacant possession price. Still, the Roses were good tenants. They paid their rent – though God alone knew how they managed to make such an uneconomic farm pay – and Betty was a great contributor to the village. In fact, he had quite a soft spot for Betty.

Ashley had not stopped at farm expansion. His entrepreneurial instinct and unquenchable stamina had meant that even a farm as big as Wyckhamby failed to keep him fully occupied. On an impulse, he bought a bookshop near the British Museum and then, with a partner who was rich with ideas but short of capital, founded a public relations consultancy, Kirkland Wild Associates. Ashley was thus able to spend part of his working time in London and he had his own secret reasons for wanting to do that. He pushed that particular thought back into the mud at the bottom of his mind. (Two separate entities. Absolutely. Scary about that boy visiting, though – must nip that sort of thing in the bud.) And now, after a series of rewarding days, especially this lunchtime, when Kirkland Wild had exchanged a five-year contract with Rutland University and a consortium of multinationals who were about to build a huge science park just off-campus, he was on his way home.

He turned into the Edgware Road and began his route home. The Mozart finished and something atonal came on – Messiaen or Schoenberg or something. Horrible! He reached for the compact disc of Verdi's *Requiem* and was soon singing along with the tenor: '*Kyrie-e-e-elei-e-e-i-son . . .!*' and later, well along the Great North Road, the *Lacrymosa*, his voice accomplishing the contralto part in an almost convincing falsetto. He had wanted to be a chorister at school but the choirmaster said he lacked the musical talent. By the time the Verdi was drawing to a close with the final fugue and the last muttered words of the soloist '*Libera me domine de morte eternam*', echoed reverently by the hushed choir, he was within a few miles of Wyckhamby.

Betty decided to walk over to the Manor because she wanted to work off her anxiety about the meeting. She reached the gates half an hour after Ashley's arrival. They were still open and she wondered whether she should close them or not. Along the drive, crocuses were closing their petals in the setting sun. Long rosebeds on either side, the reddish shoots of the rose bushes beginning to emerge, had been under-planted with wallflowers whose scent was just noticeable. She walked up the steps to the front door and pressed the bell button. The ring seemed to come from a long way away inside and it was nearly a minute before she realised no one had heard. She pressed again, for longer, and then spotted someone approaching from the garden. It was Elaine, carry-ing a trug basket and border fork.

'Betty, hullo. Are you looking for Ashley? He's probably still over at the farm buildings. He always goes there to check up on everything when he's been away.'

'Should I go to find him?'

'Better not. He's a bit funny when he first arrives home. Come in and have a gin. I'm gasping.'

'Isn't it a little early?'

'Nonsense. Sun's well over the whatsit. I've been weeding and have a stiff back. I've earned my gin.'

'Well, I wouldn't say no,' Betty said, out of politeness. She was not a great drinker.

Elaine put the basket on the ground and leant the fork against the wall of the house. 'Let's go in the back door.' She led the way round the side of the house. The whole of the west wall was clad with a vast wisteria, reputed to be one of the first specimens planted in England, which was beginning to come to life, its flower buds enlarging like big catkins and promising a mass of fragrant, mauve blossoms. 'You may well look, and it does make a fine show—'

'It's going to be smothered in bloom, how lovely!'

'As I said, a fine show, but look at what's going on underneath. It's pulling the house to bits – look at the brickwork!'

'Worth the trouble, though. I adore wisteria.'

'Me too, but not if it wrecks the house.' By the time Betty had been shown into the little room they called Ashley's study, and a large gin and tonic – clinking with four ice cubes and a slice of lemon – had been thrust into her hand, there was the sound of another door opening and brisk footsteps. 'In here, darling!' Elaine called. Ashley came in.

'This is very matey,' he said.

'I'll leave you two in peace,' said Elaine and went out. Betty wanted to shout, *'Please stay!'*

'How are you?' he said over his shoulder while he fixed himself a whisky. Then, turning, 'Cheers!'

'I'm very well.' Betty couldn't think what else to say. She could feel him looking at her and forced herself to meet his gaze. She decided to come to the point as quickly as possible, before her nerve failed. 'Has Andrew spoken to you?'

'I haven't seen him yet.'

'Oh. Well, it's about your Range Rover.'

'My Range Rover?'

'Yes. I'm afraid I drove into it on Monday morning.'

'You can't have, it's in the stables. Nobody uses it except me. That's one of my little foibles.'

'I know. But I drove into it on Monday because Andrew had it.'

'I think you're getting confused. Andrew uses the farm truck. That'll be what you drove into. Red thing, with an open back. No one hurt, I presume?'

'No, no one.'

'Well, don't worry. Was it Andrew's fault?'

'No, mine.'

'Hard luck. Still, you're insured, no doubt.'

'But I'm afraid it *was* your Range Rover. Andrew had it out without your permission.'

'I see.' Ashley paused a moment but showed no sign of anger. He got up, walked to the window, stared out for a moment and then turned to her. 'Betty, how thoughtless of me. Let me freshen your glass.'

'Oh no, really. I'm fine, thank you.'

'Well, please don't think any more of this. I suppose Andrew asked you to break the news to me?'

'Oh no, Mr Kirkland, it was my idea. After all, I caused the accident.'

'Really?' He seemed sceptical. 'Well, you can leave Master Andrew to me.'

Betty stood up. 'I should be going. I came on foot.'

'Lordy! How badly damaged is your car?'

'Oh no. I walked from choice. It's such a lovely evening.'

'Yes it was, but it's getting dark now. Let me run you home in the car.'

'No, it's kind of you but that really won't be necessary.'

'I'd like to, Betty.' He opened the door for her.

'I'd really rather walk. I love it in the twilight.'

'Tell you what,' he followed her out of the room, 'I've had a stuffy week in London. I'll walk with you.'

'There's no need.'

'But I *want* to.'

'Well, why not come halfway?' She waited while he collected his shooting jacket – the cowdung colour looking incongruous with his charcoal double-breasted suit – and they set off down the drive. The wallflower scent was stronger now dusk was falling.

They walked in silence for a while, then Ashley spoke. 'Betty, about the other night, at the dinner party.'

'Yes?'

'That boy. Did he talk to you very much?'

'Who – Andrew?'

'No – the boy who turned up at the end, just before they all went home.'

'Oh, him. No, he was so cold he could hardly speak. It was a filthy night, if you remember.'

'Did he say where he'd come from?'

'I can't remember. He sounded London-ish. Oh yes, Brixton. He said he'd come from Brixton.'

'Brixton? Are you sure?'

'Yes, quite sure. Why?'

'What did you make of him?'

'Very little. He'd been wet for too long. I wouldn't have let him in but I didn't like to leave him shivering on the doorstep while I found you.'

'And you didn't notice anything else about him?'

'No . . . Oh yes, he asked for someone called Wilson. He wanted Wyckhamby Manor but asked to speak to Mr Wilson.'

'Wilson? How odd!' They walked on in silence for a hundred yards or so, then, 'Wilson . . . I expect that was someone in the charity. Betty, I say, have you—'

'Mentioned him to anyone? No. You asked me not to, so of course I haven't.'

'I appreciate it, Betty.' Silence resumed until they reached the junction of Main Street and the Kendale Road. 'Well, here we are. This must be about halfway.'

'Rather more. It was kind of you to come.'

'My pleasure.' He stood for a moment, as if unsure what to do next and then said, rather stiffly, 'Well, good night to you.' She smiled and watched him turn and begin to walk briskly home. Poor Andrew, she thought.

Walking back alone to confront his son, Ashley felt the joy of the earlier part of the day tarnish. Dishonesty, that was the worst thing. The deceit, and the gutlessness – leaving Betty to break the news. Unforgivable!

In the kitchen at Cartwright Farm the girls had laid the table and were cooking supper, sausages, bacon and mashed potatoes, with tinned peaches to follow. 'Bless your hearts,' Betty said, wiping her feet on the doormat. 'Where's Jim?'

'In the workshop with Dad,' they chorused. Mandy said, 'They're making a frame.' Gill clarified: 'For a hide. So Jim can watch the Bum Barrel's nesting. He wants to try and take pictures with Daddy's camera.'

'I thought Daddy was seed-drilling?' Betty feared something must have stopped him.

'All done,' they said. 'Dad finished just after six. He says it's gone in really well.'

Chapter Four

Returning from an emergency call at 8.50 a.m. on 18 April, Dr Leonard Bates drove into the car park behind Bridge House so slowly that his engine almost stalled. The weather was glorious – the sky blue as a dunnock's egg, with fleecy white clouds lining up on the horizon – but he was not in a spring-like mood. He parked, switched off and prepared for the twinge in his shoulder as he reached across with his right hand to release the seat belt. Then he sat quietly for a whole minute, willing his headache to diminish and summoning up enough energy to get into the surgery.

On the whole, it had been a good idea to build a surgery in the grounds at Bridge House. It was convenient; the rates were lower than they would have been at the new health centre in Kendale and anyway, he didn't see why his rural patients should have to travel to town when he and they lived either in Wyckhamby or the surrounding villages. But there were also disadvantages, the chief one being a loss of privacy when patients took to arriving at the house expecting treatment at all hours, even for trifling problems. In spite of a clearly marked boundary with tall hornbeam hedge and wicket gate, surgery visitors were inclined to stray into the garden, especially on fine days, to wander among Maggie's mixed borders and even into the greenhouses, much to her irritation. Then there was the cost. It had been horribly expensive to erect a building which managed not to offend the refined sensibilities of the local Planning Committee but, once it was up, Leonard soon grew to love the little four-square edifice, with its steep-pitched roof, soft-coloured limestone walls and mullioned windows. Furthermore, it could easily convert to a 'granny annexe' and accommodate servants – assuming they could afford them when they retired – or they could live in it themselves if it became necessary to sell off the main house. That way, Maggie could at least keep part of the garden she had spent so many years developing.

Her idea of installing a bench seat – expensive hardwood in a *Chinoiserie* style – outside the front door, sheltered by a jasmine-clad border, had been appreciated by several of the older regular patients who would sit on surgery days like *tricoteuses* at Madame Guillotine, keeping tabs on who came and went and speculating on their diseases. Today, despite the spring sunshine, the seat was empty, thank God!

The effort of climbing the steps to the door, for it would have been too undignified to walk up the disabled person's ramp, caused a crescendo of throbbing in Leonard's temples and behind his eyeballs, so that he staggered for a second or two, his hands resting on the rail. Last night's wine sampling had been a mistake. What was that really earthy one? Bulgarian? His stomach heaved at the memory and he could feel the glands under his tongue switch into action and fill his mouth with unwelcome saliva. The trouble with the Kendale Wine Appreciation Society was that the members never took the tastings seriously. Instead of sipping, slooshing and spitting out, to keep their judgement objective, everyone swallowed and re-filled until samples became glassfuls and the discussions degenerated into social chat. Leonard seldom bought at the club, preferring to collect wines in their countries of origin and to haunt salerooms on the lookout for wise investments, but he had been a loyal and generous member since its foundation. In fact, it was really he, with a Kendale auctioneer and a local solicitor, who had got the club going in the first place.

He went in and found himself standing among a scattering of glass marbles. A small boy, from whom a sharp smell of stale urine emanated, was in the act of flicking another one up the passage.

44

'Ooh Doctor, I'm ever so sorry,' said the boy's mother, from her seat in the corridor.

'Get him to pick 'em up, Mrs Collins. Someone could have an accident.' A foetid and ill-behaved child was all he needed this morning. He had no doubt there'd be several more back in the waiting room.

'Yes, Doctor. I'm ever so sorry.' She scolded the boy and bent to pick up the marbles.

'Perhaps you ought to take him into the waiting room.'

'There aren't no more seats in there, Doctor. It's a full 'ouse.'

'I see.' Leonard strode through the door marked *Private*. Holy Wednesday, he thought. They'll all be trying to get off work for a few extra days before Easter.

Mrs Pollitt, everyone's stereotype of a doctor's reception-ist, formidable in white coat with her hair pulled tightly into a complicated knot at the back, was dismissing someone's problems over the phone with forbidding brusqueness. She hung up without saying goodbye and picked up the notepad with telephone messages. 'Six calls this morning, Dr Bates, but nothing very pressing.' In the seven years she had worked for him she had developed considerable skill in knowing which patients needed urgent help and which did not, regard-less of what they said over the phone. 'The hospital rang.'

'Market Wilton?'

'No, St Simon's. Mrs Bell. There's no change.'

'OK. I'll call anyway, on the way back from Wilton this afternoon. What else?'

'Nothing very special. Mrs Rose rang for more Ventolin but Mr Rose is here, so he can take it with him. There are two more children in Midwood Close with temperatures. Very few calls to make really,' she shot an appraising glance at him over her specs, adding, 'Just as well, I suppose. You look pretty awful yourself.'

'Self-imposed, I'm afraid, no sympathy due. I sampled a batch of Cabernets and Riojas. Fine bouquets – earthy and oaky with a velvet texture, but oh God, the histamines!'

'I'm sorry, Dr Bates. I haven't the faintest clue of what you're talking about.'

'Wine, Mrs Pollitt. Fine red wines from Spain and Australia, and from elsewhere,' he shuddered, 'less fine.'

'Oh, I see. You have a hangover.' She shuffled a file and pressed the buzzer, cue for the first patient to compose his features into an unwell expression and shuffle along to the consulting room.

Just over the hedge, Maggie Bates was working on one of her borders. She had been toiling since Leonard had left for his call just before seven and was pleased with her progress, weeding by hand, taking care to avoid pulling out seedlings of the plants she cherished but exterminating groundsel, chickweed and shepherd's purse. Bees worked among the deep blue scillas and wild primroses which flowered in patches at the border's edge. Some of the shrubs were already breaking into leaf and although it was too early in the season for lushness, the garden burgeoned with promise.

Maggie's was typical of the best English gardens. It ran to five acres in total and combined formal elegance with an impression of wildness which at times approached disorder. There were symmetrical areas enclosed by clipped yew hedges and formal terraces paved with old stone and bordered by cool lawns. The rose garden was laid out in geometric shapes and there was a wooded area with serpentine path winding down to a small backwater of the Venn which it then followed to the main river. Besides arranging the plants according to their stature, Maggie had given careful consideration to colour, texture, flowering season and the special character of every species. The result was a harmony which pleased the eye and an exuberance of growth which made the garden as fascinating in midwinter as on the longest day of the year. Where a less imaginative gardener might grow a single climber on a wall space, she would plant five: a honeysuckle for scent, two clematis – one for spring, the other for September – a rose which provided fragrant buttonholes all summer, and wintersweet or Japanese quince for midwinter blooms. Her woodland garden grew both native and exotic wildlings, so among the oxlips and nodding violets a visitor would find the startling white blooms of American wake robin and later, Himalayan blue poppies would blend with the wild ferns.

Her waterside planting harmonised even more closely with nature and, after securing ungrudging permission from Ashley Kirkland who owned the meadow on the opposite side of the Venn, she planted its bank with all the most attractive river wildflowers, from gaudy purple loosestrife and yellow flag irises to the subtly marked burr reeds and water grasses. Among the wild white willows overhanging the home bank, she had planted musk roses from which July bees, drunk with too much nectar, fell into the water below to be snapped up with an audible plop by chubb and brown trout.

It was all very idyllic. Callers found the garden's allure almost impossible to resist and to Maggie, life without it was unthinkable. But it was also a millstone. In spite of two able part-time gardeners, she had to work long hours to keep it maintained and, with each passing year, the task grew heavier. In her thirties and still childless – she and Leonard had tried everything to make her conceive, from science to mumbo-jumbo – developing the garden had been a refuge from the disappointment of not having a family. She had worked with an unnatural energy, doing most of the heavy contracting jobs like slab-laying and hedge planting by herself or with the help of one of the village apprentices. She had been fitter in those days than ever before in her life, able to dig and hew all day while Leonard was on his rounds, and then happy to take long evening walks with him after surgery, along the banks of the Venn. Her broad hips and stocky build, though hardly the ideal of feminine beauty, her mother had been prone to point out, had given her a physical strength which could match the average male. In those days, when her hair was still the colour of a conker and her complexion creamy, and when Leonard, though hardly an athlete, was still paunchless and rosy-cheeked, they had made a handsome enough couple. And they had been in love, he courteous and helpful, she supportive, getting up with him whenever a small-hours' call dragged him out of the house. He encouraged her efforts in the garden and listened with full attention to her plans. She comforted him in the strain of overwork, often by coaxing him into bouts of gentle sex in which she took the initiative at first but gradually gave way and turned compliant as his arousal grew.

Nowadays they spoke less. She was far too tired to go walking in the evenings and he liked to watch television or go to his wine club. But there was still the garden.

She stood up and felt virtuous about the ache in her back and the satisfying pile of weeds in the wheelbarrow. She straightened her shapeless tweed skirt, rolled up the sleeves of the shirt she was wearing – an old Viyella one that Leonard had discarded because it made him itch – turned to the sun and closed her eyes to feel its warmth on her face. But after a second or two, images of unkempt flowerbeds and dishevelled hedges impinged and she bent to her task again. In spite of having worked for several hours, she had achieved far less than she had hoped and the weight of all the outstanding work bowed her down. She tried to speed up but grew careless and, before her brain could stay her hand, pulled out a Christmas rose seedling. 'Bugger!' she muttered and then, when she snagged her wrist on the thorny lower branch of a rose bush, 'Oh, sod the bloody thing!' She decided to reward herself with a break and went into the empty house.

The uncleared breakfast table reproached. Hastily, she piled everything into the sink before plugging in the kettle. She called, 'Len! Are you up there?' But he was still bogged down in the surgery so she took a single mug off the Welsh dresser and then rummaged among the buckets, Vim and Jeyes Fluid in the cupboard under the sink until she found an unlabelled bottle containing a clear amber liquid. She poured a little into her coffee mug and, after a furtive glance at the door, took a hasty swig directly out of the bottle before replacing the screw top and putting it back behind the buckets. She added a spoonful of instant coffee to the whisky in the mug before topping up the tarry goo with hot water, creating a vinous smell in the kitchen. The cuckoo clock on the wall chimed eleven and she toasted it: 'Cheers!' adding, 'Repetitive little bugger, aren't you!' and went back into the garden.

Over the hedge, Leonard was reaching the end of his surgery. His headache had gone but the queasiness in his stomach, not helped by some of the unsavoury ailments brought to his attention, was still there. The waiting room was empty at last but Jack Rose, drawn by the urgency of his farmwork, had slipped out promising to return by eleven. Mrs Pollitt came into the consulting room.

'Eleven o five, Dr Bates. Am I to close up the hatch?'

'Jack Rose promised to come back. Let's give him another five minutes.'

'As you wish.' She made An Exit, managing to pull the consulting-room door to with a sufficiently loud bang to startle him but not quite severely enough to be a deliberate slam. Next door, he could hear filing-cabinet drawers being shut noisily, then Jack's Landrover came back into the yard and within a moment Mrs Pollitt's shrill voice was saying, 'Doctor will see you straight away. He's been waiting for ten minutes.' Jack Rose came in and was invited to sit down.

'Well, Jack. This is a rare occasion, a visit from someone in the Rose family, apart from little Jim, of course. How is he?'

'Very well, thank you, Dr Bates.'

'Splendid! There's a prescription for him out on the dispensary shelf. Could you take it?'

'I suppose so,' he looked anxious, 'but it might be difficult.'

'How so?'

'Well, I'd rather Betty didn't know I was here.'

'Oh?' Leonard's tone changed to archness. 'Have you been doing something you didn't oughter?'

'Sorry?' Jack looked blank.

'Joke!' A gaffe. He tried to laugh it off. Most patients who asked him to keep things from their wives had been indiscreet and wanted to make sure they hadn't picked up anything catching. 'Not a very good one, I'm afraid.'

'Yes. I see.' Jack made no attempt to smile. His face was

pale, with deeply-scored rings under the eyes and a down-
ward sag to the mouth. He sat on his hands, shoulders
hunched, legs moving restlessly, first under the chair, then
stretched out in front and finally crossed at the ankle.
Leonard waited for him to kick off but the pause merely
lengthened and threatened to become a chasm.

'How can I help?' he said at last. The silence continued.
Leonard broadened his smile and waited. Jack seemed to be
frozen, unable to unload. Leonard made encouraging noises.
'Mmm?'

'I've got a problem. I think it's my heart.'

'My dear fellow, I'm quite sure it isn't. You look a picture
of health. Besides, a farmer leading an active outdoor life like
yours – heart trouble's the last thing you can expect.'

'But the symptoms. They—'

'What are the symptoms?'

'Well, it's hard to explain really. I wake up in the middle
of the night and . . .' He trailed off. It really seemed so silly
to talk about it here, in broad daylight and with someone
else. But it was different in the small hours. That was when
the monsters came out to taunt him. They weren't nightmare
beasts with bloodlust in their eyes and gore dripping from
their teeth, but they might just as well have been for the fear
they induced. It usually started with a simple image in his
mind's eye: a Kendale Oil Supplies invoice, a rent reminder
from Ashley's estate agent or, more usually, a bank statement.
In the cold, dark bedroom, with Betty breathing evenly
beside him, he saw the print swinging in front of his eyes, the
digits at the bottom in sharp focus. Then he would begin to
tot up the larger of the unpaid bills, struggling with the
mental arithmetic, to see by how much they exceeded the
overdraft limit. He would try to comfort himself by adding
up the value of stocks and as many debtors as he could
remember but that usually led to the 'supposing' game.
Supposing Midland Grains, which had yet to pay for sixty
tonnes of wheat at £122 per tonne, went bust. He'd be ruined.
Ruined. That other Lincolnshire firm went under last year
and bankrupted larger farms than Cartwright. So his thoughts

would run until he was wide awake and in the grip of fear – stark, buttock-clenching fear which made him sweat and shiver at the same time and made his heart beat so hard he thought its knocking would wake Betty.

Lately, the mode of these night horrors had changed. Now there were other physical symptoms. After some minutes of palpitation, his heartbeat would go irregular and his chest begin to feel full, as if it were being pumped up with air until he felt sure he would burst like an over-inflated balloon. Breathing out became nearly impossible, his legs would begin to go numb and his hands and fingers tingled with pins and needles. He couldn't be sure, but he suspected the feelings were worse on his left side. Usually, these attacks would end before morning and he would drift into a doze or even sleep for half an hour at a time but on several nights lately, the feeling had persisted until morning. In desperation on these days, he had got up before five, creeping about the room to avoid disturbing Betty, and gone out. When she inquired later he would say he'd gone to check over the ewes which had all lambed within the last few weeks.

He knew he needed help but now, after taking days to pluck up the courage to come, he felt he couldn't explain. It was all too silly. Hysterical, in fact.

'Jack, I'd like to help you, but you must tell me what's bothering you,' Leonard said. He was beginning to be mildly alarmed by the colour Jack was turning and by the rigidness of his shoulders.

'Well, as I said, I wake up and get this feeling of doom.'

'Not uncommon.'

'But my heart beats like mad. I can feel it bumping in my throat. Also, it sounds irregular. It keeps skipping a beat and then sort of, fluttering.'

'Well, let's have a look at you.' Jack stripped to his underpants and submitted his body to Leonard who sounded his heart and lungs, measured his pulse and blood pressure, checked his reflexes and probed and prodded before allowing him to dress again. 'You aren't quite as physically fit as I would have expected, but your heart sounds absolutely fine. I'm quite sure you have nothing to worry about on that front.'

'Oh.' The tone was noncommittal but the relief was obvious. He even relaxed fractionally.

'But your blood pressure's a bit high.'

'Oh?'

'Of course, the worry of being here will push it up a little but I think we should play it safe.'

'So there is something wrong.'

'Is there? I haven't said so. Now look, worry is one of the best ways to push up blood pressure. So, relax! There's no reason to get yourself wound up. You, of all people, I would have thought, have nothing to worry about. Now, I will give you some tablets to reduce the blood pressure but that won't make a long-term improvement. What we need to do is get to the bottom of the problem in here,' he tapped his forehead. 'Are you working too hard, do you think?'

'All small farmers work too hard. We have to, to make ends meet.'

Leonard chuckled. 'You farmers! Always pleading poverty but I've yet to see one go broke.'

'That's a common fallacy. Most small growers are under constant pressure and quite a lot do go broke.'

'But you must be doing all right, with two girls at Capelstowe. Besides, you've got potato quota – that's a profitable crop, surely?'

'We've survived so far.'

'Of course you have. What about family life?'

'Fine.'

'Do you smoke?'

'No.'

'Drink?'

'Very little. A beer on Sundays. Glass of plonk now and then.'

Leonard's stomach twitched at this. 'What about bed?'

'Well, as I told you, I wake up too early and can't usually get off again.'

'I meant with your wife. How's your sex life?'

'Oh. Fine.' Embarrassed, Jack folded his arms and uncrossed his legs, then crossed them again at the knee. 'My, er, love life is fine.'

Outside, Maggie, who had made another brief visit to the cupboard under the sink, jabbed her border fork into the ground to lift a large and stubborn delphinium root. Under the strain, the handle broke in two and still holding onto the shaft, she fell forward, grazing her leg on the jagged wood sticking out of the business end. 'Fuck the bloody bastard thing!' she shouted, loudly enough to shock Mrs Pollitt who was still lurking in the dispensary.

'Lucky you,' said Leonard to Jack. 'I wish mine was.' Jack didn't smile. Leonard went on, 'Look, I think you may have a bit of depression. I wouldn't mind talking to Betty about this, or to you and Betty together.'

'No! Absolutely not! I *cannot* allow it!' Jack had leapt to his feet. Both men were surprised by his over-reaction.

'OK, fine. You can rely on my confidence, of course, but I do think you should see a specialist. Just to get your heart thoroughly checked – for your own peace of mind more than anything else.' He began to make a note. 'The hospital will contact you soon. Meanwhile, don't worry.'

Calmer now, Jack said, 'Betty has more than enough on her plate just now. I really don't want to worry her with anything else.'

'No, quite. I appreciate that, but I'm pretty sure a lot of your trouble is in your mind and Betty is a capable type. Don't you think she might be able to help you sort your anxieties out?'

'Maybe. But now is not the time.'

'As you wish. I quite understand.' Leonard glanced at his watch. This was taking longer than it should.

'There's another aspect.'

'Ah.'

'Have I your absolute confidence?'

'Jack, I've already said that you have. Anyway, you should know well enough that doctors are like priests at confession.'

'It's about the tenancy.'

'The what? That's nothing to do with me.'

'You see, if I fall ill, seriously ill, and have to stop working, the tenancy of Cartwright Farm could be forfeit.'

'Nonsense!'

'No, it's true. To keep the tenancy, I must go on farming.'

'So you shall. Really, this is fanciful. Not a medical problem at all, and certainly none of my business.'

'Oh, but it is. Don't you understand, you might be required to give evidence at a hearing.'

'At a hearing? Aren't you being a bit irrational?' Leonard was beginning to think this geezer needed a shrink as well as a cardiologist.

'It may seem so, but Vacant Possession is something Ashley Kirkland would be a fool not to want. It would nearly double the value of the farm, so any opportunity to dissolve our tenancy would tempt him. He would gain upwards of a couple of hundred thousand and we would be out!' The pitch of Jack's voice lifted as he spoke, making the last word almost falsetto. *'Ruined!'* Veins pulsed in his temples and the whites of his eyes were visible all round his irises.

'I really think you should forget all this. You seem to be disturbed quite unnecessarily. Besides, Ashley Kirkland is far too decent a man to do anything like that, whatever the gain.'

'Every man has his price.'

'This conversation has gone quite far enough.' Leonard's voice developed an edge. 'I think the consultation is at an end.' Then, more kindly, 'Try to take a little more rest. Lie in on Sundays, take some gentle exercise and try not to worry. You don't know how lucky you are. Some of my patients really suffer and yet, you know, it's often the ones who have most cause who make the least fuss.' He stood up and opened the door for Jack. Making sure he was out of earshot of Mrs Pollitt, he said, 'I'm going right past your front gate later today. I'll drop the Ventolin off myself.'

Jack drove slowly home to resume his work. Leonard, now quite late, spent the rest of the day trying to catch up with his calls and not succeeding. He was grateful there would be no evening surgery and hoped to get home in time for a cup of tea at about five. When he arrived, Maggie was just leaving with an armful of red and white tulips, cherry blossom, pheasant-eye narcissus and assorted greenery.

'What about tea?' he inquired.

'Have to do it yourself. I'm off.' She shifted her load and a narcissus fell to the ground. He lifted it for her but instead of putting it back into the bunch, smelled it and placed it in the buttonhole of his shabby jacket. Such flowers were two a penny at Bridge House.

'Gorgeous scent,' Leonard said. 'Where are you going?'

'Church. Betty Rose and I are on the flower rota. I hoped these might last for three weeks. They've a better chance in the church than out here in this heat, anyway. 'S always bloody freezing in there, even in summer.'

Leonard watched her walk, slightly unsteadily, to the gate which led to the towpath along the river. Her gait puzzled and slightly worried him. He wondered if she was developing an inner-ear problem and then dismissed the idea. It was surely nothing more than the awkwardness of carrying that huge bunch of vegetation.

Two days later, Ashley was settling down to an afternoon's work at the farm. His office, a former harness room, was rustic with a flagstone floor and bare brick walls, but comfortably furnished. It was tucked away in a collection of farm buildings almost half a mile from the Manor House. The original barns, byres and granary had been built with the same honey-coloured bricks as the house, in the prosperous years before the 1846 Repeal of the Corn Laws. Their dimensions were handsome and the brick had mellowed after more than a century of frosts and summer heatwaves, but for modern farming methods, they were of limited use. Nowadays they were dwarfed by a range of steel-frame sheds clad with midnight-blue asbestos, accommodating tractors, combine harvesters – all with air-conditioned cabs – and other modern farm tackle.

Close at hand, a huge cattle shed housed the dairy herd,

each of the 120 cows having her own cubicle in which to rest. They were milked, sixteen at a time in a parlour, not, as the name suggests, by a romantic bevy of merry milkmaids, but by machines which piped the milk to a huge storage tank. Here it was chilled before being pumped into a Milk Marketing Board tanker and driven off for processing. Each cow had one calf per year, reared on the premises, first on milk substitute and later, weaned with manufactured feed pellets. The males were castrated and fattened for beef. The best of the heifers were kept to replenish the herd but the majority were sold off after weaning.

The amount of dung and urine produced by the animal population at Wyckhamby Farms was prodigious. Since hygiene in the dairy parlour was crucial, the whole floor area had to be washed down with hundreds of gallons of water every day. The resulting effluent was stored, with the rest of the muck, in a vast, foetid pond known as the slurry lagoon which, though its contents were pumped out over the grass-land at regular intervals, always seemed full to the brim. Although the pumping operation caused a frightful stench, at other times the yard was not the stinking pit one might have expected, despite the numbers of farm animals there. Indeed, the strongest smell, and pleasantly sweet at that, usually emanated from the silage clamp – a stack of cut, fermented grass, conserved under plastic sheeting.

Ashley checked the contents of his in-tray, lifted the microphone of his dictating machine from its cradle and was about to compose the first of a pile of letters when there was a timid knock at the door. It was Andrew, slightly out of breath and looking dishevelled. 'Has Mardle been here yet?' he asked between breaths.

'No. You'd better sit down. Catch your breath.'

'There's a crisis.'

'Nonsense. You're dramatising.'

'I think he's resigning.'

'Piffle!'

'He'll say it's my fault but really, it isn't.'

'What are you talking about?'

The boy began to explain in a rush. 'He told Fred, you know, the new driver from Wiltshire, to finish rolling the barley this morning, but the two men on the tractor hoe had problems. Well, one of them's fallen and sprained his wrist, and so the tractor hoe had stopped with one man idle and the other out of action and I went and, and . . .' He stopped to gulp in a couple of lungfuls of air. 'Anyway, I went and got Fred off the rolling and told him to go and steer the tractor hoe and when he did, Mardle got in a right paddy and countermanded my orders and—'

'Countermanded your orders? Just who exactly do you think you are?'

'It didn't make sense. The hoeing is more urgent than the rolling and—'

'Why exactly are you giving orders?' Ashley cut in.

'Why? I . . . well, it seemed quite wrong.'

'One term at Cirencester and you know the farming business?'

'But Dad, you know which job is most urgent. You're always on about controlling weeds early.'

'That's not the point. Mardle's my foreman. I expect him, and only *him*, to give orders to the men.'

'But what do you expect me to do?'

'Your role here is still undetermined. You elected to walk out of college.'

'But I've been trying to help.'

'I know,' Ashley tried to sound kindly, 'but you mustn't chuck your weight about.'

'I wasn't. I was right. I *am* right.'

'Tactically, perhaps. But as a man manager, I'm afraid not. You should have *consulted* Mardle – you know, got him to think that it was his idea to pull Fred off the roller.'

'Dad,' the boy's tone whined, 'you've got to back me up on this one. I'm family!' There was a loud knock on the door.

'Yah!' Ashley shouted and then signalled Andrew to keep quiet by miming a zip fastener on his mouth. Bert Mardle came in, cloth cap on the back of his head, deep brown eyes darkened with suppressed rage, a scrubby beard spoiling the outline of his chin, which was thrust forward. He never shaved between October and May. 'Ah, Bert, do come in, find yourself a chair.' Ashley signalled to a hard one near the telex, hoping Mardle, with his dirty overalls, wouldn't choose to sit in the soft-covered armchair by his desk but not liking to offend his foreman. Mardle made no attempt to sit down.

'Oi'd sooner talk alone.' As he eyed Andrew, the chin was thrust out further.

'Oh, don't mind the boy, Bert. Now, what's on your mind?'

'Am I your manager or am I not?'

'My foreman? Yes, of course you are.'

'So it's me what gives the orders?'

'Naturally, once you've received instructions from me.' Mardle folded his arms while he digested this. Ashley continued, 'We discuss all the factors, of course, but I put great value on your advice and judgement.'

'Judgement, huh?'

'Indeed. You're here all the time, with your ear to the ground, so to speak. Naturally I rely on your judgement.'

'So what about Mas'r Andrew 'ere?'

'What about him?'

'Giving orders. Getting people off on the wrong jobs. What'm I s'posed to do about that?'

Andrew reddened and jumped up. 'You know very well, Mar—'

'Shut up, son!' retorted Ashley, and fixed him with a hard look before smiling at Mardle. 'Carry on, Bert.'

'Well, sir, it boils down to this. The men daren't disobey Master Andrew, 'im being family 'n all, but if he goes against what I tell 'em, I won't get no respect, 'n tha's just what 'e's done. It's about the new—'

'Yes, I know, and you were quite right to come and see me. The boy was wrong to—'

'Father, that's not *fair*. You said I was right just now. Tell him!'

Ashley took a breath and started again. 'Andrew *is* family and we all value his input. But in this instance he was wrong

– and you must see that, Andrew – quite wrong to give direct instructions to the men. I've just told him that from now on, he must consult you in every case.' Ashley pre-empted the boy's protests with a dismissive gesture. 'Now, what action have you taken?'

'Well, sir, naturally I thought to come and see you first, but it's really the barley what needs rolling. Grandfather always used to say it had to be rolled before you heard the cuckoo.'

'Father, that's folklore. You *know* the hoeing is priority. You said so yourself just now!'

Ashley ignored him. 'Quite so, Bert. But since the tractor hoe is running now, don't you think it would be more sensible to let it be?'

'But what about that barley?'

'The solution is right here. Andrew wants to contribute: let him roll the barley.'

'But, Dad, I'm not a tractor driver.' Andrew was nearly tearful at being asked, in front of Mardle, to do such a menial task. 'Can't one of the men do it?'

'Well, I suppose it won't matter if the driving ain't that good,' Mardle said, 'not just with rolling, but it's your risk, Mr Kirkland. Them new 'ydraulic rolls is valuable.'

This was too much for Andrew, who strode out, slamming the heavy door so hard that a little puff of dust fell from the open rafters onto Ashley's desk.

'Temper, temper,' muttered Mardle, a sneer appearing briefly on his face before he composed his look into one of concern. 'What are we a-goin' ter do wi' im, Mr Kirkland?'

'My problem, not yours.' Ashley gestured towards the door and then bent his head to his dictating machine.

Andrew ran home to change out of his tweed jacket and cavalry twill trousers into old clothes. Tears of humiliation and self-pity kept welling up and he ran faster and faster, working himself into a crescendo of rage. As he threw open the back door, Elaine emerged from the morning room. 'Darling? Whatever's the matter?' She followed him halfway up the stairs. He stopped at the top and looked over the mahogany bannister rail.

'That fucker Mardle!'

'Andrew, really!' Elaine came up the rest of the way and took hold of both his hands. 'Darling boy, you're shaking. What *is* the matter?'

With his mother's touch, he began to calm down. 'It's that bloody Mardle. He made a mistake and Dad *knew*. I was right but he told Mardle I was an idiot and then they both turned on me.'

'Are you sure?'

'Of course I'm sure! Now they've given me a filthy job to do. Well, I *won't* do it!'

'What have they told you to do?' Elaine put his hands on her own shoulders. Instinctively he felt for her earlobes and held each one gently between finger and thumb. It was something they often did – had done since he was a very little boy.

'Roll the barley,'

Elaine laughed. 'You silly, that's not so bad. Your father used to love that job. He said you could almost do it with your eyes shut.'

'I won't do menial jobs. I'm family.'

'My sweet, is that quite the right attitude?'

'What d'you mean, attitude?' The whining tone had returned.

'One does have duties.'

'Oh, so you're going to side with them too, are you?' He took his arms off her shoulders.

'My love, nobody owes you a living. If you hadn't thrown in the sponge, you could still be at Cirencester, having fun with your friends as well as learning.'

'It was a waste of time.'

'Aren't you rather wasting your time here?'

'Only because Dad won't give me a proper job.'

'Now that's not fair, my darling. We didn't want you to leave college and under the circumstances, it was very decent of your father to let you come on the farm at all.'

'But he won't give me a proper job.'

'Proper job? Like what?'

'I could do that bloody Mardle's, easy as wink.'

'Could you? He may be a bit of an oaf, but he's a man of tremendous experience.'

'A yobbo, and nasty with it! He hates me.'

'Not at all! You've got such a lot to learn. Couldn't you try to co-operate with your father a bit more – for my sake?' Elaine stroked the back of his neck. That little twist of hair at the nape, just above his collar, so like Ashley's, so vulnerable. 'Please?'

'Mum, I don't know what I'm supposed to *do*. Nobody *listens*.'

'I know.' She stroked his hair again. 'Tell you what – why don't you get in that new car of yours and buzz down to London this weekend? Annabel'd be thrilled to have you at the flat.'

'I can't. I'm skint.'

'What's happened to your allowance?'

'I had expenses.'

This made Elaine laugh. 'You live and move and have your being exclusively at our expense.'

'Mum! I *work* here.'

'If you can call it that. Anyway, I suppose I could lend you a bit, just so you don't sponge off Annabel. Fifty should do it.'

'Hundred!'

'Absolutely not. You've got to learn the value of hard-earned money, my lad.'

'Have you? Has Dad?'

'Andrew!'

'Hundred.'

'Seventy-five. And I want it back on the first of May.'

'Mother, I love you!'

'Yecchh! By the way, there's a condition.'

'I might have known.'

'You must go, now, and do whatever it is your father

wants. If he wants you to roll the barley – that's what you've got to do.'

'Oh, Mum!'

'I mean it, Sonny, you really must.' She gave him a little shove towards his bedroom and went back to the morning room, making a mental note to talk to Ashley. The boy needs to know where he stands, she thought. He must have something specific to do. But she was quite unable to think of anything.

Chapter Five

Later that afternoon, as Andrew was using his father's oldest tractor to pull a cranking set of rollers up and down the hundred-acre field of young green barley, Sally Doncaster was getting ready to meet Ashley. She wanted, she had said at the Kirklands' dinner party, to find out all about farming. Ashley had agreed to give her a guided tour – on condition, he had insisted, that she told him all about her own business activities. 'You never know where there might be common ground,' he had said and she agreed wholeheartedly. With such a fascinating man as Ashley, she thought, there was bound to be common ground . . .

The question was, what to wear. She needed to look sensible and countryfied but wanted to be alluring. Eventually, she selected a pair of pale blue, form-hugging denim jeans and a rust-coloured shirt which she cinched round her waist with a python-skin belt. She wasn't sure exactly how big two and a half thousand acres might be, but suspected there'd be a fair bit of walking. One thing she was sure of: it would take a lot longer for her to study Ashley's assets than it would to review her own empire. Still, she thought, one hasn't done badly.

In a decade of conscientious wheeling and dealing, she had developed, from scratch, a business which now enjoyed a turnover of nearly seventeen million. She travelled extensively, mainly to Africa, for her bread and butter, but also to any other part of the world that was interesting from a business point of view. Raylon Tropicals manufactured nothing and only carried a staff of thirty-one.

The secret of the company's success lay with the products it exported. Sally had begun to identify certain needs in some of the poorer tropical nations when she was working for a firm of travel agents. As company perks in those days, agency staff were allowed free trips from time to time and, while her colleagues were manhunting in places like Antigua or Mustique, or gambling in Las Vegas, she would spend her leaves flogging round some of the less delectable of the world's resorts. Dakar was the basis of her first trip; it kindled in her a fascination for the tropics in general and West Africa in particular.

A year later, she flew to Lagos. The steamy squalor of Ikeja airport might have frightened anyone else into hiding in their hotel until the return flight, but not Sally. On being mobbed by illegal moneychangers at the airport doors, she entered into the spirit of the occasion and haggled vigorously until, one by one, they dropped away, realising they were wasting their time with her. From an expatriate who worked in the chemical industry, she learnt about the ways of the country – who was bribing whom, who was corrupt and who was not. She had no particular plans at that time but was captivated by the different culture and wanted to learn more. At the same expatriate's suggestion, she flew north.

'I know someone over the border, in Mudando,' he said.

'Where's that?'

'Mudando is a small independent state. You get there from Kano; there are no direct flights. Anyway, this chap wants to buy irrigation equipment but no English firm has been willing to help him.'

'Why not.'

'Who knows? Lack of trust, perhaps. Mudando has strict currency laws so it's difficult to get money out.'

When she returned to Britain, Sally found a firm which specialised in small irrigation systems and tried to arrange a shipment. The firm told her that it was not possible to trade with Mudando because of currency problems.

'But there's no problem,' she explained. 'My client will obtain import licences and I will see that you are paid in advance. However, fifteen per cent of the sum must be paid to me as my commission.'

'Fifteen? Isn't that rather excessive?'

'It certainly is, but how else are you likely to sell your goods in Mudando *and* receive payment in advance?'

Sally then shared her commission with her foreign client, who was thus able to put some money aside in England for his family to use on foreign trips. Through him she came to know the ruling family of Mudando and, though her business empire spread to other parts of the tropics, this little African principality always remained her favourite spot.

But all that gruelling work took its toll. One afternoon, she jumped up to help her secretary pick up a tray of files which she'd dropped, and fainted. Scared by this, and scared too by the three-month gap since her last period, she went to Harley Street where a physician in an impressive office – all mahogany and *Country Life* – gave her a costly checkup.

High blood pressure was diagnosed, caused by stress. 'When did you last have a holiday, Miss Ray?' She could barely remember when she'd had a weekend free, much less a holiday. Thus, admonished, frightened and rather sorry for herself, she had set all her business activities on 'hold' and flown to Australia for a five-week break. 'Take lots of exercise, but relax,' she'd been told.

So there she sat, on a dreamy golden beach not far from Cape Byron, the Pacific Ocean pounding away in front of her and Apollo-like surfers, their bodies bronzed and beautiful, cavorting in the waves. Captain Cook had followed this coastline nearly 200 years before, on his way home after landing at Botany Bay. What would he think now, she wondered, of the beach cabins, the skyscrapers of Surfers Paradise, the avocado and banana orchards?

She lay dozing, bikini-clad. Voices rose and fell, sometimes a yelp of delight from the roaring surf, sometimes a child's voice. Near her a girl of about three, she supposed – she really knew very little about children – was playing with sea shells on the sand. She was talking to herself and singing snatches of a wistful tune. She looked up and caught sight of Sally staring at her. 'Look,' she said, 'shells.'

'So I see. You've collected quite a lot.'

'I'm taking them home.' The accent didn't sound quite Australian.

'Where's your Mummy?' Sally asked.

'Heaven,' the child replied. 'She died and went to heaven.' There was no sign of grief so Sally concluded that the mother had been dead for a while.

'What about your Daddy?'

'Over there.' The child pointed to a rather thin figure reading the *Sydney Morning Herald* under a hired umbrella. He was well tanned but had neither the sun-pickled complexion nor the brute muscularity of the young Australians. He looked up from his paper.

'Hope she's not disturbing you.' Rich tenor, an English voice.

'Not in the least,' Sally replied and chatted to the girl who was called Camilla, who lived in Wagga Wagga – no, she didn't make it up, there really was a Wagga Wagga only it was just called Wagga – who had no Mummy, just Daddy, and who hated cats, really hated them because they scratched and had horrid eyes that stared. Then she stared at Sally.

'Your hair's the same colour as mine, look!' she said.

'So it is,' said Sally, stroking the sun-bleached curls and marvelling at the directness of the child's gaze. She had never, until now, felt the slightest pang about being childless.

That evening, she ran into Camilla's father at the hotel. 'I'm just going to the bar,' he said. 'Come and have a drink.' He was called Jules Doncaster, had emigrated to Wagga from Cheshire, lost his wife in a sailing accident at thirty and, so far, had brought up Camilla on his own. He was an accountant, quite strait-laced really, and had very little of interest to tell about himself but had achieved partner status at a fairly tender age. She told him about her adventures in Africa and elsewhere and they continued their conversation through dinner. He found her fascinating. He'd never met a truly liberated woman before, and furthermore, one who had done many more exciting things in the last few years than he would have dared to do in a whole lifetime. She found his leanness interesting and his soft voice and gentle manner tempting. He seemed so incredibly considerate.

They repaired to the lounge for coffee. A chemistry was obviously working between them because when he said, 'I must go upstairs and check on Camilla,' she had to resist an impulse to beg him to stay.

'Will you come back and have some more coffee?'

'Oh, please, if I'm not boring you. I won't be long.' She watched him weave his way through the hotel lounge and disappear into the lift. He was back within five minutes. 'Dead to the world,' he said. They ordered more coffee and talked in a relaxed fashion. She was concentrating so intently on him she barely noticed the time pass until she realised everyone else had gone from the room. It was almost midnight.

'Another Cognac?'

'Actually, I'd as soon have a cold beer. I've grown rather fond of this Aussie lager.'

'I'd like one too. Shall I get some? I think the bar's still open.'

'Well,' Sally said, 'in the fridge in my room there are about ten cans of it. "Tubes" I think they call them over here. Some frightful name like Tooth and Retch, or something similar. Wouldn't that be more fun?'

'In your room?' His voice had become slightly husky. 'I'm not sure I can be trusted.'

'I was rather hoping you couldn't.' He caught hold of her hand: she couldn't tell whose pulse was racing harder. Upstairs, they made love with fierce urgency. Neither had enjoyed a sexual relationship for some years and in each, the tide of pent-up emotional frustration burst alarmingly. Later, calmer, they lay and held each other.

'I haven't had a bedfellow for three years,' she said.

'Neither have I really.' He thought of the half-hearted attempt he'd made the year before, ending in failure and mutual scorn.

67

'I suppose it would be ridiculously corny to call this "love at first sight", wouldn't it?'

'Why?'

'Storybook rubbish!'

'You may have doubts. I hardly know you. But what I know, I love.'

'Gertcha!' She kissed his ear. 'You've got tidy little ears,' she said.

'I must go – it's Camilla. If she wakes in the night she'll be scared.' He got out of bed. 'Do you mind if I shower?' He went into the bathroom and a few minutes later emerged carrying one of the hotel's big bath towels.

'Hey, that's mine,' she said. He grinned at her. His hair was sleek from the shower and water dripped from him making a dark stain on the carpet round his feet.

'Plenty more in there,' he said, 'brand clean.' She watched him dry himself, dabbing and mopping with detailed thoroughness. She had not had a great fund of experience in the love department – she'd been too busy with her career – and the sight of a male body was still enough of a novelty to interest her. Even though Jules's figure was slight, he had a pleasing taper from shoulders to waist. She was glad he wasn't too hairy – no more than a shading on his chest and an exciting dark line beginning just below the navel and thickening over his groin so that his prick, contracted by the coldness of the water, peeped out like a nestling bird. He turned to lift his cotton slacks off the sofa.

'Neat little bum,' she remarked.

The romance sustained itself, almost but never quite reaching again that summit of passion on their first night together. They began to make plans. 'You'll have to give up here,' she said. 'I earn more than you in England anyway so you might as well set up shop with me in London.' Within three months they were married.

All that was eight years ago. Now here she was today, her business still growing, with an adored stepdaughter and a fine home in the country. She and Jules still loved each other in their way – that first night in Australia would always be with

68

them – but she had other commitments. He had decided not to be a partner in her firm, probably just as well really, but instead developed his own consultancy, advising small companies in difficulty and arranging emergency financing while they remedied their faults.

For Camilla, surprisingly, Sally became the mother she lacked. She was firm, patient, generous-hearted and loving. In fact, she admitted to herself with a twinge of guilt that she loved Camilla more than she did Jules. If a fire broke out at the Old Rectory, she was pretty sure she'd want to rescue her stepdaughter first, but perhaps that was natural anyway.

As middle age approached, Sally's hunger for men increased but although she needed more from sex than Jules could provide, she did not become promiscuous. Rather, she flirted, teased and dallied with her male associates, enjoying the hunger in their eyes but never granting more than a brief glimpse of the delights that a deeper relationship might offer them. At first, this pattern had begun with Ashley but within the briefest time, she felt quite different about him. She sensed that she was more attracted to him than he to her, and nothing like that had ever happened to her before.

To set off her neckline, she chose a sky-blue and beige silk scarf which she tied loosely, raffishly, over the collar of the shirt. Thinking of her feet, and of all the acres she might have to walk, she selected a pair of heavy brogues but decided to take her green wellingtons and shooting jacket as well. She went into her kitchen, glanced at the clock and saw with a lurch that she only had five minutes before the appointment, but then remembered with relief that to get to Ashley's office would take all of a minute. She scratched out a note for Camilla who was playing with Mandy Rose at Cartwright Farm until teatime – the two girls had become close friends – and fixed it to the fridge door with a magnet. Instead of walking, she decided to take the BMW, shunning the more direct back route because of the unbridged ford.

Ashley was waiting outside his office as her car turned into the yard and parked next to his Range Rover. He walked over and opened the driver's side door. 'Perfect timing,' he said. 'I was just looking out for you.' Then, taking in the quality of her clothes, 'I say, you do look rather glamorous.'

'Nonsense, these are my ancient gardening duds.'

'Well, it'll be a bit muddy in places, so I hope you've brought your wellies.'

'But of course!' She accepted his offered hand and climbed out of the car. 'Thank you, kind sir!' A mock curtsy followed. 'Where to first?'

'I thought a quick tour of the farm and then a cup of tea in the office.'

'Sounds divine.'

'Right. If you'll just grab your wellies we'll make a start.' He opened the door of the Range Rover.

'Aren't we walking?'

'Not all of it. You could do ten miles and still not cover it.'

'Heavens. How far do you stretch?'

'About halfway to Kendale along that road and along the Venn that way,' Ashley made a sweep with his arm, 'right the way up into those hills.'

'But that's half England!'

'Hardly,' Ashley laughed, 'but you see that little wood, way over there, the one with the trees on the skyline?'

'Mmm.'

'That's my northern boundary. When there's a shoot, we always draw that wood last. It looks small from here but actually has the best pheasant cover so the guns can usually end on a high note.' Sally didn't quite understand what he was talking about but smiled anyway. Ashley motioned her towards the Range Rover. 'Jump in, milady, or we'll never get this tour done before dark.'

They travelled a confusing route along bumpy tracks, short tarmac roads, through narrow gates and over cattle grids. Every few minutes, they stopped to look at the crops, all appearing uniform and healthy. There were fields of winter wheat, sown in rows almost touching, like deep green corduroy, acres of oilseed rape which smelt of cabbage and had yellow flowers just emerging, bright emerald seas of barley, and grass fields dotted with contented piebald cattle or with sheep. There were lambs, galloping together in posses until their mothers admonished them with throaty gurgles and they ran back, butting the ewes' udders to encourage them to let down milk which they suckled with aggressive gulps, tail stumps twitching with excitement. In the hills the soil was pale and stony, but in the valleys it was rich and dark and had been worked to a crumbly tilth. In one of these lowland fields, a machine with two workers riding on the back was creeping across the land and pulling it into deep grooves and ridges. 'They're planting potatoes, one of our most important crops,' Ashley explained. 'Ours all end up as crisps or oven chips.' Elsewhere, on a sunny south-facing slope, potato plants were already beginning to push squat, greenish-black shoots through the land ridges. These were the early crop, planted to catch the new-potato market in late spring when London shoppers would pay big premiums for delectable, waxy tubers whose skins sloughed off at the merest touch.

'Why don't you grow all earlies, if they're so much more expensive?' Sally asked.

'Low yields. Besides, the price drops quickly so you can only catch the early market if you grow them on land in a favoured position. That's why so many new potatoes come from Cornwall and South Wales – and Jersey, of course. They have a huge climatic advantage. We're tail-enders, really, living up here.'

As they drove deeper into the hills, the landscape changed. There were larger, less disciplined hedges with trees planted in them at intervals. The land was mostly down to grass, rougher than the faultless swards of the lowlands, with a rich variety of meadow grasses and wildflowers. Sulphur-yellow brimstone butterflies flew with intent along the track, looking for the more sedentary, greenish-white females of their species.

'Oh, but this is lovely,' Sally said. 'Look at the flowers in the hedgerow.'

'Wood anemones. This is our conservation area. The land

hasn't been ploughed for more than a hundred years, if at all, and we don't allow pesticides in this section.'

'Oh, do let's walk!'

'In a moment. We just have a few more yards to go.' The track, shaded by tall hedges on both sides, became more deeply rutted, and Ashley changed into four-wheel drive to improve the vehicle's traction in the mud. She noticed his hands on the gear stick, brown and weathered but surprisingly sensitive with long fingers and neat nails. He bit his lower lip as he concentrated on avoiding the deepest ruts and, while she was studying his profile, he turned, met her gaze and smiled.

'It's a bit uncomfortable but I think you'll find it worthwhile in a minute.' He smiled again, the winning Kirkland smile. After about half a mile, when the hedges seemed to be closing in on the vehicle, they stopped and got out. He passed her wellingtons out from the back and then held her arm for support while she put her feet into them. She staggered slightly on the left one but he was quick to steady her with a hand on her waist. Instinctively she held to him and, with a gentle but decisive movement, gave him a little stroke in the small of the back.

'Thank you kind sir, again!'

'Not at all.' He stiffened at her touch and moved away as soon as she had regained her balance. 'Now, this,' he said, 'is why I brought you up that track.' He led the way to a gap in the hedge where a stile nestled among the hawthorn. 'You first,' he gestured her to climb the stile.

'Oh, how *divine!*' In the last mile, they had climbed much more than she had realised and were now atop the hill from which they could see the whole of Wyckhamby, cradled in the valley with the Venn curved round it in a great bow. 'Fancy people saying Lincolnshire is flat!' She gazed for a while and then said, 'Ashley, what a romantic spot. I'll bet you did a lot of your courting up here.'

'Some.' He began to walk. 'This wood is the one I pointed out from the yard. It has some lovely wildflowers at this time of year.' They strolled together through the grass toward the trees. As they entered the wood, and the shade, she shivered slightly. 'Not cold, surely?' he said.

'Not at all. It's just that I find woods a bit, well you know, scary.' The idea of someone so extrovert being scared of a collection of trees amused him so much he laughed out loud. 'But they *are* sinister!' she insisted, and sidled closer to him, taking his hand. His first impulse was to take his away but that seemed impolite. Then he noticed the primroses studding the mossy floor of the wood and tugged his hand free to point them out.

'Let me pick you some.' He stooped to gather a few of the pale blooms. Among them he found sweet violets and, selecting flowers with the longest stems, he gathered a dozen or so – both purple and white kinds – to add to the primroses. She watched him bending to pluck and then walking a few more steps, head bowed in search of the right bloom. What a graceful mover he is, she thought, and fit as a fiddle, almost like a ballet dancer or an athlete.

As soon as he had offered to pick flowers for her he realised his mistake. Walking with her alone into a wood, giving her bouquets, she'd be sure to think he was making a pass. He cursed his own stupidity. 'Here you are,' he handed the little posy to her. 'The violets have a bewitching scent but actually the primroses have a faint, er, fragrance of their own.'

'Why, Ashley!' The voice was creamy smooth. 'Is this what I think it is?' She took the hand which held out the flowers, keeping a grip on it while she bowed her head to smell them. He cleared his throat and tried to release his hand.

'Sorry?'

'This looks open to romantic interpretations.' She gave him what she hoped was a winning look. 'You said you wanted to discuss common ground, but I never for one instant thought, well . . . you know.'

Her other hand was reaching round to the small of his back again and he was aware of her perfume overriding the clean scent of the spring flowers. He resisted the impulse to recoil but her nearness unnerved him and the brilliance of her lipstick clashed with the soft woodland colours. Besides, he suspected that this flirting was cool and deliberate. Gently he took her hand away from his waist, and as gently placed the bouquet into her other hand.

'Ashley?'

'I'm sorry if I've misled you. I was clumsy, I just thought you'd enjoy the wood and the . . . the flowers at this time of year.'

'Misled?' Sally's voice developed an edge. 'What *can* you mean?'

'Well, your interpretation.'

'Of what?'

'Oh really, it doesn't matter.'

'No – tell me.'

'It's just that I'm quite happily married—'

'Me too. Frankly, Ashley, I'm not at all sure what the hell you're on about.'

'Neither am I really. P'raps we should go back.' He led the way to the Range Rover and soon they were bumping down the track.

Back in his office he made tea which they drank, not out of rough mugs, as she had expected, but from a set of Victorian china cups and saucers with fluted sides and a gilt and maroon pattern. 'Old, but not especially valuable,' he said. 'They were my great-grandmother's. She had the set made for her but over the years, most of them got broken. My parents were less interested in old things than I am.'

'You surprise me, Ashley.' Sally accepted a second cup, poured from the silver teapot. 'You are clearly a brilliant farmer but you are about the most unfarmerish person I've ever met.'

'What exactly is a farmer supposed to be like?'

'I don't know. Rough, I suppose – boorish, perhaps.'

Ashley laughed. 'Farmers are just business people.'

'But guardians of the countryside, too.'

'Nonsense! The land is merely a raw material to use for maximum profit. Business is business, whether you're growing peas or making soup ladles. Which reminds me, talking of business, when can we do the return match?'

'Soon as you like. In fact, I can probably tell you all you need to know about my firm here and now.' They spent another hour discussing common business interests while afternoon slipped into evening.

Over at Cartwright Farm, Jack Rose walked across his best potato field and kicked a clod of earth. It broke into three clayey lumps, one of which stuck to his foot. Not ready. It would take at least two more days of this sunshine before the land was dry enough to crumble into the fine tilth needed for planting the tubers. Bringing machinery onto damp land was unwise because its weight compacted the soil which would then grow stunted plants. But late planting also reduced yield, so deciding just how soon after rain it was safe to cultivate was always tricky. Some of his sugar-beet land was already suffering from being worked too soon and, after a few warm days, cracks were beginning to appear between the rows of young seedlings. If there were a drought, these would open wider and the land would parch before the plant had time to develop a strong root system.

This was a worry, but not half so unnerving as the impending visit from the bank manager. Once a year, Geoff Woods had to be escorted over the fields before looking through the Roses' budgets and cash-flow forecasts. On the strength of the annual visit, he would decide whether to continue to back them. For a healthy farm, even one with a large overdraft, this would be a mere formality and financing would present no problem, but Cartwright Farm was *not* healthy, and try as he might, Jack could not see how the family would be able to get through another year without increasing their borrowings yet again.

He walked through the rest of the potato land into the neighbouring field where the wheat was responding well to its dressing of spring fertiliser. He had hopes for a reasonable yield, as long as there was enough rain in summer to keep the crop growing on such light land. Further on, the barley was not so good. Drilled into a poor seed bed, it had emerged unevenly and now rabbits were making inroads into the crop by grazing along the headlands. He should have taken steps to eradicate them in February but there never seemed time to do those odd jobs even in midwinter. Rounding a corner, he saw two rabbits side by side, eating the young barley plants. In a burst of rage, he yelled and sprinted towards them waving his stick, hoping to club at least one of them, but they scampered into the hedge before he was within twenty yards of them. Pain speared him, suddenly, between the shoulder blades and for a moment, he thought he would faint. He sat down on the grass by the hedge and waited for the dizziness and the ache to pass. Out of habit, he felt for the pulse in his wrist but he could sense his heart beating fast and irregularly in his throat, as if a moth were stuck there, fluttering its wings. It would be at least five minutes before he would feel able to get up and walk slowly back home.

These attacks happened nearly every day now, but he knew he could handle them as long as they didn't get worse. Just blood pressure, Dr Bates had said, and nothing to worry about. The difficult part was keeping them secret, especially from Betty. He couldn't bear the idea of her anxiety being sharpened any more but he hated being underhand. This very evening, for instance, he'd have to tell her that everything was looking fine on the farm, when he knew that the wet spring had already caused some serious problems.

Chapter Six

South London in late April. The tropical summer flavour common to all large cities, regardless of latitude, had begun to emerge. Sugar-pink blossom had fallen from the street trees to become brown trash which swirled in the gutters whenever a lorry passed. Shop windows were bright with cheap summer clothing. The smell of hot pavements blended with doner kebabs, sweat, fresh bread, traffic fumes. Parties of noisy drinkers sat at tables outside the pubs, vaunting naked beer bellies and everywhere, young blacks, long-limbed, lissome, in sleeveless tops and Rastafarian colours, lolled and chatted in groups, paced the pavements, shadow-boxed, danced, laughed, cheered and jeered.

Ashley Kirkland, walking from Brixton station towards Clapham, felt incongruous in his charcoal business suit and quickened his pace. In spite of the bright weather and all the gaiety around him, there was an underlying menace. Recent riots had reminded everyone, even the stolid inhabitants of villages like Wyckhamby, that law and order in Britain could no longer be taken for granted. The villagers regretted the state of affairs, blaming the disturbances on violent television, lack of parental discipline, sexual incontinence and above all, on troublesome racial minorities. But they were comfortably isolated. Nothing sordid ever happened in the country, and it was easy to judge from a distance. Unlike them, Ashley knew this area well enough to see how little it would take for repressed rage to erupt into violence. Legislation had not reversed the sense of inequality round here, and with such high unemployment and a police force which disliked all minorities, especially blacks, he was surprised that the riots had been so limited. What motivation had these people for keeping the peace, he wondered.

He turned up Thistleton Road whose grimy brick houses always reminded him of 1960s films like *The L-Shaped Room*, and went into Number 24. On the second floor, he took a key out of his wallet and unlocked one of the doors, calling, 'Rick?' It was clear from the musty smell and the layer of dust over the furniture that the little one-room flat had been empty for some time. Puzzled, he peeped into the bathroom before going into the tiny kitchen where Rick often left notes. There was a reporter's pad on the draining board. He picked it up and read the neat writing on the top page but soon realised it was from an earlier time. He leafed through, looking at previous pages. *'Dearest Guy,'* they began, or *'Guy my love,'* and often ended with a *'can't wait!'*

'Mucky little tyke,' Ashley said, and dropped the pad into the waste bin. He went back into the bed-sitting room and began to undress. After pulling on a dressing gown, he set about cleaning up the flat. It was not untidy but needed dusting, and the decayed contents of the fridge had to be thrown away. Within half an hour he had it all freshened up and ten minutes later, had showered. In the chest of drawers he found a pair of jeans, a soft cotton shirt printed with a small red Paisley design on a black background, and a short-length denim jacket. He dressed and then stood before the mirror, setting about his hair with brush and comb, changing the style from swept back with parting to a more raffish wave over his right eye. As he combed, he made a series of adjustments to his expression. The eyes narrowed slightly, the mouth set a fraction firmer, the chest lifted a little. He transferred wallet and keys to his jeans pocket and, with a wink at the mirror said, 'Hello, Guy.'

He took the Victoria Line to Green Park and strolled in the evening sunshine along Piccadilly and then up through London's little Chinatown. He hoped he might get some news from one of the pubs he and Rick used, and went first into the Hackney in Old Compton Street. At the bar – an old and knocked-about mahogany affair which was embellished with much frosted and patterned glass – stood two middle-aged men in shiny business suits. They had attaché cases at their feet and from time to time, their eyes glanced furtively round the room. Soon a youth with cropped hair, tattooed neck and a leather jacket strolled in, gave one of the men a mock punch in the midriff and had his greeting returned with backslaps and a pint of lager. He sat on a barstool between them, while they joshed him and squeezed his knees.

Ashley caught the barman's eye and orderd a small Scotch. It was not the usual man but he had seen him several times before.

'You haven't seen Rick here lately, I suppose?' he asked.

'Wouldn't know 'im from Adam.' He put the change into Ashley's hand and turned to serve an overweight woman.

After a few minutes Ashley looked round one more time, in the hopes of seeing a familiar face, but drew a blank and left without finishing his whisky.

He retraced his steps, going back almost to Trafalgar Square before calling in at Dorothy's. The atmosphere at the Hackney was ambiguous, but at Dorothy's there was no doubt: it was strictly for homosexuals. In the late 1970s, the décor might have been chic, but now the chrome trims were tarnished, the mirrors dulled and the black ceramic panelling smudged. There were two bars, one at street level which seemed to be crowded whenever the place was open, and a smoky, noisy basement. Customers had overflowed onto the pavement near the entrance and he had to sidle through the press to get inside where the buzz of conversation was almost drowned by juke-box music. There were plenty of couples, many locked in intense conversation, some holding hands, others embracing and even kissing but there was not a woman to be seen.

He decided to go down to the basement bar, hoping it would be quieter. As soon as he recognised Ashley, the barman, a dark lad dressed in very tight jeans, rent at the knees and with further tears just far enough below the buttocks to avoid indecency, served him ahead of everyone else. He wore a little leather cap with the peak turned up, reminding Ashley of a photograph he had seen of the playwright Joe Orton. The barman knew Rick but hadn't seen him for several weeks. He said, 'What's your gripe, love? There's plenty of talent in here and with your looks you can still pull 'em!'

Ashley took his drink to one of the little alcoves at the back of the room and brooded on the last brief exchange he had had with the boy when he'd appeared on his doorstep that night, with a dinner party in full swing, no less! Thank God it was only Betty who saw. 'How the hell did you find out where I lived?' he had asked.

'I looked in your wallet. I had to come. I *have* to talk to you.'

'Impossible, I can't take the risk.' Then at the sight of him, so wet and forlorn, shivering: 'Hell, Rick, how could you be so daft as to come here?' He had taken his hands, gently unhooking one from the ring slung round his neck. 'You still wear it?'

'Till I die!'

'Rick, I only have a second. Someone's actually waiting to come out.'

'That lady? She's nice. I thought you had a wife for a minute but she said she just worked here.'

'Rick, *listen*. You can't stay here, you'll have to go back to London. How did you come?'

'Hitched.'

'Mad! Got any money?'

'No.'

'Look,' he had reached into a back pocket for his wallet and had taken out two fifty-pound notes.

'Too much,' Rick had said, taking one.

'Rot! Take them both and get back to Brixton. I can't see you for about a month because of spring work here. Will you be all right?' The boy had nodded, mute. His eyes were streaming, but Ashley couldn't tell whether it was from the driving rain or from tears. 'There's a shortcut down that little track, past our farm buildings onto the road. Get a lift to Kendale, then wait for a train. Now off you go!' And off he'd gone. Thank you and goodbye! Ashley wanted another drink.

Returning to his alcove, fresh whisky in hand, he began to adjust his mind to the loss. He would forget the whole thing – even get rid of the flat. Fear of detection plagued him these days, especially since that dreadful moment at Wyckhamby when Rick had brought the two halves of his double life within sight of each other. Ashley drained his second whisky and decided to go for another. The downstairs bar of Dorothy's had been filling up and was now almost as crowded as the one at street level. Young men looking as ordinary and jovial as rugby club members joked, back-slapped and flirted with each other. He took his whisky back to his alcove and decided to hunt for some talent. Before long, he noticed a face watching him from the crowd. The features were pleasant and, when the young man emerged from the other bodies, Ashley could see that the fairly broad shoulders, narrow waist and close-cut auburn hair were enticing. He smiled and the boy walked over.

'Hi! Anyone sitting here?' The voice was soft with an American inflection.

'Be my guest,' said Ashley then, after a minute, 'that's a fine watch you've got there. Mind if I have a look?'

'Sure!' The eyes were green, the clothes clean and neat. The boy offered his wrist. 'Go ahead!' With a caressing movement, Ashley traced the veining on the back of the hand and the long fingers. A musician? Artist, perhaps. The boy must have been about eighteen, he thought, perhaps twenty.

'What's your name?'

'Brett.' He made no attempt to take his hand away. 'Yours?'

'Guy,' said Ashley. 'Guy Wilson.'

'Darling! That would be simply *divine*,' Sally Doncaster's voice rose to a shriek. 'June twentieth, then . . . Yes, just over a month . . . Love you love you *love* you!' She put the kitchen phone down and turned to Betty with the gleam of conquest in her eyes, 'Got him!'

'Michael Chetwynde?'

'In person. Delighted to come. He says,' here she lowered her eyes in modesty, ' "anything for an old friend".'

'But that's wonderful.' Betty sounded doubtful. 'Only—'

'Only what?'

'The Parochial Church Council – they don't like anyone to act without their approval.'

'Fiddlesticks!' The Rectory doorbell rang. It was Elaine Kirkland, armed with clipboard and notebook. Sally ushered her in but instead of indicating a kitchen chair, said, 'It's such a lovely day, why don't we work on the terrace? You two go first and I'll bring us a jug of coffee.' Sally shooed the two women outside where they found sumptuous padded garden chairs arranged round a low, stone table.

'What do you make of this, Betty?' Elaine jerked a thumb at the house.

'Well, it's kind of Sally to let us have the Old Rectory for the fête, but—'

'It's a hijack.'

'Oh, I wouldn't go so far as to say that.'

'I would. The fête's always been at Bridge House. Maggie's garden is one of the main attractions. She's absolutely fuming.'

'Poor Maggie.'

'Refuses to do a thing for the fête now, just when we need her most.'

'We've got Sally to help, at least.'

'But can we depend on her?' Betty thought of the disproportionate number of school runs she was making, and the extra journeys with Camilla to dancing classes, riding lessons or taking her home after playing with Mandy. Reciprocal favours were rare.

Sally arrived with a large thermos jug, plates and biscuits. The women sorted themselves out with cream and sugar. 'By the bye,' Sally said, 'I did tell you I won't be here for the actual fête, didn't I?' Both women stared at her. 'I'm afraid

I'll be in Mudando. Still, you'll be able to manage without me, won't you?'

'We'll have to,' Elaine said, after a silence. 'But you'll be able to help over the next few weeks, won't you?'

'After today? What more is there to do?'

'Everything really,' Elaine said. 'All the bookings, fixing the marquee, arranging the stalls, and there's quite a lot of chivvying up to do as well.'

'I doubt if I'll have very much time.' Sally employed her 'deeply regretful tinged with a soupçon of reproach' mode. 'I do have a business to run.'

'Ye-es, I see. I wonder who else could . . . um,' Betty was alarmed at the prospect of extra work. 'You see, we were rather counting on you. I mean, when you said we could rely on your—'

'And so you can. It's just that I have other commitments.' She broke a biscuit and toyed with the fragments. 'I do so envy your relaxed country ways, especially yours, Betty. You seem to have time for *everything*. We've lived here for nearly three months, but I still haven't slipped out of the rat race into your gentle pace of life.' She ended her speech with a tinkly laugh.

Elaine met Betty's eye. 'Perhaps we should get down to business,' she said. And so, to the sound of cuckoos in the warm May sunshine, the women discussed details of Wyckhamby's annual fund-raising exercise. After almost an hour, they had perfected their plans and the meeting was ready to split up.

'Yes, that's another thing, Elaine,' Sally said. 'You will be able to look after Michael up at the Manor won't you, when he comes on the day?'

'Michael? Who's Michael?'

'Chetwynde,' Betty explained. 'The television man from *Michael Meets*. He's agreed to come and open the fête.'

'Really?' Elaine looked surprised. 'I thought the PCC had invited the Bishop of Lincoln.'

Betty shrugged and glanced at Sally. 'They did invite the Bishop ages ago,' she said, 'and since he's accepted it's going to be a bit difficult to put him off. I mean, it's quite an honour really, we've been wanting him for years.'

'Pooh, we don't want a fusty old Bishop when we can have a telly star, do we? What we need is a crowd-puller.' Then, on a different tack: 'By the way, Betty, you said you'd get your husband to mow the Rectory paddock so that visitors can use it as a car park.'

'Jack is in no condition to do anything,' Elaine said sharply. 'I thought you knew he was ill.' Betty looked embarrassed.

'Betty, you never told me.' Sally's voice dropped a tone. 'What's wrong?'

'He thinks he's got a heart condition,' said Betty. 'There's nothing physically wrong, apparently, but he has high blood pressure and now he's got depression as well. What's so awful is that he's been feeling ill for months but didn't tell me until a fortnight ago.'

'Sounds like a clear need for mind over matter to me,' Sally said.

'That's none of our business,' Elaine cut in and began to gather up her notes. 'Have we finished here? Ashley gets home from London today and I need to be back at the Manor.' She thanked Sally for coffee and began to walk with Betty down the long Rectory drive. Once out of hearing Elaine said, 'Bloody woman! Betty, I'm so sorry.'

'Actually what she says is true, really. If only Jack could stop worrying, I'm sure he'd feel better. He's had a heart scan and everything but he's still convinced there's something wrong.'

'Poor you!'

'Oh, we'll manage somehow.'

'But you do so much for the village, Betty. Are you sure you can cope?'

'Quite sure.' They came to the end of the drive and stopped by an old lilac which threw its shade over the entrance. It was in full flower, a double white, and Betty breathed deeply of its fragrance.

Elaine said: 'Old Abbey Farm – I presume you know all about it?'

'Yes, of course.'

'Are you interested?'

'Elaine! We couldn't even afford to buy one of the field gates, let alone the whole farm. Anyway, I didn't think it was on the market yet.'

'The Church Commissioners aren't selling, they're looking for tenants. It's to be let from next Michaelmas. I'm surprised you hadn't heard.'

'I've been so tied up with Jack. Anyway, we couldn't possibly take it on. With things as they are I—'

'All the locals will have a go. They'll probably offer exorbitant rents, just to get the tenancy. I hear, for instance, that Clarke – you know, the Kendale Road Clarke – has already offered eighty-five pounds an acre.'

'But that's ludicrous!'

'For Old Abbey, yes, but averaged over his eight hundred acres, the rent looks tiny and the extra land is bound to make him more efficient.'

'Well, it's beyond our pockets. We couldn't possibly bid, not at any rent.'

'Pity. It's just what you need to bring your acreage up to a profitable size.' Elaine might not have had much practical experience, but she had grown up on one farm and married into another. The economic facts of life were as clear to her as to Betty, who lived at the sharp end.

'We simply couldn't afford it.'

'Perhaps not, but don't you see? Whatever the outcome, it's bound to put all the local rents up.'

'That's true.'

'And your own rent is up for review this year.' Elaine was trying to sound kindly but her words struck a bleak note.

'But Ashley's our landlord, thank goodness. He's a fair man.'

'He has been, as far as you and Jack are concerned, so far. But he *is* a businessman, Betty.'

'Of course.'

'Nothing to do with me, I know, and I've no intention of being disloyal to my own husband, but you should understand the implications.' She gave Betty's arm a little squeeze. 'Forewarned is forearmed.'

'I'm grateful.' A cock chaffinch flew to a branch in the lilac and began its urgent little song. 'As it happens, Jack and I are supposed to be meeting Ashley later today, about the rent. D'you think we should mention this?'

'Better to wait and see what happens, don't you think?' Elaine glanced at her watch. 'Heavens, I must dash.'

By the time Betty had got home, seen to the pigs, cleared up the mess the children had left in the house and done her daily quota of weeding in the garden, it was nearly dark. Jack had been in bed all day again. He had tried, he said, to get up at lunchtime but had had another attack and thought it best to rest.

'I'll be OK tomorrow,' he said. 'If only I could sleep at night, I'd be fine.'

'What needs doing on the land?'

'Not too much, but the cereals should have been sprayed for weeds a fortnight ago and the beet still needs steerage hoeing. We'll have to get contractors to do the spraying.'

'I'm sure we'll manage.' She tried to sound cheerful but felt the odds against their survival weighing more heavily than ever on her shoulders. 'What about tonight?'

'What's happening tonight?'

'Our visit to Ashley Kirkland – surely you hadn't forgotten that?'

He groaned. 'I don't really feel up to it. Could you handle it on your own?'

'Jack! It's about the rent. He'll expect you to be there.'

'But I feel so bloody awful. I don't think I can get up.' She looked at the deep lines in his face, the hunted look in his eyes and tried not to let the exasperation show in her voice.

'I know.' She stroked his head. 'I'll go. You rest. And try not to think too much. You'll only make yourself worse if you do.' She went downstairs and began to sort out the children's supper before getting ready to go over to Wyckhamby Manor.

*

When Elaine got home, Ashley's Daimler was parked outside the front door. She put her own car away in one of the stables, converted before the war into garaging by widening the doorways, and went into the house through the back door. He was in the drawing room, formal in his worsted suit.

'There.' He kissed her on the lips and took her arm. 'What do you think of that?' He had placed a small picture on the mantelpiece. It was a water-colour portrait of a youth, full-length, in a dilapidated hat and velveteen jacket, smoking a clay pipe. His stance was cocky, left hand thrust deep into his breeches' pocket, a tambourine under his arm. By his costume, he looked mid-nineteenth century.

'Oh, Ashley, he's beautiful!'

'A fairground boy – William Hunt, 1827. Signed and dated.' He picked it up again and turned it to face the window. 'There's a small tear, though.' Elaine put her index finger on the glass. 'No, not there, that's his shirt collar. Look, there, just below the hat brim.'

'Oh yes. Still, it could be restored.'

'Not likely. I'm keeping it as it is. I don't like the idea of restoring something as special as this. It seems dishonest somehow.' He sat on a chesterfield and relaxed.

'Tired?'

'I'm bushed. Elaine, be a treasure and pour me a whisky, I'll take it up and have a bath.'

'The whisky you'll have. The bath, not a chance.'

'Why?'

'The Roses are coming.'

Ashley groaned. 'What the hell for?'

'Jack's got this heart thing and from what Betty was telling me today, he's got depression on top.'

'Awful, especially for Betty – but what has it to do with us?'

'Well, you know they're struggling to survive . . .'

'And I suppose they want to delay paying the rent?'

'I expect so.'

'Well, Hector sees to all that – although I *do* know that they are already five weeks overdue.'

'Ashley, Betty's a friend of mine.'

'All the more reason for letting Hector deal with it. It's fairer through a land agent.'

'Hector Enfield will just be businesslike.'

'Precisely. And fair.'

'But, Ashley, this is a human thing. Betty does so much for everyone around the place. Jack's illness could finish them.'

'Mmm. I do feel for Betty. Poor bloody woman – whatever made her pick such a wimp for a husband?' He put the watercolour back onto the mantelpiece. 'But after all, we're not a charity.'

'I'll fetch you a Scotch. By the bye,' she indicated the picture, 'how much?'

'I hardly like to admit. Still, it's a fine investment and it was relatively cheap because of the damage.'

'A William Hunt. Six thousand? Seven?'

'Less. About five, actually.'

'Really? Not much more than the rent on Cartwright Farm.' She went to find his drink. A few minutes after she had returned with a silver tray on which she had placed a small decanter, jug of water and three thick, crystal tumblers, Betty arrived and began by apologising for Jack's absence. Ashley dismissed her explanations with an impatient gesture and indicated the decanter. She declined with a brief headshake.

'Well, Betty, how's everything looking over your way?'

'Fine.' It wasn't but she didn't know how to get started. 'Well, reasonably fine.'

'How are the pigs?' Ashley smiled. He must have known that the pigs were her special concern.

'They really are fine. We've had even better results so far than last year.' She went on to give chapter and verse of her achievements with her livestock and as she talked, she began to relax. Ashley's estimation of her abilities grew as she spoke.

'What about the rest of the farm?' Her face fell slightly but she recovered herself quickly.

'The farm's all right. All the crops seem to be—'

'Seem? Don't you have details?'

'Of course not. It's impossible to tell at this stage how well they'll do.'

'We can forecast our yields to within twenty per cent.' He wished he hadn't taken quite so aggressive a stance. He softened his tone. 'Are you expecting a good harvest?'

'I don't see why not, but it hasn't rained for a while. We could do with more water, especially for the potatoes. But we . . .' She didn't know how to continue.

'But you have a problem now?' he prompted.

'So it seems.' A pause.

'Jack?'

'Yes.'

'How ill is he?'

'Physically, not.'

'Oh? Oh well, that's good. I'd heard he was bedridden.'

'But he is.' She described Jack's depression and his illusion that he was suffering from cardiac asthma. Ashley listened.

'Betty, I'm so sorry,' he said. 'It's another burden for you and I sympathise, really I do. But what exactly do you expect from me?'

'Work is not falling behind on the farm, not yet, but it's going to be a struggle and there are extra costs. We haven't yet paid our rent for the last half-year.'

'I can't get involved in that. As you know, our land agent deals with it.'

'Hector Enfield, I know. But I felt I owed you an explanation. I hate the thought of being in arrears without telling you – in person, I mean.'

'Well, I appreciate it, Betty.'

'And I also needed to tell you that we would find it difficult to pay for a little while yet.'

'Ah, now. As I said that's really a matter for—'

'—But we *will* pay. You have my word on that.' She looked directly into his eyes. He held her gaze. The grey eyes were gentle but there was an undercurrent of defiance. She was sitting erect, on the edge of her seat with her chin held up, breasts pushed against her blouse. Again, his admiration for her courage grew.

'You really care about that little farm, don't you?'

'It's our livelihood.'

'No, there's more to it than that. And it's got to you more than to Jack, hasn't it?'

'I'm not sure what you mean.'

'Aren't you?' he smiled. She continued to look straight at him. 'Cartwright Farm belongs to you—'

'Technically it belongs to *you*.'

'But you feel that you belong to it. You are part of it, the land, the whole concept of the farm. Living off the land, putting heart back into the soil, giving and receiving – isn't that how you see yourself?'

'Our lives are brief, the land is for always.'

'Exactly. You put husbandry first. For you, "long term" means several generations.'

'But isn't that what farming is supposed to be about? Stewardship?'

'Not these days, Betty. My long term is no more than five years. With fertiliser and pesticides we maximise yields without knowing what the residues will do to the land. We shave costs, we keep labour to the minimum. Profits are falling and business is tough. Your concept is romantic – admirable, but unrealistic.'

'How do you think your grandfather and his forebears developed your empire?'

'Most of this "empire" as you call it is of my making.'

'But you had a fine farm on which to build – one which had been in your family for generations.'

'Is that what you're trying to do, create an empire? Cartwright is a pitiful little patch to start from. Besides, you're probably too late, farming's going into decline. All those generous subsidies of the Seventies – you won't see the like of those again.'

'Not an empire.' The zeal in Betty's eyes made him want

to hug her. 'I, we, all love it here. We just want to do the best we can.'

'Scratching a living, against the odds?'

'We *will* pay our rent. I'm only asking for an extension, while we get over this present problem.' She stood up, ready to leave.

'I admire your pluck and I'm sorry about Jack. It's damnable for you to be so burdened, but you,' he rose and stood opposite her, placing a gentle hand on each shoulder and looking right into her grey eyes, 'you seem to be the very heart of that place.' He walked to the window and then glanced back at the water colour. 'But, as I told you before, it really is in the hands of the agent.'

'Of course.' Her voice sounded flat.

'Technically, he could give you notice to quit.' He paused while she digested those chilling words.

'Technically, we are rather in your hands.'

'And I appreciate your plight. I really do.' He looked again at the water colour and she followed his gaze. 'Let me have a think about it.' He opened the drawing-room door for her, then hesitated. 'Stay for a drink?'

'Thanks but I must get back. There's so much to do.'

'Fair enough.'

'He's a pretty fellow, isn't he?' Betty said, pausing in the doorway.

'Who?' Ashley looked puzzled.

'Your new picture.'

'Oh. Oh yes. I fancied him the moment I saw him in St James's Street.' They walked to the front door. 'Well, good-bye, Betty, I do hope Jack is soon better.'

'Thank you, so do I.'

'And I *will* give it some thought.' He squeezed her hand and smiled. Involuntarily, she returned the squeeze, her hand lingering in his for a moment, her level gaze directed into his hazel eyes.

'Thank you.'

Chapter Seven

'If there's Anyone there,' said Betty, walking alone to the church, 'thank You for all this.' The still air was full of birdsong; orange-tip butterflies danced among the cow parsley, the green and white flecking of their underwings matching the lace of the flowers, and overhead, swallows were gliding high – a sure sign of settled weather. The sky was cloudless but the heat of the early June sun was tempered by dappled shade under the huge chestnuts which lined Church Lane.

The beauty of so many English churches, even if they are ancient, depends not so much on the quality of their architecture as on where they are. At Wyckhamby, St James's was an unexciting building with squat nave and a foursquare, Romanesque tower but, standing in a watermeadow, with the Venn gliding past to the east and flanked by the outline of the Old Rectory garden whose collection of rare trees had been planted more than a century before, the setting was perfect. The building material was a soft local limestone, composed of billions of microscopic fossils which had withstood centuries of frost but which, these days, crumbled in acid rain. The building's two exceptional features were a sanctuary ring and a vaulted ceiling. The former, dating back to the twelfth century, looked like a doorknocker – which it was – in crudely wrought iron, depicting two lizards or dragons whispering into the ear of St James. The wooden ceiling, a Victorian addition, hid the structural roof timbers; it tended to darken the interior but was, stated the Official Guide, typed and photocopied by a zealous and largely accurate local historian, 'unique but for one similar and inferior structure in Holland'.

Before going into the church, Betty paused for a moment in the porch. She found it impossible to believe in an actual God as such, and had never swallowed the ideas of a virgin birth or a man who could work miracles. Neither would she subscribe with more than a token nod to the mumbo jumbo connected with the Eucharist, nor to the whining and breast-beating of the Catholics, and certainly not to the concept of original sin which she regarded as a particularly morbid form of self-hatred. Yet, in spite of her apostasy, she practised a kind of Christianity which would put many an evangelical hardliner to shame. She attended church regularly, to appease a social conscience rather than to worship and, throughout her life, she tried to devote herself to the needs of others. She did believe in some kind of organising influence on the world – Whoever or Whatever it might be – but as far as piety was concerned, she felt that fellow humans, rather than an abstract deity, should be the target of her love. She believed that everyone had a moral duty to serve others in society, not just by making hopeful utterances of good intent each Sunday but by action whenever it was needed.

The coolness of the church's interior was refreshing but it was dark after the sunshine outside, so she decided to sit in one of the back pews to allow her eyes time to adjust. Out of the sun, thoughts of her problems came flooding back. Jack had spent most of the last couple of weeks sleeping and seemed unable to exert himself at all without turning dizzy. Once this week, while attempting to couple the three-ton trailer to the tractor, he had passed out. Luckily, he had fallen away from the draw bar but the incident could have maimed or even killed him. He had been back to hospital, this time for a brain scan as well as for further tests, but still no one could find anything physically wrong. In fact, with all the enforced rest, his blood pressure had returned almost to normal. And yet, the symptoms of cardiac asthma persisted and intensified in moments of stress or exertion.

Betty had managed to do some of the farmwork herself

but had fallen behind and had had to employ contractors for spraying and for weeding the sugar beet. That meant higher costs. They needed another driver – well, more than a driver really, someone who could step into Jack's shoes for a while without costing more than a minimal wage. She had written to various acquaintances from the past just in case they knew of any students or indeed anyone who might come to help out, even for a few weeks, while Jack recovered. It was harvest she was dreading most.

She was also worried that all the stresses in the family might begin to affect the children. Gill and Mandy's summer uniforms, second-hand when Betty had bought them from the school clothing pool, were beginning to look shabby and some of the pupils at Capelstowe had been teasing them. Betty knew the girls felt ashamed of their parents' second-class appearance and the rusting family car, and that they resented not being able to go on any of the school trips. Whenever she delivered them to Capelstowe and saw the looks on the faces of some of the mothers, with their elegant clothes and full maquillage even at nine in the morning, she couldn't help feeling she was letting her own girls down. At least Jim was all right. He didn't care what his clothes looked like and neither did any of his mates.

Much to her surprise, Camilla had turned out to be a great friend. Gill and Mandy adored her and even Jim liked her because she seemed willing to muck in with whatever they wanted to do. She had a pony and an expensive bicycle, and most of her clothes carried designer labels, but whenever she came to Cartwright Farm or the children played at the Rectory, she either shrugged off her wealth or allowed her friends generous access to all her possessions. The four children became one gang, doing everything together. Arguments flared up, of course, but these were shortlived. Mostly, they seemed to be laughing – running everywhere and always laughing.

Betty smiled and glanced at her watch. She had agreed to meet Maggie here at eleven but it was usual for her to be late. She decided to wait a little longer, to rest in the coolness.

Financial worries kept surfacing but she tried to push them under, and to meditate on a more restful theme. Then she thought she heard a clink. She listened more carefully, hardly breathing. Yes, there it was again. Unmistakable: the sound of glass clinking. This was frightening. For some time, communion wine had been disappearing from the vestry cupboard. It was too easy to force the antiquated lock and the Rector had not got round to replacing it with something more secure. Now it sounded as though the thief was right there with her in the building. Curiosity overcame her fear. Surely, a thuggish burglar would be more interested in the silver or the alms box. This was probably some kid who'd been doing it for pranks and hadn't heard her come in. Well, his game was up! She walked to the vestry and pulled aside the curtain.

'Good Lord! Maggie!' The doctor's wife was sitting on the vestry floor, back leaning against the cupboard, legs comfortably apart, bottle raised halfway to lips. 'What *are* you doing?'

'Cheers!' Maggie, evidently drunk, waved the bottle. 'Want a swig?'

'That's stealing.' Betty went to take it from her. 'Has it been you all the time?'

Maggie snatched the bottle back and cradled it like a child on her bosom. 'Piss off! It's mine! Finders keepers.' She pulled the cork and took another swig.

Betty tried to prevent her. 'You can't do this. Come on, you need to stand up and get some black coffee down you.'

'Why don't you fuck off, you and your do-bloody-gooding ways. Makes me want to puke.'

'Maggie, your language! In church!'

'Just bugger off!'

'No.' Betty was firm. 'I can't possibly. You need help.' She took the bottle from her friend and helped her up. Maggie was much drunker than a couple of swigs of altar wine would account for. In fact, she could hardly stand. 'Come on, let's get you home. We can talk about the flower festival later.'

'Flower fessiv'l? Wa'ya bloody talking about? Flower fess'val!'

'It's what I came to church for – to meet you and talk about the flower festival. You know, when the fête's on.'

'No, no! You're quite wrong. There's no fête. Bloody Donc'ster woman pinched it, silly tarted-up bitch! Nobody wants an old bag like me doing fêtes any more.' She began to cry. ''N now you won't want me any more either. My best friend 'n I've buggered it with you now.'

'Come on. We've got to get you home.'

'No!' Betty was surprised at her vehemence. 'Leonard'll see.'

'You've been doing this quite a bit lately, haven't you, this sly sipping?'

'Sly, bollocks! Just d'screet, s'all.'

'Maggie! I want to help you.'

'Well, you can't. I'm perfec'ly a'right. Bollocks!'

'You can swear all you want but I'm not leaving you like this. Come on, we're getting you home.' Betty had difficulty supporting her since Maggie, though no taller, was quite a lot fatter than she, but they managed to stagger along the towpath of the Venn. As they went, the fresh air helped Maggie, if not to sober up, at least to get a little more control of her movements. Once she had to stop to vomit into the river while Betty held her head, and once she lurched too far for Betty to be able to hold her upright and both women sprawled in the meadow. Luckily no one saw.

Back at Bridge House, Leonard was just finishing his lunch of cheese on toast washed down with a chilled Sauvignon de Touraine. His first reaction, thinking both women were tight, was to laugh. 'What on earth have you two wicked females been up to?'

'We need to get her to bed. She's not in very good shape,' Betty said and Leonard then realised that it was more serious than just a giddy lunchtime bash. They got her upstairs and, eventually, settled off to sleep. Back in the kitchen, Betty said, 'She was in the church. Drinking the Communion wine.'

'Communion wine?'

'She's got a problem, hasn't she?'

'Not that I know of.'

'But this has happened before.'

'What *can* you mean?'

'The drinking. This isn't just a one-off.'

'What are you suggesting?' Leonard was getting angry. He pushed the cork into the wine bottle and jumped up to put it into the fridge. 'What business is it of yours anyway?'

'If I find one of my best friends semi-conscious on the vestry floor, I think it is my business.'

'Doesn't that sound rather pious to you?'

'It isn't meant to. I'm concerned.'

'There's no need to be.' This was hassle he didn't want. 'Anyway, haven't you got enough troubles of your own? How is Jack?'

'Jack? You're his doctor.'

'I'm sorry, Betty, you don't deserve this.'

'Leonard, the Communion wine has been disappearing for weeks. Nobody minds a rave-up and heaven knows, I'd drink more if I could afford it. It might be a useful crutch amid all the angst of my life these days, but *secret* tippling – that's sinister.'

Leonard sighed, sat down and pushed his unfinished lunch to one side. He indicated the other chair and Betty also sat. It was like a consultation with the rôles reversed.

'I suppose I've known for months really,' he said slowly. 'I just haven't attempted to face up to it. She's always been prone to alcohol – we both are. If we decide on a slap-up meal at home or go to a decent restaurant, we invariably split a bottle for the starter and another for the main course. And we have brandies and pre-dinner cocktails as well. She always keeps up with me, tot for tot, but I've never thought of her as being, you know, actually hooked. I suppose I should have. With her lighter body weight, it's like her having half as much again as me.' He thought for a moment. 'I should have seen what she was up to. God, what a mess!'

'Do you know how long it's been going on, this secret tippling?'

'Haven't a clue. Not a clue. She's been more irascible lately, given to fits of fruity language, but I put that down to pressure in the garden. It's such a bloody great plot to look after. I've watched her stagger, even smelt it on her breath but . . .' He faltered. None so blind, he thought, as those who don't want to see.

'Does anyone else know?'

'Don't think so. It would be awful if people began to laugh at her in the village.'

'They could be doing that already,' Betty said, 'but the villagers can be pretty unobservant and anyway, Maggie's language has always been known to be, well . . . eccentric.'

'She'll have to stop. Outright. Cold turkey.' He considered the prospect. It would be difficult, very – a stony row to hoe. 'In the church you say? Dear God!'

Betty got up. 'I have to go, Leonard, let me know if I can do anything.'

'Thanks, I will. But this is a problem which Maggie must sort out for herself. We can only support her.'

'That's rather what I meant. It'll be hard. You'll need support too.' Betty left.

As she opened the gate and stepped into the road, a low sports car sped round the corner and she had to leap out of the way into the verge, scratching her leg on a bramble. It was Andrew Kirkland. Bored with Wyckhamby, he had just phoned his sister and been invited to London for a few days.

He and Annabel arrived at the door of her flat in Pont Street at the same time. She was laden with Harrods bags full of expensive groceries. 'Here,' she said, once they were inside, 'make yourself useful.' She handed him a bag of over-ripe avocados. 'Cut these in half and spoon out the flesh. There, into that basin.' She unpacked her carrier and began to sort out packs of fresh raspberries, a small tin of Beluga caviar, quail's eggs and a bloody parcel which contained a large piece of fillet beef. This she unwrapped and cut off about a pound and a half, saying, 'Look, our supper, courtesy of International Tubes PLC.'

'You'll get nabbed one of these days,' Andrew said, his juices beginning to flow at the thought of sizzling steak.

'Not I!' She rummaged in the fridge and brought out a bottle of champagne, Laurent Perrier 1980. 'Left over from Imperial Drugs' little bash on Thursday. A breakage, don't you know.' She tossed it to him. 'Open it up, weed, we'll start on that now. I've a useful little Burgundy to go with our meat.'

'Pinched as well, no doubt.'

'Not exactly. I filched it from home.'

'Stealing, from your own family!'

'Don't be such a prig. Just open the fizz and let's get ratted. I'm utterly worn out.'

'Not before we've talked.'

'Talked? That sounds heavy. What've you been up to, Baby Bro? Shagging the dairymaid, I shouldn't wonder.'

'Don't be so coarse!'

'Oh, what a little prude it is!'

'Can't you be serious for a minute? It's Dad.'

'What about him?'

'He won't take me seriously. Won't let me *do* anything.'
He began a series of gripes but Annabel soon stopped him.

'This is just whining. If you've got a real problem, talk to me about it. If you don't like being at home, get a job somewhere else. Even you could find *something*. You can lodge here if you want, just while you get fixed up, but for God's sake don't moan. Now open that champers.' She placed the bottle into his hands.

Andrew put on a sour face.

'If that's the way you feel I'm going!' He banged the bottle down again but made no attempt to leave.

'Suit yourself. But remember, as long as you are at home you may have a meal ticket, but you have to play their game. It's all part of growing up. Take it or leave it.'

'I'm sick of being told to grow up. I've got more ability than any of you think – you just wait and see.'

*

When Maggie Bates woke up two weeks later, the first thing she thought about was Bucks Fizz. Leonard had been up for a while, and morning sunshine was already streaming through the window. Outside, a cuckoo was going berserk with a run of *cuc-cuc-cucs* before singing the second note. My fourteenth day without a drink, she thought, and imagined the pop of a champagne cork, the muted fizzing as it poured into the glass, the creamy foam rising to the rim and almost but not quite overflowing, and then the dash of pure orange juice clouding the liquid. She shut her eyes and tried to blot out the nagging pull in her body, a pull which made her feel sick and her temples break out in sweat. The image of the illicit whisky under the sink returned for the umpteenth time. It was still there, she knew: *Leonard didn't.* I've been so good so far, she thought, surely a tiny sip won't break anything? There must be an inch, yes, a whole inch in the bottom of the medicine bottle ... surely a liqueur glass of Scotch is hardly going to pickle my liver. She sat up. No, it'll be OK. Just that, to help me get up, then no more. The phone made her jump.

'Mags? Betty. How are you this morning?'

Maggie's heart sank. The bloody woman wouldn't leave her alone. 'Godawful!'

'It's a wonderful morning.'

'I didn't need telling. I've been kept awake for hours by a mentally-bloody-retarded cuckoo.'

'"In June, change my tune. In July, prepare to fly, in Aug—"'

'Yes, yes! Did you want anything?'

'Just making sure you're all right.'

'Of course I'm not all right. I'm bloody. It's hellish. I don't think I can manage much longer.'

'Take it by the day. I'll drop in for a few minutes after delivering the children. Bye!'

The phone clicked and Maggie got up. Betty's interfering ways made her angry but she knew now that she wouldn't need the whisky. She went into the bathroom and slammed the door.

Betty went to see Jack, who nowadays slept in the guest-room, and was surprised to find him up and dressed. He had lost so much weight that his shirt collar seemed a size too large and the creased skin of his neck made him look old.

'This is a nice surprise,' she said, walking up to him and undoing his top shirt button. 'Why not leave it open? Suits you better.'

'Thought I'd walk the farm, get some fresh air. Can you come?'

'Not just now. I've got to take the girls and then go to see Sally and then Maggie. Perhaps this afternoon.'

'Have you *got* to see those women this morning?'

'I said I would. There's the pigs and everything to do as well.'

His face fell. 'I suppose I'll have to go without you.'

'Why not wait until this afternoon? I'd love to walk the farm with you.'

'No. I want to go now, while I feel strong. It really would be good if we could walk together. Why not visit the women later?'

'Jack, I need to see them both today. Next week's going to be so hectic with the bank manager coming – that'll wipe out a day – and then there's the fête the week after. Not to mention your next hospital visit. I really can't change any-thing now.'

He sat on the bed. 'I don't think I'll go after all.' His breathing shortened, was becoming irregular.

'Jack!' She sat beside him on the bed. 'Same trouble?'

'It's like a steel band being tightened round my chest.'

'You'd better lie down again.' She took off his shoes and laid the covers over him. 'I'll bring up some tea before I go. Jack, I do have to go.' She left him and delivered the children, returning to check up on him. He was asleep by the time she got back. He seemed to sleep most of the time now, fitfully at night and on and off all day. She hoped the new set of tests at the hospital would come up with something so that they knew what they were up against.

She checked over the piggery as quickly as she could and

then changed into a flowery skirt and plain green cotton top before setting out for the Old Rectory, where Sally was completing preparations for her visit to Mudando.

'Betty, darling, it's so good of you to see to Camilla like this. Now, let me tell you,' she reeled off a litany of instructions, 'this is my contact number in Mudando. Jules will be home about seven-ish each evening. I've explained all the details to him but if there's any mishap or you can't take her for any particular reason, he will come home from his office especially to deal with her. But it is a long way from London, as you know, so I hope you'll be able to cope all right. How's Jack, by the way?' She did not wait for an answer, but continued, 'I leave on Saturday and aim to return on the twenty-ninth, but it might be necessary for me to stay a little longer.' On she went until Betty felt quite exhausted. Then, 'Now, lovey, how about a cup of tea? Or a gin if you'd rather?'

'Tea. I'll come and help you make it.' In the kitchen, under the forest of dried flowers, Betty broached a new subject. 'Remember when you first came here, you wanted to do something about the garden?'

'And how! It's so neglected. We can't wait to renovate it.'

'Have you approached anyone yet?'

'Don't know who to ask. There are so many cowboys about, masquerading as landscape gardeners.'

'It's just that I know someone who is a really gifted designer and has a huge knowledge of plants.'

'Is he reliable?'

'I think so. She's looking for another project at the moment.'

'She? Mmm. If she's looking for work, that doesn't say a great deal for her reputation.'

'Doesn't need the money. What she wants is something to occupy her. Something to motivate.'

'Well, what I want is someone who will turn this eight acres of mess into a respectable garden which will look after itself. A man's job, surely?'

'I don't mean the physical work, though she could supervise that all right. I mean a garden designer who will plan your renovation and reorganise everything so it is easier to maintain. That's something she could do really well.'

'Sounds a possibility. Expensive?'

'As I said, she doesn't actually need the fees. She needs an occupation. I'm sure she'd be good.'

'And who is this paragon?'

'The doctor's wife, Maggie Bates.'

'Big tweedy woman who drinks too much and swears? Not a chance!'

'She doesn't drink at all nowadays. She's re-starting her career. She's good. She actually designed some fine gardens in her youth.'

'Such as?' Sally was barely listening.

'Two of the Cambridge colleges – St Radagund's, I think it was, and Trinity Meadows.'

'Really?'

'And she's worked for the Royals.'

'Royals?' Sally's interest was rekindled.

'She advised the Queen Mother on a rose project and created a colour theme garden for one of the lesser ones, Princess Michael or somebody.'

'Impressive. It would be good to have this garden done by someone who advises royalty. I might talk to her when I get back.'

'Or you could talk before you leave so that she can draw up some plans while you're away.'

'Good thinking, Betty.'

At last, Betty got away and went straight to Bridge House to tell Maggie the good news. She was working among her old roses, a small scratch on her brow from a thorny briar that refused to be dislodged caused a dribble of darkening blood to run like a tear onto her cheek. After a fortnight, the alcholic puffiness was receding and her face was developing a hardened, weathered look which suited her and made her appear younger, or would have if she had not been wearing such dreadful clothes; a bashed straw hat, torn tweed skirt and white cotton blouse pulled open at the buttons, showing a grey bra beneath, and stained yellow at the armpits. When she spotted Betty, she was tying back a long branch garlanded with fragrant pink blooms. 'Here, cop hold of this string and wrap it round while I hold up the branch.' She stretched to her full length – a couple of inches shorter than Betty – and held the rose branch to a post while the other woman tied it in place. 'Bloody wind broke the wire. Thanks, Betty.'

'Don't they look gorgeous?' Betty admired the rose garden. Every bush and climber was covered with bloom and the scent, in spite of a stiffish westerly breeze, was heavy on the air. Most of the roses were old varieties with romantic or odd-sounding names like 'Hebe's Lip', 'Souvenir du Docteur Jamain', or 'Ispahan'. Betty pulled a bloom close to her nose and breathed in the fresh perfume. The crowded petals were white with a suffusion of pink. 'Mmm . . . this is gorgeous.'

'One of my favourites – 'Maiden's Blush'. Bloody silly name, been grown for centuries, probably since Botticelli's time. The French call it *Cuisse de Nymph Emuée* – "thigh of the passionate nymph". More like it but too racy a name for our cold English manners.'

'A rose by any other name,' said Betty, moving onto a brooding purple-red moss rose. 'Now here's one I do know – William Lobb.'

'Bang on.' Maggie seemed jollier than she'd been since that dreadful morning after the vestry incident when Leonard had told her she must stop drinking and stop outright from that moment. She had screamed and raged all over the house and had smashed two of his bottles of Bordeaux on the porcelain sink, chipping it and cutting her thumb to the bone. Betty, who arrived later that day, hoping to reorganise their date for planning the flowers in the church, was railed at for being the cause, with her interfering know-it-all ways, of such deep unhappiness. It took courage to keep coming back, or to phone, but Betty had made contact every day through almost a fortnight of rage alternating with gloom and self-pity. Was this new confidence and that flush in the cheeks significant?

'Maggie, you are all right, aren't you?'

'You mean have I sneaked a crafty swig?' Betty was silent. 'Well no, I haven't.'

'But you seem . . .'

'High? Pissed?'

'Relaxed. More confident.'

'I'm beginning to feel better. I woke up today dreaming of champagne but after you phoned, it went out of my head and I haven't thought about it since.'

'You're on the mend.'

'What I need to do now is to get stuck into something challenging. I thought of re-doing part of the garden.'

'What about taking on a few clients?'

'Designing?'

'Mmm.'

Maggie thought for a moment. 'Nar! I'm too old. All the youngsters are doing it now. I'm forgotten.'

'There *is* a potential client in this village.'

'Don't be bloody silly. Nobody actually pays to have their gardens designed round here. Oh, unless you mean that painted bloody harlot at the Rectory.'

'Maggie!' Betty giggled. 'But yes, that is who I mean. I happen to know Sally Doncaster wants someone to redesign the Rectory garden.'

'What is it – eight, ten acres? It's a mess. The last three Rectors were worse than useless and then it stood empty for a year before the Church decided to sell it.'

'Quite a challenge.'

'You bet it is. All they've done is tart up the terrace by the house; the rest is jungle.'

'Beyond your average college kid fresh from Merrist Wood.'

'Mmm.'

Having set up the opportunity, Betty changed the subject. 'Flower festival. We ought to plan.'

'Got it all thought out. I'll provide the stuff but I'll need you to help with the actual arranging.' The two women planned their work for the weekend of the fête but after a short time Betty had to go to collect the children from school.

Handling other people's problems afforded relief from her own but back at home, Jack was still asleep and the bank manager's annual tour was only two days away. None of the children had made their beds that day and now, after returning from school, they simply dumped their satchels down on the kitchen floor, opened the biscuit tin and began to squabble over who was to have the last Bourbon creme. Betty told them to tidy their rooms and begin their homework. Then, armed with a cup of tea, she went to get Jack out of bed.

'I'm all done now. Why don't you get up and we'll look at the crops?'

'I don't think I can face it now.' He turned his head to the wall.

'Oh yes you can.' She sat on the bed and shook his shoulders gently. 'Come on, Tiger. Up and at 'em!' She pulled him upright and held his cheeks in her hand. His eyes avoided hers but she bored into his skull with her intense gaze, willing him to look back. Eventually their eyes did meet and for a brief flash, she saw the old Jack, the idealist who had come into this farming venture, dangerous as it was with their limitations of capital, with zeal and determination. But then the lids drooped and the face looked old again, nearer fifty than forty. She shook the head a little and kissed his mouth, sensuously, probing with her tongue until his lips softened. His arms went round her and she began to feel his body shaking with dry sobs which made a hoarse gulping sound. She held him tightly and let him howl like a schoolboy after a beating. Her reserves of tenderness were being heavily tapped. If only he could come to terms with the challenge they were facing, they might survive. But she must not goad him. That could make things worse.

'We need to walk the crops together,' she said. 'I don't think you'll be well enough to talk to the bank manager.'

'We can put them off.'

'If we do that, he'll suspect something is badly amiss. He already knows our financial predicament.'

'What can we do?'

'I'll see him alone. But I'll need to be briefed.' She put her arms round him again and squeezed him, slipping one hand into his pyjama jacket, stroking the hairs on his chest and tweaking a nipple. 'You can depend on me for now, but I can't cope with tractors and things. We'll have to borrow a driver if you aren't better before harvest.'

He stroked her cheek and ran a hand down over her shoulder, outlining a breast with his forefinger. 'You're so strong.'

'So are you really; you've just lost your confidence. You'll get it back.' She wished she could pack more conviction into what she was saying. She undid his pyjama jacket and ran her hand down over his navel. 'Do you know how long it is since we made love?'

'I don't know, a few weeks.'

'Almost three months.' She let her hand stray lower while he traced the outline of her nipple through the green blouse.'Maybe that's what you need.' She brought her face down to his and tugged on the cord of his pyjama trousers but he pulled her hand away.

'No! I'll get up now. Let's get on down to the fields.' He showered and dressed and soon they were walking through healthy crops of wheat and barley. Parts of the sugar-beet field were less good, with weeds choking the rows of plants, and the potatoes were patchy but were recovering well from late planting. There were skylarks singing above the arable and a line of white clouds on the western horizon promised rain which would help to sustain their crops through to harvest. All in all, it looked as though they could forecast an average, or even slightly better than average, harvest. But to survive, they needed more – bumper crops, top prices and then a break of immense good luck on top of that.

Chapter Eight

On the morning of the Shires Bank's visit to Cartwright Farm, Betty got up two hours earlier than usual. On top of all her chores, she wanted to go through the farm records one more time, just to make sure she was well-rehearsed and able to field difficult questions. She also needed to give the house a final dust over, so that everything looked its best.

She had put a vase of rosebuds on the study desk and had stood a large bunch of paeonies and lupins in a glass jug in front of the sitting-room fireplace. Their peppery scent greeted her as she entered the room and she was gratified to see that none of them had drooped – as lupins so often will – overnight. A good omen, Betty hoped and, after glancing round the room to check that everything else was in good order, she shut the door on them.

The fine weather had returned, after a brief wet spell overnight, and everywhere the countryside looked refreshed and clean. The lane leading to Cartwright Farm was especially beautiful in late June; the wildflowers were at their best and Betty hoped that the sight of scarlet poppies, blue cranesbills and mauve scabious would give Mr Woods a good feeling when he arrived.

Jack, relieved that she seemed able to cope with the forthcoming ordeal on her own, had been encouraging, almost supportive, the evening before, running through likely questions and reminding her of the strengths of their business as well as its weaknesses. By the time she got into bed, Betty's head was full of so many different fragments of information that she felt she would burst. She had slept fitfully, woken by a hooting owl and later, by rain beating on the window panes, but the morning sunshine was encouraging. She took a cup of tea to Jack, still sleeping in the spare room, and woke him gently. He sat up and drank. 'You'll be all right?' She stroked his brow.

'Yes, I think so. I'll just keep out of the way.' She tidied his bedclothes and opened the curtains.

'If you do get up, try to keep quiet. It's perhaps better that he doesn't see you at all this time. You can always fix a meeting when you're better.' She was not keen for Mr Woods to see how much weight Jack had lost. Last time they had met, he'd had so much breezy self-confidence, even though the writing had been on the wall for them.

She got the children off to school, fed the pigs, made coffee which she poured into a Thermos jug, and then sat and waited. At eleven precisely, a gunmetal Audi pulled up outside the front door and two men got out. Mr Woods – 'Do call me Geoff' – was about the same age as Betty, grey-suited and stiff-looking, with gold-rimmed glasses and thinning hair, but jovial and friendly. 'This is our Regional Adviser, Agriculture, Peter Lumley,' he said, introducing a much younger man of studied rural appearance, like something out of *Country Life*, Betty thought, and bound to say, 'Yah!' Sure enough, he held forth a damp hand, said 'Oh, yah, hi,' and condescended to sit in the offered chair while the three of them exchanged pleasantries, enthused about the weather and then ran out of things to say.

'Is Mr Rose joining us?' Lumley asked.

'He's not at all well, I'm afraid,' Betty explained, 'but he has briefed me so I'm sure I'll be able to provide you with all the information you need.'

'That's a pity. I had hoped—'

'—Betty is a partner in the business,' the bank manager cut in, 'and quite able, I'm sure to be our guide.' He permitted himself to smile at her and then inquired, 'What is the programme?'

'I thought we'd walk the farm first. Then I've prepared a

cold lunch after which, if you like, we can look through the records.'

'Fine.' They finished their coffee and walked slowly through the yard. Betty had decided to start at the piggery. It was the area she had most confidence in.

'What weaning policy does your husband use?' Lumley asked, before they went into the first building.

'We settled on seven weeks. I can keep my results up to scratch that way. These buildings wouldn't really do for weaning piglets any younger, besides, I think it's unnatural.'

Lumley gave an indulgent smile. 'Yah, but Mrs Rose, we have to divorce romance from commercial practices, don't we? Most modern systems have moved over to five, or even three-week weaning.'

'I think you'll see that our results compare well with larger, commercial units,' Betty's voice was calm and confident, 'even those with modern buildings and a huge capital outlay.'

'Sure,' drawled the expert, 'but no doubt your husband would want to give the idea of modernising some thought.'

'I doubt it. He has nothing whatever to do with the pigs. This is entirely my venture.' Betty felt the flush of anger burning and hoped it didn't show too much. She walked them briskly through the buildings and showed them the sows, the feeding equipment and then led them outside again. The bank manager seemed impressed and said so.

'Useful thing, having visitors round,' Lumley drawled. 'Gives you a stimulus to clean everything up.' They moved out of the yard and began to walk the crops. After close discussion with Jack, Betty had preplanned the route so that they saw the best cereals first, then skirted the sugar-beet field, avoiding the low-lying corner where the weeds had got such a hold, and, after a brief look at the twenty acres of potatoes, finished with the barley crop which looked like a soft green ocean with waves rippling through the shimmering ears. Last night's rain had not knocked any of the crop down and augured well for a high yield.

The men were not only pleased with what they saw, but were also taken with Betty's grasp of the farm business. What they didn't realise was that she was surprising herself. Armed with first-hand knowledge and with Jack's coaching, she had been able to reel off variety names, discuss their plant disease policy and forecast likely yields. Time and again, Lumley asked probing questions about a particular crop or the history of a certain piece of land and each time she was able to provide an answer. But this was the easy bit. Looking into the finances, even after a congenial lunch, would be far more gut-churning.

They returned to the farmhouse where Betty transformed herself from farmer to hostess and showed the men to the lavatory while she busied herself setting out the dishes she had prepared early that morning: smoked mackerel pâté, salads, home-made oat cakes, fresh fruit, including the first pickings of her own strawberries, a wedge of farmhouse cheddar and a jug of home made cider.

In the privacy of the downstairs cloakroom, the men exchanged glances. 'Pathetic, really,' said the manager. 'They may not be very solvent but their husbandry is as good as anyone's.'

'Mmm. If it all looks as good as the bits we saw . . . Did you spot that bottom land – decidedly weedy.'

'The pigs looked great. She has a real grasp.'

'Yah, but what about him?'

'Competent. This illness is a bit disconcerting, though. Gone on a long time now.'

'Well, the figures tell all. I can't see how a little unit like this can possibly survive. What makes them go on?'

'Guts.'

'Desperation, more like. They're things of the past, peasant holdings like this. They ought to quit while they're ahead.'

'We'd better go in. We've been missing for too long.' The manager led the way into the kitchen. 'Ah, that looks delicious,' he said, rubbing his hands. 'Good country fare!'

Betty poured them cider and offered food. There was much overstated appreciation and expressions of amazement that she should be able to cook and keep house as well as act as stand-in manager. They discussed country matters throughout the meal and during coffee, after which Betty took them through to Jack's little study where she had laid out all the relevant papers. As they entered the room, the atmosphere changed from conviviality to cool politeness. The manager kicked off by fishing in his briefcase and bringing out a fat file.

'Well, we've had a most enjoyable visit, but I think it's time to get down to business. I have your latest accounts here. Not very good reading, as you know.'

'Last year was difficult for various reasons.'

'I know, I know,' he looked stern, 'and we asked for a cash-flow forecast which, if I may say so, seemed to me at the time rather optimistic for land of your quality.'

'But now that you've seen the farm, I'm sure you'll agree that the crops look promising.'

'Indeed, they're a credit to you.'

'On the whole,' chimed in Lumley, 'but there are, as I'm sure your husband would admit, a few ribby areas.'

'But our yields will be above average. We're sure of that.' Betty knew that income had to cover their costs – that was the crux.

'Very probably,' said the manager, 'but how will that affect your cash flow?'

'It will bring more money in.'

'Of course, but will it bring enough?'

'With your continued support, I'm sure we can survive.'

'But my dear Mrs – er – Betty. You are already above your overdraft ceiling, with nothing more to come until after harvest. How will you manage until then?' There was no answer to that. Betty sat in painful silence. The manager continued, 'We could foreclose.'

'But you won't.'

'How do you know?'

'Not before harvest, it wouldn't be logical. You'd need us to get the harvest in or your losses on our debt would be the greater.'

'We could use contractors to get the harvest in.'

Betty felt a thrill of despair which surged up inside her and became a wave of nausea. 'You wouldn't, though,' she whispered. Tears were close now.

There was a silence, then: 'Peter has some suggestions.'

'Indeed I have.' Lumley took over. 'Small farms like yours are no longer commercially viable. Even with specialist cropping, a largely arable unit like this needs to be at least seven hundred acres and is better at a thousand.' He warmed to his theme. 'One of the advantages of size is that you can survive the hard times that are undoubtedly coming to all farmers in the Common Market. You should quit while you're ahead, Mrs Rose. You could come to terms with your landlord and agree a surrender price—'

'Are you suggesting we should give up?'

'It's not giving up. You could secure a useful surrender price in return for Vacant Possession on this land. With that and your stock in hand, you could fund your borrowings and retire.'

'Retire?'

'Well, find something else to do of course, but you could wipe out your debts.'

'And what would happen to this farm?'

'It's part of the Kirkland Acres already, isn't it? They would, presumably, farm it themselves. They might let you stay in the house – buy it even. You could afford to do that if you negotiated good terms.'

'No.' Her voice was no more than a whisper and her hands were shaking so much, she had to sit on them. 'No!'

'Well,' said Lumley, 'it's either that or expand to a viable size. There's Old Abbey Farm coming up for rent, of course.'

'Oh, that is out of the question, I'm afraid,' the manager dismissed Lumley's suggestions. 'Unless they were able to get their hands on more capital.'

'It is, as you say, out of the question.' Her voice was flat.

'Well, we do – and I want you to know that it gives me great pain to have to say this – we do have an obligation at the bank to safeguard our lending. Your business is approaching the point where it will, in my view, be almost impossible to keep afloat. Even if your harvest breaks all records, you have a huge hardcore debt and—'

He was interrupted by the door crashing open and Jack staggering in as though drunk. His face was ravaged, the eyes black-ringed, the mouth in a rictus as he fought for breath. Both men stood up, alarmed.

'I've just heard what you said,' Jack muttered between laboured breaths. 'Every word . . .'

'Jack, Jack! Sit down. You're not well.' Betty tried to restrain him. The bank men, anxious to avoid a scene, made ready to leave. 'Gentlemen, please!' Betty fought back tears. 'Please bear with us. I, oh, come on Jack, come back to bed.'

'No. I want to stay to hear the end of this.'

'Jack!' She looked directly into his eyes, willing him to obey, forcing her voice to keep steady. 'Jack, I can handle this. You must get to bed.' She led him to the door and turned to the men who were staring, embarrassed, and said, 'Please give me a moment.' Back in the bedroom she said, 'Jack, don't you ever do anything like that to me again! You promised to trust me and now you must.'

She returned to the study to find that the bankers had packed their papers back into their briefcases and were leaving. 'I'm so sorry. He doesn't mean what he says, he really isn't very well.'

'We felt we ought to go,' said Woods, 'but I hope you will consider everything we've discussed.'

'I've been considering little else for months.'

'And?'

'We do not intend to get out of here unless we are evicted.'

'Mrs Rose, I should warn you it could come to that. In the case of insolvency, your tenancy could be void.'

'I must have your support. At least until harvest.'

'I can't really give you an answer now, not off the cuff. But I admire your courage and I will be in touch. Soon.' They hurried down the path, got into the Audi and drove off, leaving Betty to gaze after them.

On their way down to the main road, the manager said,

'You've got to admit it, that woman's got more balls than all our male clients put together.'

'Yes. But no hope.'

Geoff Woods eased the Audi gently over a rut, brushing the long flowering grasses and disturbing flocks of dark brown butterflies as he went down the narrow lane. 'Nice spot just here.'

'Difficult approach for a big modern combine, though. This track needs widening. A bulldozer could do it in half a day.'

The Audi accelerated, leaving a layer of dust on the wild flowers which lined the lane.

Betty went straight upstairs to find Jack sitting bolt upright on his bedside chair. 'Well, you certainly created an impression.'

'Betty, I'm so sorry, I . . .' He broke into tears. She stood by the door watching him. 'I'm sorry . . . sorry . . . sorry.' She did not move towards him.

'I'm angry, Jack, angry!' And by God she was. Not just with him but with everything. In fact she was livid with rage. She wanted to scream and break things. She wanted to pour forth a torrent of abuse like Maggie Bates had when she was forced to come to terms with her alcoholism, or to smash a window like a frustrated youth committing mindless vandalism. If she were a man, she might have shouted or got drunk. Instead, she looked Jack in the eye and said, 'I will not be beaten. Not by this crisis and not by you. I *will* stay here. You have a choice – a choice only you can make. You can either get better or you can—' can what, she wondered. Die? Go? No, she couldn't suggest he should go. That would be cruel. But was this depressive creature with his psychosomatic disease really the man she had married? 'Or you can stay as you are,' she concluded. 'There's nothing anybody else can do for you. It's up to you.' She did not wait for a reply but swept out of the room, went downstairs, picked up the telephone and dialled.

'Capelstowe House.' The voice was assured and patrician.

'Oh,' said Betty, 'I wonder if I could have a word with the Principal. It's Betty Rose here.'

'Speaking,' said the voice.

'Ah, Miss Durrant. I felt I should contact you as soon as I had made a decision. I'm afraid that Gill and Mandy will have to leave the school.'

There was a slight pause, then: 'This is rather sudden. Is there anything wrong?'

'Nothing. Nothing at all. It's just that I will need to make other arrangements. There are only three weeks left of the summer term and I'd like them to stay for that, of course, but—'

'Mrs Rose, you may have overlooked it, but we do require one complete term's notice, in writing, if you are to take your girls away.'

'I see.'

'It is stated quite clearly in the prospectus and printed on the termly bills.'

'But I have no choice. I will not be able to let the girls come after this term. There are personal reasons.'

'A term's fees will still be forfeit.'

'Even if their places are taken by other pupils?'

'It's most unlikely that they would be.'

'You have a waiting list, surely?'

'On a school-year basis, yes, but I don't think we could fill your girls' places at such short notice.'

'But if you *were* able?'

'That would not absolve the debt. Rules are rules.'

'Let me explain,' said Betty, fighting to keep her voice even, 'that I have an invalid husband who is unlikely to recover for some time and as a result, we face a crisis in our family finances.'

'I sympathise, but your personal problems are no concern of mine.'

'I see.'

'Perhaps Gill and Linda—'

'—Mandy.'

'Perhaps Gill and Mandy would feel more at home in a state school.'

'Are you saying they don't belong at Capelstowe?'

'From the behavioural point of view, and with their work, perhaps, but children, even nicely brought-up ones like most of my pupils, can be beastly. It's all a question of fitting in. The threadbare uniform, the, ah, down-at-heel shoe does tend to reveal much about the wearer. Children are quick to spot those of a different, shall we say, background. We try to curb any victimisation, of course, but it's not always easy to detect.'

'Do you know, Miss Durrant, I believe you are right. My girls would be far happier away from Capelstowe.'

'I'll still need notice in writing. They could leave at Christmas.'

'Oh no. They have left as of this moment. And if you want your fees you'll have to sue me for them. Good night to you!' She hung up and sat very still. What *had* she done?

At the same moment, the phone in Ashley's study rang. He grunted with annoyance and put down his copy of *The Times*. 'Kirkland!'

'Ashley? Hector Enfield.'

'Well, old rogue, how's the land-flogging business?'

'Better, now that interest rates are coming down. I don't feel half so depressive about Monetarism as I did when it was hurting more. She is turning out to be a godsend after all, our Iron Lady.'

'Ha ha! Wait 'til it all turns out to be a flimflam boom, just like last time. Remember the Barber fiasco in the early Seventies?'

'No way. This is different. Enterprise is alive. Houses and land are on the up and up. Listen, I thought I ought to tell you, though it's not official as yet, about Old Abbey Farm.'

'Aha! Do we get the tenancy?'

"Fraid not!'

'Damn!' Ashley had been confident of winning the tender. He had bid a steep rent and had put forward, through

Enfield, a meticulous budget. His credentials were, after all, faultless. 'Damn! What went wrong?'

'It seems we didn't offer enough rent.'

'Ridiculous! We bid nearly seventy quid an acre!'

'We were nowhere near. We weren't even under bidders.'

'What was the winning offer?'

'Eighty-six!'

'Eighty-six pounds? Per *acre*?'

'It throws new light on local rents,' Enfield said. 'From the landlord's point of view, I mean. You need to bear that in mind.'

'Meaning Cartwright Farm?'

'Exactly. Your tenants will have to face a rent review before much longer.'

'But they're struggling on forty-two pounds an acre! Are you suggesting we should double their rent?'

'Not necessarily, but you, and they, should know what has happened to the market. You can be sure this will push up other rents in the district. Theirs would be more realistic at what, sixty-five? That would mean they'd have to find another five grand a year. Would that break them?'

'Probably.'

'Don't you believe it. Those sort of people always manage to stump up, somehow. They love a challenge.'

Betty had had more than enough challenges for one day, but she had to talk to the children right away. She called them into the sitting room.

'Oh look, Mum,' Gill said. 'The lupins have dropped petals all over the carpet.'

'Well, at least they haven't drooped,' Betty said. 'Now quiet, all of you. I've got some news.' They sat in a row on the sofa, eyes round and attentive. 'We're in a crisis. I can't go into too much detail but Dad's ill, as we all know, and there's not enough money coming in. Dad's illness is in his mind as well as his body so we must all will him to get better – to *think* himself better. We'll have to make sacrifices too. If we don't, we may have to leave here and live somewhere else.

Do any of you want that?' The heads shook in unison, eyes even rounder.

'What sacrifices?' asked Gill.

'Well, you girls will be asked to make the biggest one. I'm taking you away from Capelstowe. As of now, in fact. I've had a bit of a row with your Principal.' The girls looked at each other. Betty waited for the reaction, expecting consternation, but watched their faces break into smiles which broadened into grins. 'You look pleased.'

'We hated it,' said Mandy, slipping easily into the past tense. 'Some of the other girls were really foul and Miss Durrant was a stuck-up old cow.'

'Mandy – that isn't nice!'

'Where will we go?' Gill asked.

'It may have to be Kendale for a while, but I'll try to get you both into St George's Community College as soon as I can. Jim, of course, stays where he is.'

'Kendale's OK. Sharon Cooper goes there. There's a free bus, too.'

'Yes, but if you're going to a state school, I'd rather you went properly comprehensive, over the county border, I mean, and not here, where they have Eleven Plus and secondary modern.' The children chatted about schools while Betty went into the kitchen to set about supper. Soon, Gill appeared.

'Mum, you look funny. Your eyes are all staring. Why don't you sit down while we do supper.'

'Do you mind baked beans again?'

'No. I'll do some poached eggs as well, shall I?'

'Bless you.' Betty had to struggle not to cry. 'Get Lazy Jim to lay the table.'

'Mum. We're going to be all right, aren't we?'

'Frankly, to keep the farm, we need a bit of a miracle just now.'

'Not the farm. I mean us, the five of us. We'll be all right, once Dad's better, won't we?'

Next morning, the third Wednesday in June, among the

post was a letter with a Nottingham postmark. The handwriting was neat and upright, in black ink:

Dear Betty,

What a pleasant surprise to hear from you after what must be at least ten years. I was sorry to read about Jack's illness and must say, your letter sounded very cheerful considering the size of your problems.

Unfortunately, I don't know of any students or farming folk who might be interested in coming to help out and, reading between the lines, I suspect that you would find it difficult to employ a worker, much less a manager to stand in for Jack.

However, your letter was timely because Karen and I are likely to split up for good. We have been living apart for nearly three months now and I do not expect us to be able to come together again. Furthermore, I have become very disillusioned about working for the government. ADAS, as you know, is being changed and I really want to go in for a bit of hands-on farming.

I wondered, when I read your letter, whether you might like me to come to spend a few weeks with you, while Jack gets better, just to help out in return for bed and board. I have a little put by and wouldn't dream of asking for pay. In fact, I would value the experience of practical farming so much that I would almost feel indebted to you both.

In case you'd forgotten, I read Natural Sciences at Nottingham University and went on to study Crop Husbandry at Cambridge before joining the Ministry.

Chuck this letter away if it annoys you, but I just thought I'd write in case you thought it a good idea.

Best wishes to all of you.

> *Yours, John Holman.*

There was a number on the letterhead. She rang it at once. 'John? I got your letter. Yes, yes, of course. But I should warn you – you may be too late. The bank is on the brink of foreclosing. We're in rather a mess. How soon could you get here? Today? Really? Oh John, that would be wonderful! From Nottingham?. Ooh, I don't know, a couple of hours, maybe less.' She gave directions and then set about her morning's work with a much lighter heart than on the previous day. But her joy was temporary. The phone rang.

'Mrs Rose? Betty? Geoff Woods here, Shires Bank.' His voice felt like a physical weight pressing down on her shoulders.

'Oh yes?'

'We've been considering your position, here at the bank and I think we should meet. There are decisions to be faced.'

'Yes, I see.'

'I'd like to come out to Wyckhamby again, tomorrow, if that's convenient. I'm afraid I can't come today because of other commitments.'

'Yes.'

'Tomorrow, then. What time would suit you?'

No time at all, thought Betty. 'Oh, after I've seen to the stock,' she said. 'Eleven?'

'Eleven, then. I'll be alone. Oh, and by the way, I think it might be better if Mr, er, Jack isn't involved. We can talk to him as soon as he's, you know, recovered.'

'Right.' The phone had hardly been in its cradle for a second when it rang again and Betty jumped like a startled cat. 'Yes?'

'Betty? It *is* you? You sounded quite strange.' Elaine Kirkland was cheerful, as well she might be, thought Betty. 'Have you got a cold?'

'No, well, actually, I do feel a bit rough.'

'Oh dear. But you're going to be all right for Saturday?'

'Saturday?'

'Betty? You *are* all right, aren't you?'

'Saturday? Oh my goodness, the fête! Elaine, I'm not sure, things are rather coming to a head. We've got a bit of a crisis.'

'Oh Betty, you're not going to let me down, are you?'

'I'll try my damnedest not to, Elaine, but you do understand, we are rather up against it. Jack took a turn for the worse yesterday.'

'I *am* sorry.'

'So I may not be able to pull my weight this year.'

'Well, if you can't, you can't. Don't worry, we'll cope.' She rang off and Betty left the phone off the hook while she cleared the breakfast things away. She went up to the spare room where Jack was just beginning to get up. She decided not to say a word about the phone call from the bank manager.

'Come on, Tiger. We've got to move you back into our room.'

'Why?'

'First, it's your next step to recovery. Secondly, I want the pleasure of a man in my bed – or a warm body, anyway. But thirdly, we have a guest. Coming today and staying tonight.'

'Who?'

'A face from the past. John. John Holman.'

'Well, I'm damned! Dear old John!' Jack's face lit up at the memory of happier times. She showed him the letter.

'I rang as soon as I read it. He's coming today!' She shooed him out of the guest room and prepared it for their visitor, changing bed linen and polishing the furniture. She left the windows wide open and put a little vase of sweet peas on the dressing table.

He arrived just after two. Lean, seven years younger than Betty, his stern, pale face belying a more giving nature within. 'You've put on the teeniest bit of weight and it suits you,' Betty said. 'You were such a skinny minnie when we were young.'

'We're young now.' His voice still had a trace of the drawn-out vowels of his native Fenland.

'Comparatively. Well, you are, John. It is so good to see you!' His face barely creased into a smile but the grey eyes, under the flaxen hair, sparkled. She held him by the waist and marvelled at the firmness of his body. 'Goodness, you are fit.'

'Farming a desk, you have to take care. Most of my colleagues have gone to seed but I keep active.'

'Come and see Jack. Oh but first, let me tell you about

him.' She described the illness and meant to do no more than touch on their financial predicament but once she had started, the whole story of their decline, gradual at first but accelerating like a big dipper in the last few months, came flooding out.

'Well, that *is* a sad story.' John was a man of few words.

'Come and see Jack.'

'No. Get him to join us in here. From what you've said, it's probably wrong to treat him as an invalid.' And eventually, Jack did join them, and chatted about old times with some animation. They sorted out a working arrangement. John would stay until after the weekend, would go home to collect his belongings and would then return and help to run the farm until Jack had fully recovered or at least until after harvest.

'What are your long-term plans?' Jack asked.

'Sort out my personal life. Then get my feet onto the farming ladder. I'll go for a tenancy eventually, or a partnership, but I'm short of capital, as all would-be farmers are.'

'After you've seen what's happened to us you'll probably think differently.'

'I don't think so.' He fixed Jack with a penetrating look. 'No, you've been undercapitalised, and you've had bad luck. You're down but not out yet, I'd say.'

'Bless you for saying that,' Betty said, when Jack was out of the room. 'But we may be tomorrow. Our bank manager is coming at eleven. We've got until then to work out how to persuade him to forestall his regional office which wants to put the skids under us.'

Next morning, Mr Woods, manager of the Kendale branch of the Shires Bank, arrived to announce that they had no choice but to foreclose and that he was appointing a receiver. He was surprised to find a radiant Betty accompanied by an East Anglian agriculturist whose professional qualifications and all his other credentials, for that matter, were faultless. He was proposing to join their ménage, for nothing, to gain more practical experience. It didn't make sense.

'It may not make sense to you,' said John, 'but I still can't reverse a four-wheel trailer and I've never climbed into the works of a combine harvester.'

'But what will you bring to this farm?'

'Muscle,' said Betty. 'A respite. It'll buy time for Jack to get better, and create a chance for the two of us to pull things round. He'll bring new ideas too.'

'I see,' said the manager, trying to make his words sound less dire than they were. 'But I'm afraid your time has pretty well run out.'

'But won't you give us a stay of execution?' Betty sat bolt upright, appealing to him with all the persuasion she could transmit through her intense eyes, willing him to relent. 'At least until after harvest?'

'I can't give you a decision now. Some of the wheels have already been set in motion.' He got up and turned to the window of the little study which looked out over the neat front garden. How the hell did she have time to look after that as well as everything else? 'But I'll discuss it with my colleagues right away and will contact you by tomorrow afternoon at the latest.' She almost kissed him but felt that wouldn't be quite the thing and so pumped his hand instead.

'Thank you. Thank you!'

'Whoa! Don't thank me! I just said I'd consult my colleagues.' He left.

The phone rang. It was Elaine. 'Betty? You sound better.'

'I'll know more tomorrow, but I think I am better.'

'What are you talking about?'

'I'll explain later. Now, the fête. How far have you got?'

'You can help? Oh Betty, I can't tell you the relief!' They talked for fifteen minutes, Betty making notes, suggestions and decisions with the flair of a professional manager. John Holman looked on in disbelief. Could this be the same person as the little farm secretary who had temped for him, and tried to mother him, what – twelve years ago? Who had laughed when he'd asked her out to dinner and then introduced her husband to him? What friends the Roses had been. Older, more mature, but so young-thinking. Young-looking too, then, when he'd been staggered to learn that Betty was twenty-eight. And now, on the brink of financial extinction, here she was, taking the lion's share of the organisation of something as trivial as a garden fête. Remarkable!

Eventually, she hung up. 'Oh John,' she said, 'I expect you heard most of that. The fact is, we've lost one of our main helpers and I'm needed for tomorrow's fête. I simply can't let them down. Would you be able to amuse yourself for half a day?'

'Of course. I can walk the farm, with Jack.'

'Oh?' She felt, oddly, a pang of resentment. Now that she was so closely committed herself, she wanted to be the one who showed him everything. 'Couldn't that wait until a bit later?'

'The sooner I get familiar, the better.'

'Yes, of course. Still, do you think Jack's up to it?'

'It's better if we assume that he is.'

'Right. Gosh, I must get over to the Rectory. Ooh! The Rectory paddock – it's to be the fête car park. It needs mowing but I'm not terribly good on a tractor.'

'Neither am I but I'll have a go.'

'We generally use the old hay-mower. It's already fixed onto the small tractor – the Massey Ferguson.'

'Jack and I'll cope.'

'I'm not sure about Jack. I'll go and see if he's up yet.'

'I should hope he is. It's almost half-past twelve!' He made an exit with purpose in his stride. Quiet, almost surly, he seems, thought Betty, but what confidence he exudes. Just what Jack needs. She went off to help with the preparations for the fête.

The afternoon was perfect. Morning clouds had rolled away by lunchtime and now it was warm enough to melt the icing on Mrs Mardle's cakes but not so hot as to bring on fits of the vapours among the older revellers. A steady trickle of visitors issued into the Old Rectory garden, many of them puzzled, having gone first to the usual venue of the annual fête at Bridge House. In fact Maggie Bates, refusing to go anywhere near the place, had had to redirect so many people that she put up a crudely written notice which said FÊTE AT OLD RECTORY and then, after a spate of anguished callers who only attended the event in order to see Maggie's garden, wrote in even untidier script under the main message, GARDEN NOT OPEN. But after further pleadings from people who had come 'such a long, long way' and others who had 'so longed to have another look at the old roses' she had relented and torn down her notice to replace it with one of last year's yellow National Gardens Scheme posters which proclaimed an official opening to the public. She spent the rest of the day guiding plant enthusiasts along her borders and redirecting revellers. The fête she was boycotting.

At about 5.30, as the press of visitors was beginning to die away and Maggie felt able to nip indoors for a cup of tea, a maroon Rolls Royce crunched on the gravel drive. Bugger, thought Maggie, someone must have opened the gate. She was about to tell them to park in the village street when the chauffeur jumped out and ran and opened the back door for his passengers – a short, tubby man in beard and sandals and a taller, dove-grey-suited man with burnished, waving hair, bronzed skin and a disturbingly familiar face. Maggie peered more closely. Where had she seen him before? Yes, that was it! He'd been on the cover of the *Radio Times* the other week. He strode forward, stretching out a hand and arranging his camera smile for her. 'Mrs Bateman, I presume.' The shorter, tubby man trotted behind.

'Bates.'

'Michael Chetwynde. I do hope you'll forgive this intrusion.'

'Not an intrusion. We're open until six.' She wasn't quite happy with the little band of gawpers that was assembling in her peripheral vision. 'You'd better come in, but I warn you, the house is like a bloody tip.'

'Oh no. We came to see your lovely garden. This is Jeremy Dubber, he's a producer for BBC Television but his main passion is gardens so, as soon as we heard yours was open, we just had to drop by. As you probably know, we've been opening your charming village fête.'

'Not actually *my* village fête. Did you say Dubber?'

'That's right,' said Dubber.

'He's based in Birmingham,' Chetwynde explained. 'Does documentaries, and *In Gear*.'

'We seldom watch. Clothes are hardly my line.' Both men laughed at that.

'*In Gear* is about cars.'

'Same thing. All we watch is drama. And gardening programmes, of course, just to see what you've got bloody wrong this week!' They laughed again. Maggie took down her Gardens Scheme poster and closed the gates before giving them the last guided tour of the day.

Over at the Old Rectory, to the relief of the organisers, the fête was drawing to a close. It was too early to say, but the takings seemed to be much higher than last year, when it had rained. What with the flower festival in the church, Elaine thought, and the extra money from Michael Chetwynde who so kindly auctioned off tickets for supper for two with him at one of the smartest London restaurants next month and a guaranteed seat in the audience of one of his TV chat shows, they should clear at least £2,000.

Betty was going from stall to stall, collecting cash and issuing receipts. As her burden increased, she looked at the mix of notes and coinage and found herself thinking the unthinkable: we could live on this for months. How much could she lift without being detected? She flushed, feeling guilty at the very notion. How could she even think that, when it was village money, freely given. She put the appearance of such thoughts down to stress. Money had been a burning preoccupation with them lately.

That morning, the bank had actually agreed to raise their overdraft ceiling to £50,000, with a review after harvest. It was early days but she felt they had a chance, now that John was here. He had already put forward some brilliant ideas and had begun to enthuse Jack who, within a day of his arrival, was visibly improving. He had even tottered down to the fête for half an hour, and seeing the wobbly mowing lines and missed areas in the paddock, had laughed. Had actually laughed!

John, who had thrown himself into the village affairs with strong but mainly silent enthusiasm, was already at work dismantling some of the stalls. There was to be a barbecue with fireworks later but before then, much cleaning up. The last of the visitors had been let in and were taking the hint to be gone, now that the whole fiesta was disappearing before their eyes. Children still flocked round the pony ride corner, hoping for a couple of free goes before the two piebald, fat, hairy little beasts were taken home to rest after a day of boring but noisy work.

Betty arrived with her cashbox at the pony rides simultaneously with John, who had been asked to take down the temporary fence. Gill, Mandy and, of course, Camilla, were also there, having helped to organise the rides all afternoon. She smiled at the gaggle of children still waiting for a last ride. 'Closing time I'm afraid, kids,' she said to a chorus of 'Ohs' and "S'not fairs". 'Oh well, just one more each.'

'They'll have to buck up,' John said.

'Won't take a sec,' Betty promised. John grunted, pushed back the pale hair and set about pulling up the fenceposts, rocking them vigorously in the ground and then heaving them up with a grunt. When it happened, it didn't seem very serious. The jet fighters had been flying past all afternoon and the local ponies were quite used to them. But the combination of circumstances made a difference: the aircraft, very low, crossed just as John yanked the post from the ground and stumbled with it, knocking the flank of one of the ponies, which bucked. The child on top somersaulted in mid-air and, as she landed, unhurt, a second child was trampled by the other pony which had lashed out with its rear end and bolted. Both ponies were caught, amid laughter, in a few seconds but the little body on the ground stayed inert as John knelt over her. Betty looked over his shoulder at the chalk-white face, quite unconscious, and noticed with nausea and shock, that one leg was twisted round and under her body. She glanced again at the face. It was Camilla Doncaster.

PART TWO

Summer

Chapter Nine

It was the wild oats that first got Andrew Kirkland acquainted with Tracy Mardle. He managed to track her down at the Wyckhamby garden fête, now back to its old venue in Maggie Bates's garden at Bridge House.

Two years had passed since Camilla's accident. After that disastrous day, the Old Rectory had never again been used for village events, even though the sum raised there had exceeded anything before or since by several hundred pounds. With visitors complaining about missing Maggie's garden or worse, having to pay two admission charges if they wanted to see it *and* go to the fête, the Parochial Church Council had decided at their very next meeting to revert to the old site. The words, 'Never again!' had been on most of the helpers' lips, especially when some minor inconvenience had happened – the obsolete plug on the tea urn not fitting the new socket in the Rectory, or there being a dearth of level sites for the Bowling for Pig. Then, when the child fell off the pony and was trampled, that pretty well put the lid on it as far as most of the inhabitants were concerned. It was as if the injured leg – fractured in two places with the bone actually protruding through a wound in the shin, so Bert Mardle had said – was all the fault of the absent Sally Doncaster. After all, if the do had been held at Bridge House in the first place, like it always was, this would never have happened.

So, at Bridge House on the first Saturday in June, under a cloudless sky and the lightest of easterly breezes, Camilla Doncaster was in charge of the pony rides at her third village fête. The accident had done nothing to douse her fascination with horses. She had made a good recovery and, although her nearest kith knew that she dragged her right foot ever so slightly, she was as lively as any other sport-mad teenager. She was more demure now, at thirteen, and undoubtedly heavier in thigh and chest, but she was still physically a girl, almost but not quite ready to develop into a woman.

Andrew had gone to the fête as much to do his duty by putting in an appearance as to find Tracy. He usually tried to get out of village functions because the locals either patronised him or sucked up to him, depending on their social status – or rather, on what they perceived to be his. The whole thing made him sick and what was worse, reminded him that he still didn't really have a place in the pecking order. He walked briskly through the garden, cutting across the end of one of the borders and knocking down a whole stem of irises. Later Maggie would find the withering buds and curse the unseen vandal.

Tracy was down in the rough grass by the river, standing with her back to him, chatting with a couple of youths a little younger than Andrew, wearing motorcycle gear and hair gel. The arms of their jackets were festooned with rows of leather thongs like misplaced epaulettes and their eyes were fixed on Tracy. She was dressed in black shorts and a pink sleeveless top which ended well short of the shorts. As he approached, Andrew found his eyes returning to that couple of inches of suntanned midriff every half second or so, especially when she turned to greet him and he could see how sweetly her navel rested in its little dimple of tanned flesh.

'Wotcher!' The word was distorted by the champing of chalk-coloured bubblegum which accentuated the pinkness of her mouth.

'Ah, Tracy. I wondered—'

'Oh ah?' She chewed with a faraway look in her dark eyes, like a ruminating ewe. One of the motorbike boys sniggered. 'Piss off, Charlie. This is Mr Kirkland.'

'I was wondering whether you could come roguing the wild oats next week.'

'Get off! They can't be showing yet, 's too early.'

'Not in ear, of course, but big enough to spot.'

'Oh ah? Wha's the rate?' He caught a glimpse of the tip of her pink tongue as it turned the pale bubblegum in her mouth, then the chewing resumed. He realised he'd been staring. Charlie sniggered again and out of the corner of his eye, he could see the shoulder of the other boy shaking.

'One seventy-five.'

'An *hour*?'

'Yes.'

'Tha's real tight, tha' is.'

'I'll be working alongside.'

'Oh ah? Tha'll be nice.'

'So you can come?'

'I'd need,' she paused to chew for a while, running an appraising eye over him until he could feel his cheeks beginning to burn, 'I should need two quid.'

He knew he should be firm but—'OK, if you promise to stay to the end of the job. It's about five days' work.'

'A'right. Monday, then. What time?'

'Ten. No point in going earlier, the dew will drench you.' A vision of himself wiping her slender, bedewed legs with a warm towel swam into his mind's eye and it took a physical gesture to wave it away. He addressed the boys: 'You chaps can come too, if you want to earn a bit of pin money.' He was trying to be friendly, natural, but the 'chaps' sounded like something from Biggles. The boys looked at each other and sniggered again.

'Er, yeah! Cheers, mate. Monday, then,' Charlie said and turned his back on Andrew. He felt awkward and walked away.

'Andrew!' Tracy called after him. 'Where is it?'

He stopped, glad to have an excuse for turning back to look at her again. 'Dean's Meadow. We'll start at the top and work down towards the river.'

Andrew went home with a head full of disturbing images of Tracy. She'd always been around, of course, but he had never really looked at her before and had not realised just how much she had grown up. He had been timid about contacting her because he knew that her father, Bert Mardle, was not exactly a devotee of the Kirklands, in spite of being their farm foreman, and that her elder brother had an ugly reputation for being what they called 'ard. But now, he was really looking forward to Monday. He hoped the hot weather would continue so that she didn't have to wear too many more clothes, and spent his weekend in a rising fever of anticipation.

In the English countryside, June is a month of climaxes. The green of the wheatfields deepens until the top or flagleaf of each plant emerges, broadens and bends over like a cock's tailfeather, reflecting light from its surface and making the fields shimmer like the sea in a westering sun. Then, as the month advances, the flowers begin to peep through the fold at the base of the flagleaf. These are paler, blue-green and arranged like the scales of an inverted fir cone. Gradually, they ascend on their stems until the foliage is hidden and all the eye can see is a continuous carpet of wheat ears, swaying in the smallest air current. At the peak of growth, all the flowers produce pollen at the same time and are fertilised in a moment. From then on begins the process of swelling and ripening the grain.

A succession of pesticide sprays will have been used, to keep the crops clean, but even the most vigilant farmers fail to destroy all their pests and weeds. The best grown acres of cereals are often decorated with a scattering of scarlet poppies or yellow charlock and along the hedgerows, wildflowers may dare to encroach a few feet into the monoculture. Mostly such invasions are harmless, but one plant species against which Ashley had a constant vendetta was the wild oat. During the previous ten years, he had spent thousands of pounds removing this pest from the farm, first by careful crop rotation, then by using chemicals so precise in their targets that they could destroy the wild oat plants without harming the closely related cereals. Wild oats are persistent plants whose seeds can remain dormant in the ground for many years before germinating but at last, Ashley had got the infestation down to such a level that the few remaining wild oats could be removed from the fields by hand. It was for this task that Andrew had recruited Tracy.

On the Monday, she arrived alone at three minutes to ten. 'I'm ever so sorry but Charlie and Darren couldn't come.'

'That's all right,' Andrew said, trying not to look relieved. 'I had a feeling they wouldn't.'

'Innit hot?' Tracy was wearing the same shorts with a different top, this time a tee shirt which hung loosely and failed to show off her outline until she moved. When she did, Andrew noticed that she was wearing nothing underneath. He handed her a couple of empty fertiliser bags and indicated her sector of the field. Side by side, about thirty feet apart, they would walk slowly through the crop, following the drill rows until they reached the other end of the field, where the Venn meandered, nearly two miles downstream from the village.

There had been no rain since early May and the hardening ground was cracking in places. The oat plants were easy to see, since their leaves were taller than the uniform wheat crop, but there turned out to be many more there than they had thought. They worked steadily, pulling up the plants and stuffing them into the plastic sacks. Within a couple of hours, they had crossed the field twice and were approaching the river for the third time. Here, their sectors ended at a crook in the bank which formed a little bay where the water was clear and shallow. The place was a natural suntrap but no picknickers or ramblers ever went there because it was so far from any road or footpath.

'Innit time to knock off for dinner break?' Tracy asked.

'We better do one more row. That'll take us back to the top of the field where we left our lunch bags.'

'Oo-oh, I'd sooner stop 'ere.' Tracy sat on the riverbank and stretched out her legs. 'I ain't 'ungry.'

'Neither am I but I'm dying for a drink. It's sweltering!'

'Come and sit down for a bit first, then we c'n go back.'

He sat beside her and undid the buttons of his shirt which

was clammy with sweat. 'I say, do you mind if I take this off?'

Tracy burst out laughing. 'Fancy askin'.' She gave him a little push on the shoulder. 'You gentry aren't half soft!' She giggled and gave him another push. 'Soft on top, rotten inside. That's what Dad always says.'

'Is that what you think of me? Gentry?'

''Course.'

'But why? We haven't got titles or anything.'

'It's the way yer talk. "I say, old chep" – you know, sort of funny.'

'But I don't talk like that at all.'

'Oh ah? You oughter to listen ter yerself.' She let fly with another peal of tinkling laughter which excited him, and then looked at him and made a little *moue* with her mouth pouting. That excited him even more. 'Aah, bless him, 'e's gone all hurt!'

'No, really. ' He sat silently for a moment, then, 'Do you think we're rotten inside?'

'Naooo! That's just Dad. 'E's Labour, see. Always on about the working man and the borgee-oise. That's you, the borgee-oise.'

'Oh.'

''E likes yer Dad, mind, 'cos 'e's fair. Fair 'n decent.'

'But still bourgeois?'

'Borgee-oise? Yeah. 'E thinks you're a spoilt brat, but I think you're *gorgeous*!' Andrew blushed again. 'Ooh, I think that's sweet the way you do that!'

'Do what?'

'Y'know, go all red.' She sidled a little closer and he felt a tress of her black hair brush his cheek. ''Ow is yer love life, anyway?'

'Oh, er fine. Absolutely fine.' Well, non-existent really. He'd never had much bottle when it came to approaching females – acceptable in a spotty fourteen-year-old, he thought, but too shameful to admit to at twenty. They both sat in silence for a while. He could feel the sun burning his shoulders. A dragonfly flew past and, in the deeper part of the stream, a fish jumped. 'Look,' he said, 'a chubb! Quite a big one,' as the fish with greenish back and pink fins rose again, sucking in a spent butterfly which had fallen into the water and was vibrating on the surface.

'Looks nice and cool in there,' Tracy said. 'In't the water clear? You can see every pebble on the bottom.'

'Tell me, Tracy,' said Andrew, 'what do you people really think of us?'

But she had leaped up. 'I'm going to paddle!' She kicked off her canvas shoes and scrambled down the bank into the shallow water. 'Ooh, it's lovely!' He watched her walk into the river until she was knee-deep. The water made her toes look white against the pebbles. 'Why don't you come in too?'

'I'll get my trousers wet.'

'So? They'll dry in no time, this 'eat.'

He got up, took off his boots and walked up to her, in the stream. The coolness of the water was refreshing and the rounded pebbles on the riverbed soothed and massaged the soles of his feet.

'Let's go a bit deeper.' He pushed further out until the water was up to his waist.

She followed, getting her tee shirt soaked. 'Not too far.'

'But it's lovely!' He turned to beckon and caught sight of her, the tee shirt wet and clinging, her breasts outlined, the nipples made hard by the coolness of the water. The shock made him feel physically dizzy.

'Oi! What're you bloody staring at?'

'You're all wet.' His voice had gone husky. He cleared his throat.

'Not 'alf as wet as you.' She stepped forward and pushed him hard. He stumbled, catching his feet in a hank of waterweed and fell. Spluttering and laughing, he struck out, swam a vigorous crawl upstream for a few strokes and then allowed himself to drift back down with the current until he was level with her. Then, he slipped underwater and grabbed her ankles. She went under and was instantly a writhing, flailing mass of arms and legs. Nails scratched his chest and belly and the kicking nearly knocked him over again. He managed to catch hold of her and help her to her feet. She coughed and retched until tears mixed with the riverwater on her face. 'Stupid prat!' she wailed. 'Don't you know I can't swim!' She sobbed a little and in spite of the afternoon heat, began to shiver.

'Here, let's get you onto dry land.' He helped her back onto the grassy bank and they sat down again. She was still shaking. 'Look,' he said, 'I think you'd warm up more quickly if you took off your wet shirt. I promise not to look. In fact, I'll go back up the field to get something dry for you. You'll be quite all right, as I . . .' She had taken off her tee shirt and sat looking directly at him.

'I don't want you to go nowhere,' she said. 'I aren't embarrassed, even if you are.' She patted the grass beside her. 'Here.' The shivering had stopped. He sat. She took hold of his hand. 'Andrew?'

'Mmm?' Surely she could hear his heart beating.

'Are you queer or something?'

'Of course not.'

'Well,' she placed his hand on her breast. 'Aren't I dropping a big enough 'int or something?'

'Oh Tracy! Tracy!' He was almost overcome. She noticed four red weals running down his chest.

'Ooh, you poor boy, did I do that with my nails? Here, let me kiss it better.' Her wet hair tickled his chest and he threw his arms round her, kissing the top of her head. 'Your trousers are wet and clammy,' she said. 'Let's take the rest of our wet things off. We can sunbathe all over.'

'We shouldn't really.'

'Why? Nobody'll come. Not here, there's no way down, only through the crops.'

'But we shouldn't.' In response she put her hand on the back of his neck and held it there while she kissed him. The sensation of her sharp little tongue darting in and out of his mouth sent a current along his whole nervous system until his fingers and toes tingled and he thought he might faint. With her free hand she undid his belt. He flinched. 'Tracy!'

'Andrew. I do believe you've never been with a woman before.'

'At my age? That's a bloody insult! What do you think I am? A sissy?'

'Sissy?' She resumed undoing his trousers. 'Not quite, seeing as 'ow this little soldier's standing to attention.'

It was all over very quickly. In fact, the actual business had been rather a disappointment, Andrew thought, after all that crazed longing. But at least he wasn't a virgin now and as for Tracy, he loved her with a sizzling ardour. He loved her dark eyes, her olive complexion, her pouting lips, her dropped aitches, her jutting breasts – majestic, they were, those breasts – and, above all else, he loved her tinkling laugh.

They resumed their work, allowing their clothes to finish drying on their bodies and, by sixish, had pulled out their day's quota of wild oat plants. It was natural that they should finish their work at the river end of the field and that Andrew should want another swim. They walked back to the little bay and after a dip, they made love, twice, and each time, Andrew got better at it. At last, they parted, Tracy to trudge down the lane to her parents' tied cottage, Andrew to walk on air back to Wyckhamby Manor.

It was after nine by the time Tracy got home. On the kitchen table was a plate on which sat a Mr Frosty Heat 'n Serve chicken pie with frozen peas and oven chips. She eyed it without much appetite.

'That's been waitin' for yer since half six. Where've yer bin?' Bert Mardle was putting a shirt on over his string vest before leaving for the pub.

'Down Dean's Medder, roguin' wild oats.'

'Oh ah? 'Ooo else was there? That Charlie Shattock, I'll bet.'

'No. No one. Only Kirkland.'

'What, roguin'? Mr Kirkland? Nivver!'

'Naoo! Andrew.'

''Im!' Mardle snorted. 'Bloody mamma's boy.'

'I think 'e's nice.'

'Nice my arse! Prob'ly a pissin' woofter. All them public school types is.'

'Dad, 'e's all right!' Tracy laughed. 'An 'e certainly ain't no woofter!'

'Oh? Well, if 'e tries anythin' with you, my girl, I'll knock 'is fuckin' 'ead off.'

'Dad!' Tracy passed him his cap. 'I c'n look after m'self!' She glanced at the cold food and switched the oven on. Then a wave of queasiness overcame her so she switched it off again and scraped the meal into the bin. The manufactured pie lost its pastry lid, revealing a congealed mush within. She'd have some bread and cheese later, she decided, and turned on the telly.

Andrew walked into Wyckhamby Manor through the front door and went straight up to his room, leaving a trail of dirty footprints. Elaine looked out of the sitting room as he passed and called after him: 'You all right, darling?'

'Never better!'

'What've you been up to today?'

'Wild oats.'

'Sowing?'

'Ha ha! Roguing them out of the wheat.' But then again, thought Andrew, thinking of his new-found manhood, but then again!

'Oh Dad, do let's!' Mandy's eyes were bright with excitement. 'It'll be lovely.' She'd been working on Jack for some minutes, since he had come in to see how she was getting on with her physics homework. 'Mum needs a rest after all that extra work at the fête and you said the farm can cope without you for a day.'

'We-ell.' Jack had already decided but wanted to prolong the suspense. 'What about the dog?'

'We can take him. He'd love to play in the sea.'

'But who'll feed the pigs?'

Mandy's face fell. 'Oh, the pigs. I didn't think of them.'

'Well, animals don't know about holidays. You can't just go away and leave them.'

'No, I know that.' She turned her attention back to the exercise book open in front of her and sighed.

'But there is such a thing as a standby pigman.'

'Expensive.'

'I think we could run to it.' He put his hand on her shoulder. 'But now isn't the time to get distracted, my sweet. You'd better get on with your prep.'

Betty came into the study. 'I do wish you brats would stop hijacking my office.' She linked arms with Jack. 'And *you* shouldn't encourage them. What's wrong with your bedroom?'

'Oh Mum! You know I can't work in there. The atmosphere's all wrong.'

'Yes, foul. You kids can't work in your rooms because they're squalid and you won't tidy them.'

'But Mum—'

'Oi!' Betty began to rifle through a heap of papers pushed to the side of the desk. 'What have you been up to here? These were all in order.'

Since Jack's illness, Betty had taken over a sizeable share in running the farm. Now, after prolonged therapy and the fitting of a pacemaker, and after a steady combined effort on her part, supported through their darkest hours by John Holman, he was back to his original vigour.

John had stayed with the Roses for almost a year, helping them through that crucial harvest, driving the combine harvester all night on several occasions and then taking it to neighbouring farms to earn extra income from contract harvesting. He had managed to steal a march on the weather throughout seedtime and into winter, getting the next year's crops into perfect seedbeds and giving himself time for more contracting work while Jack, then able to do an occasional day, kept Cartwright Farm ticking over. But above all, it was John, taciturn but goodnatured, patient but ruthlessly efficient with what he called 'time management' who seemed most able to push Jack out of his depression. It was he who refused to admit that there was anything seriously wrong with Jack, who wouldn't listen to his excuses and who wouldn't put up with any backsliding. Even when the hospital had fitted him with a pacemaker, John had refused to admit that it was anything other than an expensive placebo.

Betty had provided the loving touch. Time after time she had listened to Jack raving with despair and comforted him with gentle tones until she felt she would burst. Between them, they had ensured a full recovery. 'We make a good team,' Betty had once told John, after an especially difficult night. 'You're the stick and I'm the carrot.'

Now she looked sternly at her daughter. 'I said these were all in order, young lady!'

'They still are, Mum. I just made a bit of room.'

'Well, just make sure you don't muddle anything up.' Mandy tried to catch her father's eye, without success, and then attempted to nudge him. Betty, quick to pick up an atmosphere, said; 'Hello! What are you two hatching up?'

'Tell her, Dad.'

'Nothing really,' Jack shrugged. 'I just thought it would do us all a bit of good if we went to the coast for a break.'

'Out of the question,' Betty retorted. 'We may be doing quite well on the farm now, and you've got your health back, thank heavens, but we certainly can't afford a holiday.'

'Dad meant just overnight – tell her, Dad.'

'Well,' Jack said, 'you know that schoolfriend Jim brought home for lunch the other Sunday – the boarder with RAF parents? What was his name – James? No – Josh, wasn't it?'

'Joss, Dad, Joss. Go on, get to the point!'

'All right, madam, give me a chance.' Jack was enjoying the suspense. 'Well, it seems his parents have a cottage at Middlestrand and we can borrow it if we want. His mother rang earlier this evening, while you were over at Bridge House, to thank us for giving young whatsisname such a lovely day. Rang from Germany, for heaven's sake.'

'But we only gave him lunch!'

'It seems he fell in love with the farm, and he must have reported on us in glowing terms. His mother spoke of "loving family relationships" and "what a wonderful mum you must be" and so on.'

'How embarrassing!'

'Not at all. You should take it as a compliment.'

'Well, it was nice to have him, poor little chap. They always *seem* quite happy at boarding school but obviously don't get much family life.'

'Dad!' Mandy said. 'Get to the point!'

'Well, that is the point really. This Mrs Wingfield said we can borrow their cottage if we want and, since the girls' school is closing for the day next Monday, I thought it would be nice for us all to go down to Middlestrand on Saturday and have a couple of days by the sea.'

'But what about Jim? His school isn't closing.'

'I'm sure they'd bend the rules, just this once. Of course, we'd take Joe or whatever he's called. He could show us the ropes. We could promise to have him back by bedtime, Monday night.'

'How would his parents feel about us taking him out of school?'

'Stop fussing, Mum. I'm sure they wouldn't mind.'

'Well, I'd mind if I were them.' Betty reflected. 'No, it isn't really on. Besides, what about the livestock?'

'We could borrow Ashley Kirkland's stockman. He'd come in and do the pigs in his own time.'

'Oh come on, Mum!' Mandy pleaded.

'It's a bit impulsive, but I must say, I'd love a break.'

'And?' Mandy sensed a triumph.

'We'll see.' Betty gathered up the girl's books and handed them to her. 'Now then, miss, you take this lot upstairs to your room and get it tidied *tout de suite*! Then, finish your homework. Dad and I have a business meeting to get through.'

'But, Mum!'

'Off!' Betty tapped Mandy's bottom with a copy of *Farmers' Weekly*. 'And not a peep from you until your room is spick and span. And you can tell Jim I'll be doing an inspection of his room too. At dawn!' She went, slamming the door. Betty turned to Jack. 'We'd better get down to business.'

'Fire away!'

'The stock looks like this,' she said, reorganising her papers and sitting at the desk. 'I've sold the last of the malting barley forward, as you know, but I think we should hedge.' She outlined her strategy to him, as she had every week since she had taken over the responsibility of marketing all their produce. That had been one of John Holman's ideas, to have long and short-term plans, and to set a time aside each week to discuss the running of the farm. At the first few meetings, Jack had been too ill and too depressed to take an active part and had stared at the floor, murmuring, 'Whatever you think right,' or, 'I don't know, I just don't know.' But gradually he had been drawn into the spirit of these meetings and began to play an active role. Eventually he took the lead, but it was agreed that henceforward, Betty would continue to be in charge of the selling.

She had had to learn the skill within a few months and had impressed everyone, even the bank manager, with her acumen. After being incredulous at first, he had watched the Roses, helped by John Holman, drag Cartwright Farm back into solvency. Now, after two bountiful harvests and some inspired marketing by Betty, they were more secure. However, they still had a large overdraft and there was a long way to go yet before they could feel really safe.

'What about this trip?' Jack asked, after they had finished talking shop. She stood up and put her arms round his waist.

'I think it's a lovely idea but can we afford it?'

'I think so. It won't cost much, just a stand-in pigman for a couple of days.'

'There's petrol. And extra provisions.' Her organisation skill clicked into gear. She began to reel through all the matters that would need sorting out before they went. Such a lot of arranging just for a couple of days. Still, it would be fun for the children. 'D'you suppose we ought to take Camilla? She's bound to want to come.'

'You dote more on that child than Sally does.'

'No Jack, that's not fair. Sally's away so much. But I'm thinking of our kids. They're bound to want her along.'

'And she is a sweet child,' Jack said.

'Mmm. I'm worried about taking that boy out of school, though. Should the parents mind?'

'It was the mother who suggested it.'

'What about the headmaster?'

'Tell the school that this is an educational trip,' Jack said, 'to study the birds of the Norfolk coast. That should secure his ungrudging permission.'

Betty thought for a moment and then hugged him. 'We'll do it!'

'Bravo!' He kissed her and stroked the light brown hair. 'There's a grey one here,' he said, massaging her temple.

'Only one? Surprise me some more!'

'The way I've led you a song and dance, it's a wonder you aren't bald!' She shushed him with another kiss.

After a few moments, they went to tell the children the trip was on. Jim was especially thrilled because Joss Wingfield, his great friend and fellow birdwatcher, had talked for hours about Middlestrand and the rare migrants which flocked on the saltmarshes along that coast. Having Joss with him, to act as host and guide would be, he said, like jam on the cake.

'Cherry,' Gill had corrected, but Jim insisted it would be jam because the cherry would be there already – or it would on any decent cake anyway. The evening passed, for the children, in joyful anticipation of the trip with questions crowding in on one another until Jack and Betty had to veto any more discussion. It was rather pathetic, Betty thought, that they should be so excited about a forty-eight-hour trip to a chilly stretch of coastline when most of their contemporaries went abroad every year.

In the next morning's post was a letter from the landlord's agent, Hector Enfield.

Dear Mr and Mrs Rose,

You are no doubt aware that, in response to instructions from our clients, Messrs Wyckhamby Farms Ltd, your rent has been held at the same level since 1981.

You will also be aware that rents in this area have risen considerably since your last review.

The purpose of this letter is to give notice that we will be making, on behalf of our client, Messrs Wyckhamby Farms Ltd, an application to review your rent for the forthcoming three-year period.

I look forward to meeting you in the near future, to discuss this matter. On a personal note, may I say how pleased I am that your farming seems to be going so much better now than it did when we discussed your last rent review?

'Oh my God!' Jack said, when he saw it. 'I'd better ring them this morning and fix up an appointment.' He picked up the phone.

'Jack,' Betty said, 'fix it for *after* the seaside trip. Let's enjoy that as much as we can – before any clouds gather.'

'Actually, my love, clouds are what we need. I know it would be a pity if weather spoiled the trip, but have you seen how dry the land is getting?'

'It hasn't rained for nearly four weeks, what do you expect?'

'Well, it needs to soon. Things could get quite serious.'

'Jack!' Betty didn't like that haunted look. It was a danger mark which needed blotting out. You had to accentuate the positive all the time, even if your own anxieties were tearing you up inside. 'It was a perfect spring and the farm has never looked better. It's far too early to worry about a water shortage, or about anything else.'

Chapter Ten

'What I've never quite followed,' said Ashley, as he stood next to Philip Wild at the urinals of the gentlemen's cloakroom in the King George Hotel in Park Lane, 'is why, along with all those physicists and what-not on the Science Park Board, they have a philosopher and a professor of Anglo-Saxon, Norse and Celtic.'

'The marriage of Academe to Industry,' Philip said. 'In fact, that's the whole nub of our role as their PR consultants. We're the ones who have to convince the public that Rutland University is geared to the needs of industry in the Eighties. It's the Enterprise Culture.'

'Oh I see,' said Ashley, who didn't. They moved out to a kind of anteroom where an attendant was filling hand basins with warm water. When they had rinsed their hands he passed each of them a small linen towel and then began brushing the shoulders of their jackets with a clothes-brush. 'I suppose it's all a question of money, really.'

'Absolutely. The Science Park will bring industry – and its lolly – to the campus, but at the same time they have to hold on to their academic integrity.'

'Hence the prestigious dons on the board.'

'You see, you *are* getting the point.' Wild felt in his pocket for a pound coin. 'That's for both of us,' he told the attendant, and dropped it onto the plate already holding several others and a five-pound note, clearly put there by the staff to jack up the going rate. At Philip's words, Ashley, who was also about to give a tip, hastily pulled his hand out of his pocket. He glanced at the young man's face, cleared now of its obsequious smile, changed his mind and fished out a coin.

'Nonsense,' he said, ignoring the plate and pressing it into the soft hand. 'This is from me.'

'Thank *you*, sir!' The receiving hand lingered under Ashley's touch for the briefest moment. He followed Philip out into the great central lounge where tired American tourists were throwing stretched vowel sounds to each other and Japanese businessmen sat in giggling groups. Bland wallpaper music issued from a Steinway: tunes by Gershwin, Irving Berlin, Cole Porter, Lennon and McCartney, all rendered down into characterless nonentities. Philip led the way to a sofa as far from the piano as possible and snapped his fingers in the face of a waiter who had materialised almost before their bottoms had touched the velour cushions.

'Earl Grey, for two. Nothing to eat.' He was about to wave him away but Ashley cut in.

'Actually, I know it's hardly the weather for it, but I rather fancy some hot buttered toast.' He smiled at the waiter. 'Is that at all possible?'

'Of course, sir. Brown bread or white?'

'Brown, please. And might I be *utterly* dissolute and have some raspberry jam?' Ashley's smile widened and was amplified by a conspiratorial wink.

'Why not, sir? Live dangerously, I always say!' They both laughed and the waiter left without giving Philip a second glance. Ashley sensed that this aimless bonhomie had snubbed Philip and regretted it. He tried to re-start their conversation. 'Tell me, Philip, do these airy-fairy dons really understand business?'

'Oh, don't underrate them. Some may be a bit naive, but Thatcher's government has put the fear of God into them. The sharper ones have been quick to learn that money from industry provides a handy buttress for crumbling ivory towers.' He looked up to see a tall, stooping figure approaching. 'Anyway, not a word to Bessie, here comes his nibs.' Then, rising, he said, 'Vice Chancellor Helmsley, how very nice to see you again!'

'Will you have tea, Vice Chancellor? Would you like to sit down?' Ashley had jumped to his feet and began to manoeuvre a chair for him. The Vice Chancellor seemed unable to respond to both questions at once.

'Tea? Ah, tea!' He hovered for a moment, looking at the chair as if it was the latest in a series of inventions designed to baffle, lowered himself cautiously and leaned back. One leg of his worsted trousers hitched up on the chair front, exposing six inches of hairless skin.

'Perhaps you'd prefer something a little stronger?'

'No, no, my dear fellow! This chair seems fine to me.'

'To drink.'

'Drink? Oh good gracious no.' Dr Helmsley was a Methodist. 'Tea will suffice.' He stretched out his legs. 'Extraordinarily expensive, these Park Lane hotels, but, um, comfortable. Very.' He relaxed for a few moments before inviting Philip to make his report.

It was an informal meeting, one of a monthly series initiated by the Vice Chancellor who wanted to keep a personal finger on the pulse of all new developments at Rutland University. They could have met on campus but he enjoyed his trips, on expenses, to London and anyway felt safer talking to these people away from his colleagues, some of whom were far too inquisitive.

Ashley knew that they could feel secure in this relationship because Philip had never failed to deliver. From the moment Kirkland Wild had been appointed Public Relations agents to Rutland University, he had made sure that the university's new Science Park project enjoyed the widest coverage possible. The result was that Rutland was often held up by Conservative politicians as a shining example of the Way Forward for all academic institutions. At Rutland could be found the perfect blend of learning, research and vocational training where young minds, instead of being diverted by useless subjects like English Literature or worse, Sociology, could be trained for the needs of Industry. Having a strong business community, Philip insisted, was the only way Britain would pay her way in the world, and that was all that mattered. After all, who was able to live off poetry or philosophy these days?

Publicly, Ashley supported Philip's views but on the quiet he was not at all sure that this neo-Victorian age, where single mothers couldn't afford to clothe their children and loonies were being turfed out of institutions to fend for themselves, didn't need a philosopher or two to be paid just to sit and think about the rights and wrongs of it all.

This month, Dr Helmsley was more than pleased. The special supplement in *The Times*, where Rutland's Science Park had been described in some detail, had been well received in the right circles and there was soon to be a television programme. But his main preoccupation today was with the land. 'We had our, um, ah, board meeting yesterday, as you know,' he said, removing his glasses, putting them down on the table and then picking them up again. 'Whereat, the main subject on the er, agenda was the landscaping of the Science Park.' He warmed to his subject. 'In order that we might, ah, be sure of an, um, cohesive design, that is to say, a design that, well, that *links* all the architecture together and um, how shall I put it, that, um *blends* with the rest of the campus, we had decided, as I am quite sure you already understand, to give the landscaping contract for all the sites on the Park, that is to say, the, ah, total of one hundred acres, to one firm.'

'I remember the original discussions,' Ashley said.

'Well,' the Vice Chancellor went on, 'there has been, ah, rather a surprising result. We approached all the well-known firms of landscape, ah, designers and invited them to enter a competition. Then, and I think this may, er, perhaps have been at your um, er, um—'

'Instigation?'

'Suggestion?'

'Precisely. On your exhortation, we made the competition more open and invited less, um, less prestigious contenders and, and, lo!' He stopped talking, turned his owl-like face to them and blinked. There was a long pause.

'And lo?' Ashley prompted.

'Ah Yes! Extraordinary! A complete outsider came up with easily the best scheme. Our first choice might have been the German firm, Grossen Linden but, vast as their reputation is, and imaginative though their drawings undoubtedly were, even they failed to, um, ah, in*spire* in the way that the winning proposal did.'

'What's the name of this firm?'

'The name? Ah yes, the name!' Dr Helmsley groped in a few pockets and eventually pulled out a wad of much-folded A4 paper. 'The address seems to be somewhere up your way, Mr Kirkland. Do not you farm in Lincolnshire?'

Ashley nodded, taking the letter from the Vice Chancellor and looking at the letterhead. 'But I've never heard of this firm, what's it called, Rumbold Venn?'

'It seems that no one has heard of it.'

'It will make a *great* story,' Philip enthused. '"University Challenge for Small Business". If you give us details as soon as you feel you can release them, we'll go public. There's a lot of mileage in this one.'

'Good God, I don't believe it!' shouted Ashley and burst out laughing. 'The firm's an outsider all right. It's our local doctor's wife.'

'Even better,' said Philip, 'a one-man show. Land of opportunity for single-minded go-getters, et cet.'

'The, ah, representative of Rumbold Venn—'

'A large woman, in tweeds, name of Bates?'

'Precisely. As I was, er, saying, Mrs Bates has been to two meetings with the board and, um, doctor's wife or no, she is certainly a most talented individual.'

'When sober.' There was a pause.

'I beg your pardon?'

'She has a bit of a reputation,' Ashley handed back the papers, 'for hitting the bottle.'

The Vice Chancellor meditated for a full minute. Her credentials were impeccable but, on reflection, she had struck him as being a rather eccentric female. At the board meeting, when the final selection had been made, he had rather stuck his neck out, since a small but vociferous faction on the board had wanted to play safe with such a large contract by appointing Grossen Linden. In the event of a foul-up here, he could be exposed. The idea of a drunkard, nay a *female* drunkard, shook him to the roots of his Wesleyan soul. 'But I, goodness me! I telephoned to Rumbold Venn this very morning, to give them the good news.'

'Well, I'm sure it'll all work out,' Ashley said. 'More tea, Vice Chancellor?'

'Oh Gawd our help in ages past!' Maggie's throaty contralto boomed across the wide lawns of Bridge House and filtered into the surgery waiting room, to the amusement of the waiting patients. One or two exchanged knowing glances but they were confusing insobriety with eccentricity. Maggie had not touched a drop of alcohol in two years. 'Our dum de dum de stormy BLAST!' The last word turned into a yell as she snagged her sleeve on a thorn. 'Blast it to sodding hell!' The words were angry but she was laughing. Even scratching her wrist was amusing today, now that she had what she called her Triumph to savour. There'd be lots more work, of course, what with visits to the site, extra drawings and so on, and she wouldn't be able to spend much time in the garden over the next few months. That was a shame but she would be able to afford a gardener now, and a good one too!

Just the bloody ticket! In the twenty-one months since the start of her design business she had been waiting for one good break. Several minor country houses had retained her services and lately, one or two local authorities had begun to invite proposals for small pieces of landscape, but what she had badly needed was a good, meaty project which would enhance her reputation and push her business into the next league. Bloody laugh it all was, really. 'Rumbaild Venn, desaign consultancea,' she told the rose bush, pinching up her lips to make a parody of her own telephone voice, 'ever so refained and naice,' and then added, 'back of envelope jobs, mostly.' All a matter of self-image, Sally Doncaster had told her. Business people tend to take you at face value and if you say you're good, they usually believe you. Sally had suggested adding her maiden name to make up a company title, but Rumbold Bates was difficult to say, so she had picked the name of her beloved river. Rumbold Venn. It had a smart ring to it, Sally had said. Maggie paused for a breather. The droughty soil was becoming difficult to work and her arms ached.

She'd sweated blood over the Science Park. A hundred acres of swampy land, neither agricultural nor industrial, to be littered with what she thought were monstrous buildings made of stainless steel and glass with all their innards nailed to their outsides. The biggest was a vast pyramid of mirror glass put up by Universal Computers. It presided over the other buildings but was squat and inscrutable, reflecting the sky from each of its glazed flanks so that you couldn't see inside, whatever the angle. Maggie thought of it as the Ministry of Truth and wondered how the hell she could use trees and plants to dilute its menace. She worked for days, drawing and rejecting sketch after sketch until that loathsome prism began to haunt her dreams. She knew that to stand a chance against the established fraternity of designers, she would need to deliver far more than they. Then, one night when she'd been working until dawn, sustained by digestive biscuits dunked into instant coffee so strong it made her gag, she found inspiration. If that bloody pyramid was the centre of the park, the answer was not to hide it but to replicate the triangular theme everywhere. She went to bed for a few hours' rest but was soon up and making fine drawings with full details of lawns, copses, lakes, formal terraces, all in geometrical shapes but without a single curve or a right angle anywhere. Within a fortnight she had made up a portfolio which contained the drawings, a well-reasoned essay on her choice of style, plant lists, names of suppliers and possible contractors. She even included one or two alternative drawings, just to show that she was flexible.

The response had, after months of silence, been an invitation to visit Rutland University where she was invited to justify her proposals and was later informed that she had been included in the shortlist for the commission. There were, she was told, only three other firms on the list. One, she had found out, was Grossen Linden but she hadn't a clue who the others were. The Germans, she knew, were strong. They seemed to be dominant all over Europe and had already transformed several unpromising sites in northern inner cities. Even the Vice Chancellor had been unable to keep a reverential tone from creeping into his voice when he kept referring to, 'Our friends from over the, ah, North Sea.' But since yesterday, the waiting was over. 'Rumbold Venn?' the girl with the nasal voice had asked, when she had answered the kitchen phone. 'Mrs Bates, please.'

'Speaking,' Maggie had said, wishing she had a receptionist to create an impression.

'Dr Helmsley for you.' Then the hesitant voice had spelled it out. Provisional appointment or, ah, rather, commission, to be ratified by the Board, of course, but she could, ah, rest assured that the decision was made and . . . And that was it, thought Maggie, bringing her hoe down extra hard on a tall, fleshy sow thistle. Just the bloody ticket!

While Maggie worked at her mixed borders, Ashley Kirkland was sitting in the Daimler with his land agent Hector Enfield. They had ten minutes to kill before their appointment at Cartwright Farm but walking over, especially in this heat, did not appeal to them at all. Besides, they felt they could talk more freely out of earshot of any passing gossip-monger, in the air-conditioned comfort of the car.

'There's far more than just money at stake here, Hector. This is family welfare.'

'The figures speak for themselves, Ashley. If a farmer can't pay a realistic rent he shouldn't be farming.'

'From the business point of view, that's right.'

'It's right from every point of view. It simply doesn't make sense for those people to struggle on. If you offer them a large surrender fee and get Vacant Possession, they—'

'They'll feel betrayed.'

'Not at all. They'll thank you for it.'

'I doubt it.'

'Oh, but they will. In the long run. They'll be free of a

burden, you see. Anyway, you'll be a lot better off, whether you keep the farm or sell it. Everyone wins.'

Ashley opened the car window and let a blast of hot June air into the refrigerated interior. 'I'm still undecided.' He closed it and felt the chill build up again. 'I'd have to give them a generous compensation figure.'

'Even so, you'd be quids in. There could be as much as a thousand an acre difference in value, you know. More perhaps, if you flogged the house separately.'

'I'm not at all sure they could be persuaded.'

'Every man has his price.'

'Indeed. But the backbone here is a woman. Betty Rose would take some shifting, I can tell you.'

'Wait till we break the news about their new rent. That'll concentrate their minds.'

'You make it sound like putting the frighteners on.'

'Not at all. It's just being realistic.' He pulled a gold half-hunter out of his trouser pocket and glanced at it without opening the lid. Ashley put the Daimler into gear.

At Cartwright Farm, Jack and Betty were bracing them-selves for the meeting. They knew that they had been living on borrowed time as far as their rent was concerned, and feared a sharp increase which they would find difficult to afford. It would take so little to make their business teeter back into insolvency. The tension of the last few days had been almost unbearable, and Betty had found herself watch-ing Jack closely and trying not to show that she was reacting, every time he displayed the slightest sign of stress. Even now, as she watched him moving the desk round to make more room in the study, she wondered whether he was wheezing or just breathing heavily with the exertion. Sensing her gaze, he looked up. 'I'm perfectly all right!'

'You were making a funny noise.'

'If you must know, I was whistling under my breath. Beethoven's *Pastoral* as it happens.'

'But you're worrying.'

'I'm perfectly all right. Anxious about this bloody rent business, obviously, but not ill.'

'We'll be all right.' She squeezed his hand.

'Unless they exceed our figure.' In the last few days, they had worked out a series of farm budgets based on different rents. Currently they paid nearly £8,000 per year and tried to keep their living expenses down to about £6,000. That allowed them to repay part of their overdraft and to cover interest charges. Any rent increase at all would be injurious but they felt they could just about cope as long as the total was less than £65 per acre. But a neighbouring farm had been let for £85 and such a level would, they knew, wipe them out.

'We've been into all that. We know Ashley wouldn't want to destroy us.'

'If he were ruthless, it would.' The pitch, but not the volume, of his voice had begun to rise. Betty opened the window a little wider and noticed that the perennials in her border outside were wilting in the hot sun. In the drought, the lupins and delphiniums had only grown to about half their normal height. 'If we went under, he would click for Vacant Possession at no cost and that would double the value of this farm.'

'*Ja-ack!*' She turned from the window. 'This is silly!'

'You're right. It is.' He smiled – a lopsided offering. She went out of the room and left him to gaze at the wall. The barometer was stuck on 'Set Fair' at almost 31 inches. It had barely moved since early May.

Betty went into her bedroom to make sure she looked decent enough for the visitors. She dabbed a little Lily-of-the-Valley toilet water onto her wrists and adjusted her hair, resisting the temptation to seek and pull out any grey ones. She stood up and pulled the hemline of her navy-blue and white cotton dress straight and then turned sideways to the mirror and stuck out her chest. The outline of her breasts, not showing the slightest sign of sagging, the flatness of her stomach, firm skin and smooth complexion reassured her. Not a bad figure, she decided, considering her age. Farming certainly kept a body fit. Then, feeling a pang of guilt for such vanity, she frowned at herself and was about to look out of the window when she heard the doorknocker.

Jack was already showing Ashley and Hector Enfield into the study when Betty came downstairs.

'As you probably realise,' Ashley began, putting on a quite different voice from his usual matey style, 'it is a little unconventional for the landlord to be present, with his agent, at such a meeting.'

'You're welcome here at any time,' Jack said.

'Thank you. As I said, unconventional, but I wanted to retain the very *personal* relationship we enjoy, not merely as landlord and tenants but rather, as neighbours and, well, as friends.' Enfield kept silent.

'I hope our relationship should continue as it has gone before, too,' said Jack, losing his grip of English in an effort to make the right response.

'Well, let's get to the point. Believe me, I do know how difficult it is to make a little unit like this pay.'

'It is, very,' Jack agreed.

'We're managing, though,' said Betty.

'Indeed. But for how long?' There was silence. 'Your rent is low.'

'Comparatively low,' Betty admitted.

'You could say that I'm subsidising your business out of my own pocket.' Another pause. 'Betty,' Ashley's formal tone was slipping and his natural charm was beginning to show, 'when you came to see me once – what, a couple of years ago? – you said that however bad things got, you would hang on.'

'So we have.'

'And how do you feel about your business now?'

'Very positive.' Betty couldn't make out where this conversation was leading but she was determined to strike a confident attitude. 'We're on a much more even footing now.'

'Splendid!'

'And I still feel as strongly. I, we, *love* this place just as much. More, if anything.'

'What about this dry spell?' Enfield spoke for the first time. 'If it turns into a long drought, it could get bad for you. Rub you out, even.'

'It could rub a great many farmers out,' Jack chipped in.

'But you're especially vulnerable.' Ashley's quiet tones were laced with sympathy. 'Any little downturn could finish you: another price drop, a virulent pig disease, anything.' The truth of these words was chilling.

'Yes, anything.' Jack was beginning to feel anger at this man's calmness. 'Even a killing rent review.'

'Ah yes, the rent review.'

'I think,' Enfield spoke again, 'that this is something you may find a bit difficult to face.'

'Nobody likes an increase in costs,' Jack muttered.

'Of course not,' Ashley said, 'especially in a marginal business.' Jack recognised the note of contempt in the word 'marginal' and fought to suppress his anger. 'But, you see, you don't have to face a killing review.'

'Oh?'

'I want to make things easy for you.'

'We don't need charity.'

'And so,' Ashley ignored the retort, 'what I'm about to suggest should come as quite a relief. As you know—' he was interrupted by a loud knock at the front door.

'I'll see to it,' Jack said, getting up. 'Do carry on. Betty and I are equal partners and she's as capable in this as I – more so, in fact.' He slipped out. Betty closed the door behind him.

'Ashley,' her eyes were shining, 'Ashley, I think I know what you were about to say. There is only one way you could make things easy for us and I *knew* deep down that you would not want to damage us.'

'Damage you? Betty, what I wanted to ask was whether you should go on with such a struggle. Wouldn't it be easier to quit while you're strong?'

'Quit? Of course it would be easy to quit. But we're not quitters. We picked a difficult row to hoe, here, we always knew that. But we *are* winning now and with your support—'

'Support? I'm not at all—'

'Oh, I don't expect a subsidy and we both know that a review is long overdue, but keeping the increase to a minimum will mean so much to us. I can't tell you how grateful we'll be.' The look of incomprehension on both the men's faces puzzled her. What was the matter? Had she embarrassed them? Did they think she should have waited for Jack to be there? She thought of changing the subject and slipping into female-to-male small talk, but she knew that would sound too contrived now. Besides, the thought of being patronised, not by Ashley, but by Enfield was an added deterrent. Instead, she attempted to steer the discussion to the next point. 'Presumably you're ready to talk actual figures now?'

'No!' Ashley's reply was too abrupt. 'That is, I think I should discuss the whole thing with Hector first.'

'But I'd assumed you already had.'

'In general terms, but not in detail.' He was embarrassed.

'In that case, can I get you some tea?'

'Um, no, thank you, I think we'd better be on our way.' Still looking baffled, the men got up. She followed them to the front door. Jack had disappeared and of the caller there was no sign. She escorted them down the path.

'Pretty garden,' remarked Enfield. 'Got a real woman's touch.'

'Dry,' said Betty. 'We need a good rain.'

'Why don't you water? There's no hosepipe ban here yet,' he said, 'not an official one, anyway.'

'No, I know, but I think it would be a bit irresponsible to hose the flower borders, don't you? In view of the national water shortage.'

'Elaine has a sprinkler running all the time,' said Ashley, 'day and night.' As Enfield walked towards the car, Ashley turned and rested his elbows on the wicket gate. Betty met his gaze and felt her pulse quicken. The hazel eyes were not twinkling, the look was intense. 'I can't quite make out what's just gone on. Am I a complete idiot?'

'Sorry?' Betty reddened. The anger in his face stirred a worrying mixture of emotions. She wanted to soothe but felt afraid and unable to fathom out why the sudden mood change had occurred. 'I'm not quite with you.'

'Aren't you?' He was surprised at how much her colour rose. 'No, perhaps you're not.' He looked into her eyes and then, as her own grey irises gazed steadily back, turned his attention to the garden. 'Woman's touch!' He uttered a little laugh. 'They've got no idea just how much you do, have they? Any of them . . .' and then, after another reflective pause, he took his arms off the gate and stood up straight. 'We'll quantify the review. You'll hear in writing.'

'Thank you. And Ashley—'

'No, don't say a word. Particularly don't thank me. Nothing's decided.' He began to walk away. Then, 'Oh, I nearly forgot.' He pulled a white envelope out of the inside pocket of his twill jacket. 'Elaine asked me to give you this.' He handed it to her and walked briskly to the Daimler.

As he opened the driver's door, Ashley looked across the roof at Enfield. 'Something of a balls-up, I fear,' he muttered.

'I was getting vibes from you to keep quiet. That was right, wasn't it?'

'Frankly, Hector, I'm still totally undecided on this one.' He got in and drove slowly down the lane to avoid making a dustcloud.

Betty walked back to the house and was about to go to change into old clothes when the phone rang.

'Darling!' It was Sally's voice. 'I'm by the pool. We all are.'

'Lucky you.'

'It's so hot, that we wondered whether you'd all like to pop over for a swim?'

'That's awfully kind of you but the children aren't home from college yet and I've got various things to do here.'

'Those bloody pigs of yours, I suppose.'

'Yes. And a meal to cook and some paperwork. Quite a bit of it.'

'What about the kids? Simon could collect them.'

'Who's Simon?'

'You know, *Simon* – our Mudandan. I promised his father we'd look after him so he's staying here for a while.'

'Oh yes, of course. Well, if you're sure.'

'Sure? My darling of course I'm sure. We'll feed them as well. In fact, you and Jack could come over when you've finished your daily toil and munch something too. What do you say?'

'Sounds lovely.' She expressed more thanks and hung up. Then she remembered the envelope Ashley had given her and she opened it. A thick white card, embossed in copperplate script, announced that Elaine Kirkland would be At Home for dinner at 7.30 on Saturday 21 June and requested the pleasure of her company and Jack's.

'Heavens,' Betty said aloud. 'That's a change from helping with the washing up,' and then wondered what on earth she would wear.

Chapter Eleven

The garden of the Old Rectory rang with a merry symphony. Squeals of excited children, accompanied by loud splashing, provided the upper notes, which were supported in the bass section by barks of adult laughter. The scent of June roses on the evening air would blend, later, with the aromatic smoke of meat sizzling on the barbecue. In spite of Maggie Bates's renovations, the main garden looked, superficially, much as it had before the Doncasters moved in but, behind the redbrick wall that enclosed the old kitchen garden, they had installed a large swimming pool.

The outbuildings had been converted to changing rooms, and the boiler room for the greenhouses – long since pulled down – was now a quaint little pavilion for summer revels. There was a bar, decorated in a *Chinoiserie* style with bamboo fittings and painted silk wall hangings but outside, the mood switched abruptly to Central American, with a paved area and permanent barbecue – an edifice of white-painted brick with its own chimney stack – next to an artifical cactus plant which concealed a standpipe, tap and hose. Lined up along the poolside were a number of floral-cushioned, white-painted day beds with wheels at one end and handles at the other.

On one of these Sally, wearing a buttercup-yellow bikini, was lounging, cordless phone held in a clinch between shoulder and ear while she made notes on a huge pad of paper. The youngsters in the pool were supervised by Jules, who was sitting on the edge with his feet dangling in the water. On another lounger, clad in turquoise trunks, lay a young man whose skin was as smooth and purple-black as a ripe September plum. He was tall, six foot three, with long, willowy limbs, large, expressive hands and a voice which made Sally think of cello music. Mandy Rose sat on a towel beside his lounger, listening and answering questions. 'What does your Dad grow?'

'Oh, the usual things,' Mandy said. 'Barley, wheat, potatoes.'

'You call them usual?'

'Round here, yes.'

'Well, *my* dad grows yams and sorghum. That's more usual, I think!'

'I thought you said your father was a prince.'

'Sure!'

'Like Prince Charles?'

At this, Simon slapped his thighs, making a loud clapping sound and broke into a rich, deep laugh. 'No, no! Not at all like Prince Charles.'

'Well, then. He can't be a real prince.'

'Why not?'

'Well,' Mandy considered, 'he just can't. That's all.'

'He has plenty of horses. He even plays polo – well, a game quite like polo, anyway.'

'That doesn't prove a thing.' Mandy leapt up. 'Come on, lazy, it's time you went in again.'

'I've only just got out. Besides,' he began to roll his eyes and shiver dramatically, 'it's so-o-o co-o-ld!' But Mandy grabbed his hand and began to pull.

'No excuse. Come *on*.' She tugged. He shivered even more. 'Hey, Cam!' she shouted over her shoulder. 'Help me get this lazy lump into the pool.' Camilla was in the water playing with a beach ball but came at once.

'Hang on!' She swam a brisk crawl to the steps at the deep end – Jules noticed how much her stroke had improved since they had had the pool – climbed the steps and ran along the side. In spite of a tendency to be over-indulged by Sally and positively spoilt by Jules, she showed no signs of selfish behaviour. Ready and willing to help around the village, and growing more pretty by the day as she matured, everyone adored her. She and Mandy were so close nowadays that they even thought together.

'Camilla!' Jules warned, quietly. 'Don't run by the pool-edge.' He leant back to watch her go past. 'It's dangerous.'

'Sorry, Dad.' She got to Simon's lounger and took his other arm. Both girls hauled him to his feet. 'Come on, Simon!' they cried in unison. 'Time for a dip!' He broke from their grasp, dived in and surfaced with an earsplitting falsetto shriek.

'Oooh! It's fre-e-ezing!' Everyone laughed. Soon an energetic game of water polo began with the beach ball whizzing to and fro. Jim, Gill and eventually even Jules got into the water and joined the mêlée. A couple of times the ball flew out of the water and once it hit the barbecue where Sally, now wearing a snow-white towelling robe over her bikini, had taken over the cooking of sausages, chops and chicken pieces. She protested. Play got wilder.

Jules soon tired and resumed his place on the edge. Jim began to wheeze and climbed out to get dry and to dress but the three girls and Simon continued, swimming and throwing, faster and faster until they could hardly breathe. Possession of the ball became the only goal, driving all else out of focus until one got hold of it. Then it had to be thrown hard, before anyone else got close. Camilla had it, then Mandy, then Simon, lunging, tackling, hurling, diving and ducking. Then suddenly it disappeared. For a few moments, no one could speak, then Gill looked at each opponent.

'Who's . . . got . . . it?' she said between laboured breaths. Simon shook his head and shrugged. Camilla ducked and surfaced after a few seconds. Pointing to Simon.

'Him . . . It's him. He's . . .' She couldn't speak for breathlessness but pointed below the surface to where Simon had the ball trapped between his knees. He looked all innocence and shrugged again and shook his head but Mandy had crept behind and, treading water, put both hands on his head.

'Down you go, your unroyal lowness!' She pushed down,

hard, shocked by the steely feel of his woollen hair under her palms. The ball surfaced and Camilla threw it onto a lounger. Simon didn't come up. Play stopped. They waited, knowing him to be fooling. He didn't come up.

'Simon!' Mandy shouted, in a different tone from the earlier joyous yelling. Sally, hearing the note sharpen to panic, swung round and ran to the pool-edge. She couldn't see into the depth of the water because of the surface glare.

'Simon!' Sally shouted and jumped into the water just as, at last, he surfaced at the far end and pulled himself out of the pool on strong arms. He turned and looked from one person to another. As soon as he had his breath back he laughed and slapped his thighs.

'Your *faces!*'

Sally struggled up the steps at the shallow end, her saturated robe hanging comically and then falling to the ground in a sodden heap. 'Simon, you are a rat!' She laughed, but it had been a horrid moment. She tried to imagine what it would be like, having to stand before the Prince in Mudando to tell him that his first-born, his heir, the light of his life and apple of his eye had drowned in her care. She turned her back and walked to the pavilion. Simon sensed her disapproval and stood, indecisive. Jules watched from the pool-edge.

'You might just see that she has a towel, Simon,' he said. Simon went to the door of the pavilion and stood awkwardly, peering in. Sally was buffing her hair with a towel.

'I'm sorry, Mrs Doncaster, really I am.'

'What for?' The boy stood, blocking the light. 'You make a better door than a window.'

'Beg pardon?'

'Oh, nothing.' She found one of Jules's robes – a jazzy affair with palm trees and manic bongo drummers printed on the thin terry – a gift he had worn once. 'What are you? Twenty-three, going on twelve?'

'Sorry.'

'Where did you learn to breathe underwater?'

'Pardon?'

'Don't say "pardon". You must have been under for minutes.'

'About a minute, no more. We used to have underwater competitions.'

'In Mudando? Where the hell—?'

'No, at Cambridge. I usually won.' I bet you did, she thought, with that great chest.

'Have you written to your father yet?' She brushed the tangles out of her hair with brisk movements and tossed it back, securing it in a rough ponytail with a towelling wristband.

'No. But I am going to.'

'Just make sure you do – tonight.' He stepped back to let her out. 'You are an overgrown baby, aren't you? Have you thought about next year?'

'No.'

'Well, Simon, you must. You can't go on being my courier.'

'It's a job.'

'Not for someone with your brains. You've got a Cambridge degree, for heaven's sake.'

'I like being a courier.'

'Just an excuse for you to go blinding about on that great motor bike of yours. You'll have to grow up soon, you know. There'll be big responsibilities – at home, I mean.' She stroked his arm with the backs of her fingers. His skin was flawless.

'I want to stay in England.'

'Oh, you're hopeless! Go and play with the other children.'

Jack and Betty arrived just as the meal was ready. The children all got dressed, began jockeying for places in the queue and soon bore off cardboard plates which buckled under the weight of singed meat, salad and a microwaved potato. Jules poured champagne for the adults and Buck's Fizz for the youngsters. Jack had brought along two bottles of Co-op Rheinpfalz, at which Sally said that it was very sweet and very naughty of him to have done it, but that all the drinks were organised. Silence fell as everyone, appetites sharpened by so much swimming and fresh air, concentrated on their food.

'Hell!' Sally said, suddenly. 'I forgot the barbecue sauce.'

'I'll go!' Camilla jumped up and sprinted along the pool.

'Camilla, walk!' Jules shouted, but she increased her speed, dodged through the narrow arch which led out of the kitchen garden and tripped, slamming her knee into the wall. The impact of flesh and bone against brickwork was audible from the other side of the pool. Jules sprang up shouting, 'Oh my God! Which leg? Which leg?' But Sally got there first. Camilla was sitting, her face white in the fading daylight, her eyes glazed with pain.

'Oh my baby . . .' Sally seemed not to know what to do. 'What have you done?' Betty, having told all the other children to keep away, had also come over.

'Can I do anything?'

'I don't know, Betty.' Jules got up and made a space for her to kneel by the child. She looked at the knee, already swelling, and at the dark trickle of blood running down from the grazed skin.

'May I look, Cam?' She felt the leg. 'Nothing broken, I think. Probably just a nasty bruise.' She helped the girl to her feet. 'Do you think you can walk?' Camilla took a tentative step and winced.

'No.'

'Have another try. Here, cling to my shoulder.' They took a step together. 'Ye-es. There you are, just a very nasty bash. Nothing more.'

They staggered back to congealed meat and cold potatoes. Everyone did their best to revive the party but little of the early conviviality returned. Camilla, subdued and tear-stained, rested on a lounger while her knee swelled ominously. As soon as they could reasonably do so, the Roses took their leave. On their way out, Betty turned to Sally.

'I'm so sorry about Camilla.'

'I know, poor lambkin! Her bad leg, too.'

'It was a nasty bang. Even so, I wouldn't have expected

quite such a swelling. Jim did a similar thing last year, when he fell off his bike, but his knee didn't blow up like that.'

'It's quite horrible. I'm going to take her back to the specialist.'

By next morning, the swelling had subsided somewhat and Camilla's extrovert cheerfulness had returned. She wanted to avoid a doctor's visit but Sally was adamant. 'We mustn't take any chances,' she said, and phoned Leonard Bates's surgery there and then.

'Oh, good morning,' she put on her creamiest telephone voice for Mrs Pollitt, 'and *such* a lovely one, isn't it? May I please speak to Dr Bates.'

But Mrs Pollitt wasn't having any of that. 'He's with a patient.'

'Ah. Well, could he possibly ring me when he's free?'

'He won't be. He's got a full surgery, then he'll be off on his rounds.'

'I see. Well, it's quite a simple matter really. I just want him to refer my stepdaughter, Camilla, to Mr Turner for another examination. She's had a bit of a bang, you see, and well . . . you know – better safe than—'

'It isn't for the likes of you to decide whether a specialist sees your stepdaughter, Mrs Doncaster. That is a matter for Dr Bates.'

'Which is precisely why I am trying to contact him, Mrs Pollack.' Sally used the wrong name on purpose because she knew it annoyed the old bat.

'You can bring her in. Doctor will not be finished here for at least two more hours.'

There was nothing for it but to comply. When, after an interminable wait among hay-fever victims and wailing toddlers, their turn came, Leonard was apologetic. 'You should have phoned,' he said. 'I know how busy you are.' He examined Camilla's knee and said, 'I'm not totally happy with that. I'll get you over to Turner right away.' He phoned, grunted a little, scratched out a note on his pad and then hung up. 'Tomorrow, eleven o'clock.'

'Damn!' Sally remembered that she had a board meeting in

London and that it was Jules's Sheffield day. 'Is that the only time?'

''Fraid so.'

'She'll be there.' They marched out, or rather, Sally marched and Camilla hobbled, ignoring Mrs Pollitt.

'Can't Betty take me tomorrow?'

'Yes, darling, I expect so. Would you mind?'

'Of course not.'

Betty agreed to take Camilla along and waited with her while the specialist scanned X-rays, prodded and quizzed. He wouldn't confide in her but she sensed that he was uneasy. 'I want to monitor Camilla's progress.'

'Of course, Mr Turner.'

'We'll need to run some tests later, when she's healed up. Meanwhile, she must be careful.'

'Yes, I see.'

'Not too much charging around, young lady. What sports do you do?'

'Netball. And tennis.'

'Tennis should be all right.'

'And riding, of course.'

'Riding? I think you'll have to give that up for now. At least until you've had your tests.'

Betty drove her tearful charge home. 'Don't fret, Cam. It won't be for long.'

'It's not me, it's Damien. He has to be exercised or he'll pine.'

On the longest day of the year, the thirty-seventh without rain, Jack and Betty were hurrying with their evening chores, anxious to get bathed and changed for the Kirklands' dinner party. Betty had visited Second Hand Roz and found a simple dress – little more than a sheath, really – in blue and white silk with a lightweight matching bolero which had close-fitting sleeves and a Chanel-style neckline. It was almost new and, apart from a grease stain on the sleeve of the jacket, was in perfect condition and still close enough to modern fashion not to look quaint.

She met Jack walking across the farmyard in open-necked check shirt and faded corduroy trousers. His clothes and skin were dusty but like all the other farmers in the neighbourhood, his face was ruddy from the sun. He was carrying a brown paper bag. 'This is yours. Agrivet dropped it off by the gate.'

'Ah, good.' She took the bag and looked inside. It contained bottles of injectable iron for baby pigs. Even in herds as well run as Betty's, anaemia was a common ailment and all her young pigs received a tonic within a few days of birth. 'I'll take it over to the building tomorrow. I've just finished there now. I need a long soak to lay the dust.'

'Me too. Talk about dry!'

'I'm sure we'll get rain soon, especially now the wind's gone westerly.'

'It changed last week, for a while, but what did we get? Cloud for half a day, then back to this heat.' He followed her into the house. She left him to make a pot of tea in the kitchen and went upstairs to run her bath. While the tub was filling, she laid out her dress, selected the navy shoes, the nearly matching handbag and rummaged in her tights drawer for a ladderless pair of the right shade. Then, removing slacks, blouse, bra and knickers she walked to the bathroom, locked the door and slipped into the warm water. She washed her hair, scrubbed her nails, soaped and rinsed her body and then sank back to luxuriate in the steamy atmosphere.

Almost an hour later, a thump on the door dragged her back into consciousness. The water had cooled to blood temperature and a grey scum had settled on the surface. 'Half an hour and we're due!' Jack called through the door.

'Oh gosh, sorry! I must have drifted off. Come in.' She jumped out and unbolted the door before picking up a towel.

'I've fed the kids,' he said, 'so there's nothing more for you to do.'

'That was sweet of you.'

'Mandy did most of the work. I just chatted while they ate.'

'Do you want my water?' She glanced at the bath. 'Yuk! No, I don't suppose you do.'

'There isn't much time. P'raps I'll just have a wash at the basin.'

He looked tired, she thought. He took off his shirt. Apart from face, neck and a reddened delta on the chest where his shirt had been unbuttoned in the sunshine, his skin was disturbingly pale. The slight bulge where the pacemaker was fitted under the skin reminded her of his frailty and she kissed his shoulder.

'You ought to work with your shirt off. Get a healthy tan.'

'Sunbathing? Fat chance we've got for that!'

'It should be a bit easier until harvest, now most of the arable work's done.' She squeezed his upper arm muscles and went to dress. Sitting at her dressing table by the bedroom window, she had a clear view of the garden below. The lawn was turning brown but there was still some colour in the flower borders. I must pick a rose, she thought, to wear on my jacket. A white one if I can find it. She dressed quickly, sorted out her hair and put on make-up. She decided to wear an old pendant that had belonged to her great-grandmother, a large aquamarine, half an inch across, cut in a heart-shape and set with a dozen small diamonds. The stone was too pale to be very valuable but she had loved it ever since she was a child when her mother had worn it on special days. By the time Jack came into the bedroom, she was ready to go. 'Will I do?'

'Fine,' Jack said, hardly glancing at her. 'I'd better hurry up.'

'I'll wait in the garden. I want to find a decent rose.' She walked downstairs and out into the evening light. On the back of the house grew an ancient climbing rose which she had identified as 'Madame Alfred Carrière'. Though reddish in the bud, the fragrant blooms were soft white. She selected one that was fully open but by no means blown, and pinned it to her jacket. Soon, Jack came down and they were ready to go.

They were the last to arrive. Jack tried to find a parking

space for the Escort, now nine years old, without blocking anyone else in and eventually managed to squeeze between the wall and a large BMW. Elaine came out to them. 'At last! How *lovely* you look. Gosh, Betty, that dress!' She faltered and recovered at once. 'So elegant!' How on earth could she afford silk? Elaine remembered having had one like that herself. Hadn't she had some mishap with it? Popped it into a Sue Ryder or somewhere? Yes, that was it. She'd dunked the sleeve in some Hollandaise and had never managed to do away with the stain . . .

'Can you keep a secret?' Betty said. 'Second Hand Roz!'

'You clever thing!' cried Elaine, craning to see whether there was a mark. 'Come and meet the others.' She ushered them to the conservatory whose double doors were wide open. In front of them, on the terrace, a table had been set with drinks and nibbles. As Elaine handed each of them a glass of champagne, the other guests fell silent and when Jack saw how well groomed the women were and how scrubbed the men looked, he wished he'd had a bath.

'Now,' Elaine prepared a round of introductions. 'Philip Wild, Ashley's partner, and Andrea, of course, and Lord Redwood – he likes to be called Douggie – and this is Susannah, and Leonard and Maggie, of course, you know and . . .' On the ritual went, until Betty realised that she had not taken in a single new name. After a few minutes, Elaine clapped her hands and said, 'Before we eat, we're all going on a garden tour. Do top up your glasses and off we'll go.'

There was a general hum of appreciation and the fourteen guests moved off, following Elaine. Jack had got caught up with Lady Redwood but Betty, standing aside to let everyone past, found herself at the back of the little procession. Ashley, who had also waited, walked beside her.

He had planned to take her aside for a few moments at some stage in the evening. At their last meeting they hadn't communicated at all well, and he needed to get it through to her that their future at Cartwright Farm was still in doubt. But seeing her now, dressed so elegantly but looking so ill at ease with these other people, he couldn't bring himself to introduce a sour note.

'Betty, I must tell you, you look absolutely terrific.' She glanced at his face but there was no hint of mockery. She smiled. He smiled back. 'May I?' He offered his arm and they began a gentle stroll. 'I don't just mean the dress, though that is pretty smart. But you look so healthy.'

'It's just the sun. Have *you* looked in a mirror lately?' She studied his bronzed features. That word 'comely' crept into her mind again. They slowed their pace to enjoy the shrub roses whose blooms flowed out from between ranks of Irish yews on either side of the lawn. There was a slope away from the house towards a lake and when they got to it, they followed the path along the water's edge. The lake was really quite small, not more than half an acre, with an island in the middle. This was planted with huge rhododendrons, some of which had finished flowering, while others were covered with brilliant flowers, their images reflected in the water, doubling the drama. The surface of the lake was scattered with fallen blooms which barely moved in the slow current. By now Betty and Ashley were some way behind the main party and almost out of earshot.

'Oh, but this is lovely!' She stopped to take in the feast of colour.

'Garish things.' He seemed reluctant to stop. 'Come further along and you'll see real beauty.' He led the way over a little rustic stone bridge which spanned the stream feeding the lake and soon they were among tall trees. The land dipped away into a shaded dell where ferns and Himalayan primulas grew among dwarf maples. The freshness, the dampness of the atmosphere reminded Betty how dry it was everywhere else. The other guests had all gone in a different direction. 'Now,' he said, 'just stand absolutely still and listen.' She stood. Gradually, the different sounds became identifiable: water burbling in the stream, the occasional rustle of a bird in the undergrowth. She could hear a water vole munching a reed stem, the cheeping of moorhen chicks and then the rattling buzz of a dragonfly. Ashley had not let go of her arm and now she was aware of his closeness. Overhead, fleecy white clouds were bubbling up in the late sunlight.

'It's like paradise,' Betty whispered.

'Sshh.' Ashley took her other hand. She was about to pull back but a bird, very near, began to sing. It was a nightingale. Her heart surged for the beauty of the sound and they listened for a full five minutes.

'The others will wonder where we are,' Betty said. 'We should go back.'

'In a minute.' Ashley let go one of her hands. 'Betty, I know this sounds awfully trite, but I want you to know that I really am an admirer of yours.'

'And we all are of you,' she said.

'No, I mean beyond the usual niceties.' He came close again. She noticed how sweetly his hair curled behind the neat ears. 'I don't know how to say this, but my feelings go deeper than just, well, than just acquaintanceship.' What was he saying? This was supposed to be a business discussion!

'Ashley,' she was embarrassed. 'Don't confuse a romantic setting with reality.'

'No, no. I know it's romantic now, with nightingales and everything, but I've felt like this for a long time.' Had he? Yes, by gosh, he had!

'This is silly. A man of your type can't possibly be hankering after the middle-aged wives of hard-up tenant farmers.'

'My *type*?'

'Well, it just doesn't make sense. Your interests run in quite another direction.'

He pulled back and reddened. Could she know? 'Just what exactly do you mean?'

'Mean?' She wondered at the mood swing, as if he were alarmed all of a sudden. 'I mean that your interests run along different lines from mine, that's all.'

'What, exactly, do you mean by "interests"?'

'Business interests. You're a clever businessman: you know what you want and you get it. I, that is, Jack and I have our goals too, but we know it will always be a struggle for us.

That's the way it is.' The sun went in and a brief but chilly breeze rustled the maples in the dell.

'Oh, is *that* what you meant.' He hoped the relief didn't show on his face.

'More or less. But while we're on the subject – and I think, once this conversation has finished we should never refer to it again – while we're on the subject, I'm pretty impressed by you. You know our situation but you've never made us feel uncomfortable about it. You've given us tacit support. We'll always be grateful for that. But,' she hesitated a little, 'there's another thing.'

'Well?'

'This isn't meant to change anything at all, so please don't think it is but, physically, I think you are pretty impressive too. I would be dishonest if I didn't say that I find you,' she paused, but couldn't find a more apt word, 'if I didn't find you *comely*. In fact, all in all, I think you are a pretty marvellous sort of fellow, and Elaine is a lucky woman.'

He took both her hands in his again and looked into her face. He felt a dangerous impulse welling up, an urge to blurt out everything. It took quite an effort to suppress it.

'Oh, Betty! There's such a lot about me you don't see. If only I could tell you but . . .' He could feel a catch coming into his voice and stopped.

'We really should go back. You're the host. What will people think?'

'Betty, you remember that boy? You know, the one who—' His words were drowned by a loud crack of thunder. 'Oh my God, the sky's gone black! Come on! It's going to chuck it down!' He grabbed her arm and, as they ran for cover, lightning flashed and a second wallop of thunder made their ears sing.

'Get away from the trees,' she shouted, 'into the house. It's safer.' The first few raindrops fell, each the size of a tot of gin. Soon it was coming down in stair rods and by the time they got back to the house they were drenched. The rest of the party had noticed the thunderclouds billowing up behind the house but even so, had not quite managed to get inside before the first drops fell. In the house, female guests and some of the vainer men scampered off to dab themselves dry and repair their turnouts. Voices were raised in cheerful protest at the suddenness of the change but all agreed that the storm was a huge relief. The drought had, at last, broken.

All over the village, noses were pressed to windows as the villagers watched the rain falling and the lightning flashing in the twilight, making eerie effects with the shadows of the trees. Soon the river began to rise and to change colour from clear to brown as water, running straight off the parched land, began to drain into it. At their tied cottage, the Mardles set out zinc baths, buckets and basins to catch as much rainwater as they could. In the Rectory garden, no one had remembered to bring in the floral print covers of the poolside lounger cushions and their colours began to run. At Cart-wright Farm, Jim Rose hoped he hadn't left his homework out on the table in the yard but was afraid, with all the thunder and lightning, to go and check.

Down at the Heron, the quiet chatter among farmhands and other locals had risen to an excited crescendo which almost drowned the noise of the storm. There was much laughter in the Public Bar and relief all round. Even the Rector had become animated, waving his half-pint tankard and singing bits of Mendelssohn's *Elijah* in a cracked tenor. '*Thanks be to God, He laveth the thirsty land!*'

Chapter Twelve

The rain was heavy but brief. Early next morning the church bells pealed to a clear sky and worshippers walking to early Eucharist splashed through pools which steamed in the vivid sunshine. By midday the pools had shrunk to puddles and by teatime the lanes were almost dry. Within a few days, the Venn had fallen back to its former level and the cracks in the land began to widen again in the summer heat. It was clear that the drought would continue, and weather forecasters promised even hotter days to come.

Although the benefit of the rain was shortlived, it had been violent enough to damage the winter barley crops, tangling their maturing stems and, in some places, laying them flat. A few days after the storm, Betty and Jack were just finishing breakfast when they were disturbed by a knock on the front door. It was Hector Enfield, looking awkward in fawn cavalry-twill slacks and a check shirt, open at the neck.

'I'm sorry to come so early, and doubly sorry to arrive unannounced.' He seemed to want to apologise for not wearing a jacket and tie. 'It's so hot!'

'Would you like to sit down?' Betty cleared a dirty cereal bowl and coffee cup from a place at the kitchen table and pulled out a chair for him.

'Actually I won't, if you don't mind. I'm just on my way back to Kendale but I thought I should give you this in person.' He fished an envelope from his hip pocket. 'I expect you know what it is.'

'Rent?' Jack moved to stand beside Betty.

'Yes. I ought to tell you that when we met last time, I'm afraid there may have been a misunderstanding.'

'Really?' Betty queried. 'What kind of misunderstanding?'

'I think you were somewhat misled – in the matter of the actual increase.' Betty's heart sank. 'You see, Wyckhamby Farms *have* to run as a commercial operation, just like any other business.'

'Of course.'

'And I think Mr Kirkland may, quite unintentionally, have given the impression that the subsidy—'

'Subsidy? What subsidy?' Jack was breathing in short gasps.

'You can't farm on an unrealistic rent forever, Mr Rose.'

'Is our rent unrealistic?' He was looking too pale.

'I'm afraid it has become so.'

Betty knew, really, that there'd been a communication gap at that meeting, a sort of glitch, like a computer when you fed in the wrong instruction, but why hadn't Ashley mentioned it the other evening, by the lake?

'Look,' Jack cut in, 'could we have the bottom line?'

Enfield looked startled. 'I'm sorry – yes, of course.' He cleared his throat. 'I'm recommending that we fix your rent at just over sixteen thousand pounds.' There was silence. Jack left the room. Enfield looked at Betty and shrugged. 'I'm sorry. It's a realistic figure.'

'Nonsense!'

'Higher rents per acre are being paid, in this parish.'

'You know as well as I do, Mr Enfield, that the one example of that kind of rent round here is based on a single large landowner grabbing a few neighbouring acres at any price.'

'Nonetheless, Mrs Rose,' his voice developed an edge, 'it is a rent that is being paid and is therefore a viable precedent.'

Betty sat down, took the envelope and opened it. The figures looked even more forbidding in print.

'We couldn't possibly find that kind of money,' she was speaking softly, almost to herself, 'however brilliantly we farmed. It simply isn't in the land.'

'What will you do?' His voice had lost its edge.

She looked up at him. 'I don't know. I have to—' she corrected herself '—we have to think.'

'It's perhaps not the best time to mention this, but I'm sure you realise that there could be a handsome settlement if you were to consider surrendering your tenancy.'

'Yes, I realise that.'

'It could solve all your problems at a stroke.'

'Yes.' Another long pause.

'On a formal basis, may I expect a response within a few days?'

'Oh, you can have that now. There's no way we can pay this sort of figure. Absolutely no way.'

'I quite understand.' Enfield put on a sympathetic face, ready to provide comfort in defeat.

'It's quite unacceptable.'

'Difficult, certainly.'

'No. Unacceptable. We will have to go to arbitration.'

'Oh, I don't think it would be necessary to go to that extreme. I'm sure we could arrive at a mutually acceptable figure among ourselves.'

'Arrive at? So this demand *is* negotiable?'

'The rent? Oh, no, no, no. You misunderstand me – I meant an acceptable *compensation* figure. For Vacant Possession.'

'We have no intention of quitting,' tonelessly. 'We will appeal for a fair rent. And we shall go on.'

'Are you sure that's a sensible course?'

'It is our only course.' She began to clear the rest of the table. 'And now, Mr Enfield, perhaps you had better leave.' She watched him walk to his car and then went off to find Jack. He was in the farm workshop, cleaning a set of sprayer nozzles.

'That poisonous little shit gone?'

'He's only doing his job. You shouldn't have walked out like that, Jack, it looks bad.'

'I couldn't stay. I'd only have made matters worse by shouting at him.' He put the brass gauze filter of a nozzle down on the bench and sighed. 'Oh God, Betty, what the hell are we going to do?'

'I don't know,' she passed him a rag, 'but I've got a feeling this whole thing is a bluff. A ploy to frighten us.'

'What makes you think that?'

'It's such a ridiculous figure.'

'But there is a precedent.'

'Barely – a one-off example. Also, he was hinting about Vacant Possession.'

'Oh?' Jack twisted the rag in his hands. 'How did you react to that?'

'I didn't take the bait.' Jack looked disappointed. 'Instead, I told him we'd appeal.'

'But, Betty,' he picked up another filter, buffed it with a wire suede brush and wiped his hands again. 'Don't you think it's time to take stock?'

'What do you mean, take stock?'

'Review our situation; reconsider.'

'No!'

'Think of the compensation. We could make quite a killing if we got out. Maybe even six figures.'

'No!' She fought back tears. 'No, no! I *won't* give up.'

'But don't you see?' His voice rose with exasperation. 'He's offering us a way out of the trap.'

'I don't feel trapped.'

'Don't you?' He began to shout. 'Don't you feel that this, this relentless, backbreaking, *maddening* bloody struggle for survival is, is,' his breath came in gasps, 'is Sisyphean?'

'But think of all we've tried to achieve,' tears flowed, '*have* achieved.'

'And where's it got us? Precisely nowhere!' He fished in his pocket and brought out a handkerchief. Betty took it and turned away from him to wipe her eyes and blow her nose.

'I'm going to talk to Ashley. Direct,' she said.

'What good do you think that will do?'

'I don't know, but I'm sure I can get through to him.'

'He fancies you, I can see that.'

Betty felt herself reddening and hated herself for it. 'What *do* you mean?'

'I could see the way he kept staring at you on Saturday.' Jack grew calmer, interested in her discomfiture. 'He couldn't keep his eyes off you.'

'Ridiculous!'

'He seemed ever so keen to escort you round the garden. In fact, you were pretty chummy with him.'

'Oh Jack, really! This is nonsense! Anyway, I can't believe Ashley is responsible for this rent fiasco.'

'If he isn't I can't imagine who is.'

'He's acting under Enfield's advice. I've *got* to talk to him.'

'Waste of time!' Jack said, picking up the rag again. 'Still, if you think you can get somewhere by giving him the come-on . . .'

'How *dare* you!' Betty's voice had sunk to a whisper. 'How *dare* you!' She snatched the rag he was twining round his hands so sharply that it gave him a friction burn. 'You just won't join the fight, will you? Well, don't worry – I can handle it even if you want to cop out!' She threw the rag to the floor and went back to the house. In the bedroom she spent a full ten minutes composing herself and then phoned Wyckhamby Manor.

Elaine answered. 'Betty, I'm afraid you've just missed him. He's gone to London until the weekend.'

Andrew Kirkland pulled up at the end of the lane. 'From here, we walk,' he said. He reached behind him and passed over a tartan travel rug. 'Here, cop hold of that and I'll bring the basket.'

Tracy opened the door of the sports car but had difficulty struggling out, partly because the seats were so near the ground and partly because her white pants were skin-tight and prevented her from bending her knees more than about halfway. She managed, eventually, to stand up, pulled her candy-striped shirt down so that her midriff was covered and tugged and patted her hair into place. Andrew fetched a portable cold box from the boot of the car and they walked together along the green lane into the woods.

'Ooh, Andrew! I en't never been up 'ere before!'

'You wait. I know the perfect picnic spot.' He led the way through some fairly thick undergrowth into a part of the wood which was so densely planted with trees that it was difficult to move forward. Outside, the afternoon was hot but in here it was cool and shady and the woodland floor was soft and mossy. Tracy's white stiletto-heeled, patent leather sandals sank into the ground and made walking difficult. Andrew lent a supporting arm. 'Only a little further,' he whispered. It seemed wrong to talk in a normal voice.

'It's ever so gloomy in 'ere.'

'And private. And quite cool too.' He led the way through a thicket of goat willow and elder into a small clearing shaped like an amphitheatre. The sky was visible overhead but they were completely surrounded by vegetation and could not see further than a few feet. 'How about this?'

'Ooh, Andrew,' Tracy said. 'We've got a whole little world to ourselves.' She spread the travel rug and they sat side by side. She put her arms around him and they kissed, her little pink tongue probing. He pulled himself out of the clinch for a breather.

'Trace?'

'Mmm?'

'Why don't we,' his voice was hoarse and breathless, 'why don't we take our clothes off? I mean all of them. Absolutely everything.'

'S'posing somebody comes.'

'What, here? Don't be daft.' He took off his shirt.

'All right,' she said, 'but you'll have to take mine off.'

With clumsy, trembling fingers he undid buttons, zips and catches and then got out of his own gear. He was, he thought, a pretty good lover these days. Tracy had taught him such a lot about it and now he was able to last until she was satisfied, or if not, to continue with caresses to give her what he called transports of ecstasy. Being completely starkers in the middle of the wood added spice to Andrew's excitement and, by the time their sexual appetites were satiated, the sun was losing some of its strength and he discovered that he was hungry and thirsty. They got dressed and he opened the cold box.

'Champagne?'

'Ha! More borgee-oise knick-knacks.' He handed her a glass which she drank off thirstily. 'More!' He refilled her glass and then took a swig out of the bottle. 'Manners!' She cuffed him. 'Use a bleedin' glass!'

He ignored her and rummaged in the box for food. 'Egg and cress or crab paste?'

'Don't mind if I do!' She took an egg and cress and scrutinised the contents before eating it with rapid little bites. 'Haven't you got no white bread?'

'Brown's better for you.' They munched and sipped, their arms round each other.

'Tracy.' Andrew put his glass down and stroked her hair. 'Tracy, I haven't asked but I presume you are taking precautions?'

'What, about keeping this quiet?'

'No, not that. Well, yes, that too but you know, the other thing.'

'What *are* you goin' on about?'

'You know, precautions. I presume you're on the pill.'

'No.' There was a thoughtful silence.

'No? But I mean I haven't done anything about it either.'

'About what?'

'Well, you know. I haven't, sort of, *worn* anything when we're, well . . .'

'You ain't worn anything this afternoon, that's for sure. Every inch of yer stark nekid!' She laughed at her own joke, 'every single inch!' She nuzzled his cheek.

'But, Tracy, be serious for a moment. One of us should be taking precautions.'

'What for?'

'Well, you know, babies.'

'Oh that. Well, that's up to you, innit?'

'What about you?'

'I aren't going on no pill.'

'I see. Well, next time.'

'There ain't no point anyway.'

'Why on earth not?'

'Can't you guess?'

He looked puzzled. 'Guess what?'

'I've got one in the oven already.' She nibbled his ear lobe.

'Are you sure?' He was too ignorant to know that barely four weeks since their first time was too short a spell to confirm his paternity.

'Sure? 'Course I'm sure!'

He was numb for a moment, then a burst of ineffable joy surged through him. *I'm a man*, he thought, *I've sired an offspring!* He looked at Tracy with renewed love in his eyes. 'Oh my darling.' His voice quavered. 'That's so wonderful!'

She was moved by the tenderness in his eyes and cradled his head in her breast. 'Shhh!' She rocked him gently. Poor spoilt little fool, she thought. Why were men such babies? Worse than little kids really. Even tough brutes like Charlie Shattock turned to jelly when you got their underpants off. And Darren. In fact Darren had turned out to be the better lover in the long run. Cradling Andrew's head she thought fondly of Darren's wiry little body and his extraordinary staying power. He did everything in quick, nervous movements, like a Jack Russell terrier. He even spoke rapidly, jerkily, but with such wicked humour. She hoped Darren was the father but she couldn't be sure because as well as those two there was – oh, shameful! – her brother Jason. She prayed that Jason wasn't the one. That just wouldn't be right . . . not right at all. Thoughts of Jason came with a mixture of guilt and an inner tingling which made her shudder.

Andrew looked up. 'Getting cold, my love?' He adjusted his position to make her more comfortable.

'No. Just someone walkin' over me grave.' How funny, she thought, that this silly boy should assume it was him. She looked down at the wavy hair on the top of his head. Still, she thought, he is quite sweet. Sweet, and ever so wealthy, even if he is borgee-oise.

After another hour of dozing, they returned to Andrew's car and drove back to the village.

If they had been less absorbed in each other, they might have noticed the stout figure of Maggie Bates in frayed gabardine skirt and grubby print blouse, shuffling towards the church. Her gait was unsteady and her face blotchy with bloodshot, watery eyes and a smudge of mud over her left brow. She didn't really know what she was doing but instinct drew her towards the one building in the village which would be cool and where she could be alone. She had to think things through but above all, she had to deal with this crushing urge, this invisible force willing her to do what she knew she mustn't. She wanted a drink, more than she wanted anything, but she knew she needed, more than anything, not to have one.

What a difference one moment in time makes, she thought. Before the phone call, life was sweet. Work was hard and there were all sorts of pressures, but she was doing what she wanted to do and it was good. Then the call: the silence, the singing in the ears, the shock – and suddenly, the need to escape from the pain. The ache for a medicinal nip. Now she was fighting the temptation but soon, very soon, she knew she would be defeated and the bottle would be opened.

Vice Chancellor Helmsley had offered little in the way of an apology. 'As I said,' he had explained, 'the, ah, commission was provisional and, after considerable reflection, the ah, the, um, Science Park Board has decided, after all, to appoint our friends from across the North Sea. As I'm sure you'll, ah, agree, they are well established in this field.' Afterwards, Maggie had sat with the phone still in her hands until the shrill alarm tone made her hang up.

'Oh, sod them all to hell!' she moaned out loud, fresh tears brimming over and adding more streaks to her face. 'Sod them all!' She got to the church and found the door locked but, as the porch was cool, she sat there and cried for a while. Then she remembered the Communion wine inside and tried the door again. Thoughts of Communion wine brought a picture of Leonard's cellar at home. She imagined what it would be like to drink rich smooth clarets, like red velvet, or sharp Loire wines with a gooseberry tang. She dried her eyes with her skirt hem, spreading the mud smudge a little more, and decided to go home. She might as well drop this whole mockery of a career now. It was well and truly buggered up and anyway, who had she been trying to fool? Career indeed! Nothing more than a silly old bag titting about with a sketchpad for middle-class nobodies. If she was going to ditch the pretence of the career, it was surely more honest to face the facts and admit to being a boozer. Besides, after such a long period of abstinence, surely she could control her intake. Of course she could! Anticipation of a comforting drink brought a spring into her step as she walked home.

'Good God, Maggie, whatever's the matter? You look terrible!' Leonard, who had been sitting over a late cup of tea and wondering where she was, leapt to his feet. 'You haven't been drinking, have you?' He'd dealt with too many recidivist patients to deceive himself that alcoholism was curable.

'No I haven't! But I'm sodding well going to!' She got a glass out of the kitchen cupboard.

'OK! OK, it's your choice.' He took both her arms. 'But tell me what the matter is first.'

'Leave me alone!'

'No way. Tell!'

'Oh fuck off, Leonard!' She tried to shake herself free and then in a jumble of tears, obscenities and fractured narrative, explained how she had lost the vital contract, clinging to him all the while until he thought she would pull him over.

'You're in shock,' he said, when he had got the gist of the story. 'I'm giving you a sedative and putting you to bed.'

'No, I'll be all right in a minute.'

'Oh no you won't.' He led her gently upstairs and got her into bed. Quickly, because he knew that she could be up and raging again within minutes, he ran down again for his bag, gave her a tranquillising shot and then sat stroking her hand until she drifted off. He disliked treating his own wife. The medical ethics were suspect but this, he knew, was an emergency. 'You poor bloody woman,' he said, stroking a wisp of hair back from the unconscious, but still puckered face. 'You really did get a raw deal.' He put her hand under the covers and then drew the curtains before leaving the room quietly and going downstairs to open a bottle of Rioja.

It had been a pig of a day. First the terrible news about that poor bloody Doncaster child and now Mags. What a lot of suffering he had to deal with! When there were genuinely ill patients to treat, instead of the usual self-pitying mob, he felt guilty because he couldn't ease their burdens. For the millionth time he asked himself Who it was up there, or out there, who allowed such vile things as disease to happen? What all-loving, divine Power could let kids suffer the agonies of cancer or the indignity of radiotherapy, chemotherapy, every bloody therapy except one that gave them back their health and vitality. If God was love, where the hell did that sort of thing fit into the divine order? Leonard sighed and took a long pull at his Rioja.

Betty had been drawn into the Doncaster drama almost as soon as Camilla and Sally had returned from the hospital. She had been about to pick up the phone to find out when Ashley would be back from London, when it had rung and made her jump. A tearful Sally Doncaster had begged her to drop absolutely everything, whatever, and please, please, come round at once.

Betty did as she was asked and within minutes was hearing that Camilla had a congenital bone disease similar to the one that crippled the artist Toulouse-Lautrec. That her bones would become progressively brittle, that her life would, almost certainly, be shortened, that she must, from this moment on, abandon all sports, all games, all rough and tumble.

'Are you sure? Is it confirmed?'

'She's had all the tests, poor lamb; she felt like a pincushion afterwards. Then today, we had to go in again, to get the results. But Betty, that isn't the worst thing.' Sally stared at her with frightening, wild eyes and streaked maquillage. 'The worst thing is, she doesn't know. They made her wait outside while Turner told me everything.' The sobbing began again.

'What do I tell her, Betty? She knows something's going on. And what about Jules? He won't be able to handle this!'

Betty slipped into caring mode and stayed to give counsel and provide moral support. It had been startling to see someone as cool and capable as Sally laid so low, and compared with these, her own problems seemed minor.

On the Friday evening, Betty decided not to leave things a moment longer and drove up to the Wyckhamby farm buildings in the Landrover. She knocked and went into Ashley's office but found that she had interrupted a meeting between him and his foreman, Bert Mardle. She hovered on the threshold, embarrassed but not wanting to pass up the chance of talking to him. 'Oh, I do beg your pardon.'

'Betty! Lovely to see you. This won't take too long now, will it, Bert?'

'No, sir.'

'Why not go up to the house? Have a stroll in the garden. I'll join you there in what, twenty minutes?' She withdrew and drove to the Manor, parking at the back and then walking slowly past the huge wisteria, now in full leaf, but with a scattering of late blossoms, and peeped in at the front door after ringing the bell. There was no response, so she wandered down the sloping lawn, following the route she and Ashley had taken during the dinner party. Most of the rhododendrons had shed their blooms now but the lake surface was still scattered with a few browned petals. Instead of crossing the little bridge, she turned the other way and came to a small weir at the tail pool of the lake. There were stepping stones here and as she was about to cross and go down into the dell, she spotted a grey wagtail scurrying and darting about at the edge of the stream which drained the lake. She watched the bird working feverishly, filling its beak with mayflies and then darting off to feed young somewhere, she imagined, before coming back to resume the hunt. Poor thing must be worn out, having to work all the daylight hours.

He found her in exactly the spot where they had had their

last conversation. It was natural that he should embrace her and kiss her cheek.

'No nightingales today.' His voice was less animated than usual and he looked tired after his week's business.

'No. It's beyond Midsummer Day. We were lucky to hear them the other night.' She didn't want a repetition of that conversation and needed to get to the point. 'Ashley, what's going on?'

'Going on?'

'With Mr Enfield and the rent.'

'Ah.' He looked away from her gaze. 'You've been contacted, have you? I didn't know. I haven't spoken to Hector since I got back.'

'Well?'

'Well?'

'You realise it's an impossible figure.'

'Betty, I really can't discuss it.'

'Ashley, you must.'

'Must?' His cheeks reddened. 'Why must I?'

'There are livelihoods at stake.'

'Now, Betty, rent reviews are strictly policed by the 1948 Act. It's in the hands of the professionals. Naturally, you will want to contest the figure and no doubt you'll get a bit knocked off at arbitration. That's all I can say at this stage.'

'But you know it simply isn't possible to produce enough on our land to pay anything like that much.'

'No. But, as I told *you* two years ago, when you were up against it once before, a farm the size of Cartwright simply isn't economic.'

'But we've managed.'

'Barely.' He took her hand. 'You can't go on sailing from crisis to crisis.' She took her hand back and folded her arms. He went on, 'Look, you'll have to decide whether to expand your business to a realistic size or to quit altogether.' Betty was silent. 'You should think of quitting while you still have the choice, you know. At the moment, your tenancy is a rich asset but soon, you could face bankruptcy. Then it would be worthless.'

'We could face a fair rent. What you propose is extortion.'

'Not really. On a bigger unit, that rent is frequently paid, sometimes more.'

'On the best soils perhaps, but not here and you know it.'

'As I said, I really can't discuss it, Betty.' He began to walk towards the house. 'Drink?'

'No.'

'Suit yourself. But Betty, here's a question – no, two – for you to think about. One, why is it always you and never Jack who wants to fight this battle? Is he using his head rather than his heart? Or is it just that you have the balls?'

'Don't be coarse!'

'What I'm driving at is this: do you think you *really* have the strength to carry the whole burden yourself?'

'I don't have to. Jack and I are equal partners.' He looked sharply at her and smiled – a knowing, conspiratorial grin – not quite a leer. She stiffened even more. 'You said there were two points.'

'Two: what is your tenancy worth?'

'What do you mean, worth?'

'On today's market, your farm, with you sitting in it, is worth about a quarter of a million. But with Vacant Possession, it's worth what, at least four hundred thou, maybe, with a keen buyer, half a million. It's a pretty house, you know.'

'That's quite irrelevant if we're staying there.'

'Oh, quite. But it would be usual for a landlord and tenant to, shall we say, split the difference on a surrender. That could leave you with a cool hundred thousand. On top of your liquidation proceeds, you could have a useful nest egg. You could almost retire.'

'Nonsense! Anyway, it's irrelevant, as I said before.'

'Suit yourself. But the offer's there.' She began to move away, towards the back of the house. He walked a pace behind her. 'Betty, must you dash?'

She quickened her pace. 'There's a lot to see to.'

'Well, talk it over with Jack. I'm sure he'll see sense!'

Back at Cartwright Farm she found Jack in the yard sorting

out triangular knife sections for the combine harvester which he had parked just outside the workshop.

'Got to think of harvest. It won't be all that long now and I want to get everything ready.' He indicated the combine. 'I've started on this already, but I'll need a hand on the overhaul. Do you think Jim is old enough to labour for me?'

'Is it safe?'

'Perfectly. It's only a question of passing me tools and so on.' He straightened up from his task. 'Where've you been, anyway?'

'To see Ashley.' His face fell and he glanced at the friction burn, almost healed now, on the back of his hand. He had apologised for his remarks and they had made up lovingly but he still felt an undercurrent of resentment at the mention of Ashley.

'Oh? Withdrawing the demand, is he?'

'No. He actually suggests we should quit. Take the money and run.' She tried to make the idea sound contemptible.

'Did he mention a surrender figure?' Jack was growing more convinced every day that they should get out while they could do so at a profit.

'Yes.'

'Well?'

'He talked about a settlement of around a hundred thousand.'

'Did he, by Jove? That means we could probably click for a good deal more.'

'I told him it was irrelevant.'

Jack said nothing, but reached for the electric angle-grinder and prepared to sharpen the blunted sections.

'I think staying on here is irrelevant,' he said. 'We're on a hiding to nothing.' Before she could reply he switched on the machine and the screech of the stone-grinding wheel on metal drowned any possible answer. He turned it off for a moment and added, 'I think it's utterly foolhardy. The strain will kill one of us.' On went the grinder again. When it stopped again, he demanded, 'Are you quite sure *you* aren't being selfish, trying to cling to an ideal?' The motor screeched again but this time she pulled the plug out of the wall.

'He also asked why it was always me and never you who fought our battles.'

'Interfering prick!' He plugged the grinder back in and switched it on.

Betty went to the house to prepare the evening meal. There was a message, written in Mandy's neat, rounded script, from Hector Enfield. Would Mr Rose please telephone him at his earliest convenience. Both office and home numbers were given. Wearily, she walked back to the workshop to collect Jack.

'Why couldn't you deal with it?' he said, walking with her to the house.

'He asked for you.' He washed his oily hands in the scullery sink and then used the kitchen phone. After a brief dialogue he rang off.

'Well?' Betty handed him a glass of home-made lemonade.

'The date is fixed for the arbitration meeting. Second of July.'

'So soon?' Betty stood, holding the jug.

'They thought that we'd have known weeks ago. Apparently, notice of arbitration is given routinely as soon as a review is raised and he's sure we were informed. We could appeal for a later date but that will take us into harvest.'

'No.' She topped up his glass and filled one for herself. 'Let's get it over.'

Chapter Thirteen

'Post,' said Leonard, coming into the kitchen at Bridge House with a bundle of envelopes and sitting heavily in the other vacant chair at the table. 'You all right?'

'Perfectly.' Maggie was buried in the *Guardian*, one hand with half-full coffee cup raised absent-mindedly to her mouth. A week had passed since the shock of losing the Science Park contract and she'd managed, with Leonard's help, to get through without having had a single drink. The disappointment had cut deeply and she still felt bitter as hell about it, but she'd managed to stay dry, and that made her feel proud, bloody proud.

'One for you here. BBC.'

'Really?' She took the envelope which was postmarked Birmingham and opened it.

Dear Mrs Bates,

A couple of years ago I visited your beautiful garden and you were kind enough to make some suggestions about the gardening programmes we transmit on BBC Television.

I was much taken, not only with your garden but with your style and, through local contacts, have followed with interest the progress of your new, or rather, renewed career since we last met.

I am in the process of making a series of programmes about garden design and wonder whether you might care to be involved. If you are interested, we could, perhaps, meet shortly to talk about it.

I look forward with pleasure to meeting you again,

Yours sincerely, Jeremy Dubber, Executive Producer.

'Well, bugger me!' Maggie handed the letter to Leonard. 'What do you think they want?'

'Goodness knows, but it could be a boost for you if they want you on TV.'

'Oh Lord, it won't be anything like that!' Maggie stuffed the letter back into its envelope. 'It'll just be advice, I expect. Help them get their bloody plant names right for once, I shouldn't wonder.'

She contacted the BBC at Pebble Mill as soon as Leonard was out of the way, and spoke directly to Jeremy Dubber.

'I'm so pleased you rang,' he said, 'because I'm planning to come up your way on July the second and hoped we could meet. Terribly short notice, I know, but things have developed apace and time is somewhat of the essence.'

'Just let me check my diary,' Maggie said, shuffling among the untidy heap of papers which had replaced some of the breakfast things on the kitchen table. She couldn't find the dog-eared calendar she used as a diary but knew she would be free. 'Day after tomorrow, isn't it? What sort of time? Eleven? Midday? Why not have lunch?'

'Why don't you lunch with me? We could go into Kendale after looking round your garden.'

She spent the rest of the day, and all the next, working through the garden, weeding, trimming and tidying to make a good impression. She wished there were more colour, but the roses needed rain to tempt them into a second flush, the lawns were brown and along the riverbank, the water garden was disfigured by a band of dry, cracked mud between the water's edge and the beginning of the vegetation. The Venn was now almost three feet lower than usual for midsummer and the shoals of gravel which had surfaced midstream on the solstice, were expanding every day. There was talk of some rivers, especially in East Anglia, drying up altogether.

On the morning of 2 July, Betty and Jack set off for Kendale. The hearing was to take place at eleven, in a hired private room at the White Hart. They were there by ten-thirty and wandered aimlessly in the hotel lobby, looking at expensive items for sale in the little glass showcases and at the second-rate landscapes – oils in need of cleaning and re-varnishing, or water colours which had faded in the strong modern lighting. No one else had arrived by eleven-thirty and they began to wonder whether they had come to the wrong place. By midday, they were seriously concerned but no, the receptionist assured them, the Oxbow Room had been reserved for a private meeting in the name of Hector Enfield but she didn't know why the other party was so late.

Then, at ten past twelve, with a flurry of apologies, Ashley entered followed by a tight-lipped Hector Enfield. 'Jack, Betty, please forgive me. What rudeness!' He shook both their hands and gave Betty a peck on the cheek, 'but I think you'll be glad when I tell you about why we're so late.'

'We wondered whether we'd got the wrong day,' Jack said.

'I'm sure, I'm sure. Now Hector has to dash but I hope you'll do me the honour of lunching with me.' Before they had time to respond, he turned, put his arm round Enfield's shoulder, and began to walk him back towards the door. Out of the Roses' hearing he said, 'OK Hector, you can leave it to me now.'

'But Ashley, don't you think I ought to stay?'

'Not at all. I'll handle it.'

Enfield seemed unsure. 'I don't know, Ashley,' he scratched his head. 'I can't make out whether you're trying to play a really clever game or just acting on an emotional whim. Why such a sudden change of heart?'

'Leave this to me, Hec, please?' Ashley guided him towards the rear door of the hotel. 'Do you remember that chap at school – Medwell or something ... no, I know, Metheringham?'

'No.' Enfield was puzzled at the irrelevance. He'd even forgotten that they were Old Boys of the same school. 'What on earth has that to do with—?'

'Of course you remember him! The boy who was accused of pinching money from the chapel collection plate. Prender-gast made him stand in full view, in the dining hall, until he either admitted it or someone else owned up. He stayed there the whole night – surely you remember?'

'Oh yes! And when we trooped into breakfast, he was still there. Had to sleep on the floor, poor little sod.' They were at the door. He paused before opening it. 'But he was in the right: Metheringham *didn't* pinch the money. Nobody owned up, but even if he knew who the culprit was – no, wait a bit.' He squinted with the effort to remember. 'He *did* know who took it, but he still wouldn't say.'

'Precisely! Anyone else would have given in but not him. He stuck it out, even though the whole school was against him. You won't find many people with guts like that.'

'No, indeed.'

'And that is precisely what we're up against with the Rose woman. Guts.'

'But Ashley, that's no cause to weaken. Quite the opposite, in fact.'

'Look.' Side by side, they walked across the hotel car park. 'This is not weakening, it's tactics. We know now, thanks to our recent quiet chat with the powers that be, that arbitration is likely to find in the tenants' favour. So, we surprise them by going for a modest rent after all and then try to restore our former relationship.'

'Well, it's your business, old boy. All I can do is advise you. But if you want my professional opinion, I think you've gone off the rails. I'm sure the husband's about to cave in. All it needs is a bit more pressure and, once he's cracked, naturally she'll follow.'

Ashley let out a little laugh. 'It doesn't work like that at all! The only way they'll ever leave that farm is if *she* wants to, really wants to. Or, if they go bust and have to.'

'And you think giving them an easy time will make her want to?'

'Not at all, but I think I might be able to find a way. There's another ploy I want to try.' Hector looked at him for a few seconds. Ashley dropped his gaze and studied the ground. 'Besides . . .' he trailed off, still avoiding Hector's eye and kicked a pebble across the surface of the car park. The image of Betty's intense gaze, the grey eyes unnervingly clear, stayed at the back of his mind. Her voice played on his inner ear too, clear and firm, reminding him of a chorister at the peak of his talent, just before his voice breaks. 'Besides . . .'

'You know, Ashley, I'm still not sure whether you really want Vacant Possession of that farm. What *is* your game?'

Ashley simply repeated his little laugh, clapped Hector on the back and strode off into the hotel.

'Betty! Jack! Once more, my profoundest apologies.' He led them into the cocktail bar and bustled round finding them seats, organising a table for lunch, and bringing menus and drinks to them while they sat uneasily. He raised his Campari, made a move to clink glasses with Betty's white wine and Jack's tomato juice but thought better of it and said, 'Well, here's to a bumper harvest!' The Roses muttered an acknowledgement, sipped and then looked at Ashley in silence. 'Heavens, I haven't said, have I?'

'Said what?' Jack's hostility was very near the surface.

'About the farm. We've been taking expert advice. That's what took so long this morning.'

'Yes, I see.'

'Tuck in!' He held out a dish of peanuts. The Roses shook their heads. He took a handful and began to munch, speaking between mouthfuls. 'Well . . . we've been advised from several quarters . . . that the rent you are paying . . . is only a little below par. Rent has to relate to profitability.' He took another handful of peanuts. 'The land is only middle quality and prices, so they say . . . are likely to fall in the future, in spite of rising costs. There's even talk of rents being frozen in some areas.'

'We all knew that before,' Betty said.

'I know.' He *moued*, a mannerism caught from Sally Doncaster, 'but there was that precedent. *So* misleading.' He sipped his drink. Betty thought the bright red Campari with its ice cubes and fussy orange slice looked far too feminine for a man like Ashley. He went on: 'You don't need to worry. I'm fixing your rent at ten K and that's that.'

'I'm sorry,' Jack said, 'I'm not quite with you.'

'Ten thousand. It's only a fiver more per acre than you pay now.'

'I can't believe it,' Betty said.

'Ah, but there's more.'

'A catch!' Jack said.

'Just a little idea I've had. But I've put you to so much inconvenience. Let me stand you a decent lunch in recompense.'

The dining room of the White Hart was busy, especially for a weekday and it wasn't until Betty had sat down that she noticed Maggie Bates at one of the window tables, lunching with a stocky little man she'd never seen before. They seemed to be enjoying an animated conversation and Betty glanced quickly at their glasses, noticed that they were drinking mineral water and then felt guilty for having had unworthy thoughts about Maggie.

'The fact is,' Jeremy Dubber was saying, 'that we are in a rather ticklish spot.'

'So you said.' Maggie munched on a breadstick. She felt quite at home with this man, in spite of the shortness and hairiness of his arms. He had a brain, for Chrissake, even if he was a bit too trendy for her liking. And, by God, he'd done his homework! Knew a bloody sight more about horticulture than the last time they met. 'How can I help?'

'Well, as I said in my letter, we are making a series of half-hour programmes for BBC2 called *Gardens of the Great*. The idea is that we visit certain famous people and look at their gardens.'

'Not exactly a new idea.'

'No, of course not. But what *is* new is that we want to take inspiration from them and show the viewers how they can make their own back gardens look great. That's why we needed a practical-minded, artistically-talented presenter – so that we can see the nuts and bolts as well as just wax lyrical about the pretties.'

'So who've you chosen?'

'Well, that's just it. As I told you earlier, we're in a somewhat embarrassing position. The series is scheduled to be filmed this summer. In fact, we're due to start shooting in just over a week's time. We had Dominic Polglase lined up but he has rather done the dirty on us. Gone off to make a film, in fact, in the States.'

'Tricky.'

'Very.'

'Still, you're well out of that one. Dominic Polglase knows sod-all about garden design.' She munched on another bread-stick. 'In fact, he knows sod-all about gardening in general. What is he? Nothing more than some jumped-up tomato-grower posing as an aesthete.' She wondered, catching Dubber's startled look, whether she had gone a bit too far.

'He's a very good presenter.'

'My arse!' Must bite my tongue, Maggie thought.

'Oh believe me, he is. But I like your style, it's gruff but good-natured. Have you ever presented? To camera, I mean?'

'Good God no!'

'Would you like to?' Dubber took a sip of mineral water.

It was Maggie's turn to look startled. *'Me?'*

'As I said, I like your style. I think you could be quite good.'

'Are you actually asking *me* to do television?'

'To present, yes. You see, the problem is the time. We start shooting so soon and all the recognised gardening presenters are unavailable. I didn't want to bring in a professional media type and as I said this morning, I respect your expertise.'

'What exactly would I do?'

'We'd ask you to present all six programmes. It would mean helping to write the material, interviewing the garden owners and then, well, just showing the viewers how to achieve the, er . . .' he waved one of his short arms in a vague circle and Maggie noticed how stubby his hands were, the fingers like bunches of sausages '. . . how to achieve the sort of results the experts have managed.'

'But I've never done anything like this in my life.'

'You'd have a director who'd be able to coach you.'

'I don't know what to say.'

'There'll be a book as well, of course, published by BBC

Enterprises. It could be ghost-written but it'd be better for you to do it – that's where the money is. Do you think you could write it?'

'Don't see why not.'

'Well if you can, you should. The BBC doesn't pay very well for broadcasting. We won't make you rich.'

'No, of course not.'

'But we could make you famous, and *that* could make you rich.'

'I'm not remotely bothered about that sort of thing,' retorted Maggie who, on reflection, was. Quite a bit.

'It'd be your own show. You'll get all the credit if it succeeds.' The publicity would be just what she needed, especially now that the Science Park commission had fallen through. Besides, it would probably be fun to do. Dammit, she *would*. She felt a surge of elation at being asked. Her mind began to fill with ideas. Her name in the *Radio Times*, perhaps an interview or two on Radio 4. People asking for her autograph! Such things were for children or egocentric twits but here she was, thinking about it and getting excited.

Dubber took her silence to be hesitation. 'Really, you'd only have to be yourself. I think you'd be a great hit.'

'Piffle! I'd be useless,' she said. I wouldn't, she thought, I'd be brilliant. I *will* be brilliant.

'You don't need fancy clothes or anything.'

'Dammit, I'll do it!' She snatched the last breadstick.

Dubber looked relieved, his thick lips breaking into a smile which widened into a grin. He had a reputation for discovering new TV personalities. He went for the quirky, the offbeat. This woman swore, wore atrocious clothes and had a deliciously jaundiced view of life. She was upper-crust without being patrician. The audience would love her. Besides, he was desperate after being let down so late in the day by Dominic Polglase.

'Well, bless your heart!' Leaping to his feet to shake her hand, he knocked over his mineral water. It took two waiters and four paper napkins to sort out their table and by the time the flood had been mopped up, their starters had arrived.

Both had confessed to loving prawn cocktail, naff though it was, and Dubber had ordered extra prawns in both. They began to discuss details.

'I can't talk about actual money here, I'm afraid,' Dubber said. 'Our Contracts Department deals with all that. They'll contact you pretty soon, but,' he forked up a mouthful of prawns, 'we need to talk about your availability. The first shot is on the tenth.'

'Of July?'

'Terribly short notice, I know. Is that all right?'

'I should think so.' She hadn't really listened to everything he said. It was such a lot to take in, but she'd make sure she was available, come hell or high bloody water. She gazed round the dining room and spotted Ashley Kirkland lunching with Betty and Jack. She wondered what on earth they could be up to.

After a frosty beginning, Ashley felt that the atmosphere was beginning to thaw. The food was reasonable, the wine adequate and after all, farming was one thing all three of them had in common. They discussed the Economic Community, overproduction, plant diseases and quite a lot of politics.

'Times are going to get harder,' Ashley said, changing at last from the routine character assassination of the Minister of Agriculture. 'The consumers are fed up with what they see as farmers freeloading. Getting paid, at first, to produce crops which nobody wants and then getting paid *not* to grow them, doesn't make any sense at all. The level of support we all enjoy can't go on, and if the government removes some of its subsidies, profits are bound to shrink.'

'There are cycles – swings and roundabouts,' Jack said. 'Pigs don't depend on subsidies and the pork price is pretty good just now, even though cereal prices are falling.'

'It's still going to get tough.'

'Tougher for small farmers than for the likes of you,' Jack commented. 'With all your resources, you could withstand a serious recession.'

'Ashley, you said you had an idea,' Betty wanted to prevent any acrimony and changed the subject.

'Later,' Ashley said. 'I'd love to walk Cartwright Farm with you this afternoon. Then perhaps we could discuss my idea afterwards.' They finished their lunch and drank a leisurely coffee before leaving the hotel. The Roses drove straight home so that they could finish their afternoon chores before Ashley's arrival.

Soon the three of them were walking slowly over the farm, heads bowed, pausing now and then to pluck a leaf or to prod the earth. On balance, the crops still looked promising but the drought was beginning to take its toll. In the wheatfields, pale areas showed where the plants were suffering from stress. The potatoes were dark in the leaf and undersized but it looked as though the sugar beet was still managing to grow, in spite of the absence of rain. Nothing was beyond help. A short rainy spell, even this late in the season, could still ensure a bumper harvest.

As usual, the pigs were in excellent condition. Betty had expanded the herd and improved her stock by purchasing expensive boars from a breeding company. She was now able to rear more piglets per litter than before and was getting them to market weight at least a week earlier. That meant lower feed consumption and, since food was about eighty per cent of her total cost, led to a significant rise in her profits.

Ashley asked all the right questions and came up with some helpful suggestions. He was impressed, finding the farm in even better heart than he had expected, and congratulated them.

'Come back to the farmhouse and have tea,' Betty said. They sat on deckchairs on the lawn. The white climbing rose on the house wall was still in flower and a pair of spotted flycatchers had built their nest among the blooms and foliage. The birds flew in short, hesitant dashes just above their heads, snapping up insects for their young.

'I think you've worked miracles here,' Ashley said, repeating his praise. 'The farm is a credit to you both.'

'Thanks.' Betty passed him a cup of tea.

'But what worries me is the future.' Jack groaned inwardly, thinking that they'd been through all that before. 'And that's why I wanted to sound you out on this idea of mine.' Betty put the teapot down and sat on the grass at Jack's feet. 'I'm not sure whether you know it but, as well as Wyckhamby Farms, I have this land in Western Australia.'

'Yes, Elaine told me about it,' Betty said. 'She loved it when you took her over to see it. Out in the wilds, isn't it?'

'Three thousand acres. Mainly wheatland, near Bunbury. It seems a lot but it's different over there. There's so much more space and the land is cheaper – but less productive, of course.'

'Still,' Jack said, 'that's a reasonable size.'

'The point is, my manager there, a chap called Billy Murphy, has inherited a farm of his own and wants to leave. I've managed to persuade him to stay until he has found a replacement.'

'How does this affect us?' Betty didn't much like the way this conversation was going.

'Well, I should have thought that was fairly obvious. I was about to fly out to interview the candidates when it occurred to me that the ideal replacements for Billy Murphy are right here.'

Betty got up. 'What are you proposing?'

'I'm not proposing anything. I'm merely saying that, knowing how well you farm here on this impossible little unit, you would make excellent managers of my Australian enterprise.'

'But we know nothing of Australian farming!'

'No problem – the principles are the same as here. Even the practices have many similarities. We could arrange a stand-in undermanager while you got your feet under the table.'

'Ashley, this isn't on,' Betty said, beginning to gather up the teacups. 'We're not interested.'

'Betty, love, hear him out.' Jack put a restraining hand on her arm and said again, in a soft voice, 'Hear the man out.' She put the cups back on the table and sat down again.

'I feel I need someone over there whom I know and can trust,' Ashley continued. 'I was dead lucky with Billy Murphy. He's one in a million, a real dinkie di Aussie, as they say, but I'd rather not risk recruiting in the dark again. You, on the other hand, are trapped, in a way, in a small unit which—'

'—which would be worth plenty more to you with us out.'

'Betty, Betty,' Ashley's tone was soothing. 'Let's not open old wounds. There's no question of your being forced out. This place is yours, and at a pretty reasonable rent I might add, for as long as you can afford to farm it.'

'Betty, do let Ashley finish.' Jack was all ears.

Ashley continued: 'I would be willing to consider taking you on as manager, or as managing partners if you wished, on a decent salary and profit-share of the Australian farm – it's call Casuarina, by the way – with full pension rights and all the other trappings.'

'What about Cartwright Farm?'

'If you gave Vacant Possession, there'd be a handsome compensation figure. Or, we could possibly come to some arrangement to farm it in hand until you returned.' He paused, waiting for a response. Betty picked up the tea tray and walked to the house without a word. Ashley looked at Jack. 'Well, Jack, what do you think?'

'I'm interested, Ashley, very interested.'

'But?'

'I would need to discuss this with Betty.'

'Of course. But there is very little time.'

'I think I ought to see if she needs a hand with the tea tray. Do you mind if I leave you for a moment?' Ashley made a dismissive gesture.

Betty was standing in the kitchen, looking out of the window, framed at the moment with white rose blooms and foliage. She turned to her husband.

'You want to go, don't you?' Her eyes were welling up.

'I don't think we should turn it down. Not outright.'

'I *knew* there was some catch. It all seemed too good after this morning, the lunch and then walking him over the farm.'

'It still is good. The rent is going to be low enough to afford if we decide to stay, but now, there's this opportunity.'

'It'd be copping out.'

'It might be doing exactly what we want – farming, but at someone else's risk. We'd gain security, and we'd be well off after the compensation for getting out here. What is there to lose?'

'Cartwright Farm!' She looked out of the window again and saw that Ashley was coming to the house. She opened the back door for him.

'I've just had another brilliant idea,' he said. The Roses exchanged glances. 'Without any commitment on your parts, why don't you go and have a look? At Casuarina, I mean.'

'How?'

'You could fly over, at my expense, and have a good look round. Check up on schools for the kids, sample the climate, social life – all that sort of thing.'

'With harvest coming? Impossible!' Betty began to wash up the tea things.

'Gosh, Betty, I've never seen you as negative as this.' Ashley seemed genuinely puzzled. 'Can't you work on her, Jack?' Jack laughed without a trace of mirth. 'Look, whatever you decided, it would still be a free holiday. You wouldn't have to pay a penny.'

'No time.'

'Of course there's time. It's only the second of July now. Your first harvesting won't begin for another three weeks.'

'What about the pigs?'

'I'll lend you Jason Mardle. He's not bad with pigs. He could look after your other bits and pieces too. You could afford to take what, ten days?'

'I don't know, Ashley.'

'Go! You've got nothing to lose. Absolutely nothing!'

Once the euphoria had died down, Andrew Kirkland began to worry. He didn't have a very clear picture of his future, but the fact that there would be an extra mouth to feed in, he calculated, about eight months' time, was something of a downer.

The evening after Tracy had told him she was pregnant he had gone home feeling rapturous, but the brightness of his self-image as gallant progenitor tarnished when he began to think, not about the consequences of being a father but about what his parents would say when they found out. That evening he had watched a wildlife film about lions and had envied the lifestyle of the males, copulating as and when required to propagate the species, but otherwise, it seemed, just lying about the Serengeti dozing while the females reared their young, caught the prey and kept a wary eye out for unwelcome visitors. As a human, he would be expected to do something about bringing the child up and that would take decades. By the time it was ready to spread its wings and get out of his hair, he'd be old. How unfair it all was!

The big worry, though, was what to tell Mum. In fact he was sure he would be quite unable to break the news to his parents and that was why he was, at this moment, speeding down the Great North Road to London to get some advice from Annabel. She'd know what to do.

He put a Boy George tape into his player – the old songs, he thought, were easily the best – and sang *Kama Chameleon* as he kept the speedometer needle at 96 mph, the perfect speed for his turbo-charged engine and also his lucky number.

Annabel was resting after laying on a buffet lunch for thirty top executives at Amalgamated Tubes and Hosing. She was not especially thrilled to see him. 'I thought you weren't coming until tonight.'

'It is tonight. It's half-past five.'

'Well, make yourself useful,' she said, flopping back down on the sofa. 'Make me a cup of tea. Then you can take me out to dinner.' He put the kettle on and then, remembering the thirty-six roses he'd bought on the way, went out to his car and returned to give them to her.

'How boring!' she said when, breathless from running

upstairs, he held them out. 'Why didn't you bring champagne?' She yawned and stretched her legs. 'There's a big jug in the cupboard under the sink.' He found it, filled it to the brim with water, pushed the flowers in without taking off the cellophane wrapping and carried them into the living room.

Seeing water dripping from the overflowing jug, she shouted, 'Not like that!' and leapt to her feet, taking it out of his hand and back into the kitchen. 'You really are useless, aren't you!' He followed and stood behind her while she tipped the water down the sink and unwrapped the roses. 'These are half-dead anyway.' She held up a bloom whose head drooped. 'You've been done.' She managed to salvage about a dozen roses and plunged these into a bucket of cold water up to their necks after cutting a couple of inches off each stem. 'More trouble then they're worth, flowers.'

'Sor-*ry*!' Offended, he flounced out into the sitting room. She cleared up the clipped stems and withered leaves.

'There is champagne,' she called, 'in the fridge. D'you want to come and open it?' There was no reply so she went into the sitting room, picked up a cushion and pretended to wallop him with it, intending to pull him out of his sulk. 'Poor baby!' she crooned, half-scornful but half-contrite, and then, noticing his bleak expression, 'My God, Andrew, there *is* something wrong.' She went to fetch the champagne and two glasses. 'Here,' she began to undo the wire which secured the cork, 'this'll help.' She eased off the cork without making a pop and poured until the foam rose over the rim of each of the glasses but then subsided without overflowing. 'Non vintage, I'm afraid, courtesy of Universal Nuts and Bolts. Cheers!' They drank. He brightened slightly. 'Come on then,' she said, sitting next to him on the sofa. 'Tell Big Sister all about it.'

He explained about being in love. About how special he felt whenever he was with this girl, how she was there, in his thoughts all the time and what a wonderful feeling he had whenever he saw her. His eyes shone brightly all the time he spoke and there was a quaver in his voice which suggested that tears were quite near the surface. Annabel was impressed. She had never seen him so involved with anything outside himself before.

'And who is this light of your life?' There was a pause.

'I hardly like to say.' Andrew stared at the cream shag-pile carpet.

'Why not?'

'It's – well,' he shifted on the sofa, put his hands behind his head and then on his knees, 'difficult.'

'Is there something wrong with her?'

'No.'

'She's a criminal? Or worse, she votes Labour?' Silence. 'That was a joke.'

'No, it wasn't.'

'Aha! A village girl.' He was still silent. She got up, put her hands round his throat and shook him gently. 'Tell or die!'

'It's Tracy Mardle.'

'Bert Mardle's daughter?'

'Yes!'

'Dear God, Andrew!' She shook him again, less gently. 'Don't you know what she is?'

'A slut? Is that what you wanted to say?' He threw her arms off his neck and leapt up. 'You see! That's just the sort of reaction I expect from the family.'

'But Andrew, she's not exactly the kind of person one might ask to dinner.'

'Typical borgee— bourgeois bloody attitude!'

'Facts of life, dear brother. You have to face up to them.' She refilled their glasses. 'And anyway, hasn't she something of a reputation?'

'No.'

'Andrew! Where've you been? She hasn't been dubbed the local "bike" for nothing. There's even been a suggestion that she and her brother—' She stopped, alarmed by the look on Andrew's face. The veins on his temples were showing in bas-relief.

'She's a beautiful girl and I love her,' he said through clenched teeth. 'We love each other but . . .' He sat down again. She waited for him to qualify his declaration but he seemed unable to go on.

'But?'

'That's just the problem. I don't know what to do.'

'That's up to you.'

'But don't you see, if *you've* reacted like this, how do you suppose Mum and Father are going to handle the news?'

'Why tell them? Much better to keep things quiet at the moment. You might not feel this way about her in a while.'

'True love is forever.'

'Oh really!' She poured more champagne into his glass. 'Go home, have your fling, but be discreet.'

'I wish it were that simple.'

'It is. If you're careful, you'd be amazed at what can be kept under cover.'

'Unless there are complications.'

'Complications? Oh my God! You've got it pregnant! How could you be so stupid?' She cuffed him with a cushion again, harder this time, so that the Dacron stung his cheek.

'It's *not* stupid. I love her and I want to have her child.'

'God, you are *sick*! She's the one who has the child. Your part in the proceedings is pretty brief.'

'You know perfectly well what I mean.' He finished his glass and stood up again. 'I'm going for a piss.'

She cleared away the glasses and bottle. The roses had perked up quite well so she rearranged them in the glass jug and put them back in the sitting room. Andrew emerged combing his hair.

'Are you sure,' Annabel asked, 'that you're the father?'

'That's a filthy question!'

'Oh, all right, all right, I'm sorry! I'll tell you what, though,' she twitched at the roses and then turned to him. 'You'll have to tell the parents.' Andrew blanched. 'Ours *and* Tracy's. You've no choice.'

'I realise that,' he looked dismayed, 'but I don't know whether I dare.'

'Oh, you'll dare. And if you bottle out, *I'll* do the telling.' She went to the bathroom, and then to her bedroom, emerging after about ten minutes looking well-groomed in a navy cotton skirt and pink blouse. 'Where are you taking me to eat?'

'Wheelers?'

'Far too snotty. I want something Italian.'

'How about that little trattoria round the corner?'

'Ricci's? Perfect!' She offered her arm. 'Oh, and another thing.'

'What?'

'Whatever dotty notions pop into your skull, do not, under any circumstances, think about marrying this bimbo.'

Maggie had so looked forward to her television début but now the day had come it wasn't going at all well. First, the cameraman had objected to her skirt. The herringbone pattern, he said, was wrong for the camera and made the picture probe or strobe – something like that. Then, when she'd been all the way back to the hotel to change, there was a technical fault with the sound equipment and everyone seemed to stand about doing nothing while that was fixed. The director had taken her to one side and gone through the words with her again and again until she wondered just why he seemed so obsessive about something so simple.

'I can give lectures without notes,' she had said, 'so this shouldn't be at all difficult.' But she hadn't bargained for the terror of that bloody lens. Unblinking, an all-seeing eye like some jealous god, it glared at her, making her body clench and driving the words right out of her head. The tension made her voice squeaky, and by the time she'd tried to present her one-minute piece to camera four times, she was breathless and shaking.

'Look, love, all you've got to do is relax!' The director's voice was calm but there was a look in his eye that hadn't been there when they started shooting. The cameraman was getting bored, and on the one 'take' that she'd got right, a jet had flown low over the Cotswold garden and the sound recordist had literally thrown off his earphones and shouted, 'Cut!' She thought he'd said something far ruder and was quite impressed until she realised it was a bit like doing films and although they didn't seem to say 'Action' at the beginning of a take, they usually said 'Cut' at the end. On any other occasion she'd have laughed at her mistake, but this day was developing into an ordeal.

'I know what I've got to do,' Maggie was near to tears, 'but I feel so bloody stupid.'

'I know it's difficult, love, but try to *enjoy* it a bit more. Just think of the lovely garden, remember what you were going to say and tell the camera. Think of it as an old friend. Someone you know really well.'

'I'll try.'

'What we'll do, to make things a bit easier for you, is to cut this little piece up. So all you need do now is the first thirty seconds. OK, love?' He stroked her arm. 'You're doing all right, really,' he said, 'but just try to relax. Come over here and do a little rehearsal, just to me, over here where no one can hear.' They walked a few steps away from the rest of the crew.

Maggie drew breath and said: 'In 1921 . . .'

'Do it to *me*, Maggie, as if I were the camera.'

'In 1921, all this was a just a piece of rough Cotswold hillside, open to the winds and weather with thin, stony soil and no more than a scattering of trees. Hardly a promising spot! And yet, Robert Millvane, youngest son of the Earl of Burfold, spent most of his life turning the wilderness into his version of paradise – Wilmincote Garden. His first step was to plant this *superb* avenue of limes. Leading up the hillside in stately procession, they seem to say "come hither! Here is something special".'

'Brilliant! And then you start to walk up the avenue. That's all there is to it. You could try to put a little more seduction into the "come hither" bit. Like this, look.' He did a slightly camp imitation of what she should do, walking sedately towards the camera position, admiring the trees and smiling all the while.

She nodded. 'You make it look so easy.' It was no comfort

at all really because she knew she would never be able to relax in front of that relentless glass eye.

'Shall we go for one?' The director was anxious to catch up on some of the lost time. 'Positions, everybody. Ready, Maggie? Lots of bounce and sparkle and above all, *relax*!' She stood waiting, feeling her shoulders rise with the tension and her knees beginning to tremble. The little red light on the camera came on and the director gave his cue signal.

'In 1921 this was hardly a hillside but – Oh God! Oh God, I'm sorry!'

'Still running,' muttered the cameraman.

'Never mind, love, count a couple of seconds and start agai—'

'In ninetee—'

'No, Maggie, we need a little pause. For editing. Start again. In your own time.' She waited for him to give the cue but he didn't. Then he did and that took her by surprise and she couldn't say anything at all. 'Cut! Never mind. Not your fault love, mine. One more go, then.' He nodded to the cameraman. 'OK, Keith? Lots of energy, Maggie. This'll be the one.'

'In 1921, this was just a piece of—'

'Sorry.' Keith the cameraman interrupted this time. 'I really am sorry, but the battery's run out on the camera. Our fault not yours, Maggie.'

It took all morning. Finally, just before breaking for lunch, she managed to struggle the words out and then walked, stiff as a plank, out of shot.

'OK, lunch everybody,' the director said, and then came and put his arm over Maggie's shoulder. 'You see! You *can* do it.'

Jeremy Dubber, the series producer, had arrived halfway through the morning but had kept out of sight until the break, not wanting to add to Maggie's distractions. Now he came up to her.

'Hullo Maggie, how are you doing?'

'Bloody awful,' said Maggie. 'I can't remember my words, I'm all screwed up and I walk like Frankenstein's monster.'

'Well, it isn't easy. I expect you are beginning to see why people like Terry Wogan and Jeremy Paxman earn so much.'

'Don't know who you're talking about.' Sulkily she fished about in her handbag, found a large red and white spotted handkerchief and blew her nose with a trumpeting blast. 'Anyway, I won't be any good to you. I'm absolutely hopeless. Ghastly!'

'Nonsense, you'll be fine, really you will.' He had watched her, covertly, and had his doubts. 'All you need to do is relax. Come and have a natter about it. Or would you rather go to the pub with the crew?'

'Good God no! I should think they've seen all they want of me for a while.'

'Let's go and sit down. There's a fine new herb garden here, opened last year.'

'I know – I designed it for the Duke.'

'Of course you did!' Dubber was trying to boost her ego, not, he felt, with much success. 'And if you did something as clever as that, you can easily tell us about it on camera.' Then, 'I've got a small picnic. Shall we?' He led the way to his car, took out a hamper and together, they walked to the terrace on the south side of the house.

The herb garden was paved with old limestone flags which reflected the heat of the sun and warmed the foliage of the herbs so that their aroma was amplified. They sat on a comfortable garden seat – reproduced from an Edwardian design – and breathed in a cocktail of vapours from the sage, thyme, mint and rosemary plants at their feet. Maggie let out a sigh so deep and heartfelt, it was almost a sob. 'Heavens, what a face!' Dubber was quite alarmed at her despondency. 'You weren't that bad.'

'I was and you know it.'

'It's just a question of being natural. Anyway, forget about it for the moment and let's enjoy your lovely herb garden.' He opened his hamper and passed her a little packet of sandwiches and a plastic beaker with BBC printed on the side. 'I've got some extra-cold orange juice,' he said, opening a thermos flask. 'When we were out in the Middle East, shooting *The Footsteps of Lawrence*, we learnt the trick of cooling it with dry ice. It should be so cold it makes your tongue ache.' He poured out a beaker for her and one for himself. 'Cheers!' he said.

'Cheers,' she whispered and took a deep gulp. The liquid was so bitingly cold that she tasted nothing, but the agony of it on her teeth made her swallow it instantly. She was terribly thirsty, she realised, and drained the beaker, swallowing hastily and panting slightly, holding it out for a refill. 'Hits the spot!' she said, slightly breathless, and then she recognised the warmth in the aftertaste. But the glow which was already coursing through her veins outweighed the alarm bells in her mind. 'Really hits the spot!'

'Just one more. You'll need to think on your feet later, remember,' Dubber warned her, and poured out another beaker.

After lunch, Maggie's pieces to camera were not only relaxed but were delivered with such verve and style that the director could hardly believe this was the same woman who, that morning, had frozen with terror as soon as the camera was set. Later, when he was discussing the day's shoot with Jeremy Dubber he asked what had happened at lunch.

'All she needed was adjusting with a screwdriver,' he replied.

As Maggie was being driven from Wilmincote Garden to her hotel at Burton-in-Wold, Jack and Betty were at Heathrow, checking into the British Airways flight to Perth, calling at Bahrain, New Delhi and Singapore. That morning, Betty had fed the pigs for the last time before leaving, shadowed by the formidable Jason Mardle who had acknowledged her instructions with grunts or monosyllables. She had been anxious about leaving them to him until he had spotted a newborn piglet that had wandered out behind its mother and had become lost and hungry. He had picked it up with such gentleness, chafing its chilled skin with his fingers to restore circulation, and had placed it by one of its mother's teats, where it had begun to suckle weakly, its colour changing from bluish-white to a healthy pink. After that she felt confident that he was a good enough stockman to be entrusted with her precious animals.

Then, after a frenzy of packing, instructing the children, particularly Gill, who, being oldest, was to shoulder most of the responsibility, and finally, phoning for a taxi to bear them to Kendale station, they were off. Off for eleven days. Betty was almost as excited about the trip as Jack, who had had a thing about Australia ever since his boyhood, when he and his classmates had listened, spellbound, to a drama series on the school radio about the Flying Doctor.

But in spite of all the excitement, she felt pangs of regret at having to leave Cartwright Farm, even for a few days. As the taxi coasted down the lane, tears pricked her eyes and when it slowed to negotiate the stone bridge over the Venn and she caught a glimpse of Maggie Bates's herbaceous borders, the tears overflowed. Those flowers would be over when she returned, just in time for harvest.

Jack noticed and held her hand. 'We'll be back,' he whispered, 'all too soon. Let's just enjoy the adventure, with open minds.' He squeezed her fingers gently.

'Oh yes, Jack,' she said, 'do let's.' But she knew that if they weren't taking Ashley's offer seriously, they wouldn't be going at all.

Chapter Fourteen

'So,' Billy Murphy asked, as he began to heave their baggage into the car, 'how d'you like Australia?' Then he laughed. 'Just a little joke of mine. Whenever a foreign celebrity visits, the journos on television news always ask that question, even when they are still in the bloody airport!'

'Here, Mr Murphy,' Jack said. 'Let me help you with those.'

'The name's Billy, Jack!' He put the last case in and closed the boot. 'We don't go a lot on surnames over here.'

'Suits us, Billy.' The Roses both knew that they would like this good-natured man. He was short but well-built, with thin straw-coloured hair, penetrating blue eyes and skin browned and pickled by the sun. He was third generation Australian and proud of his native status.

'Me grandad came over from Liverpool in 1920,' he said. 'He'd been wandering around England looking for work after the Great War, fell in with a couple of mates and all three decided to try their luck Down Under. Worked their way across, of course, on a P and O.' He drove out of the airport exit and turned towards the city. 'Ashley said this would be your first visit.'

'Absolutely the first,' Betty said.

'Well, I don't suppose the farmers are all that different here from your mob at home.'

'We've got such a lot to learn, though,' Jack said.

'Yeah, but I reckon we share the same common enemy.'

'Politicians?' Jack suggested. They all laughed.

'No, no! Well, yes, those, but I was thinking of the

weather.' He turned on the windscreen wipers as he spoke. A thin drizzle had started and was getting just heavy enough to obscure his view. That had been the first big surprise. After the heatwave of England and tropical humidity of Singapore, where they had ventured out of the air-conditioned terminal buildings for no more than a few minutes before scurrying back inside to cool down again, Perth was positively chilly.

'It's all so green,' Betty exclaimed as they drove towards the city.

'Of course, this is midwinter. We had more than an inch of rain last week. The bush gets pretty brown and dry in summer.'

'And the flowers everywhere – they're so lovely!'

'Ah, you wait 'til tomorrow, then you'll see some. Western Australia has the best of all the wildflowers and this is the time of year for 'em.' They were going to stay in Perth for one night and drive down with Billy to Jackson's Creek next day. It would be a long journey and he had suggested they should rest overnight first, to get over their jetlag.

Billy woke them early next morning and, after a huge breakfast of scrambled eggs and bacon, they began their journey southwards to Jackson's Creek and Casuarina. On the way, Jack sat in the front beside Billy and they chatted about farming matters. At first, Betty had tried to join in the discussion but soon she was absorbed by the landscape. The further away from Perth they travelled, the more she realised what a wonderful place this was. Here was unspoilt countryside by the hundreds – no, the thousands of square miles. Here was beauty too. The vegetation in the bush was so varied, and so alive. She had expected an arid landscape but there were trees in flower, green grasses and flocks of extraordinary birds, many of them members of the parrot tribe. What looked like a flock of seagulls turned out to be white cockatoos. There were green parrots with long tails, called twenty-eights, and lots of smaller species with feathers so highly coloured they looked as though they were dyed.

Betty loved the bush. This was no gradual dawning, no

growing appreciation but rather, a sudden realisation. Long before they had arrived at Jackson's Creek, she knew that she could be perfectly at home in this habitat, even though they hadn't yet set foot among the unforgiving rocks and thorny scrub. She told herself that this was the greenest time of year, that everything was temporarily out of character and that all would be brown and dusty in a few months' time. But that didn't matter. She still loved it and she longed to get into it. The eucalyptus trees had trunks marked with bold patterns of grey, russet and brown where the bark sloughed off. Tiny orchids grew under the trees, white and pink everlasting flowers bloomed in drifts all over the bush and the creeks and gullies were thick with rush-like plants with orange or white flowers. It was all so fresh, so untrammelled, so big and roomy.

They travelled through towns which had wide main streets and reminded her of the sort of one-horse joints you see in cowboy films. But their residential zones were like British suburbs of the 1950s, with little brick bungalows and neat front gardens where roses grew alongside lemons and palm trees. What neat gardeners they all were!

When, at last, they arrived at Casuarina – Jack having shared the driving with Billy – it was almost dark. Betty could just make out a long, curving lane, not unlike the one that led to Cartwright Farm, but lined with flowering trees: jacarandas, bottle brushes and silk oaks.

Lights were on in the house, a single-storey building of generous proportions with a shallow pitched roof and a wide verandah running all the way round the outside. This was edged with a gallery of decorative ironwork tracery, painted white, with swags of climbing plants – jasmine, she was sure she could smell – growing over it at intervals.

'It's the oldest place in Jackson's Creek,' Billy said, 'but I think you'll like the house. It's got plenty of, you know . . .'

'Atmosphere?' Betty prompted.

'Too right!'

Billy's wife was on the front doorstep, ready to greet the tired travellers.

'G'day!' she cried. How wonderful, Betty thought, that they still actually said 'G'day'. She was only fractionally shorter than Billy and quite stout but obviously full of energy. She bustled about, helping them carry their baggage to the guest room and then offered them a welcoming beer. They ate a light supper and, since Billy was pretty tired with the long round trip and the Roses were still feeling the effects of the flight, they all went to bed.

Betty was up at dawn. She couldn't wait to see what Casuarina looked like in daylight. The garden delighted her with its flowering shrubs and, looking beyond the fence into the paddocks, she told herself that she could walk a thousand miles and still not be halfway across this vast island which had fewer people in it than Greater London. A pair of twenty-eights flew to the tree above her head and called to each other. She still saw them as escaped cage birds rather than common native species, especially as the tree stood in the centre of a bed of pink English roses surrounded by a neatly mown lawn.

The more the Roses saw of Casuarina, the more they liked it. Billy showed them over the farm – an exercise which took a full day – and then ran through the management side with them. It seemed far more simple, with its one main enterprise, than the complications of Cartwright with all the different crops and livestock.

'Wheat's the game,' Billy explained, 'and the whole bloody thing depends on the rainfall. That and the Wheat Board.' They quizzed him about shopping, about schools and the social life. There were, it seemed, good schools – most of the country kids boarded – plenty of friendly people around and plenty to do.

The Roses' preconceived notion of Australia had been flavoured by pioneer tales but Casuarina, though a couple of hours' drive from the nearest large town, was not exactly in the Outback. What Jackson's Creek had to offer was a lifestyle which was closer to the genuinely rustic than had been possible in England for thirty years or more. Here was a truly interdependent community, without the pseudo-rural commuters who, with their residents' associations, Best Kept Village competitions and censorious attitudes towards planning, had tried to mothball the English countryside into a theme park fantasy where a smithy was considered 'in keeping', even though nobody wanted horseshoes, but where new petrol stations were unacceptable, in spite of life in the country being unthinkable without a car.

'This is so unlike anywhere we've seen,' Betty said, as they got into bed on their sixth night. 'And yet, it's already beginning to feel like home to me.'

'Me too,' Jack said. 'Everyone's so nice.'

'Pretty house, too.'

'So what do you think? Are you near a decision yet?' But she had opened her book, Peter Carey's *Illywhacker* and was too engrossed in its oddball Australian narrative to reply. Jack didn't like to press her further. He was so anxious for her to want to stay, but was afraid of influencing her the wrong way.

At Wyckhamby, as in most of England, the effect of the drought was intensified by record temperatures. Several East Anglian rivers ran dry and the press was full of pictures of their muddy beds, now hard and crazed with cracks. Domestic water supplies had been cut off in dozens of villages and towns in Wales and Cornwall, where people had to queue at standpipes set up in the streets.

Ashley Kirkland was less affected than most of his neighbours. His was some of the best land in the district, meaning that his crops would hold out for longer in the absence of rainfall. He also had an efficient irrigation system and, since late May, had been supplying his potatoes and sugar beet with water pumped, under licence, from the Venn. The lack of rainfall would reduce national crop yields and therefore ensure high prices, giving those with irrigation equipment a strong advantage. But today, a Water Board official had arrived with a legal document forbidding all further extraction of water from the river. That, thought Ashley, rather put the mockers on things.

He had been on the point of leaving for London when the writ arrived and signing for it, and then instructing Bert Mardle to pack all the equipment away had delayed his departure. He had told Elaine that he planned to stay in town for several days, possibly even over the weekend, because of the need to sort out his London business before harvest, which would then demand his undivided attention at Wyckhamby for several weeks on end. The truth was that he had quite a lot to think about and needed a few days, if not on his own, at least away from the family.

The drought had caused weeks of frustration but another worry was Andrew. What on earth was he to do with the boy? He had neither the ability to manage nor the skill to do much in the way of farmwork so where on earth would he fit in? He'd have to think of something soon or Andrew would become even less employable. If only he'd find a steady girlfriend, Ashley thought, that might make him grow up a bit or at least, develop a sense of responsibility.

Then there was Betty Rose. What a conundrum! He couldn't understand why he felt the way he did about her. There was an element of desire, certainly – she was strangely attractive to him – but that wasn't totally it. He missed her, longed for her to come home from Australia and even half-hoped they'd refuse to move out there. Why did she have this effect on him? Was it the strength of her character? Was it guilt that he felt, pressuring the Roses to give up their tenancy purely for business reasons, especially when he knew that she cared more about Cartwright Farm and about Wyckhamby than he ever could?

He had reached a decision, too, over the flat at Brixton. It had been empty for far too long – ever since Rick had done a bunk – and, although it was useful as an occasional overnight pad when he wanted somewhere discreet to take his short-term male partners, he couldn't really justify keeping it on. Not that he felt especially guilty about what he got up to during these brief encounters. It was a means of retaining his sanity, enabling him to keep up appearances in his other, 'normal' life, and nothing more. But using family money for something as secretive as a private pied à terre was wrong, he knew, and it was time to appease his conscience. Besides, reminders of Rick were still a bit painful.

He had booked a room at the Agrarians' Club for ten days. Tomorrow he would spend at the offices of Kirkland Wild but for the rest of today, his time was his own. So why, he wondered, was he driving this fast? He cut his speed, put a cassette of Rossini's *Petite Missa Solennelle* into the machine and began to sing, '*Quoniam tu solus . . .*'

At the Club, they were as effusive with their welcome as usual, but Ashley didn't want to stay. He needed air and a change. He went to his room, unpacked hastily and shed his suit, pulling on navy slacks and a fawn cotton shirt. Back downstairs, he smiled at the Club receptionist, handed in his key, and strode out towards Trafalgar Square.

On the corner of Whitehall, a group of American tourists were poring over a street map. There was a middle-aged couple and two girls in their teens or early twenties, Ashley thought, quite pretty, with dark hair and brown eyes. Sisters? Twins, possibly. There was also a boy of similar age, wearing a blue denim shirt and clean white trousers which hugged his form. 'Need any help?' Ashley asked.

'Oh,' said the middle-aged woman, 'thank you so very much. We wanted to walk to St Paul's.'

'St Paul's is quite a way from here,' Ashley said, 'but your best bet is to follow the river because that makes for a lovely walk.'

'Could you show us, sir?' said the boy, bringing the map to Ashley. He had cropped blond hair, intensely blue eyes with long, sweeping lashes, and a little vein that pulsed in his neck. London, thought Ashley, is the most marvellous capital.

'Of course I can, but you hardly need a map. You can almost see the river from here.' He showed them where to go, daring to put an avuncular hand on the lad's shoulder, then, having been thanked by the grateful tourists and having watched them make their way downhill, he crossed Trafalgar Square and walked to Dorothy's. The feel of the boy's shoulder, firm and warm under the denim, had sharpened his appetite.

At Perth airport, the Roses' flight had just been called. The Murphys' farewell was nearly as emotional as those of the relatives sending their loved ones back to the Old Country. Among the tearful grannies and brave-faced grandpas saying goodbye to their expatriate offspring, Billy Murphy was giving Betty Rose big beery kisses.

'I know you'll need a while back home to confirm yer decision, but make sure Jack gives us a call, Betty, when you've finally set the deal with Ashley.'

'We will. I promise.'

'Make sure he gives you a fair go.'

'He's a fair man, Billy,' Jack said. 'I think he'll see us right.' The final call came for their flight so they passed through the departure lounge and joined the queue of passengers shuffling slowly into the huge airliner. After all the broad Australian vowels, the British Airways stewardess sounded odd.

'Good morning, madam, good morning, sir! May I take your jacket?' They squeezed into their seats and prepared for the first leg of the flight to Singapore.

Betty's mind was reeling. She had been so captivated by the openness of the Australian country people and so absorbed with trying to understand as much as possible about Western Australian farming that she had not, for one second, thought about home. Even on the long lonely drive she and Jack had taken into the bush, when they sat alone, miles from anywhere with a cold box of lager and picnic lunch between them, the subject of home simply hadn't come up. Her present surroundings had been far too new and too fascinating for her mind to have deviated from them at all. Even the children had been out of her thoughts for most of the time. She knew they would be perfectly safe and happy for the few days that their parents were away.

Now, on the British Airways Jumbo, with purse-lipped stewardesses and grumbling Brits all around her, thoughts of home came flooding back with such a violent rush that she

223

gasped audibly. The children! The farm! Guilt soon followed and she began to berate herself for having abandoned herself so totally to this exciting new world. She hadn't even sent a postcard to anyone – not a single one!

Jack was babbling gaily next to her, oblivious of her sudden mood swing. 'I say, Betty, you were miles away.'

'Sorry, I was just thinking.'

'Well, I was saying, the first thing we need to discuss with Ashley is terms. I mean, what about Cartwright? We'll have to decide what figure we think . . .' but she was unable to concentrate. She kept seeing the image of the white climbing rose by the kitchen window of the little stone farmhouse at Wyckhamby. She thought of her pigs, even trying to conjure up the ripe, sweetish smell of the piggery and to hear, in her mind's ear, the soft huf, huf, huf of the sows lying content with their litters suckling. The more these pictures played across her thoughts, the more sharply she felt the need to be home. Jack tried, without success, to elicit responses from her. After a while he said, 'Perhaps this isn't the time. You don't seem able to concentrate.'

'I'm sorry, love.' She squeezed his hand. 'I feel a bit uneasy about flying.'

'Of course. I should have thought.' She stayed downcast long after they had become airborne. Even when they were heading towards the Malay peninsula, she was still subdued. Jack was puzzled because, though he was profoundly nervous about flying, especially at takeoff, he had never noticed any lack of confidence in her. Furthermore, she seemed depressed rather than frightened.

In Singapore, where they had planned a twenty-four-hour stopover – how she wished now that they were flying straight through – she began to take a little more interest in her surroundings. Ashley had booked them into one of the most expensive hotels in the city, the Shangri La, which had a garden with palm trees and a swimming pool. Because they were tired, and because there was too little time for much serious sightseeing anyway, they spent most of the day dozing by the pool, ordering iced drinks and having regular dips to keep cool. Jack would have liked to discuss their move to Jackson's Creek but he sensed that the time was not quite right. Not yet.

Back on the aircraft – same flight, one day later – pangs of longing for home hit Betty with renewed strength. The eighteen-hour journey stretched before her like a prison sentence and, when the captain announced over the public address system that there would be a forty-five minute delay before takeoff she felt she would burst.

'Hell!' she muttered.

'Relax,' Jack said. 'We're in no hurry.' The chief steward announced that drinks would be served before takeoff so he ordered a large whisky and soda for both of them. 'Make you feel much better,' he promised.

Betty was puzzled and distressed by the strength of her own emotions. They had been quite bowled over by every aspect of Western Australia, and in particular, Jackson's Creek, and had told Billy and his wife that they would, almost certainly, be taking the job as soon as they had cleared things up at home. At one point, Ashley had phoned from England but, to play safe, Jack had said they wanted a few more days to think things over before making their final decision. But now, Betty sat with an open magazine on her lap, gazing at the print without seeing it. Jack noticed a tear fall onto the page, making a blister on the glossy paper. He reached into his pocket and fetched out a large handkerchief. Absently, she took it and turned her gaze to the window. Outwardly, barely a dozen tears fell but inwardly, she was grieving more bitterly than she would have felt possible. She was guilty and ashamed for having even considered forsaking her home, but couldn't think how to let Jack know what she felt. Whatever she told him, he would feel betrayed. It was like the anguish she imagined someone might feel, wanting to come back into a happy marriage after an inexcusable but still highly pleasurable affair.

After a while, she was weeping more copiously and Jack began to feel exasperated. 'What *is* it?' he had asked a dozen times. Now, again, he pressed her. 'Betty, darling, you must say. What's the problem?'

'I . . . I . . . can't . . . do it.'

'Can't do what?'

'Can't . . . go.' Jack's heart sank. 'I know . . . our . . . farmhouse is . . . is . . .'

'Draughty? Inconvenient? Dilapidated?' His voice rose slightly with each word.

'Yes, yes, I know all that. But I can't . . . bear the . . . thought of leaving.'

'You'd rather be cold, wet and broke at Wyckhamby than bronzed and comfortable in Australia?' His voice was still raised, his tone sarcastic. In response, she wept more openly. Heads were beginning to turn so he kept silent for a while. Later she calmed down.

'I'm sorry, Jack. I know it's emotional and silly but I feel so distressed at the thought of leaving.'

'Do you think you can bear to leave at all?'

'Yes. I can *bear* to.'

'Let's talk rationally about it.' Calmer now, he continued in a low tone. The rest of the passengers were locked into a film about robots. 'The children would love it out there. It would be good for our health, and healthy for our finances. What is there to go home to, apart from financial worry?'

'This may not seem rational to you, Jack, but *home* is what it is. The farm, Cartwright, I mean. It's what we've struggled to retain. We're succeeding, too – I know we are.'

'Times are going to get tougher. You heard Ashley say that.'

'I know they are but I still think we can survive. We're a tough family.'

'You're tough. I'm quite ready for a softer option.'

'Not just softer, Jack, better. I know. That's why I'll come to Australia if you really want to go. I'll come loyally, I'll even come happily.'

'So what's the fuss all about?'

'I won't ever be able to see it as home.'

'But you loved it. You were the one who wanted to drive all night through the bush, remember?'

'I *know* all that. But home is . . . is . . .' She began to weep again.

He put an arm round her shoulders, comforting her as much as he could. 'I knew you felt strongly about Cartwright – we'd have given up years ago if you hadn't – but I felt sure you'd fallen in love with Jackson Creek.'

'I have – that's what's so impossible about it all. I loved it there, *loved* it. But if we leave home it will be like . . .'

'Like a betrayal? Of all we've struggled for? Crap!'

'People like us were born to struggle. We need to do things for ourselves. You'd be hopeless with a boss.'

Jack thought about that. He hadn't worked for anyone else for years but could remember the frustration of managing farms for owners with plenty of clout but with limited abilities.

'That's true,' he said. He sipped his Scotch. 'But with Ashley it wouldn't be like that. We'd be ten thousand miles away, for heaven's sake!'

'It won't be easy all the time, even with a fair man like Ashley.'

'Easier than struggling to earn interest for the bank.'

'Will it?' She turned a tear-streaked face to him. 'Do you really think it will? You don't get on very well with him.'

'I'll manage. We'll manage. After all, we are going to be managing partners.'

'And as for security,' she was more rational now, 'if farming does go sour, won't he shed his more distant assets first, to keep Wyckhamby going? Where would that leave us?' They talked intensely for a while and then fell silent, each ruminating on the dilemma. Gradually Jack began to see other pitfalls. They had such a lot to learn about Australian farming; supposing they made a mess of Casuarina? What would happen if Ashley did decide to sell up, or decided to send Andrew, that idiot son of his, over to farm the place? They could find themselves out on the street without a single asset, not even a mortgaged house. By the time the flight was approaching Kuwait he, too, was growing cold feet. Discussion turned to home.

'What about the drought?' Jack asked.

'I'm sure it will have rained by now. It must have.'

'Yes, of course it must.'

By the time they had taken off from Kuwait, they were both convinced that they would be happier, ultimately, living at Wyckhamby. They would even be far better off there, in the long run, of course. Not being regular world travellers, they had no idea that long flights can play havoc with people's judgement and that at 30,000 feet, thought processes often become quite irrational.

At Heathrow they landed under a brassy sky. The airport grass was browner than it had been at Perth and, when they bought newspapers in the terminal building, they read of fights breaking out among people queuing for water and saw pictures of dry riverbeds lined with dead fish.

Ashley was there to meet them and soon they were cruising quietly along the M25 in the back of his Daimler. 'Well?' he asked.

They both took a deep breath.

Chapter Fifteen

In the time it took to travel between Perth and Cartwright Farm, Betty had been through the full emotional spectrum, but when she opened the back door and went into her own kitchen, she was too drained to be capable of any sort of emotion at all.

The children – all into their teens, but she would always see them as 'children' – had cleaned up after their last meal but had not put away the pots and pans which were neatly stacked on the draining board. They had arranged some wildflowers – field scabious, knapweeds and purple loosestrife – in a jam jar which anchored a sheet of plain white paper on which they had written 'Welcome Home'. It was decorated with a little drawing from each of them: a pencilled violet by Gill, a pony's head by Mandy – the most talented artist in the family – and a shark chasing a terrified swimmer by Jim. The children themselves were not there.

Betty sat on a kitchen chair and stared at the flowers. On the flight home, everything had seemed so clear-cut. She loved Australia, would pine for it in the years to come, but Wyckhamby was where they belonged. That sense of 'Home' had been at the core of her feelings, but now, sitting in the kitchen with the latest bank statement waiting among the pile of brown envelopes in the mail, with not a green blade of grass to be seen, and with some of the crops actually dying for lack of water, she felt she had made a terrible blunder.

The journey home with Ashley had been an ordeal. She wished he had left them to make their own way back from Heathrow, so that they could have re-acclimatised themselves to the realities of their life in England before having to face him. As it was, he had pressed them for an answer on the Australian job almost before they had pulled away from the airport car park. At the back of her mind was this terrible feeling that if they had gone home first, before seeing him, they might have reversed their decision and emigrated.

Ashley had been incredulous at first, then contemptuous. 'I can hardly believe my ears!' he had said when, gripping each other's hands in the back of the Daimler, they had chorused their resolve to stick it out at Cartwright Farm. 'What makes you think you have any chance of sticking it out?' he had asked, with scorn in his voice. 'Haven't you seen what's going on?' The parched landscape on either side of the motorway told them clearly enough. The harvest would be small and yet there was, in these days of food surplus, no guarantee for high grain prices. 'A year like this will wipe out stronger farmers than you.'

'We're all in the same boat,' Jack said. 'The drought affects everyone.'

'Everyone in England perhaps, but they've had thunder-storms all over the Continent. The French are forecasting a record wheat crop. That'll swell the surplus and push our prices even lower.'

'Well, everything looked pretty good on the farm when we left,' said Betty, 'so it may not be half so bad as you suggest.'

Ashley snorted. 'Just wait 'til you see it.' The journey had continued in silence.

When they had pulled into the lane at Cartwright Farm, both their hearts had sunk. The grassland had not grown at all and looked brown and crisp. The cereal crops were prematurely ripe – not the golden straw colour of a healthy harvest but pale parchment with heads standing erect, signi-fying abnormal lightness of grain. In bountiful summers, the wheat ears would nod with the weight of the grain they contained.

In the garden, the plants were covered with a thin layer of chalky dust. Rabbits, an increasing problem of recent years, seemed to have discovered Betty's flower borders and had nibbled whole areas to ground level and burrowed in several places. Their pellety droppings were scattered over the dying lawn.

'Now how do you feel?' Ashley asked. Then he had laughed – not his usual, captivating chuckle but a cynical, sneering guffaw. Betty was shocked. She couldn't understand why he was so bitter.

Out of politeness, but really hoping he would go, she said, 'Won't you come in and have a cup of tea? Or a drink, perhaps?'

'No, you'll need to be by yourselves. God knows, you've enough to worry about!' Then he softened. 'It *is* kind of you but I ought to get home. I've been in London almost as long as you've been abroad.'

They refused his offer to help lift their luggage out of the boot but, while Jack was stacking the cases, bags of souvenirs and bunches of Singapore orchids by the door, Betty went back to the Daimler to thank Ashley before he left. He was sitting in the car with the windows closed, using the air conditioning to keep cool. She tapped lightly on the window, making him start.

'Sorry to startle you, but I just wanted to say—'

'Betty, I'm worried about you.' He looked up at her, craning his head out of the car. 'Really worried.'

She froze and replied in a low, flat voice, 'There's no need to be.'

'Betty, Betty! You've made the wrong decision.'

'Have we?'

'Have *we*? Oh no, don't drag Jack into this. It's you.' She was silent, staring at the ground. 'The decision has always rested with you and this time I'm sure you know, deep down, that it's the wrong one.'

'We will survive.' Betty, who said these words at least once a day, found them hard to believe now.

Ashley sensed her hesitancy. 'Change your mind!' She shrugged, unable to look at him. 'Go on! Change it, now!'

'I need more time.'

'Nope! When I pull away from here, I start recruiting at once. I've already got someone in mind.'

'Just the rest of today, please, Ashley. We've only just got home.'

Jack had taken their luggage into the house and came to the Daimler now to add his thanks to Betty's.

'Jack!' Ashley called. 'Betty seems to be back on the horns of a dilemma. I've suggested that you reconsider. What do you think?'

Jack glanced at Betty who remained silent, still looking at the ground, and lowered his head to window level.

'The fact is, Ashley, we discussed this all at great length on the flight coming home. We know that things won't get any easier here, but, for various reasons, we have made up our minds to soldier on.'

'Is that what you *both* want?'

'I need—' Betty was about to say 'more time' but hearing a faint shout, she looked up and saw her children running along the lane waving. Before she could continue, Jack pre-empted her reply.

'That is precisely what we both want, Ashley.' He stepped back from the car door. 'We are going to stay.'

Ashley drove slowly away. Betty watched the brake-lights flicker as the Daimler squeezed past Jim and the girls in the narrow lane. She felt that she had betrayed everyone. Jack, who was standing just behind her, encircled her waist with his arms and, as she waved to the youngsters said, 'Here they come,' and then, with as much conviction as he felt he could muster, 'now we're all home at last. Thank God!'

Harvest at Cartwright Farm began three days later. News from the Continent, where crops had already ripened, was that yields were even higher than hoped for and the resulting grain mountain would therefore grow to even more politically embarrassing proportions. British taxpayers were sick of subsidising over-production, and the anti-farming lobby was gathering strength. There was even talk of making cereal farmers pay a levy to cover the cost of storing the surplus.

'Typical,' Jack had snorted, 'to pay people to grow more and then penalise them for success.'

In normal years, Jack hired a labourer at harvest-time to cart grain from the combine harvester to the granary, but this year, when they were unlikely to make any profit at all, he decided that they should try to get the harvest in on their own. This meant that Betty would have to drive the tractor which pulled the corn-trailers. She would have to reverse them into the building – a job requiring considerable driving skill – tip them and then, with grain-rake and shovel, level the heap as the grain-store filled up. It was a man's work – and a powerful man, at that.

Unless it was dried to less than 16 per cent moisture content, a pile of grain would heat up – rather like fresh lawn mowings – and spoil. Ashley Kirkland had a sophisticated drying system, computerised so that every ounce of grain could be dried and stored at precisely the right moisture level. There were useful premiums for extra-clean, extra-dry grain and at Wyckhamby Farms, quality control was taken seriously.

The system at Cartwright was more hit and miss. It consisted of a series of meshed steel tunnels, laid out across the granary floor and topped with sacking. As the grain covered them, air from a powerful and very noisy fan was blown down these tunnels and allowed to filter up through the grain. Each day, Betty would take samples and read their moisture levels on a meter. As a backstop, she relied on the cruder method of plunging her bare arm into the corn to see whether it felt warm or cool.

This year, with the endless heatwave, cereals were coming in dry but hot from the sun. To cool the harvested crop in the store it would be necessary to run the fan at night. Without extra help, Jack and Betty would be working for at least eighteen hours a day.

The house, Betty decided, would have to stay dirty for the duration. Meals, such as they were, could be prepared by the children. She and Jack would probably live on the occasional sandwich, snatched before collapsing into bed at midnight or later. Jim, after a fortnight at Scout Camp, had taken to frying big breakfasts and every morning of harvest, he promised to stoke up the workers with a blackened mix of bacon, eggs, mushrooms, sausages and fried potatoes, all done in the same pan and mostly at the same time. Any queasiness Betty felt at the sight of these offerings soon went when she thought of the hours of exhausting work that stretched ahead.

They started on the winter barley. After five days, they were halfway through the crop. 'The heap won't even be half the size of last year's,' said Jack, inspecting the granary on the fifth morning, before going off to grease up his combine.

'It isn't that bad,' Betty said. 'Don't forget we had twenty more acres of barley last year.' She didn't much like the look of Jack's colour this morning. He was grey after less than three hours' sleep and had deep black rings under the eyes. 'Do you want a hand greasing up?'

'Don't be stupid, you've got to get the other side of the store ready before the first load. I doubt you'll have time even to do that, with everything else to see to.'

'All right, there's no need to work yourself up.' She handed him a sampling spear – a device which you plunged deep into the heap of grain and then, with a twist of the wrist, opened to collect a couple of ounces from the exact spot. 'Go and have a probe,' she said. 'See if you can find a hot spot.' She wanted a word of encouragement, praise even, for handling a tough job.

'I haven't time. I'll have to take your word that it's all good and dry.' He strode off towards the Landrover.

She began to lug sections of steel ducting into the other side of the granary ready to receive the next portion of grain. The work was hot and dusty and made her back ache. She spent more than an hour preparing the floor of the building and then fixed a layer of tarpaper round the stone walls to prevent damp from coming into contact with the grains.

She glanced at her watch. Almost eleven! He would be starting at any moment and she hadn't yet been into the pigs. She ran to the house to wash her hands and relieve herself.

The piggery was abuzz with flies and the heat made the smell overpowering, even for an experienced stockman. One or two of her charges were showing signs of heat stress but, in general, the sows seemed happy and the weaned piglets, even the youngest ones, looked healthy enough. She topped up feed-hoppers, checked once more for any sick piglets and then looked at her watch again. 'Oh Lor!' she muttered and went to the tractor shed to get the trailer out.

She hated driving tractors. They were terrifyingly large and powerful, with controls so stiff she needed all her strength to operate them. You wanted eyes in the back of your head to make sure you didn't hit any gateposts with the trailer, and driving on the public road was unnerving because it was usually impossible for a motorist behind to know your intentions. She particularly hated turning right, since she had once nearly collided with an overtaking motorbike. But the most difficult job of all was reversing with a trailer. At first, Betty had been close to tears, trying to remember which way to turn the steering wheel. It was the opposite way round to a car but, once the trailer was pointing in, more or less, the right direction, you had to turn the steering wheel back the other way. Jack had tried to teach her but he had only shouted, adding anxiety to confusion. Eventually, she had realised that she could only learn by practising on her own.

She drove out of the yard and headed towards the last barley field. For all its size and might, the tractor was agonisingly slow, trundling along the road at twelve miles an hour, leading a growing crocodile of impatient motorists. In the field, Jack was waiting with a full combine. He pulled the discharge lever almost before she had stopped under the spout and, in a second, golden grain was pouring into the trailer.

'Where the hell have you been?' he shouted from the driving platform. 'I've been waiting for nearly half an hour.' He hated the combine to be idle at any moment during harvest.

'I'm going as fast as I can, dammit!' Betty rarely swore. Jack said nothing more and, as soon as the combine tank was empty, threw the threshing drum into gear and with a roar of the diesel engine and hundreds of moving parts, the great machine lumbered away to devour more of the standing crop. The rows of threshed straw which patterned the field in stripes were valuable as livestock bedding and fodder, and would be baled and collected later.

At two o'clock, the combine began to overheat. Breakdowns were common enough with new models but this twelve-year-old machine was becoming increasingly unreliable. Betty had emptied three trailers into the granary and had levelled much of the crop, raking until she felt her arms would pull out of their sockets. Now she had returned to the field to find Jack tinkering with the engine. She climbed onto the driving platform. 'What's wrong?'

'Muck on the radiator. There's a hole in the screen.'

'Can you fix it?'

'Easily. But it's too hot now. It wants leaving for an hour to cool off.'

'Let's have a break then.'

'No chance!' He sounded agitated. 'We can't afford to stop.'

'Yes we can. It's going ever so well. We're days ahead of last year.'

'Only because there's bugger all to put in the store.'

'And because this is perfect harvest weather, Jack. Be thankful for some things at least. How much more barley have you got to cut?'

'Eight, ten acres – no more.'

'Is that *all*? The store's barely half-full.'

'You see what I mean? The grains are so starved and pinched, it's a wonder there's any crop at all.' He looked at her, ashen with fatigue, the eyes staring, whites showing above the pupils as well as below. The reproach was eloquently expressed in them.

'We could have had our flights booked by now,' Betty said. 'Is that what you're thinking?' He looked away and slammed the engine cover down, then, thinking it would cool more quickly in the fresh air, opened it again.

'Let's look at the wheat. Some of it may be ready.' They began to walk through the adjoining crop of sugar beet to the first of the wheatfields. Here, the soil was a heavier loam, retaining its moisture for longer, enabling the crops to fare better. Betty walked briskly but after a while, Jack began to lag behind. She turned to see him stagger. She ran back.

'What's the matter? What is it?' She saw him drop to his knees. His breathing was coming in wheezy gasps.

'Nothing . . . just breathless. I . . . can't . . .' She helped him into a sitting position. He gasped and struggled until slowly, his breathing settled down. 'It's my old heart trouble.'

'Nonsense. You've got a pacemaker now. It's probably just exhaustion; and a panic attack.' She knew she must not, under any circumstances, let him entertain any thoughts about his old disease recurring. Last time he was ill, John Holman had convinced her that it had been purely psychosomatic, but this new development was disconcerting. A meagre harvest she could handle; a poor year too, even with impossible weather, but she didn't think she could take another of Jack's breakdowns. Not now. 'Feeling better?' she asked brightly.

'A bit.' They walked on, more slowly now, passing through a gap in the hedge which separated the sugar beet from the wheat. They were quite relieved to see that the crop would not need combining for at least another week. It looked more promising, too, than the barley. Betty threshed a couple of ears in her hand and bit the plump grains. They were still quite soft and dough-like.

The next few days were spent baling, carting barley straw into the yard and stacking it into the pole barn. This needed one worker to stand on the stack while the other tossed up the bales, each weighing nearly half a hundredweight, with a two-pronged bale fork. Their working days were shorter than when the combine was running but they still toiled until nine or ten each night. With practice, Betty got better at manoeuvring the tractor and trailer, even when it was stacked high with bales and threatened to topple over whenever she drove through a pothole. Skill alone was not really enough, however, and she was afraid that the brute strength she needed to keep up with the work was beginning to run out.

At night, she lay sweating in the sultry atmosphere, overtired but unable to sleep, worrying about the farm. In Jackson's Creek, she kept thinking, the young wheat crop will be coming through. I must write to Billy Murphy when I've got a minute. I suppose I've let him down too. She screwed up her eyes to stop the tears.

Four days later, just when the Roses were getting stuck into the wheat crop, Mandy came running across the field with a thermos flask and three plastic beakers. 'Mum, Mr Doncaster rang,' she said as she poured out tea for them and for herself. 'He sounds terribly upset. He says he must speak to you.'

'Well, I'm sorry, love, but it's harvest.' Betty sipped the tea. 'I'll come as soon as this trailer is full. Shouldn't be more than about half an hour.'

'He was actually crying, Mum. On the phone.'

'Oh, for heaven's sake!' Betty was tired and irritable. 'I'll come up now. Want a ride?' Mandy hopped on board and, with the trailer only half-full, they drove back to the farmhouse. She went to the kitchen phone and rang Jules.

'Betty? Oh thank God! Betty, it's Camilla.'

'What's happened?'

'She's had a horrible accident, horrible!'

'Oh Jules, I'm so sorry!'

'She's broken her leg – the bad one, in several places. The bone is virtually pu-pu-pulverised.' He wept and shuddered. Betty waited for him to compose himself. 'It wasn't a bad fall – only out of a tree – but with her illness, you see . . .'

'What about Sally?'

'Still in Mudando, miles from anywhere. We can't even reach her by phone. She goes completely incommunicado when she's out in the bush.'

'Yes, I understand. Camilla's at Kendale, presumably?'

'Yes, Queen Elizabeth Ward.'

'Well, I'll try to get in to see her, but the trouble is, Jules, we're in the middle of harvest.'

'Oh I see. Does that entail a lot extra work?'

'A certain amount.'

'You see, she's asked especially for you. She really needs a mother.'

'Jules – at any other time I'd manage.'

'Yes, of course. I suppose Jack needs your support.' You don't know the half of it, thought Betty. 'But I don't know who else to turn to.' His voice quavered again. 'I'm desperate, Betty, desperate!'

She sighed. 'I'll do what I can.'

'God bless you, Betty. God bless you.' The last words were whispered just before he hung up.

'Mandy, did you hear all that?' The girl nodded, her eyes brimming. Camilla was almost a sister. 'I think I'd better go to the hospital on my own, though, don't you think?' She nodded again and Betty kissed the top of her head. 'Will you talk to Gill and Jim?'

Betty emptied the half-filled trailer, drove it out to the combine and took the tractor straight back to the farmyard for the second one. When she returned to the field, to her surprise, the combine was in exactly the same spot as when she had left. She hurried over to see Jack lying on his back under the front axle. 'Jack!' she screamed. 'Jack, are you all right!' There was no response but when she shook his leg, he stirred and sat up, bumping his head on the bottom of the great machine.

'Oooh!' It was almost comical and Betty giggled, on the edge of hysteria. Then she noticed that beneath the grime, his face was ghastly.

'I must have passed out,' he wheezed.

'Poor old thing,' she said, determined not to appear concerned. 'You're worn out. Still, it's not a bad wheat crop – much better than we dared hope.'

'It's this heart thing again.' He grimaced. 'It's come back.'

'Probably just stress. You'll be all right.' She stroked his hair. 'But I think you ought to pack up for today. We can afford to take half an afternoon off. There hasn't been a single day of rain.'

'Can't stop the combine.'

'Yes, we can. Anyway, I've got to go to Kendale now.'

'Kendale? What the hell for?' She explained about Camilla's accident.

'And you've promised to go hospital visiting? In *harvest*?' The last word came out as a shriek.

'There's no one else. Do stop now, Jack, come and have a rest.'

'Can't stop the combine.'

'I don't like the idea of you working when you feel ill like this. I don't think it's safe.'

'Can't stop the combine.'

'Well, just fill these two trailers, then stop. Please?' He was silent. She walked back along the footpath to the house and washed the dust off her face before jumping into the Escort to drive to Kendale.

On the way out of the village, on a sudden impulse, she turned into the yard of Wyckhamby Farms. The grain-drier was humming and a huge trailer was tipping 15 tonnes of grain into a cleaner which removed dust, debris and alien seeds, spilling clean wheat onto a rubber conveyor that whisked it off into the grain-store. Ashley was standing just outside his office, talking to Bert Mardle. She waited while the two men conversed. Ashley had spotted her out of the corner of his eye but continued his conversation for several more minutes. At last he strode over. 'What can I do for you?' he asked curtly.

'I'm not sure, really. I just dropped in.'

'You're lucky to have time to "just drop in" in the middle of harvest.' He looked as though he was about to turn away.

'The fact is, I've got a problem.'

'I've been telling you that for years.'

'Jack is ill.'

'Your problem.'

She swallowed and began again. 'Jack is ill. I have no relief combine-driver.'

'Hard luck!'

'I can handle a tractor but I don't know how to operate a

combine. Even if I did, I would need someone to cart the corn to the store.'

'Well, I'm sorry but I really can't help. All my equipment is in use and, obviously, we have no spare drivers.'

'Believe me, Ashley, if I could, I would carry the harvest on my back rather than give in. But the fact is, I do need help.'

'And the fact also is, that I am quite unable to assist.' He looked closely at her. She met his gaze. The stare of those grey eyes, their directness, made his heart skip a beat.

'Yes, I see. It was silly of me to think you would.'

'What will you do now?'

'I have to go to Kendale Hospital, to see the Doncaster child. She's broken her leg in several places.' He studied her face again. There were deep lines round the eyes.

'You look terrible,' he said, not unkindly. 'How on earth are you finding time to see this child? Why can't its mother go?'

'*Her* real mother died years ago. Sally, her stepmother, is in Africa.'

He kicked a small twig away from the doorway, took his tweed cap off, scratched the back of his head and looked at her searchingly. Still she met his gaze.

'You could have Cyril. He can't drive a combine but he could do some carting for you. That'd help you, wouldn't it?'

'Any spare pair of hands would help.'

'He's a bit thick, but capable with a tractor.'

'I can't afford to pay full wages.'

'You can't afford to haggle. He'll be there tomorrow morning at seven. Still in my employ. We can discuss money later.'

'Oh . . .' She suddenly threw her arms round him, kissed his cheek and then ran for the car. He stood gazing after her, absently rubbing his face.

She drove quickly, wildly, to Kendale, worried now that she had spent too much time on her diversion. There was one free space in the hospital car park but she was afraid of making some poor old thing with bad legs or a heart condition have to walk any distance, so she drove to a public car park three streets away.

The ward sister took Betty to Camilla's bedside and explained that she could stay for as long as she liked and that there were no strict visiting hours so she could just pop in whenever she had time. She was a kind, motherly woman with plump features, thick plastic specs and a messy hairdo under her headdress.

'We hate to discourage visitors,' she whispered, for Camilla was dozing. Betty was shocked at the paleness of the child's face. Her leg was encased in white plaster from ankle to groin and suspended on a sling.

'Is she comfortable?' Betty hissed. 'That looks an awkward position to have to lie in.'

'Not too bad, but she has had quite a bit of pain.'

'Is she having painkillers?'

'Yes, but with her condition I'm afraid worsening pain is something she will have to endure.'

'Oh, how horrible!' Betty's eyes pricked with tears.

The sister seemed anxious to get on with her duties but gave Betty's shoulders a comforting squeeze before she left. 'Just call if you need help.'

Betty stood by the bed and watched. Camilla was sleeping lightly, breathing with shallow, rasping breaths. When she awoke, startled for a moment by Betty's motionless figure, her eyes were bright and glittery with pain.

'How are you, love?'

'Auntie Betty!' The face lit up and she tried to raise herself on her elbows. Again, Betty's eyes pricked.

'No, don't move.' She pulled a chair up to the bed and sat. 'There, that's better, I'm down to your level now.'

'I'm glad you came.' The girl spoke with a conscious effort. 'They make me have pills and injections all the time. The pills make me feel sick.' There was a long pause. 'Especially if I talk.'

'Then don't talk.' She held the child's hand. It was so hot and dry that the contact with her own calloused palms rustled like paper. After a while, she said, 'Is there anything you want?'

'Just to see you,' Camilla said, 'and Gill and Mandy,' and then after a pause added, 'and Dad of course.'

'When is Sally coming home?'

'Mum?' Another silence while images of her stepmother filtered through her drugged mind. 'Twenty-ninth of August.'

'Well, that's not too long to wait, is it?' Betty put on the bright voice she used for Jack when he was displaying his symptoms.

Camilla began to cry. 'It's . . . ages.'

'Only about two weeks. The time will fly and you'll be feeling loads better by then!'

'Will you come again?'

'I'll try, love, but we are a bit busy.'

'Yes. Harvest.' Betty watched the girl's features working. She was fighting back more tears. 'But if you *do* get time.'

'Of course.' Camilla managed a weak smile and Betty felt a surge of pity for her. 'Of course I will. Every day if I can.'

'Every day?' The smile widened and she put her arms up to Betty who leant over and they hugged each other, Camilla whispering, 'Thank you, thank you, thank you,' over and over.

Betty stayed for a while longer. Not much was said but her presence was a healing comfort. Then, with a guilty start, she remembered home and harvest and Jack. 'I'm sorry, Camilla, but I have to go.' She kissed the child's hot brow and then ran for the car.

On the way home, she switched on the car radio to listen to the weather forecast but must have missed it because the announcer was trailing programmes to come later in the evening. It hardly mattered. The cloudless sky, turning coppery in the west, promised further days of heat and for once, thought Betty, the weather was serving them well. What had been a disastrous drought for the growing period was now, at least, working perfectly for harvesting.

Next morning at seven, Cyril arrived. He was a silent man

with buck teeth and thinning grey hair who, even on a chatty day, never managed more than a handful of monosyllables. He was of less than average height and slight of frame, but had surprising strength. The Roses had known him for years but had seldom conversed with him in the past other than to nod or to comment on the weather.

'You know where we're harvesting today?' Jack asked.

'Oh ah!'

'Fine. Well, if you could empty these two trailers into the store and then take them up to where I'll be with the combine?'

'Ah!'

'There's hardly any dew, so I expect to be able to start cutting as soon as I've greased up.'

'Oooh. Ah!'

'Yes, well, I'll see you up there later on, then. Meanwhile, could you do Mrs Rose a favour and level this corn for her?'

'That I will!' Betty saw him handle the grain-rake with expert ease and left him to get on while she put a load of sheets and pillowcases into the washing machine. She hoped she might have time to get a couple of rooms cleaned up as well and to prepare a proper supper for once.

Over the next few days, a new working routine developed. Cyril drove the tractor and trailers all day, giving Betty a hand between journeys to manage the growing heaps of grain in the store. The fan only needed to run for a few more days on the early wheat. The barley, much of which she would be feeding to the pigs, was already dry enough to keep indefinitely without spoiling. In more fertile years, they would be approaching crisis point at this stage of harvest, running out of space in the store. The decision would then have to be made, whether to erect a makeshift bin in the implement shed to hold the surplus, or whether to sell off a couple of lorryloads at depressed harvest prices just to create a bit more room. Their finances usually necessitated early sales anyway, just to reverse the cash flow. This year, even if the remaining wheats broke all records, the store would be nowhere near full.

The situation was the same at Wyckhamby Farms except that Ashley knew, almost to the last hundredweight, how much grain they had. His foreman, Bert Mardle, had weighed and recorded every trailer-load on the farm weighbridge as it came into the yard. Ashley calculated the loss of weight through drying so that, by the end of their harvest they would know precisely how much crop they had to sell. Some of it Ashley had already sold forward, to be sent out from the store at regular intervals from November onwards, but the bulk of the crop he intended to keep, speculating on a rise in prices next summer. They also sent regular samples to test for protein content and for the dough-making quality of the wheat. Most of Ashley's wheats went to be ground into strong flour for breadmaking, and therefore commanded a premium over the normal price.

Three days after losing Cyril, albeit temporarily, to Cartwright Farm, Ashley and Bert were checking over a gadget that fed insecticide onto the conveyed stream of grain as it whizzed along the rubber conveyor belt into the granary. The chemical would prevent weevils from infesting the corn.

'Is this stuff safe for 'umans?' Bert wondered.

'God knows,' Ashley replied, 'but it's approved by the Min of Ag and that's all that matters!' They made a few adjustments and then went into the office to check over the records.

'We'll be nearly thirty per cent down on last year,' Ashley said.

'To be expected, Boss. You can't do ought about the weather.'

'No. Still, it's been the easiest harvest we've ever had.'

'We ain't finished yet!'

'We'll be done by lunch tomorrow – you'll see!'

Back at Cartwright Farm, the end was not quite so close. 'If everything holds together,' Jack said over breakfast on the day Ashley finished, 'we could fetch in the last of the wheat in, what, three days – four at the most.'

'Well, don't overdo it.'

'No need to, the weather's perfect. Mind you, if it rained now, the rest of the crop would be ruined.'

'Nonsense!'

'No, it would. Half of it would be knocked out of the ears – it's so ripe, you see – and what is left would sprout overnight. I remember that happening in 1976.'

'Well, it isn't raining.' Betty pushed the blackened fry to the edge of her plate and made a mental note to suggest to Jim that he might like to have a go at doing boiled eggs tomorrow, just for a change. 'That's one thing we needn't worry about, rain.'

By Wednesday, when the end was two days away, a slip clutch shattered on the combine and damaged several other parts. Jack had to call at two machinery stores in Kendale and one further afield before he could find all the replacements he needed. He worked on the repair all evening, getting the combine back into commission just before one in the morning.

Next morning, they both got out of bed at six, as usual, and listened to the first news on Radio 4. 'The drought is finally broken,' said the newsreader. 'Rain is already falling in the Scillies and is expected to move to other parts of Britain over the next twenty-four hours.' The 6.55 weather forecast bore the news out, promising rain over the whole of the country within a couple of days.

Outside it was hard to believe. The mist was burning off to reveal a duck-egg sky over a golden landscape. Cyril was already in the yard, stacking wheat straw in the Dutch barn, tossing the bales up as if they were empty cardboard boxes. He grinned at the Roses.

'Heard the forecast?' Jack asked. 'They talk of rain.'

Cyril put down the bale and stared at the sky, running his eyes round the horizon before looking back at the Roses. 'Nivver!'

'Well, we can't take any chances. I want to start the combine early this morning. I'll probably go on until it's done.'

'Jack, you can't! It would mean working all night and most of tomorrow,' Betty objected.

'We've no choice.'

'What about Cyril? Couldn't he drive the combine for a bit, to give you a break?'

'That Oi can't!' said Cyril, looking terrified at the notion.

'He's never handled one before,' Jack said. 'It wouldn't be fair to ask.' He drove off in the Landrover and was cutting into the wheat crop within the hour. At lunchtime he felt optimistic. The combine was running like a sewing machine and the crop was surprisingly heavy for so dry a year.

At two he had his first real attack: a sharp pain in the chest, quite different from his earlier symptoms, coupled with a vice-like grip on his lungs. It took him by surprise but he managed to stop the threshing drum and put the machine into neutral before getting off to sit on the ground for a short rest. He fell asleep almost at once but woke when he heard the sound of Cyril's tractor approaching. He discharged what little grain there was in the tank. Cyril looked puzzled. 'Another breakdown,' Jack lied. He didn't want Betty alarmed with second-hand tales of 'being took queer'. 'I've got it fixed now.'

Cyril waited until the combine had gone round the field once more and left with a full trailer. Jack worked on. The day wore into evening and then into night. There were two more breakdowns, genuine ones this time, caused by tangles of wheat straws jamming in the works and breaking chain links. Though trifling, they held him up and then, when a small V-belt snapped and the engine began to overheat, he lost his temper and threw himself off the driving platform, the frustration making him bellow into the darkness. He had no spare belt with him but knew there would be one in the workshop.

In the yard, the welcoming lights from the house windows proved too much of a temptation and he went in to find Betty in bed, reading. 'Why the hell aren't you asleep?' he shouted. 'It's nearly two o'clock!'

'When you're out there slaving? Don't be daft!'

'You need sleep.'

'Not as much as you. Come and lie down, you look terrible.' He took off his jacket and trousers, went to the bathroom to wash his face and hands and then came back to lie beside her, rigid with tension. He smelt strongly of sweat and diesel. Betty stroked his hair, massaged his shoulder and kissed him on the lips.

'You're a bit gamy,' she whispered. 'The sweat I don't mind, but you're a bit like an old tractor, or an oily rag.' She kissed him again and squeezed his thigh. 'Try to relax. Then you'll be able to sleep.' He turned away from her. She ran her fingers gently up and down the backs of his thighs and then lightly over his crotch. There was no response. Nothing stirred, not even when she stroked his abdomen and slipped her hand beneath the elastic of his underpants, so she just lay and held him, willing him to relax and drift off to sleep.

By dawn, although neither had slept, they had dozed and felt slightly less fatigued. Jack got up and put his trousers back on without changing his underwear. 'Be finished tonight,' he said, 'then I'll have a long hot bath.'

'And then you can have another one, straight away but with me in there with you!'

'Tart!' he said, and went to kiss her.

'Go away! You're like a ferret that's fallen into the diesel tank!'

Outside, the sun was shining brightly and a breeze was beginning to stir the plants in the garden. After a snatched breakfast of bread and Marmite – Jim had taken offence at Betty's gentle criticism of his burnt fry-ups and withdrawn his services – Jack went off to begin the last day's cutting.

At Wyckhamby Farms, there was a crisis meeting. Ashley had Bert Mardle and most of the workforce assembled in the yard and was addressing them. 'Change of plan, I'm afraid, everyone. There's going to be rain.' That elicited a murmuring of dissent as a dozen countrywise heads turned to search the azure sky for signs of a change.

'Nivver 'appen.'

'Not a chance!'

'Be dry while Christmas.'

'As I say,' Ashley continued firmly, 'rain is forecast and I've no intention of taking any chances. We must get as much of the straw burnt off as possible before the weather breaks. Bert, er that is, Mr Mardle has to be in Kendale this morning and so I'm taking charge myself. I'll take one party up to the north end to fire the stubbles there. Andrew here will take the rest of you to fire the land between us and Cartwright Farm. Now, I don't need to remind you all that straw burning is highly unpopular and also dangerous unless you obey the safety regulations.' There was muttering among a couple of the hands about what the regulations were.

'Really,' Ashley continued, 'it's just common sense. Burn against the wind. Make sure the fire breaks we've ploughed round the fields are adequate, and be ready to put out any fires which threaten to cross a fire break. Corners of fields are especially dodgy. And above all, don't try to burn too much at once. Four or five acres at a time is plenty.'

Off they went, armed with matches, pitchforks and broomsticks to which flat pieces of canvas webbing had been attached, for beating out fires which crept the wrong way.

A mile away, Jack had his second attack as his combine was trundling towards the last and largest of the wheatfields. He stopped the engine, sat on the platform floor, put his head between his knees and waited for it to pass. The pain was sharp and his breathing difficult. He gasped for air, willing his lungs to open and let it in. Gradually, the grip on his chest ebbed, his breathing eased and he felt well enough to continue.

The crop was standing erect, giving him a sense of satisfaction as the combine crept forward, cutting the first swath of the last thirty acres. Cyril had left two trailers at the gate and was at the other end of the farm, tilling the barley stubbles while Betty worked in the store.

The westerly breeze stiffened and the light began to grow clearer now, and the air fresher than it had been previously. On the western horizon was a thin, dark line. An hour later, this was visible as a cloud bank. Jack spotted it halfway through his fourth round. Anxiety clutched. He tried putting the combine into a higher gear but soon found that he was overloading the threshing drum and losing precious grains over the back of the sieves onto the ground. He prayed for nothing to go wrong and calculated that he had a couple more hours of dry weather. But the breeze increased and the clouds grew, their outlines gleaming with white billows, their centres dark and pregnant.

Glancing behind, he was startled to see what he first thought was another huge thundercloud rearing up to the east. He stared for a few seconds until he realised it was a column of smoke from the stubble fires at Wyckhamby Farms. 'Filthy practice,' he muttered. 'Ought to be banned.' Then, with an ear-piercing shriek of slip clutches, the threshing drum seized up and the smell of burning rubber caused by the huge V-belt slipping on the pulley and friction-burning made him hit the Stop button. A tangled mess of bindweed and wheat straw had clogged the combine. 'Oh God help me!' he yelled. He had spotted the green patch in the crop on a previous round and had planned to skirt round it next time to avoid a jam like this. He climbed down to investigate. The tangle of vegetation had twisted round and round and was iron-hard. He needed the crowbar that travelled with him on the platform floor and climbed back up to get it.

A mile away, panic was breaking out in Andrew's burning party. Failing to make adequate fire breaks within the huge fields, they had lost control of the blaze which was now engulfing an acre every few minutes and sending vast columns of smoke hundreds, no, thousands of feet into the air. Andrew was flailing ineffectually at one of a dozen areas where, against the wind, flames had crept across the ploughed fire breaks and were threatening the neighbouring fields to the west. Over the road, where Jason Mardle had been given the job of burning the roadside fields, partly because he was so formidable a figure that members of the public were less inclined to stop and complain to him than they would to anyone smaller, fire had crept into the hedge bottoms and was blackening the vegetation right up to the edge of the road. Soon the air all round Wyckhamby was fouled with acrid smoke and cluttered with suspended smuts which blew through villagers' open windows, blackening their curtains, and ruining washing hung out on clothes-lines.

Jack was too preoccupied with his combine to realise that he was in danger. The fire worked quickly through his land. His barley stubbles burnt over in a flash and within moments, it was only two fields away from his standing crop and closing in fast. He half-heard a fire engine siren but concentrated on his own immediate problem. He poked at the mat of tangled stems with the crowbar until a few strands broke loose. These he clawed away, almost pulling off a fingernail in the process, and then gradually teased out more stems until, with a wrench, he managed to yank the blockage clear. 'Got it!' he shouted. And leapt up the steps onto the driving platform to start up.

Overhead, the advancing rainclouds were invisible now because of the smoke pall, but he knew from the chill that the sun had disappeared behind them. He did not realise how close the fire was, so preoccupied was he with trying to finish harvest before the weather broke. Every minute counted. He put the threshing drum into gear and set the knife running. Then he spotted the crowbar still lying on the ground in front of the combine. 'Oh, sod it! Sod it!'

It was at that point that he cottoned on to the advancing fire. 'Bloody idiots!' he shouted. 'Dangerous fools!' He had left the engine running but now, distracted by the fire, he forgot to shut it down, or at least put the knife-drive out of gear, before scrambling down the steps again to pick up the crowbar. In a single moment of carelessness, he stooped, almost beneath the paddles on the front of the machine, took hold of the crowbar safely but then straightened up too soon. He knew he had made a fatal mistake before he felt the blow on the back of his skull which, almost playfully, tossed him forward onto the moving augur above the knife. The engine was only idling but before the combine stalled with this new obstruction, he was dead.

The first heavy drops of rain began to fall. They made little impression on the advancing fire as it consumed the wheat crop. They hissed as they landed on the hot parts of the engine and turned dark red as they pattered in increasing numbers onto the torn back of the inert body.

Chapter Sixteen

Driving back from her daily visit to Camilla, Betty felt more contented than at any time since her return from Australia. Harvest was all but finished and even though rain threatened, she felt sure they would be able to get the last of their wheat in without much loss. In fact, a good downpour would lift everyone's spirits: she was sure of that. It would also soften the ground and encourage the weed seedlings to germinate so that they could then be destroyed during autumn cultivations.

Soon after turning onto the B4315, she was overtaken by two fire engines heading, she deduced, for that huge pall of smoke on the skyline. The nearer she got to Wyckhamby, the more concerned she became, especially when she noticed that the smoke was blotting out the view of St James's spire. An ambulance went past, flashing its blue lights. Somebody was hurt, obviously. She wanted to accelerate but now, with the gathering smoke, it was like driving in thick fog. Spots of rain, some of them black with smuts, began to hit the windscreen. She turned on headlights and windscreen wipers, finishing her journey along the farm lane at a snail's pace.

The whole place seemed to be on fire. Hedges were smoking, the cornfields were black, even the dry grasses in the water meadows were burning fitfully, crackling, hissing and generating huge volumes of smoke. There were several fire engines with crews training hoses on the fields which came right up to the villagers' back gardens.

With a clutch of anxiety, she saw that the ambulance which had passed her had stopped outside Cartwright Farmhouse, its blue lights still flashing. She got out of the Escort and ran across the yard. Cyril who, an hour earlier, had driven the Roses' tractor at top speed across the wheatfield to warn Jack of the approaching fire, was sitting on the grass by the ambulance with a blanket over his shoulders. The skin of his face was like chalk, its pallor amplified by dark smudges of burnt straw and, when Betty got close, she could see that he was weeping and trembling. An ambulanceman sat beside him, offering comfort, but when he spotted Betty, Cyril began to howl in a high, keening voice. A policewoman came out of the house, recognised Betty, hesitated for a moment, swallowed, and then walked over to speak to her.

At the hospital in Kendale, Sally had missed Betty by no more than half a minute. Those few steps across the children's ward to Camilla's bedside made up the last stage of her arduous journey from Africa. Coming out of the bush into Mudando City, she had been told about Camilla's accident and had set out for home at once, travelling without reservations and contacting Jules wherever she spotted a telephone. At first he had been incoherent but gradually, over several calls – the last at Heathrow – he had told her the whole story.

Now, at last, she was with Camilla. She had been awake for twenty-seven hours and was feeling the strain, having driven directly from the airport to the hospital, where she planned to spend an hour with her stepdaughter before heading home for Jules, a bath and a long sleep.

'Auntie Betty's been seeing me every day,' Camilla had said. 'She's been really nice.'

'You're lucky she's got the time, my precious.'

'Well, that's just it, she hasn't really. She says they're ever so busy. Sometimes she came in wearing old jeans and a flannel shirt, still dirty from the fields.'

'How sordid!'

'Oh, I didn't mind even if she was grubby. But sometimes she looks ever so tired and then I feel really sorry for her.'

Sally had been almost too fatigued to listen. 'I'm sorry, my pet, but I really have to go home. I've been awake for days, literally!' Then she had walked out into the rain – typical bloody England – and had driven home in thickening smoke.

She arrived at Wyckhamby in time to see the aftermath of the holocaust. The fire brigade had quenched the flames but had re-grouped their vehicles at Cartwright Farm, standing by in case the landscape rekindled. Betty and the children were being treated for shock. The fires were no longer dangerous now that the rain was heavy enough to saturate the ground, but smoke from the smouldering vegetation was still obscuring everything and making breathing uncomfortable.

In the drawing room of the Old Rectory, Jules was pacing up and down, waiting for Sally. She walked in, kissed him and said, 'God, I'm done for! Pour me an obscenely large gin, would you?' Then she burst into tears.

On the evening of Jack's fatal accident, Maggie Bates was enjoying a bit of a thrash at the Cat and Custard Pot in Shipton Moyne. The pretty Cotswold village was near the last location to be filmed for the television series *Gardens of the Great* and now, after the director had said, for the last time, 'OK everyone, that's a wrap,' the production team was ready to let its hair down.

Maggie had already let hers down – quite a bit, in fact – at lunch-time. Now she was standing in the middle of the Public Bar, telling filthy stories in a coarse voice to the crew who egged her on with double whiskies and salacious taunts. It hadn't been an easy series to shoot, Jeremy Dubber felt. The guests on the programme had tended to be difficult to interview, either shy and tense or too garrulous, but that was usual, especially with gardening people. The biggest problem had been Maggie. Sober, she was unable to perform – too tense, couldn't remember her lines, either. With a couple of stiff vodkas inside her she could deliver her pieces to camera, often impromptu, with wonderful energy and perfect wit. However, one vodka too many and everything she did was untransmissible. The problem was, that fruitful period between being frozen with fright and too pissed to perform, got shorter with every day's shooting. By the last couple of garden visits, she was becoming an embarrassment to everyone.

In the middle of some anecdote which had the lighting engineer giggling like a schoolboy, she spotted Jeremy sitting by the bar and sauntered over to him without finishing her tale. She lifted her glass. 'Cheers, Dubber ol' thing!'

'Maggie!' He nodded with as jovial a face as he could muster. The pity of it was, when she was good, she was *really* good. The viewers were going to love her; the programme controllers already did. No doubt they'd all want his blood when she was dropped for the next series.

'Here's to th' next series-is-is-is!' she giggled.

'Here's to it,' said Dubber, raising his tomato juice.

'Wha's that? Bloody Mary? Poncy kind 'f drink!'

'Bloody without the Mary.'

'Well, here's to the nex' run an'way.' She tried to catch the barman's eye. 'Oi! Gorgeous!'

'Steady, Maggie.' Dubber was embarrassed. 'Why not have something soft?'

'I'd sooner have something *hard*,' she said, ogling a well-knit man at the bar. 'I bet *he* could provide something hard.' A raucous, throaty laugh followed and she staggered. 'Whoopsadaisy!'

To create a diversion, Dubber got down from his barstool and clapped his hands. Everyone in the crew and all the regular drinkers, for that matter, looked round. Conversation died.

'Chaps and er, chappesses,' he said. 'Not a speech, but I'd just like to say what tremendous fun it has been, making this series, and I want to thank you all: Keith and the camera crew, our director Mike, of course, our researchers Debbie and Kate, the production assistants and by no means least, our illustrious presenter, Maggie here, for such a splendid effort. You all faced a big challenge, to shoot this series with an horrendously short timescale and I must congratulate you, every one of you, for such professional work. Now, some of us,' here he rolled his eyes meaningfully at Maggie, 'are rather tired and I hope the rest of you won't mind if we break up the party at this stage.' With that he gave every possible dissenting face a stern look and then, taking Maggie by the elbow, steered her out of the pub to his car outside before she realised what was happening.

'What the fuck are you doing, Dubber?' she asked angrily, at last.

'Taking you to your bed and breakfast,' he said. 'You've had enough.'

On the way, she appeared to sober up. 'When will you start doing the next series?'

'It's too early to say just yet. I'll let you know nearer the time.' His mind began to formulate the letter he would have to write. *My dear Maggie*, it would begin, *I'm so sorry to have to tell you . . . circumstances outside my control . . . my painful decision to use a new presenter etc etc. Naturally, if we are doing anything else that might suit you, we will, of course, contact you etc.*

At the bed and breakfast, the landlady fixed her with a stony stare. 'Breakfast at eight-thirty, then, madam,' she said, blocking the way through to the lounge where there was a self-serve bar with an honesty box for the guests' personal use. 'Good night!' Dubber got her safely delivered to her room and then escaped back to the Cat and Custard Pot, where the crew were settling down to a late supper of gammon and chips.

Practically everyone in Wyckhamby went to the funeral. Not that they had all been especial friends of Jack; indeed, several of them hardly knew him, but they all knew and liked Betty. It had rained incessantly since the accident and now the Venn was almost back to its normal flow. The landscape was black where every field of stubble had burnt. The fires had jumped across roads in some places and even where they hadn't, trees on the opposite sides had seared foliage. In autumn, these singed leaves would fail to drop, making the half-dead branches look unnatural until the following spring.

The Kirklands were shamefaced. Andrew had actually been

arrested for arson by an enraged local policeman, and spent several hours in a police cell at Kendale before being rescued by Ashley, who came to explain everything. Ashley had been told that he could expect a summons and a substantial fine. He published a letter of apology in the local paper and made a public promise to abandon the practice of straw-burning altogether – as soon as they had developed an alternative means of disposal at Wyckhamby Farms.

The congregation filed slowly into St James's Church, shaking umbrellas and wiping wet feet on the tattered door-mats before shuffling to the pews, filling the church from the back. The Mardle family were all away except for Tracy who arrived alone, wearing black shoes, a short black cocktail dress and a strange hat shaped like a Rowntrees Fruit Gum, with a little black veil over the eyes. Whispering in the body of the kirk turned almost to a hiss as she walked up the aisle to sit just behind the Kirklands.

When the mourners came in behind the coffin, the whispering died away. Betty and the children walked with bowed heads and dry eyes to their reserved pew at the front of the church. There were few other mourners: Jack's mother, a brother and Betty's sister.

After the service, there was a desultory gathering at Cartwright Farm where the relatives and close friends stayed for an hour or so, drinking cheap sherry and talking in hushed tones. They left as soon as it was polite to do so and Betty stood alone in the empty sitting room. Mandy came in, then Gill. All three held each other for a long moment and then Betty said nobody would mind if anybody went to bed. Silently, the girls crept upstairs. Jim was already in bed. He had shut himself away immediately after the service and needed to be left alone for several hours yet.

In the late evening, Betty went out to check over the livestock and to see that rain wasn't leaking into the grain-store. Everything seemed all right in the yard and she was about to go in again when she spotted headlights in the lane. It was Ashley's Daimler. She expected to feel unable to communicate with anyone at the moment, but for some strange reason, she was relieved to see him, jumping out of his expensive car, assured and smartly dressed.

'Betty, I'm so sorry, I know this is an appalling time to call.' He embraced her and was quite taken aback when she held onto him. Usually, she stiffened when he had any physical contact with her.

'Thank you so much for coming,' she said, holding the door open for him. 'The house is a tip, I'm afraid. We have hardly cleaned up after harvest or anything you know, since . . . since . . .' She made an effort to regain control. 'Can I give you a drink?'

'Let me pour them,' he said. 'Have you any Scotch?'

'A little. Otherwise it's cooking sherry.' She pointed to a sideboard. He discovered a bottle with about two inches left in the bottom and a pair of crystal tumblers, chipped and cloudy with age.

'Scotch!'

'I'll get a jug of water.' She went to the kitchen and returned with a cracked porcelain milk jug. He had divided the remains of the bottle equally between the two of them. 'Heavens, Ashley, I can't manage all that!'

'Poppycock! It's exactly what you need. Cheers!' He handed her the glass and they sipped. 'We need to talk. I would have left this for a week or so but I've got to go to Australia, to sort out a successor for Billy Murphy. I fly tomorrow at seven.'

She sat down heavily, slopping a little of her whisky out of the glass. Australia was too painful to think about just now. 'Oh yes?'

'The fact is, I need to tell you a couple of things.' He sipped again, still standing. 'Your wheat crop – the one that burnt in the field – how much do you think it was worth?'

'What? Oh, I haven't really thought about it yet.'

'Well, don't think about it now but, Betty, listen. This is important.' He sat beside her. 'I have informed my insurers that it was a record-breaker. I said that you had thirty-four drilled acres and that it was coming in at four tonnes to the acre.'

'But that's a gross exaggeration. We've never taken more than ninety tonnes off the entire field, even in a good year.'

He held up his hand to stop her. 'Do you *know* exactly what weight of grain you had there? Before the fire?'

'Well . . . no.'

'Was it a variety you've grown before?'

'It was 'Avalon'. No, we've never grown that one before.'

'So you can't possibly know, not for sure. It might have been the perfect one for that field.' He folded his arms and lifted his chin. 'And I say that it was, and was therefore set for an unprecedented yield. You should say so too.'

'That would be untruthful.'

'Not at all! Who can prove otherwise?'

'No one can. Not actually *prove*—'

'Precisely! And you, Betty, must corroborate my evidence. You'll make me look a complete clot if you don't. The difference in compensation could be as much as five thousand pounds. You *need* that money.'

'But it isn't right.'

'Well, they may not even investigate very thoroughly. After all, it's usual for the perpetrator of the damages to get off as lightly as he can. They may not realise that I'm trying to do the reverse.' He pondered a moment. 'I say, do you think they'd believe more than four tonnes per acre?'

'No!' He laughed at her vehemence. She took a prolonged sip. He glanced at his watch and fidgeted. 'You don't need to stay, Ashley, not out of duty.'

'It isn't that.' He stood up again, looked at her, looked away and then felt his gaze drawn back to those grey eyes. 'The fact is, under these, er, new circumstances, your farm tenancy will expire. What I want to say is that you can stay in the house for as long as you like. I wouldn't dream of asking you to leave.'

She looked at him in amazement. None of these matters had yet entered her mind. 'What are you saying?'

'Oh gosh, gosh, gosh! I'm so *sorry* to do this now but, you see, I'll be away for three weeks and I didn't want you to be worried about your security.'

'I wouldn't have been much more worried than I usually am. As you've so often pointed out, Ashley, this is a difficult farm to run.'

'Well, at least you won't need to worry about that.' He shifted his weight and looked uncomfortable. 'But farming *does* need to go on, you know that.'

'Of course.'

'So we would like to come onto the land as soon after the eleventh of October as we can, so that we can sow autumn crops before it's too late. Of course, if you were to let us on sooner, it would help enormously. I'd even waive three months' rent for that.'

'Am I hearing you right?' Betty was beginning to shake, not with fear, or grief, but with rage. 'Did you say you wanted me to "let – you – on"?'

'Well, yes. Obviously, *you* won't be farming it. Not now.'

'Oh, won't I?' Ashley opened his mouth and shut it again. She gulped the rest of her Scotch, took several deep breaths and then stood up. 'This is probably the lowest point of my life, but what you see here is not – and get this straight, Ashley – is *not* despair.' She patted her chest, just below her throat. 'This is a cornered woman, but *not* a beaten one. I am legally entitled to inherit Jack's tenancy, as you should know.'

'But how can you possibly want—?'

'You were always fond of telling me I was the brains behind Cartwright Farm – well, I'm going to need them now. Nothing here will change. Even if we don't make much profit, the children and I will have a good way of life. And, what's more, we'll do it without setting the whole of Kirkland Acres on fire.'

Ashley wanted to hug her. He made a nervous move towards her but she glared so fiercely at him that he simply mouthed a silent good night and let himself out. He drove straight to London to stay overnight before catching the early flight to Perth.

Betty went upstairs to the bedroom. Reaching under the bed for a slipper, she came across one of Jack's tee shirts, wedged between mattress and divan. Sometimes he used to sleep in one, bottomless, and if they made love he would pull it off and stuff it under the mattress, heavens knew why. It must have been there since before harvest. She held it to her face. It was clean but there lingered a faint tang of diesel mixed with sweat. She sat on the bed motionless while the tears flowed. When the sobbing began, she stuffed the shirt into her mouth, not wanting to wake the children.

PART THREE

Autumn

Chapter Seventeen

After four weeks of almost continuous wind and rain, the September equinox brought an Indian summer. Crowding swallows twittered and chattered along the telephone wires, waiting for the impulse to begin their journey south. The house martins seemed less anxious to gather and were still swooping down to the Venn, skimming the surface and snapping up insects as if summer would never end and they could stay until Christmas.

Betty Rose was in her garden, looking for flowers to pick. The rain had freshened everything and now she was enjoying a late flourish of colour from penstemons, heleniums and Michaelmas daisies. Seven or eight years ago, she couldn't remember when exactly, she had bought a dozen nerine bulbs from the Kendale Woolworths, and had planted them at the base of the wall on the south side of the house. Jack had scolded her for extravagance, saying that three would have done just as well. Over the years they had multiplied and every autumn, a wide drift of the delicate pink lilies nodded in the breeze. After this summer's drought, they had been reluctant to appear and she wondered whether they might have perished, but now, in the sparkling sunshine she spotted several blooms opening and dozens of buds emerging from the ground. They were Jack's favourite flowers and seeing them here, Betty made a mental note to tell him they were coming out as soon as she saw him. Then she remembered.

Grief came in bursts these days, rather than the constant, grinding pain of the first few weeks, but when it did come, it was so intense that it felt like a physical blow. Sometimes, like now, these jags were prompted by a particular reminder but, just as often, they came from nowhere and took her by surprise. At these moments, she had to get away, to be completely alone so that she could let her feelings out. Besides sorrow, she felt rage from time to time, and was inclined to fly off the handle with minor annoyances – especially with the children. Then remorse would make her over-compensate, and she would bake them special cakes or take them on treats to Kendale to see a film.

She hesitated over the nerines, stroking their smooth stems, but decided instead to pick a small bunch of blue Michaelmas daisies and half a dozen border pinks to put in John Holman's room.

How relieved she was that he had agreed to visit! Now that she had committed herself to staying on as tenant of Cartwright Farm, professional advice was something she needed more urgently than anything else and John was an obvious choice. After his last stay, during Jack's illness, he had got to know the farm and its limitations. He had a clear, analytical mind and, though hardly talkative, was likely to be frank and direct with his recommendations.

But she was glad, too, that he had agreed to come back because she had felt awful about his premature departure at the funeral. During the gloomy gathering after the service, she had suddenly felt the overwhelming need to be by herself for a while and had slipped into the kitchen. John had come in to find her sitting with her hands on the table in front of her.

'Betty, I—' but she had given him a look of such anguish that his tongue froze.

'John. Please don't be hurt, but I rather want to be on my own.'

'Of course.' Crimson-faced, he had opened the kitchen door and without another word, had walked out and down the lane towards the church where he had left his car.

He had phoned a few days later. 'I wanted to explain about last Tuesday.'

'Nothing to explain,' she had said. 'It's for me to apologise.'

'No! I was tactless.' There was a pause. Pauses were pretty frequent during conversations with John. His phlegmatic Fenland nature prevented him from expressing more than a portion of his feelings. 'Are you all right?'

'In the circumstances, yes.'

'What are you going to do?'

'I'm not sure how, but I intend to stay here on the farm.'

'Do you?' Another silence had ensued while John thought through the implications of her decision. 'Not easy.'

'Not at all.' Another pause, then, 'But what about you, John? What are you up to?' And he had talked briefly, very briefly, about the farm he managed for a landowner in Sussex, not far from Betty's birthplace, as it happened. He had charge of all the arable acres and a 180-cow dairy herd to look after as well. 'Sounds an interesting job,' she commented.

'Yes.' Another breath or two and then, 'Well, as long as you're all right.' And he had hung up.

Over the next few weeks, while rain prevented any field-work, Betty began to analyse her situation. It was not good but it was, she felt sure, redeemable. She had acquired considerable farming skill – both managerial and practical – during Jack's illness and, more recently, during harvest. She could, for a while, run the farm single-handed but that would mean an almost unendurable workload and she didn't think she had the stamina to go on alone for very long – certainly not long enough for any of the young to grow up and take over.

She also needed to make the farm more viable, heaven knew how, but she just had to. The old regime of cereals and pigs wouldn't produce enough income to pay the rent, let alone provide something to live on. Jack's insurance money gave her a temporary breathing space but the overdraft was still there and would soon begin growing again. She needed inspiration, quickly.

The Ministry of Agriculture turned out to be useless. She went to visit their advisers at the Kendale offices and was told that her farm was too small to pay, that its soil quality was too poor to diversify and that the climate at Wyckhamby was wrong for pretty well any crop that she wasn't growing at present. Most irritating of all, they had suggested that farming was man's work and that she would find it much harder to do than she thought. Her best bet, they advised, was to get out while she could.

After a brief period of dejection she had thought of John and, while rain beat on the windows and the wind tore leaves from the trees and scattered them along the lane, she had written:

Dear John,

I'm not sure whether you could spare the time, but we'd be so glad if you could come down for a weekend.

We all want to see you again, of course, but the fact is, I need advice about the farm and want to pick your brains. I would consider this a professional consultation and would expect to pay a fee.

Friday 21st September would be a good date for us, if you happened to be free.

By return of post, a card arrived.

The 21st is fine but I'm due some holiday and could stay longer than just the weekend if you thought it helpful.

She had phoned him straight back.

She took the flowers into the house and arranged them in the chipped porcelain jug she had used for Ashley's whisky water a month earlier. A peacock butterfly had flown into the guest bedroom but although she opened the window to let it out, it fluttered slowly into the darkest corner of the room and settled there, folding its wings so that the colourful eyes were concealed. It looked like an old brown leaf stuck to the ceiling.

'I wouldn't hibernate there,' she told it. 'You'll wake up when the central heating comes on and then regret it when there aren't any flowers.'

Gill, just home from sixth-form college, came in and hugged her mother. 'First sign of madness,' she said, 'talking to yourself.'

'I wasn't. I was chatting to that butterfly.'

'Oh, that's all right then. Quite normal.'

'How was college?'

'I think I've picked the wrong subjects, Mum.'

'Everyone says that when they've just started. You'll be fine. Just stick with it.'

'But Mum!'

'I've got to prepare supper. Come and chat in the kitchen while I work.'

John arrived in mid-evening, carrying a brace of partridge and a bottle of Rioja.

At Wyckhamby Manor, the first of Elaine's autumn dinner parties was in full swing. Most of the guests were locals but from the outside world, or at least, a different inside world. Dr Steven Webb, Professor of Anglo-Saxon, Norse and Celtic at Rutland University sat opposite his dowdy wife and blinked at the bowl of wild cyclamen blooms in the middle of the table.

Maggie and Leonard Bates had been invited at the last minute when the Doncasters had had to drop out because of a crisis with Camilla. Maggie, who had guzzled a couple of fortifying whiskies before leaving home and two more in the Kirklands' drawing room, was well into her third glass of Sancerre. 'Bloody decent drop of plonk, Ashley!' She took a piece of Melba toast. Three other pieces slipped onto the tablecloth and reaching to put them back on the silver tray, she knocked the crystal wine glass with her wrist, nearly spilling the wine. 'Whoops a *daisy*! Mustn't spill the nectar!' She grinned at Dr Webb whose expression froze. He fingered his water glass.

'Interesting, that you should give so powerful an agent as alcohol so bland a name as nectar,' he said. His voice, a penetrating tenor, was inclined to bray. He sipped his sparkling water.

'Fiddlesticks!' Maggie retorted.

'"They are so brief, the days of wine and ros—"'

'"Not long,"' Maggie chipped in.

The professor looked startled. He was not accustomed to being interrupted. 'I beg your pardon?'

'The quote is, "They are not long, the days of wine and roses." It's Dowson.'

'Tennyson, surely?'

'You're the professor,' Maggie retorted and turned to her neighbour, a barrister from the neighbouring village. 'Do *you* know anything about poetry?'

Presently Annabel, down from London to help her mother, brought in a large oval dish on which sat three brace of roast partridge, garnished with watercress and sitting on a nest of the thinnest potato chips Leonard thought he had ever seen. 'Annabel,' he said, 'each time we come you surpass yourself.'

'What a delightful bird is Perdix perdix,' Dr Webb brayed, 'but what a pity to shoot a vanishing species.'

'These are Red-Legged Partridges,' Ashley said, 'and they are common enough. We don't shoot Grey Partridges on this farm.' He walked to the sideboard and began to carve the birds into portions while Annabel distributed the plates and offered vegetables. The professor declined any meat but took generous helpings of red cabbage, game chips, celeriac and leeks.

'Dr Webb, I'm so sorry you dislike partridge.' Elaine was concerned for her most important guest. 'Can I offer you anything else? Some cheese, perhaps, or an omelette? I'm sure Annabel could rustle something up.'

'Thank you, no. It is not that I dislike poultry.'

'But you disapprove of shooting?' Ashley asked. Everyone else in the room either shot regularly or was at least involved in the more social aspects of shooting parties. There was a difficult silence relieved by Elaine.

'Darling, Leonard's glass is almost empty.' So's mine, thought Maggie.

'Oh, I do beg your pardon!' Ashley was happy to skate over the embarrassing moment. 'I haven't poured the new wine for anybody.' He picked up two crystal claret jugs and filled a fresh set of glasses, managing, just in time, not to pour any 1967 St Emilion onto the back of Dr Webb's hand. 'Whoops, sorry!'

'As I think I said before, I do not partake,' said the professor.

'Like your Vice Chancellor,' Ashley said.

'Exactly so.'

'And how is Dr Helmsley?' Ashley asked, when he had seen to everyone else's glass. Maggie's had been the first to be filled, but she managed to drain it before he had come full circle, and thus secured another refill.

'Our Vice Chancellor? Speaks most highly of your firm. You have, it seems, exceeded all expectations on the publicity front. The Science Park, even though some of us had the very gravest doubts about it, is likely to become one of our richest assets. Yes, it is simply splendid, although there is rather more German involvement there than British, I'm afraid.' Maggie's hand tightened on the stem of her glass as he spoke. 'And the Japanese, of course, are deeply involved,' he concluded.

'Inevitable, surely,' Ashley said smoothly. 'Both countries are well ahead of us in technology.'

'Indeed, but the public image we must convey is that the Science Park is a *British* venture. And we, ah, hope that your firm will continue to serve us in that respect.'

'We shall be delighted to. The University is one of Kirkland Wild's most valued clients.'

'One little point.' The professor dropped the pitch of his voice a semitone. 'I know not whence they come . . .' Maggie guffawed. Dr Webb threw her an angry glance and started again. 'I know not, as I said, whence they come, but we have heard – that is, the Vice Chancellor has heard – a rumour that Kirkland Wild was in financial difficulties.'

Ashley laughed. 'News to me! I'll show you a balance sheet after dinner.'

The professor shook his head. 'It was, as I stated, a rumour,' and he dabbed his thin lips with his table napkin.

'Rivals,' Ashley said, 'especially in public relations, like to undermine. It's all a matter of confidence.'

'I'll say it's a matter of bloody confidence!' Maggie's voice was, very nearly, raised more than was seemly. The wine was joining forces with the Scotch already in her system. She was flushed and breathing heavily. The other guests fell silent. 'I mean, it's a bit of a damned cheek, coming out with crap like that, at a bloke's own bloody dinner table!' She was shouting now. 'I mean, you and your arty-farty speech and your snotty attitude.'

'I beg your pardon?' Webb's voice had sunk to a whisper. He had gone quite pale.

'You're the one, aren't you?'

'Maggie, please!' Leonard was trying to catch her eye.

'It *was* you! With your fart-arse attitude about shooting and drinking. I might have known you for a humbug.'

'Maggie, what are you trying to say?' Ashley asked, wishing he hadn't as soon as the words were out. The woman needed shutting up, not egging on. He'd been told she'd given up booze, but knew that once hooked, you never could. What *had* Elaine been thinking of, inviting her to such an important dinner party?

'I'm not *trying* to say anything. I'm succeeding in saying that this creep, or other creeps of the same ilk at that poxy little technical college they've got the neck to call a University, didn't have the confidence to let me landscape their Science Park—'

'Ah! I see!' Ashley tried to intervene.

'Even though they knew, they bloody well *knew*, that my scheme was inspired.' Maggie got to her feet. 'You people make me want to puke!'

'Come on, Maggie.' Leonard was on his feet. 'It's time to go home.' He helped her out of her chair and walked her to the door.

Elaine jumped up to help. 'Um, do have more of anything you want,' she told the silent guests. Ashley began to stand up. 'No, darling,' Elaine said, gently pushing his shoulders downwards again. 'Stay and look after our friends. I'll be back in a moment.' She ushered the couple into the hall and closed the dining-room door behind her. 'Can she walk?' she asked Leonard, her voice icy.

''Course I c'n fucking walk!'

'Elaine.' Leonard's voice quavered. 'I can't tell you how—'

'Just take her home, Len. I have to get back to my guests.' She watched Leonard help his drunk and heavy wife into their car and went back to try to glue together the shards of her broken party. It was soon over.

When the last of the guests had gone, Elaine retired, saying she had a headache but Ashley went into the kitchen to help Annabel.

'Quite a party, I gather,' Annabel said, nibbling a partridge leg. 'Want some?'

Ashley shook his head but reached instead for the cooking brandy and poured out a slug for each of them.

'The trouble is,' he paused to sip, grimace and then sigh gratefully, 'in a way Old Ma Bates is right.'

'She often is. Besides, that professor'd be enough to drive anyone to drink.'

'Mmm. In a way, I feel responsible.'

'For what? You didn't make the scene.'

'No, responsible for Maggie not getting that project. When their Vice Chancellor told me about their choice of landscape designer, I might have undermined their confidence.'

'Did you question Maggie's ability?'

'Of course not.'

'Well, there you are then.' She drained her tumbler and held it out. 'This stuff is utter filth. Can't we have some Armagnac?'

'Can't be bothered to go to the dining room again, can you?' In response she waggled the glass and Ashley slopped a little more Three Star into it.

'Dad, I rather wanted to have a quiet word with you.'

'Oh lor! That sounds ominous.'

'Not really.' She sipped. 'Well, a teeny bit perhaps. It's about the firm.'

'What firm?'

'Daddy! Our firm, Designer Diner.'

'What about it?'

'Well, we've got a bit of trouble with the accounts.'

'In what respect?'

'Daddy, don't go all formal.' She drank more brandy. 'We've got plenty of work and I know our prices are right – in fact, most of our clients don't seem to care what they pay – but the fact is, we appear to be a bit strapped for cash.'

'You're obviously milking your business too hard. What are your drawings like?'

'A bit high.'

'Annabel, I must ask you this and please don't jump down my throat, but is that partner of yours absolutely straight?'

'Well, that's the problem. I *think* so, but her meals always seem to cost so much more to lay on than mine.'

'Fishy!'

'Actually, I wish I was on my own, but I just couldn't do the work single-handed. If we could just get an injection of cash, to get the bank off our backs, we'd be on an even keel again.'

'What sort of an injection?'

'Oh Daddy, you'll be cross.' She walked over to him to refill his glass. He shook his head but put his arm round her waist.

'Try me.'

'Ten would do it.'

'Ten *thousand*?' He stepped away from her. 'What the hell are you up to?'

'I *knew* you'd be cross but, you see, I wasn't really experienced enough to know how to run a business before. We both know so much more about it now but, boy, are we paying for our earlier mistakes! I owe the bank fifteen—'

'Not "I", "we". "We, the partnership owe the bank" is what you should be saying.'

'I, we, what's the difference? I'm so worried about it I can't sleep and that's interfering with my work. Daddy, you must help!'

'Now look here.' Ashley circled her waist again. 'I know you've got talent enough to solve your own problem. Unlike Andrew, you're gutsy. I admire that in a woman.'

'Don't patronise!'

'I'll lend you eight thousand. At ten per cent per annum, repayable within two years.' She hugged him. 'But you mustn't put it into your partnership. Use it for survival and draw nothing out of the firm while it builds up its liquidity again. And get an auditor in to check up on all your practices.'

'Right.'

'I'll arrange something tomorrow and post a cheque to you next week.'

'Can't you write one now?'

'Certainly not. I need to see that the transaction is as tax-efficient as possible. Besides, I'm not the bottomless pit of wealth you lot all think I am.'

'Come off it, Dad!'

'No really! The drought has made us actually lose money on the farm for the first time in decades. It isn't serious but it *is* food for thought. Farming is getting tougher and my other businesses are still very much at the development stage.'

'But, we're all right aren't we? As a family, I mean?'

'Lord, yes!'

'If it all worked, you could be all right, as a family, in spite of everything.' John Holman put the last of the saucepans away on the shelf in Betty's kitchen and picked up the kettle.

'Don't you dare!' Betty took it from him. 'Go through and sit down and I'll do the coffee – or would you rather have tea? It is getting rather late.'

'Coffee won't keep me awake.'

She took a jar of Maxwell House out of the cupboard and found a couple of mugs. 'Only Instant, I'm afraid!' She knew there would be no answer but that it would be all right.

What a relief, she thought, to be taken seriously. They had talked earnestly over the supper table about her prospects. Chances of survival were slim but there *were* chances, provided she made fundamental changes. Most of the farm would have to carry on growing cereals and sugar beet: the soil just wasn't good enough to launch into higher-value crops like vegetables or soft fruit. But there was a small pocket of rich land lying along the B4315 and that could make a useful Pick Your Own centre.

'Loads of people want things for their deepfreezes,' John had said. 'Autumn-sown broad beans would be ready by late May, then there'd be strawberries and green peas in June, raspberries and French beans in July and so on.' With crafty planning, they could raise expensive produce for cash customers right up to the last days of autumn.

Then John had talked of livestock ventures, of tourist potential, of developing a shoot and various other ways in which Betty's activities at Cartwright Farm could be broadened to make the business able to survive.

She took the two mugs of coffee through to the sitting room and handed him the least chipped one. 'Of course, in the meantime, I've got a hell of a lot of catching up to do. This rain has put us behind with the autumn work.'

'I'm here for the week – I'll help you.'

'No, that wouldn't be at all fair. You're on holiday.'

'I said I'd help.'

'We'll talk about it tomorrow.' They drank their coffee. She finished hers first and got up. 'I'm turning in – I'm done for. I hope you'll excuse me. You know where your room is and everything.'

'Of course.'

'John?' She hovered at the door. 'Thank you for coming.'

He nodded and looked slightly embarrassed. 'That's all right.'

Chapter Eighteen

The weather held, apart from a brief gale at the beginning of October, and on the morning of the eighteenth, Leonard Bates was busy in his wine cellar. On the morning after that frightful scene at the Kirkland dinner party, he had decided to make a final bid to cure Maggie of her alcoholism. He knew that the prognosis was not good and that the chances of her slipping back into drunkenness, even after years of abstention, were pretty high, but he also knew that failure could kill their marriage and would probably kill her. So, in spite of his lifelong passion for collecting and drinking wine, he had decided to abstain with her. Well, actually, he'd be giving up ahead of her because he knew she wouldn't be able to stop drinking until she really wanted to, and that wouldn't be for a while yet. There would, Leonard reckoned, have to be quite a lot more degradation before self-disgust could give her the will to change. Then he would be needed to convince her that she *could* give it up. Meanwhile, he just hoped her liver would be able to take the punishment.

His gesture was not only a huge personal sacrifice, but it also involved a good deal of physical work. He had contacted Roland Clarke, the Kendale wine merchant who had driven over within the hour. Nobody, even those who knew Leonard well, had ever been invited into his cellar and speculation about its size and value was a popular pastime among local wine-traders.

Clarke was not disappointed. Even to his cold, commercial gaze, the sight of all those bottles, stacked and arranged according to age and provenance, was stirring. 'I've never seen such a collection in amateur hands,' he said, adding, 'but then, you're no amateur.'

'Best part of forty years collecting. All of it still perfectly drinkable. Look at this,' Leonard held up a bottle of Château Talbot. 'Nineteen forty-seven! The first bottle I ever bought to put down. That was before I went to medical school.' He stroked the dusty glass before laying the bottle back in the rack.

'You'll keep that one, surely? As a memento?'

'No, it has to go. Every bottle.' He looked round the cellar. 'Every last drop.'

'There must be more than two hundred cases here.'

'Considerably! The cellar goes on round the corner.'

Roland had advised Leonard to make an inventory so that he could write a catalogue. The middle-range wines he could sell through his own business in Kendale but the grander labels would go to a London auction house. 'We'll need to put a reserve price on them, just in case the best buyers aren't there. If they don't sell the first time, I can hold them for you.'

'I'm not sure I want to prolong the agony,' Leonard stated quietly. 'Let them go at any price.'

'You really mean business, don't you?'

'It's a matter of life or death. I should have done this years ago.'

'But your wines mean – *meant* everything to you.'

'Not quite everything, Rowley.'

They had taken a bottle of Corton, Clos du Roi 1967, upstairs to the kitchen. Leonard drew the cork, decanted the wine into a crystal jug and took two glasses down from the Welsh dresser. Slanting sunlight glinted on the jug which glowed like an outsize garnet. 'Let's sit outside.' He held the door for Roland and followed him out to the table and chairs on the terrace.

'Nearly as warm as August,' Roland declared, taking in the view of the garden. He was surprised at how scruffy it looked.

'She hasn't done anything in it for weeks,' Leonard said,

278

following his gaze across to the mixed borders. 'There's the odd burst of energy on a decent morning but then she's so pissed by elevenses she loses motivation.' He filled the glasses. 'Let's let it breathe and warm a little in the sunshine.'

They had sat until Roland could wait no longer and had raised his glass, sipped, sloshed the wine round his mouth, and swallowed. 'A classic!'

They had refilled their glasses twice and then, before his was half-empty, Leonard said: 'Rowley, how long have we known each other? Fifteen, twenty years?'

'At least.'

'And you know more about wine than anyone. That's why you're the bloke I wanted to share my last drink with.'

'I'm honoured.'

Leonard held up his glass and watched the sun glinting through the rich redness. He noted the way the wine moved, colourless at the very edges of the liquid and moistening the sides of the glass without sticking. He held the rim to his nose, closed his eyes and inhaled slowly, sensing the bouquet and, in his mind's eye, seeing fleeting images of the Burgundy hillsides, the glare of the sun on the limy soil, the coloured slate rooftops in the villages, the rows and rows of vines, all trimmed back in July, their clusters of grapes still small and hard, like green pearls. When he had sipped, savoured and swallowed, he lowered his glass, still nearly half-full. 'That was a good mark to go out on.' He wanted to say more but couldn't trust his voice. Roland stayed silent too, even when Leonard emptied his glass onto the ground.

Now this morning, with more than half the cellar contents listed, Leonard was beginning to realise that he had underestimated the value of his collection by thousands of pounds. The prospect of so much money might have neutralised the bitterness in some people, but in Leonard, it did not. He counted the contents of yet another bin and added to his list, *Trotanoy, Pomerol 1961, 57.*

Camilla was having a better day and was even able to walk in the Old Rectory garden for a little while without crutches.

Her disease had advanced with frightening speed during the autumn but now she seemed to be having a remission. Everyone knew it was only a temporary respite but the relief was immense.

Sally was in Africa, working with the Prince in Mudando. As well as looking after her own business interests there, she was in almost constant demand nowadays as adviser to the ruler of that small but, she felt, highly civilised African state. She was drawn to the place in a way that affected her far more than any other part of the world. Whenever she arrived there, she felt a quickening of pulse and a catch of emotion that made it feel almost like coming home. The Mudandan royal family were friends with whom she shared a closer, warmer relationship than with anyone back in England. And she approved of the way the Prince ran things. Admittedly, he reserved the right to order public floggings, even hangings, and did so from time to time, but nobody starved and there was little crime.

But being so frequently needed in Africa made her spend even less time than before at home. Camilla missed her, and Sally missed her stepdaughter, sensing that every hour with her needed to be cherished because there were so few left. Her work in Mudando, she knew, was crucial for business, and for maintaining her family's wealth, but she also loved the arid little state and its people with an ardour that eclipsed the feelings she had for her true home, and this made her feel guilty.

Betty Rose had done much to fill the gap while Sally was abroad, and Camilla had become nearly as dependent on her as on her own family. Visiting the Rectory every day had added an almost intolerable burden to Betty's workload but it had helped her to come to terms with her loss of Jack.

Jules was less able to cope. Instead of sharing the pain, he bottled it up, driving the splinters of suffering more deeply into the quick. Camilla's decline – not steady, but with sudden dips between spells of relative stability – sickened and terrified him, but he was unable to express his love for his daughter for fear of breaking down in front of her and alarming her. As the pain increased, his inhibitions grew and he felt more estranged. His gratitude to Betty was tainted with envy for her easy relationship with his daughter. Betty touched her a lot, kissing the top of her head, stroking her arm, cuddling her and sometimes, when he saw this, Jules felt he would burst. Yet, when he was with Camilla, all he could do was hold her hand, rather formally, and give her a chaste kiss on the forehead each night and morning.

This morning, he was working at home and had taken a break from his papers to have a chat with Betty while Camilla tottered in the garden.

'Aah!' Betty took a sip of coffee, brewed from fresh beans, processed a moment before on a complicated but noisy apparatus in white and gilt.

'That was heartfelt,' Jules said.

'Mmm. I'm beginning to feel almost human.'

'Things going any better on the farm?'

'Not yet, but the prospects are looking brighter.'

'Good. Um, Betty,' Jules hesitated, stirring his Royal Worcester coffee cup with slow, deliberate circular movements, 'I'm so grateful to you for helping with Camilla.'

'I know, Jules. You don't need to thank me.'

'The fact of the matter is that I would rather like to do something in return.'

'There's really no need.'

'And, since you presumably need professional advice on your business, um, now more than ever I would imagine, I'd be glad to offer my services. I know nothing of farming, of course, but quite a bit about finance and accounting.'

'Oh, Jules, that's sweet of you,' Betty put her hand on his, 'it really is. But I think I'm all right for the moment.'

'Are you sure?'

'I've decided to look for a business partner.'

'Really?' He sounded doubtful. Caution was the very basis of Jules's existence.

Mmm. Someone with physical strength to come in and help with the heavy work.'

'I see your point of view,' he took his hand away, gently, 'but do be careful. There are lots of pitfalls with partners.'

'I know. I haven't made my mind up about it yet, not completely anyway, but I'll need to pretty soon.'

'The problem with partners is that they're rather hard to get rid of. Are you sure you wouldn't be better off employing a manager?'

'Couldn't possibly afford that. I need someone who'll take a risk, who can live on thin air. Someone as headstrong as I am, in fact.' She giggled.

'And someone who will introduce capital?'

'If possible.'

'I'm still not sure you wouldn't be better off with a manager, even if it's just a temporary measure while you get yourself sorted out.'

'I can't afford a salary! I can't pull a single penny out of the business.' A few drops of coffee had spilled onto the table and with her spoon, absently, she traced a pattern in the flecked marble surface, connecting them up. 'John Holman is staying with us at the moment. He's a professional farm manager.'

'That East Anglian chap? The silent one?'

'Yes.'

'And you're thinking of him as a business partner?'

'Absolutely not! He's far too clever to want to struggle with a hopeless little farm like mine. He's just helping us while he takes his holiday.'

Carrying a drink in each hand, Andrew picked a cautious route through the crowded Saturday-night bar. In spite of his care, someone jogged his elbow and a dollop of sticky cocktail slopped over his fingers. The Crooked Billet was not his kind of pub at all but it was far enough from Wyckhamby, he judged, to be fairly safe and certainly not the kind of establishment that any of his parents' friends would have frequented. There was a quarter-sized pool table on one side of the room with a noisy game in progress.

'Here we are.' He put Tracy's cocktail down in front of

her and sat beside her on the scuffed banquette. As he did so, he noticed with a shock that her waist had noticeably thickened. Was it the way she was sitting? No, there was, quite distinctly, a bulge. 'Cheers!'

'Cheers!' She sipped, licked her lips and snuggled close, putting her arm round his waist. 'Nice'n romantic here, innit?' Andrew looked across the smoky, noisy room at the cardboard Babycham advertisement behind the bar and wondered what she meant. 'I could go for this place.'

'It's a bit noisy for me.'

'Naow, not this pub, silly, the village.'

'Little Greaveby?'

'Mm. There's some good 'ouses 'ere.'

'Really?'

'Yeah. On the estate, round the back o' the village.'

'Oh? I thought they were council houses.'

'They are! Or they was, but they've been sold off.'

'I see.' He took a long pull from his pint of draught lager and snuggled closer. 'What's that perfume you're wearing?'

'Can't you be serious for a minute?' He nibbled her ear. 'Be'*ave*!'

'Well? What is it?'

'Never mind that. What do you think?'

'Think? About what?'

'Them 'ouses!'

'What houses?'

'Oh! You're useless. Look, we gotta think about little Fred, 'ere.' She took his hand and laid it on her belly. He experienced a surge of love, mingled with terror. She pressed on with her theme. 'We can 'ave a look, can't we?'

'It's dark.'

'There's street lamps.' She gulped down her cocktail, stood up and pulled his hand. 'Come on, Andrew!' He went meekly.

A brief silence fell over the room as she clacked across the quarry-tiled floor in her stiletto heels, negotiated the double doors, still leading Andrew, and then told him to shut them behind him. As play resumed at the pool table, a brawny labourer said, 'She's got that one by the balls!' Outside, Andrew heard the burst of general laughter and suspected it was at his expense.

They walked down Little Greaveby High Street, past the small shop-cum-post office, the war memorial and the rows of half-timbered cottages with their miniature front gardens tidied up for winter. At the end of a side lane, they came to the council estate where several For Sale notices were on display. Some of the houses boasted new, clear varnished doors with oval-topped glass panes and brass letter slits. One or two had had their cheap brick walls clad with imitation stone. Tracy pointed these out and said, 'See! See what you can do with these 'ouses, if you use yer imagination, like. They can be really nice.'

'They're so crowded together.'

'Well, we've got to think about an 'ome.'

'Have we?' He felt depressed at the prospect of living on an estate like this. A man of about thirty came out of one of the houses and climbed into a ten-year-old Ford Capri. He had a cigarette sticking out of his mouth, dark greasy sideburns and a sagging beer belly. Andrew couldn't really imagine him as a potential neighbour. 'Wouldn't it be better to look at some of those pretty cottages in the High Street?'

'I ain't cleanin' one o' *them* every day – them beams is terrible dust traps. Besides, the rooms are dark and they ain't sanitary, really.'

'Oh.' They walked on in silence for a few steps. She stopped by a lamp post.

'How about a little bungalow? Could we afford that?'

'Mmm, no.' Andrew wasn't sure. They hadn't really discussed much about their future at all – apart from that first afternoon when he had said that he would never forsake her, never. He rather wished that bit could be unsaid. But then he caught sight of her face, draining of natural colour in the bilious light of the sodium street lamp. She looked so earnest with those huge eyes, the brows raised in query. He felt a fresh surge of love and put his arms round her. 'I don't know really.'

284

Later, they went back to Wyckhamby and, since Ashley was away in London, made love on the Persian carpet on the farm office floor. Afterwards, they held each other for quite a long time, enjoying the afterglow. She was so tender and so passionate that sometimes he almost wept with love. But now that summer was over and they could no longer screw *al fresco*, their assignations seemed so furtive. They would not be able to keep their relationship secret much longer. 'You won't dump me, will you?' She nibbled his ear-lobe as she whispered.

'I promised, didn't I?'

'So. When are you going to tell?'

'Soon.' He went home and worried about it for most of the night.

They met again on the following Saturday and instead of driving her straight to Little Greaveby, he stopped the car in Wyckhamby, by the river.

'Git moving!' She was agitated. 'Someone'll see us.'

'Let them. Let them all see us!' he said, and turned to face her and braced himself for a speech. 'Tracy, will you marry me?'

''Course I bloody will, but get out of 'ere. I don't want me Dad to find out.'

'He'll have to – sooner rather than later.'

'Look, there's someone coming!' She sank lower in her seat and rested her chin on her chest. 'Pull away, *please!*' He drove off. After a safe interval, she sat up. 'I'll need to talk to Dad first, OK?'

'OK.'

She steeled herself to broach the subject with her father that evening.

'Dad,' she said, after serving him his tea. Bert Mardle looked up from his *Exchange & Mart* and took the plate from her. 'I need to talk.'

'Wha'?'

'I thought about . . .' the words died. She felt her body tensing. He poured some Daddie's Sauce onto his sausages and began to eat, holding his knife and fork as if they were pencils. She tried again. 'Maybe I should be thinkin' . . . about settlin' down.'

'You? Ha!' he snorted, lifted his teacup, and held the saucer just below his chin as he drank.

'I got a steady man, now, Dad and—'

'Steady my arse!' The empty cup was banged down in disbelief. 'Different steady-'un each week, more like!'

'Not now, Dad.'

'Who is it? That Charlie?'

'No.'

'Darren then, or is it that little blond bugger, plays football?'

'No, Dad.'

'You was with 'im night before last. Bill seen yer – in the bus shelter at Kendale.'

She coloured a little. 'No, Dad.'

'You sayin' Bill's a liar?'

'No.' She hung her head.

''Cause he says he seen yer there with Charlie as well. Last week.'

'So?'

'So who's the poor mug yer want ter "settle" down with?' She stared at him. He stared back, his anger rising.

'Dad, don't get in a temper!' She held his gaze but began to tremble. 'Please!' he stared. The fear on her face fed his rage.

'It's never *'im!*' He jumped to his feet. 'It *is* 'im! That little sod Kirkland!'

She cringed. 'He's not little.'

'You leave 'im be!' Mardle's face was empurpled with rage. 'You 'ear? LEAVE 'IM BE!'

'I can't, Dad.' She began to cry and shrank back further from her father, bumping her head on the glass-fronted food cupboard. 'I can't leave 'im be. I'm expectin'.'

'You little bitch!' He smacked the side of her head so hard that it hit the cupboard door and broke the glass. 'Mucky little bitch!' Then he shook her roughly. They were both trembling. He thrust his face up to hers so that they were

286

nose to nose. She caught the sharp tang of Daddie's Sauce on his breath. Between clenched teeth he said, 'If 'e comes near you again, I'll cut 'is fucking bollocks off!' He strode out of the kitchen, slamming the back door.

Later, when he had returned from the pub after swallowing five whiskies in quick succession, he had calmed down enough to be able to talk more rationally. Tracy, contrite and tearful, made him a cup of tea. 'I'm afeared to tell Jason,' she said.

'Leave him to me,' Mardle replied. 'But are you sure you're . . . you know?' He indicated her midriff.

'Yes, Dad, I'm sure.'

He put his head in his hands and sighed deeply. 'It'll end in tears, girl, you mark my words.'

Later, when he broke the news to Jason, the reaction was more or less as he expected. At first, he turned pale, then he started rummaging in the sideboard drawer.

'I'm not 'aving that,' Jason hissed. 'I'm not fuckin' 'avin' it,' and he found the flick knife he was looking for, slipped it into the top of his right cowboy boot and strode out of the house. The sound of his van revving soon drowned anything that might have been said in the kitchen as he roared away into the night.

The van, which was not easy to control at normal speed because of faulty brakes, too much play on the steering, and balding rear tyres, lurched from side to side as he drove, flat out, along the village street.

The Heron would be the first place to look. The bastard wouldn't be in there 'isself – he never went there, being too stuck up for pubs – but someone in the bar might know where he could be found.

Jason jerked the wheel over, making the van's tyres squeal as it swung into the pub yard. A figure tottering by the entrance came into his vision too late and at the same moment that his boot crashed down onto the brake pedal, the van smacked into flesh. He had hit the woman hard enough to throw her a couple of yards through the air and saw her land on her back in a flurry of limbs and skirts like an oversized child's doll.

He leapt out of the van and ran over to her. By the time he had knelt to see how badly she was hurt, several people had emerged from the side door of the Heron and were running over. 'We heard the crash,' someone said. 'Is anyone hurt?'

'I didn't 'ave a chance,' wailed Jason, his mission forgotten. 'She danced out straight in front of me.' Jim Hutton, landlord of the Heron, came up and pushed through the clustered drinkers.

'I didn't 'ave a chance, Jim,' Jason was wailing. 'Didn't 'ave a—'

'Get out the bloody way!' Jim knelt by the inert figure. 'Oh blimey, it's Mrs Bates. Jason, go and get the doctor. No, don't drive – run across the meadow, it's quicker. Fred? No, you, Bill, go inside and call an ambulance.' He loosened her collar. She had vomited all over her clothes and the reek of alcohol, tinged with sharply foetid stomach juices made his own stomach heave. One arm was quite badly jammed under her body and was obviously injured but she didn't appear to be bleeding.

Leonard arrived before the ambulance. He was breathless from running over the meadow and could hardly speak. He checked his wife for vital signs and then began to assess the injuries. He straightened her arm and felt the fracture. The rest of her seemed unharmed and her colour, as far as he could tell by torchlight, was satisfactory. She would be badly bruised and might be a little concussed but was probably unconscious as much because of the alcohol in her system as the blow her body took from the vehicle.

As he moved her limbs to make her more comfortable, she began to come round. 'Don't try to talk,' Leonard said. 'You're all right. I'm here.'

She focused on him, her head wobbling. 'My mouth tastes revolting. Get me a drink, will you?'

'You've had more than enough.'

'Don't be a prat . . . I need water.'

'In a moment.'

'Hell'va piss up.' She began to giggle and then to cry. 'Bloody well hurts, Leonard. Give me something for Chrissake.' Then she passed out again.

When the ambulance came, Leonard said to the driver, 'Don't take her to Kendale General, drive her to the Fairhaven. I'll go on ahead by car, to see to her admission.' If he could use this incident to get her launched on a drying-out programme, he might save months, even her life. Then, to the little knot of spectators, he said, 'Um, could someone give me a lift back to Bridge House, to pick up my car?'

They were discreet at the Fairhaven and quite used to well-to-do drunks who were admitted on a variety of flimsy pretexts. They would care for Maggie as well there as anywhere and besides, a couple of days in the comfort of a private health-care hospital wouldn't come amiss if she really was going to dry out. The first days would be the worst and she would need all the pampering and support she could get.

They set Maggie's arm and checked her over for internal injuries. At the moment of impact, it seemed, her body was completely relaxed. Had she been sober, she might have been maimed, killed even. Leonard sat by her bedside all night and when she woke, he spooned a light breakfast into her before going home to take morning surgery.

Ashley glared at the new dairyman, standing on the other side of his desk. 'Do you realise what this will cost?'

'With respect, sir, the problem started before I came.' He had been working at Wyckhamby Farms for almost a month now and in that time the milk yield, which had been declining gently but inexplicably throughout the autumn, had suddenly plummeted. Under normal circumstances, this would have been a minor annoyance, a mere hiccough, but with the farm having done so badly after the summer drought, every fall in yield on every enterprise mattered. He had, after all, been employed to stop the rot after his predecessor had caused heavy calf losses simply because of poor hygiene. That had cost enough, but this latest mishap would leak tens of thousands from their reserves.

'We're adrift by more than two hundred gallons a day.'

'It'll come back, sir. Now we know what caused it.' The young man shifted awkwardly and looked over Ashley's right shoulder, avoiding eye contact. 'They're resilient beasts, Holstein Friesians.'

'They need to be.' Ashley indicated that the interview was over and watched the young man walk out, closing the door quietly behind him. In spite of faultless credentials, including a degree from Reading University, this one would never be good with animals. Stockmanship was innate, could not be learned and, even though he was competent in every other respect, he just didn't seem to have that special quality. He could not be blamed for the fault in the automatic feed-mixer that had unbalanced the nutrition of the cows' rations, but a good stockman would have spotted their decline much sooner – certainly before their milk almost dried up. Ashley wished he could dismiss this man before anything else went wrong but that, he knew, would hardly be fair.

To clear his head, he decided to walk over to Cartwright Farm to get a breath of fresh air and, hopefully, to have a chat with Betty. Lately, he had been so immersed in his own affairs that he had seen little, far too little of his tenant.

The lane up to the farm was quite muddy from the rains but the fields looked dry and workable. He was surprised to see how well ahead Betty was with her work and wondered how on earth she had had the stamina to get it all done. He knew that she had borrowed that Fenland chap but wasn't sure how good he was. Quite often, these qualified managers were all theory and no practice.

The front door of Cartwright was wide open, letting in the chill, so he called 'Anyone home?' and walked in. The hall and kitchen were empty so he tapped on the study door and opened it. Instead of finding Betty at the desk he looked straight into the gaze of John Holman. 'Oh!'

'Hullo?' John was not smiling. Blue eyes stared into hazel ones.

'I was looking for Mrs Rose.'

'Betty's not here.' He made no effort to elaborate.

'As I see.' There was a painful silence. John lowered his head to his work – combing the Yellow Pages for a local electrician. Ashley felt his hackles rising. 'Is it possible to know when she might be back?'

'Soon.' John kept his attention on the directory, running a stubby finger with blackened nail down the fine print between the advertisements. The lemon-blond hair was falling slightly forward and he flicked it back with a swift movement of the head – a mannerism which for some reason Ashley found irritating.

'Well, you seem to have got your feet well and truly under the table.'

'Sorry?'

'I was under the impression that this was Mrs Rose's desk.' Ashley's voice was quiet but not without menace.

John looked up again and met his angry stare. 'It is. I've just looked in to find a phone number. As you probably know, I'm helping Betty out.'

'Yes, I bet you are!' John's face paled slightly but he said nothing. After a long pause, Ashley continued, 'What exactly *is* your rôle in this ménage?'

'Helping out, as I said.'

'Then perhaps you'd help Mrs Rose out a little more by telling her that her landlord called and would like to speak to her as soon as is convenient.' He swung round and walked out, leaving muddy footprints across the hall.

He seethed for the rest of the day, angry with himself for having made such a stupid scene out of nothing and then, when his emotions had cooled, trying to analyse why he had reacted that way. God knew, Betty wanted support. He just felt it was he who should be the provider of it.

Back at the office, late in the afternoon, there was a message on the answering machine: 'Gosh, I hate these things . . . it's er, Len Bates. Ashley, could you collect your wine as soon as possible? Um, today if you can.'

Ashley picked up the phone and dialled. 'I can be with you in five minutes. Is it all ready?'

'Been ready for days, old boy.'

He drove to Bridge House in the Range Rover, overdue, now, for renewal but being kept for an extra year because of the poor harvest.

'Ashley, thanks for coming so quickly.' Leonard showed him into the house. ''fraid I can't offer you a drink.'

'It's a bit early for me, anyway.'

'I didn't want to bother you but the fact is, Maggie comes out of hospital tomorrow and I rather want to get it all cleared out before she arrives. You do understand, don't you?'

'Of course. Hell of a thing for *you* to have to give up, though.'

'Not really.' He uttered a bleak little laugh. Ashley noticed that Leonard's paunch had already begun to shrink, presumably as a result of having stopped wine-bibbing.

'Well, I'm most grateful to you for keeping some back for me. It will come in handy at dinner parties, speaking of which, Elaine wants me to say that Maggie is quite forgiven. But you know that, don't you?'

'Ashley, I have never felt so bad as that night.'

'Forget it.'

'God knows, Maggie's ability to embarrass, even sober, is unbelievable but I was *mortified*.'

'I said forget it.' He pulled his chequebook, folded in half, out of his hip-pocket. 'That professor? What an insufferable little turd!' Both men laughed but found it difficult to meet each other's eyes. 'Six cases, wasn't it?'

'One Chassagne Montrachet, two Sancerre, one Morgon and a couple of cases of Beaune.' Leonard helped him to carry the wine out to the Range Rover and as the last case went on board, said, 'That concludes the purge. This house is now dry.'

Roland Clarke had already sold much of the collection. As a favour to Leonard, he had merely taken a small handling commission which enabled the cheaper bottles to appear in his shop at bargain prices. The finer wines were to be auctioned in November and had total reserves in excess of £20,000. All in all, Leonard would clear at least £30,000.

There'd be enough, after paying Capital Gains Tax and footing Maggie's bill at the Fairhaven, to go on quite a little spree. A world cruise, perhaps. But as he dialled the Kendale travel agents, Leonard felt quite sad.

Chapter Nineteen

Cruising up the Tagus into Lisbon, the P&O liner *Brisbane* caused quite a stir. Her huge white bulk – she was nearly a quarter of a mile long – dwarfed all the other craft on the river and the stylish twin smokestacks at her stern made her look far more modern than she really was.

Leonard and Maggie had one of the better staterooms. Instead of portholes, it had windows which flooded the cabin with daylight and provided a series of changing views. Even at sea, Maggie was wont to sit in one of the two comfortable chairs and stare at the ocean gliding by. In the three days since they had cleared Southampton, steamed out of the English Channel and followed the coast of Spain, she had gazed and gazed, watching grey, choppy seas give way to darker, almost black-looking swells, foam-topped and angry. Then the skies had gradually lightened and now, in brilliant sunlight on a fresh autumn morning, she and Leonard were drinking breakfast coffee and watching the banks of the river slip by.

'Marvellous when they bring the views to the window,' Maggie said. There was a tremor in her hand and a constant, grinding ache at the pit of her being. She wanted a drink so badly she felt she could scream. But she'd been here before. She knew that the sharpness of her craving would lose its edge, eventually, but that the deep-seated drink-longing would never really leave her as long as she lived.

'You all right?' Leonard asked, and wished he hadn't. It was a stupid question in the circumstances.

*

Ashley sat brooding in his seat as the Lincoln and Clee-
thorpes train pulled out of King's Cross. He had been
travelling to London by rail since harvest, because it was
cheaper than driving the Daimler, and had discovered that
second-class seats were nearly as comfortable as first-class
ones.

Until recently, days spent at Kirkland Wild had provided
relief from the anxious times at Wyckhamby Farms. While
agriculture had suffered from drought and low prices, public
relations had been buoyant and profitable but now, with the
cracks in Britain's over-heating economy beginning to widen,
confidence was ebbing in most businesses. A slump in
advertising pointed the way to recession and closer to home,
several of Kirkland Wild's best clients were either cutting
back or dispensing with their services altogether, preferring
to organise their public relations internally. Ashley's parting
conference with Philip Wild had been full of foreboding.
Wild had even hinted that he would be open to the idea of
winding up the partnership and, more sinister, suggested that
he was likely to be headhunted and might be available to a
higher bidder.

Partly to find distraction from his business worries but
also to feed a growing appetite, Ashley had spent much of
his spare time on this week-long sojourn looking for sex. He
had visited a basement flat in Earl's Court, where a naked
and almost hairless Thai boy had given him a questionable
massage and, two days ago, at Marble Arch, a black with
dreadlocks had led him up a car park emergency staircase
where he had pulled a knife and demanded all his cash. It was
not wholly unexpected. The danger added spice to the sexual
excitement and no harm was done, really, because Ashley's
other persona, Guy Wilson, never carried a wallet or credit
cards, or, for that matter, any means of identification.

Apart from Rick, and he'd long since disappeared, he never
saw his partners again. The affair with Rick had, at first,
stunted the growth of his promiscuity but, later, fed it. Rick
had been compliant, almost meek, but Guy needed rougher,
more masculine company. Finding it was easy: the problem

was lack of time. Lurking in the right pubs, hanging round the gay sections of pornshops or loitering in mainline railway stations wasted hours. The identification of a likely quarry, the eye contact, the 'chance' remark – it could all take such ages, but for what? Some encounters, in dark alleyways or lavatory cubicles, lasted less than five minutes. His appetite was not satiated by such frequent assignations, but heightened. With Guy Wilson, sex was a habit, a drug, and it was getting harder to control. As he grew older, he needed more, not less.

When he arrived at Kendale station, Andrew was waiting with the Daimler. Ashley would have preferred to make his own way home, but disliked the idea of leaving a vehicle in the station car park. He needed a while to adjust to Wyckhamby, to get rid of Guy and to step back into his rural niche.

He greeted Andrew who, quite out of character, leapt from the car, took his baggage and loaded it into the boot. He seemed tense. Ashley got into the driving seat. 'Everything all right?'

'On the farm? Oh yah, fine.'

'How's the milk yield?'

'Um, I'm not sure. OK, I think. Why, was anything wrong with it before?'

Ashley drove on in silence. As they were entering the village he said, 'I'll drop you at the house. I want to go to the office for a bit before I come in.'

'Well, actually, I wanted a word with you and Mum together, if that's OK.'

'Can't it wait?'

'Not really.'

Ashley sighed and drove to the Manor. The lights in the drawing-room windows were inviting. Outside, a chill, stinging rain had begun. He walked in, leaving Andrew to deal with his luggage. Elaine offered a perfunctory kiss and a large whisky in which four ice-cubes tinkled.

'Andrew wants to talk to us. I think it's pretty big.' She sat next to him and stroked his hair. 'Tired?'

'A bit.'

'The milk yield's coming back up, Bert Mardle told me this morning.'

'Good.' He drank some whisky. 'What's this all about?' But before Elaine could say anything Andrew came in from garaging the car. He looked at his parents, poured himself a drink and sat down opposite them. 'Help yourself,' Ashley said.

'Darling, don't be unkind,' Elaine said.

'Well, what's the problem? Got a girl in pod or what?' It was meant as a joke, of course, but Andrew jumped like a timid hare and forgot his carefully rehearsed speech.

'It's Tracy. I . . . I don't know what to do.'

'Tracy? Who's Tracy?' To Elaine, 'Do we know a Tracy?' Ashley repeated the word with contempt. Elaine shrugged. Andrew looked at the floor and whispered something inaudible. 'What?'

'Tracy Mardle,' he said, still in a whisper.

'How long has this been going on?'

'Since June.'

'Since *June*? You've been having a hole-in-corner affair with my foreman's daughter for nearly half a year? How deceitful can you get?'

'We love each other.' Andrew was shaking now, and still whispering.

'Say that again!'

'I've asked her to marry me.'

'Well, she can't!' Ashley's voice was brittle. Andrew looked up to meet his father's gaze, saw the anger on his face and looked down at the carpet again.

'She has agreed to be married.'

'I bet she has,' Ashley stood up. 'But I won't allow it. It's ridiculous – laughable!'

Andrew also stood up. 'Let me remind you, Father, that I am twenty-two. I can do as I please.' His voice caught and croaked on these words. 'You can't stop me.'

'And let me remind *you* that you depend on us for everything. Everything! Without us, you'd have nowhere to live. You've no qualifications, no plans and now, after carrying on in secret like this, you've shown that you're dishonest. What's more, you're unemployable.' Andrew tried to say something, swallowed, and began to walk out of the drawing room. 'Don't you *dare* leave—'

'Oh, let him go, Ashley.' Elaine ran to the door, and looked after her son who turned. They exchanged glances and she said, softly, 'Go upstairs. I'll talk to you in a minute.' He nodded and walked off, making a little sound in his throat halfway between a sob and a moan. She closed the drawing-room door and took Ashley's glass for a refill. He watched her busying herself with decanter and ice-tongs.

'We're the ones who brought him up,' he said, taking the glass. 'What the hell do we do now?' He railed for a few minutes while she made sympathetic noises. When he had burned out his rage with talk, she made a suggestion.

'Why not let this run its course?'

'Are you mad?'

'If you try to stop it, they may stiffen their resolve. As it is, I dare say it's merely an infatuation.' She let him digest that for a moment and then tried him with another idea. 'I think he should be given some responsibility on the farm.'

'You *are* mad!'

'Andrew's not stupid, not really. He just has no rôle. He needs to have a proper job.'

'But he's so hopeless with people.'

'Can't you think of *something* he can do on his own, without having to give orders to anyone?' She was putting on her most persuasive tone.

Ashley thought for a while. 'Nothing springs to mind, but I'll think about it.'

'Promise?'

'Promise.'

She took hold of his ears and kissed the top of his head. 'He needs to learn about integrity from someone,' she murmured. 'You should take him under your wing more.'

Andrew did not go upstairs. He put on his Barbour and wellingtons, planning to go for a walk in the dark. Outside, the rain had turned into a heavy downpour and he changed his mind. Then, dithering on the doorstep, he thought of Tracy. He would go over to the Mardles' tied cottage right away, and have it out with the family. He had nothing to lose. They might even let him stay there with Tracy until they got fixed up with somewhere to live. Surely the family would come round in the end. Meanwhile, Tracy had said there were council houses. He thought of the man with the Capri and beer belly at Little Greaveby and shuddered. It was so unfair! His father had loads of money, and there were several empty cottages on the farm. Ashley could give them a roof over their heads at a stroke if he wanted to.

The Mardles were watching television when he arrived at their back door. Mrs Mardle showed him in and sent Tracy upstairs. Mardle was perfunctory. 'What are you going to do, young man?' But before Andrew could answer, there was a squeal of brakes outside as Jason's van arrived. 'Oh Christ, what's 'e doing coming 'ome this early?' Mardle looked rattled. 'You'd better clear off. It's Jason. 'E can be a bit violent, like.'

'Can't I talk to him as well?' Andrew didn't like the alarm in Mardle's eyes.

'Best if you go. For now, like.'

Andrew opened the back door to see Jason's body framed by the lintel. He looked even bigger than Andrew remembered, partly because of his leather World War Two flying jacket.

'You!' Jason lunged forward, grabbed Andrew's clothing at breast-level and yanked him outside. His sweater was stretched and three buttons were pulled off his shirt which also ripped along one seam. Andrew felt a tuft of chest hairs being pulled out.

'Ouch! Jason!'

'I've often wanted to kill,' Jason breathed a mix of beer and salt-n-vinegar crisps into Andrew's face, 'an' I wouldn't mind killing *you*.' Keeping hold of him with one hand, he slapped Andrew's face with his open palm. 'You bin round our Tracy, an' that I . . . will . . . not . . .'ave!' He punctuated the words with more slaps, forehand and backhand. Andrew cringed. He could feel his nose starting to bleed. He sniffed and tried to speak, but Jason wasn't done yet. He changed hands on the sweater clinch and caught hold of Andrew by the crotch.

'Oh, please!' Andrew whined.

Still clutching his privates, Jason grabbed Andrew's neck and pulled his head forward so that their noses were touching again. 'You obviously know what *this* is for,' he squeezed harder, "n if you come near our Tracy again, you won't be needin' it no more!' His grip tightened until Andrew squealed. Then he brought his knee up hard into his stomach and as he doubled up, winded, Jason stepped back, breathing heavily from his exertion. In a while, Andrew straightened up. His face was bloody and his eyes wild with fright and pain. He began to walk down the cottage garden path but Jason said, 'Where d'you think you're going? I haven't finished yet.'

'Oh, for Chrissake!' Andrew's voice was thick and clotted with tears.

'Do you get my meanin'?' Jason came up behind him and spun him round so that they faced each other. He took hold of Andrew's shoulders, gently, and shook him a little – not roughly – and squeezed them as a football coach might do to one of his team. 'Well? Do you get my meanin'?'

'Yes.'

'Sure?'

'Yes, er, Jason.'

'Good!' said Jason, softly, still keeping hold of his shoulders. Then, before Andrew could blink, he fetched him a crashing head-butt. Andrew saw a white flash and collapsed.

He must only have been unconscious for a few seconds because when he came to, he heard the Mardles' cottage door closing quietly. He lay on the path for about a minute and then realised that it had been raining all the time and that he was very wet and cold. But he couldn't go home, not like this. He had to get cleaned up. He stood up and felt his face. The skin of his cheek was raw where Mardle's head had hit it, but his nose didn't seem to be broken and both eyes were in working order, although he could feel one closing up. The ache in his balls had spread deep into his abdomen and this worried him a lot.

He began to walk, passing the farm buildings and going into the meadow along the banks of the Venn. He didn't know where he was going or what to do. The rain was so hard now that he gave up trying to keep it out, indeed, looking upwards, feeling the cold water sluicing down his swelling face was quite relieving.

Gradually the intensity of the pain subsided to a series of aches and he turned back. Before going home, he thought of slipping into the farm office to clean up a bit. He began to think up an explanation. He would say that some of the cattle had broken out of the buildings, and when trying to round them up, he had fallen and been kicked.

He knew a short cut into the farmyard. Between the huge slurry lagoon and the back of the implement shed there was a narrow catwalk which, for the sure-footed, provided access. He approached the slurry lagoon, felt for the post-and-rail fencing at its edge and soon found the walkway. At one point his foot slipped on the wet concrete and he nearly lost his balance. He teetered on the edge of the lagoon – an evil-smelling lake of cowshit and water – and clutched at the wooden rail for support. It cracked ominously but held. If he had fallen in, his chances of survival would have been slim. The slurry would be too thick to swim in, but far too liquid to support him.

Up to that point, Andrew had been wishing he was dead, but this narrow escape changed his mind. He thought of Tracy's wonderful breasts and sighed. Then his aching body reminded him of Jason and he knew he wouldn't dare to carry on with her.

He let himself into his father's office. It was chilly, without the stove burning, but at least it was dry. He was about to look in one of the cupboards for a teacloth or something to dry himself when he heard the outer door open. He froze, not wanting anyone to disturb him. When he saw that it was Tracy, he felt fear rather than relief.

'You poor thing!' Seeing his darkening bruises, she was all sympathy.

'How on earth—?' He was on the brink of panic.

'I followed yer. After Jason left.'

'Where is he now?' Tracy shrugged. 'Christ, girl! Don't you realise what he'll do to me if he finds us?'

'Wha' about me? Don't I count?' Her lip trembled. Tenderness welled up in him but he dared not touch her.

'Of course you do.' She stepped towards him but he recoiled, folding his arms. 'But, Tracy . . . I don't think we can get married.'

'Wha'?'

'I think we must part. Pack it in. My people are against it. And so, it seems, are yours.' She stared at him. 'It's better this way, really it is.'

'But what about me?'

'I'll . . . I'll make sure our baby's all right.'

'But what about *me*?'

'I'll provide for him, of course. He'll have to be educated, naturally, but I can pay the fees.' He spoke faster as he warmed to his theme. 'And of course, he'll need a helping hand from time to time but we Kirklands will see to that. I've read a story like this somewhere. He may not know what his origins are but he'll have reason to be grateful, believe you me. He could even get a commission in a crack regiment or study medicine or – aaah!' On his bruised and broken face the slap of Tracy's hand stung fiercely.

'You feeble little *shit*!' she hissed. 'You and your soddin' storybook notions! Well, I ain't havin' the baby's 'ead filled with no daft borgee-oise notions and I ain't havin' nothin' more to do with you! If you wasn't so shaggin' ignorant you'd know the baby couldn't be yourn anyway.'

'What d'you mean?'

'I ain't sayin' nothin' more to you.' She swept out, leaving both doors open. Her slap had rekindled the pain in his body but that was nothing to the pain of seeing her go.

Chapter Twenty

Two years later to the day, Maggie and Leonard Bates were taking a siesta in Kenya.

The coconut palm outside their bedroom window sighed and shifted in the sudden breeze like a sleeper stirring before waking. This happened every afternoon at about the same time. The sun would dip towards the horizon, turning the Indian Ocean from turquoise to platinum; the breeze would come and soon, the little green lovebirds would arrive and chatter in the palm until the rapid tropical dusk swept away the colours and turned up the sound.

It was a signal to get up from the siesta bed, shower, decide what to wear, read awhile and then, to saunter down for a pre-dinner mingle with the other guests at the hotel. Disdainful in his faultless white jacket, the Muslim barman – inevitably known as Abdul although his real name was Ibrahim Yusif – would be dishing up daiquiris, Campari or gins and tonics for the tourists, and Tusker beer or Scotch for the old colonials.

For Maggie and Leonard, he reserved a special smile. On their first visit to East Africa, they had dithered at his bar, unable to decide what to drink. On the *Brisbane* they had satiated themselves with endless Cokes and Seven Ups, but had disliked the ship's canned fruit juices. When he had suggested one of his special cocktails, their abstinence from alcohol impressed him. Most of his customers were unable to get through the daily grind of holiday-making without a midday session and an evening of steady tippling. He had mixed pineapple juice with soda and added a dash of lime and a teaspoonful of passion fruit pulp. Maggie had eyed it. 'Looks foul,' she had said, 'specially with those passion fruit seeds.' She tasted. 'Mmm! Nothing a good slug of rum wouldn't put right.'

The barman's face had fallen. 'You want I put rum, Memsahib?'

'Not at all! Joke!' By the end of their twenty-four-hour respite from the ship, on that first trip, they had fallen quite badly for Kenya. The *Brisbane* had been due to sail for Colombo at dawn but the prospect of getting back into the confined community of dreary cruisers and misfit crew, surly now after four weeks with the same passengers, was not uplifting. Boredom had begun to load stress on top of Maggie's fight against alcoholism, and that concerned Leonard. It was only a few weeks, after all, since her drying-out had begun and she was still vulnerable, would always be vulnerable.

'Tell you what,' he had said, as they carried their fruit drinks into the hotel garden. 'Why don't we jump ship?'

Maggie had reflected for at least five seconds. 'Bloody brilliant idea,' she chortled. 'Another day with those blue-rinse widows and nancy-boy stewards and I'd have jumped overboard!'

After dining at the hotel, they had gone back on board, collected enough clothing to survive for a few days and told their astonished cabin steward that they'd see him in Sydney, where they would pick the ship up again in a couple of weeks.

Now, two years later, here they were again, sipping one of Abdul's fruity cocktails and anticipating a weekend by the sea before driving upcountry for ten days of plant-hunting and wildlife-watching. Maggie lifted her glass. 'Cheers Abdul,' she said, 'and good hunting to us!'

In Wyckhamby, on 21 September 1988, while the Bateses were foraging in the foothills of Mount Kenya, Cartwright Farmhouse was abuzz with chatter. Geoffrey Woods the bank manager was there with Elaine Kirkland, Jules Doncaster, the Rector, Betty's solicitor and a handful of selected friends. Ashley was in London and therefore unable to come and Sally Doncaster had had to decline because of a most *frightful* headache which had taken her quite by surprise that very afternoon.

The Rose youngsters were dispensing sparkling wine – less than four pounds a bottle but still *méthode Champenoise* – and ferrying hot canapés from the kitchen. With her back turned, it was almost impossible to tell Gill from her mother. Her shoulders had the same set and when she laughed, her chin came up and her head moved back in exactly the same way. Face to face, though, her features were more like Jack's, with dark, slightly sunken eyes yet holding Betty's open expression and innate appeal. She moved slowly among the guests, carrying a battered stainless steel dish of tiny sausages on sticks and, wherever she lingered, was quizzed about how she was enjoying Medical School and when she would qualify.

Mandy, eighteen now, was going to Leeds University in a couple of weeks to read History. She had always been the most balanced of the Rose children but was also closest to Camilla and felt the pain of her illness more keenly than the others. People who knew her well could detect the sorrow which underlay her placid temperament and understood the reasons for her frequent pensive spells. In contrast, Jim had become more extrovert. Asthma attacks were rare nowadays and, after a relaxed and largely trouble-free puberty – Betty had discovered girlie magazines under his mattress and had detected stains on his bedsheets but had turned a blind eye to both – he was developing into a personable young man. His passion for wildlife, and birds in particular, and his insatiable thirst for knowledge about them gave him a strong sense of purpose. Like the girls, he had agreed to help with the guests at his mother's party but unlike them, he had extracted the promise of a wage. There was, later in the year, to be a birdwatching trip to Costa Rica, and Jim was saving like mad, to buy a ticket.

When everyone's glass was full, Mr Woods tapped his with

a pen and the conversation died. 'Ladies and gentlemen,' he began, 'Queen Victoria once said, "We are not interested in the possibility of defeat." Two short years ago, this farm was facing a crisis.' He dropped his voice a semitone. 'There was a tragic accident and Betty here was left facing ruin.' He restored his pitch. 'Now you are all country-dwellers and as such, know very well that farming is not, as so many of my townee customers think, a piece of cake. I'm sure Betty won't mind me saying that back in the early Eighties, I didn't rate the chances of Cartwright Farm very highly.' He paused, put the pen into his breast-pocket, took a sip of his wine and continued: 'But I didn't allow for her resourcefulness, her determination and her growing business acumen. And I did not reckon on the common sense she was to exhibit, looking for a business partner. And what a lucky choice she has made.'

'Hear hear!' muttered someone.

'John Holman here has done much to help her to reconstruct her business. In two short years – just two years, ladies and gentlemen – this pair have salvaged a foundering venture. Not only have they been professional, timely with their cultivations and prudent with their management, but they have also been innovative.' He pronounced the word with the accent on the second syllable. 'Motorists can stop, now, at their Pick Your Own centre to gather anything from raspberries to Brussels sprouts. Next season, the farm shop opens, and there are various other plans afoot which I know about but which are still rather hush hush.' Geoff Woods ran on while the guests' attention began to wander.

'Seems almost like a wedding speech,' one muttered behind her hand. 'They'll be publishing the banns next! Mind you, partner or not, she'll need an 'usband.' Her neighbour sniffed and pretended not to hear. Betty was undefilable and infallible as far as she was concerned.

'And so,' Woods was grinding to the end of his homily, 'I offer Betty and John, on the formalising of their partnership, my heartiest congratulations and a toast to Cartwright Farm.'

'Cartwright Farm,' everyone said, although most of the

glasses that were raised were empty by now. There was ragged applause as Betty and John bent to sign the partnership documents laid out on the table. In the ensuing silence, Betty was expected to respond. She straightened up and put the lid back on her fountain pen.

'Well!' She felt rather flustered. It was embarrassing. 'Thank you all for coming. We are now, as you see, partners, and, well, that's that, really. Oh, Gill, Mandy, do see to everyone's glasses.' John did not speak. He simply nodded to the group of faces before him and went to help hand out nibbles.

There were several young children at the function and of these, the youngest, but not the smallest, was the twenty-month-old, dark-haired, beetle-browed Wayne Everitt, son of Tracy Everitt, née Mardle. He had already choked on a crisp, snatched from a fat child almost a year his senior and hit a fellow toddler over the head with a toy telephone, giving her a nasty bruise over her left eye. Now he was trying to dismantle the Roses' old-fashioned wooden playpen.

'That child has all the Mardle traits and not one of its father's,' Elaine Kirkland said. 'Isn't that odd?'

'Odd and rather a pity,' the Rector agreed. 'The father's an excellent boy. Works for you now, doesn't he?'

'Darren Everitt? Yes, he's second cowman. Small and wiry he may be, but what a worker! Dotes on Tracy, and he's *wonderful* with the cows. Ashley's delighted. He wants to put him into college so he can come back and take charge of the whole herd.'

Tracy Everitt came up to Elaine a moment later and said, 'I better take Wayne home now, Mrs Kirkland, 'e's gettin' a bit naughty.' She looked tired, Elaine thought, but that wasn't surprising. She was such a young girl to be in her second pregnancy. The baby must be nearly due now too.

'Good idea, Tracy. It isn't right for you to be standing up for too long.' Elaine smiled at her. 'When is it now?'

'Next week, or the week after. Darren'n I ain't sure.'

'No. Well, perhaps you should take your leave of Mrs Rose.'

'Take what?'

'Just say goodbye and thank her for having you. And make sure I get to say goodbye to Wayne before you take him.' She wanted another chance to scan the little boy's face for any trace of Andrew. It seemed that no one in the Mardle family had ever raised the question of the child's paternity, nor were they likely to now, but she wanted to set her own mind at rest. So far, she had not been able to spot the slightest hint of Kirkland blood. The child resembled the dreaded Jason Mardle more than anyone and seemed, already, to be exhibiting his nature as well as his looks.

A few days later, on a blustery Saturday morning, and with her unerring knack for bad timing, Sally Doncaster phoned Betty, who was wrestling with a cropping programme for the Pick Your Own project for next year and resented the break in concentration. She tossed her pen down and snatched the study telephone.

'Yes?'

'It's about Camilla. Not good.'

'Oh, Sally!' Betty forgot her pea and bean rotation. Camilla was confined to bed or a wheelchair these days.

'They want me to let her go into Kendale General.' Sally was agitated. She had resisted hospitalisation for as long as she could, feeling that the child would be so much more comfortable at home. 'She's very weak.'

'Don't you think that might be the best thing?'

'It would be for good, you know.' Betty stayed silent for a while. 'Are you still there?'

'Yes. What does Jules think?'

'Oh Jules, Jules! He doesn't know. I can't get any sense out of him at all.'

'It probably hurts him too much.'

'Oh I know, I know. But he can't . . . express anything. He just bottles it up. He's lost so much weight this year. I'm worried sick about him. I feel so *guilty*.'

'Why should you feel guilty?' There was no answer, just a sort of gulp. 'You have a loving relationship. You're lucky to have that.' Betty was surprised to hear a cackle of bitter laughter.

'Loving? That's hilarious, that is. We haven't touched each other for ages. Not since, oh, I don't know.' She paused, 'Well, I *do* know really.' There was a long gap, then, 'Christ, I've never told anyone this . . . but there's no one to tell, except you.' Betty changed hands and put the phone to her other ear. 'Remember that barbecue? When Camilla had her first nasty fall?'

'That was years ago.'

'Well . . . I, well . . .' Sally's voice wobbled and she stopped speaking.

'Don't tell me if you don't want to.'

'No, wait.' Sally pulled herself together. 'Just before Camilla's accident, Simon, you know, the Prince's son? He played that silly trick, if you remember, and I was a bit harsh with him? Well, after everyone had gone home he went to his room and I was afraid he might be sulking, so I went to see whether he was all right and—'

'Don't tell me, Sally. You don't need to.'

'No, Betty, I want to, I do.' She blew her nose. 'Betty, that kind of beauty, I can't tell you. That boy's body was the most perfect—'

'Sally, I shouldn't be hearing this. You're overwrought. I ought to ring off.'

'No, don't! Please don't! I'll spare you the details. But, you see, afterwards I felt so miserable and guilty that I went and blabbed to Jules and instead of hitting me or screaming at me or going out to screw some doxy, the way most men would—'

'Would they?'

'Betty, don't be naive! Anyway, Jules didn't do or say anything. Or did he? Yes, I think he just said, "I see," and that was that.'

'Oh.'

'And he hasn't touched me since. He's cold – inside, I mean. Cold as ice.'

'Sally, I'm sorry.'

'And now, with Camilla so ill, he's just eating himself alive.'

'Like the Spartan boy.'

'The what?'

'With the fox under his cloak.'

There was a puzzled silence. 'What *can* you mean?'

'Doesn't matter. What about Camilla?'

'Oh Betty, that's the biggest worry. I don't want her to go to hospital. I can't bear to think of her going through all that . . . that indignity.'

'No, but it may be better for her. Have you asked her what she wants?'

'Won't say. Poor sweet, she's so drugged up she doesn't really know what she's doing. But there's another complication.'

'Oh?'

'I've been spending too much time at home. My business is suffering.'

'I'm sorry.'

'The October crash last year was bad for Jules, too. We're nowhere near as liquid as we should be. The fact is, I've got to give the firm more time or we'll be in financial trouble. That means not being able to spend as much time as I should with Camilla.' She paused. Betty heard rustling and then nose-blowing sounds. 'I might even sell my business.'

'But it's your life's work!'

'I can't neglect Camilla.'

'No, I see that.' There was another silence. 'Are you still there?'

'Yes. You know, Betty, I envy you.'

'Oh!'

'No. I do. Things have really fallen into place for you.'

For Ashley, things were falling out of place. The worldwide 1987 stock-market crash had shocked his London world and confidence continued to ebb as the business community talked itself into recession. The clients who remained with Kirkland Wild were, by and large, loyal, but were working with much tighter budgets these days, reducing profits for the firm. And, as if outside events were not disconcerting enough, Ashley's partner Philip Wild, who did most of the work, had been expressing dissatisfaction. The PR industry was getting altogether too competitive, he felt. He had talked, several times, of selling his share and doing something else. Ashley knew that the firm depended on Wild for survival.

At home, thank God, things were better. He had enjoyed two easy farming years with good autumns and bountiful harvests. Commodity prices were far too low, but Wyckhamby Farms were efficient enough to be able to perform well, in spite of that. He was coming down to London for two or three days a week nowadays and had his own flat in Hampstead, above board this time and occasionally used by Elaine when she came here to shop or do a theatre. When she wasn't there, the flat's location was convenient for Hampstead Heath, particularly the spot where homosexuals were wont to gather.

Guy Wilson's personality had developed, now, in such detail that he seemed not only more real to Ashley, each time he adopted the Wilson mantle, but was ever more sharply contrasted with Ashley's respectable self. His promiscuity continued to grow, driving him to hunt for partners, blunting his selectivity and pushing him into taking bigger risks. This morning, as he worked through his post at Kirkland Wild, he thought of the ginger-haired boy he'd been with last night. The sexual encounter had had the usual anonymity but afterwards, the young man had wanted to talk about his background. It seemed that he had been unable to face telling his parents or his girlfriend about his sexual orientation and had slipped away to London where he now worked as a waiter. There was nothing very unusual about that, but when the boy told Guy that his family farmed in Lincolnshire, not far from Louth, Ashley felt a jolt of unease.

Ashley's frequent absences suited Andrew. His father was still an uncomfortable presence but they had, over the last couple of years, developed a level of respect for each other.

Since he had been beaten up by Jason and brushed off by Tracy, Andrew had kept himself aloof from the Mardles, and the rest of the villagers for that matter.

After that night, when Andrew had limped home and refused to discuss his injuries or their cause with anyone, Elaine had gone over to the Mardles' cottage to speak to mother and daughter. She had quizzed Tracy about what had been going on with Andrew. Tracy had stonewalled.

'But you *are* pregnant?'

'Oh ah!'

'And Andrew is the father?'

'If you say so.'

'What do *you* say?' But the girl had sat glaring at her. She was a pretty thing, Elaine thought. Such a pity about that awful voice, though.

Less then a month later, she heard from Bert that Tracy was going to marry Darren Everitt, another village boy. The pregnancy was not alluded to, neither was the beating up. Clearly, thought Elaine, there was more to all this than they were admitting to. But she had left it at that.

Ashley had begun to introduce Andrew to commodity trading – buying and selling futures. At first, it bored him – everything bored him – but after a while, he began to understand the market systems. As soon as he discovered that everything depended on price movements, he began to find out what caused such movements. He started to read the agricultural and business press, following a select list of commodities.

'Go for crops that we grow and know,' Ashley had advised, 'like wheat, barley, potatoes. They should keep you occupied for now. Don't do any real trading yet – follow the prices and keep a record of what you would have bought and what you would have sold, and when and why, and show me in a month how you've done.'

Andrew did as he was bid, getting prices from the *Financial Times*. His first month's figures showed a substantial loss, and he thanked God it was only make-believe. He fudged his results to show his father how well he had done. It was easy:

all he had to do was go back over the pretend transactions and re-do them with the added advantage of hindsight. The exercise taught him his most important lesson – that he who knows most about *everything* pertaining to the market is the most able to predict its movements.

By the time he was ready to start trading for real, with his father breathing firmly down his neck, he had developed a level of acumen which surprised everyone. Within a year, he was a relatively competent trader, earning a respectable income in his own right, as well as dealing with the farm's crops. He branched into other products and burnt his fingers a time or two, wiping out his entire year's income on one particularly injudicious deal. That scared him, and thereafter he stuck mainly to the three original commodities that had started him off: wheat, barley and potatoes.

He also began to deal a little in soya-bean meal, a by-product of the vegetable oil industry which was used as a protein-rich animal feed. A couple of lucky transactions aroused his interest and he soon became learned in all matters relating to the commodity: which countries grew it, where most of the processing took place and, above all, what factors dictated price changes. Soon he recovered all the money he had lost in his early trading and was beginning to build up his own capital.

But now he was playing the dangerous game of over-speculating. A sharp, unexpected movement in the market could wipe him out and, since he was trading with his father as guarantor, he was not just steering himself into jeopardy but was putting the whole of Wyckhamby Farms at risk. On this gamble, there was much to gain, he knew, but he managed to make himself forget that there was also everything to lose.

Chapter Twenty-one

As Betty Rose opened the stiff, frosted glass doors of the Royal Horticultural Hall in Westminster, a scent of chrysanthemums, blending with the bitter tang of evergreens and the earthiness of peat compost, brought back memories of childhood and her father's greenhouse in Sussex.

The hall burgeoned with colour. 'I can hardly believe it's November,' she told Maggie, taking in the huge displays of autumn flowers, shrubs covered with berries in a range of colours from blood red through scarlet and amber to yellow, and trees, transported whole from nursery and arboretum, looking glorious in their autumn livery.

'It's still pretty early,' Maggie said. 'Guy Fawkes' Day tomorrow.' She opened her scuffed leather handbag and took out a spiral-topped secretary's pad. 'Got your notebook?'

'Rather!' Betty fished for it. 'I want to get lots of new ideas.' They had come to the Late Autumn Flower Show to select plants for a couple of borders she wanted to replant. Now that Cartwright Farm was profitable, she felt she could afford to spend a modest amount on revamping part of the garden, to make it easier to maintain but still interesting, particularly in autumn and winter. Maggie, who was back in business in a very small way as a garden designer, had agreed to help her with the planting plan.

'You need some bold greenery. Something that'll shout at you in winter but make a decent background in summer,' she had said, when they had looked, together, at the garden in mid-October. 'Your borders are all perennials at the moment – very pretty in June but bugger-all to look at on Boxing

Day.' Then she had suggested a trip to London. 'Some of the best nurseries exhibit at those flower shows, every month. Let's go and see what they've got to show us.'

'I don't know whether I can get away.'

'Go on!' Maggie urged. 'Christ knows, you need a break!' It would be Betty's first day away from the farm in seven months.

'We-ell. There's the pigs – but John could do them.' She pondered; warmed to the idea. 'Why not?' The next show was less than a week away.

'Look at all these different kinds of holly,' Maggie said, leading the way to the first of the big trade stands. 'Now these would make a marvellous backdrop, especially this.' With her calloused thumb, she traced the edge of a leaf. It was nearly thornless with a cream border and a trio of dark red berries at its base. 'This one's a cracker but you'll need to plant a male tree nearby if you want it to berry like this at home.' They moved slowly from one stand to another, making notes, talking to the nurserymen and enjoying the plants. During the morning, several people from the horticultural world recognised and greeted Maggie but one or two looked shifty and scuttled away. As noon approached, they decided to take a breather.

'Perfect spot for a sandwich downstairs,' Maggie said, and led the way to the cafeteria. They bought snack lunches, found an empty table and sat down. Sod it,' Maggie said, 'we didn't get drinks.'

'I'll go.' Betty jumped up again, just a touch too quickly. 'What do you want?'

'Mineral water. And a coffee.' Betty was soon back, and after they had talked at length about her garden, the subject turned to the village and then, for some reason, to Ashley. Betty usually shunned talk behind others' backs but here, in London, it seemed somehow less wrong. Since Jack had died she had had no close relationships and often felt a longing to express herself to someone on an intimate level. John Holman was a good listener, of course, but that was a business relationship. She had no interest of a romantic nature in anyone, but she still harboured a special fondness, in spite of everything, for Ashley. The physical magnetism was still there, stronger now than before, actually, and the mysterious side of his nature fascinated her. Try as she might, she had never managed to fathom out the reasons for his changeable character. She wondered what Maggie felt.

'What do you make of our squire?' She tended to think of him as a Victorian squire, powerful in country life but, on the whole, benevolent.

Maggie shrugged. 'Ashley? A good egg, definitely.'

'A curate's egg, I sometimes think.'

'Good in parts? No, surely not.'

'He nearly destroyed us. Did you know?' Maggie looked up from her sandwich. Betty corrected herself. 'No, that's too strong. He did give us a worrying time, though, a couple of years ago.'

'But he offered you a job, too. In Australia.'

'Oh yes. That's the extraordinary thing about the man. He seemed hellbent on getting rid of us one minute and then was all over us the next. There was no rhyme nor reason to it.'

'Well, it doesn't really matter now, does it?'

'No, except that he *is* our landlord.'

'Well, as long as you pay your rent.' They drank their coffee and Maggie lit a cigarette. 'You don't mind?' she gestured. Betty shook her head. 'You see, I happen to be a big fan of Ashley's. I think he's one of the few truly benevolent people. He actually tries to do good, I mean literally, do good. The village would be buggered without him. Well, without the two of you. I don't know how you manage to do so much for everyone.'

'Oh, really!' Betty flipped a dismissive hand.

'And I'll tell you something else.' Maggie leaned forward to stress her point, covering her sandwich plate with a tweed-clad bosom, 'I'm fairly sure he helped me with that big landscape project at Rutland University.'

'But you lost that!'

'Yes, but not because of him. It was that prick of a Vice Chancellor. Him and his dons – load of bloody wankers!'

316

Betty glanced anxiously round as Maggie's voice boomed across the Royal Horticultural Society's cafeteria. 'If you'll pardon my French!'

'More coffee?'

'No thanks. Don't want to be piddling all afternoon. Let's go and finish the show.' They gathered their notebooks and bags and returned to the plants.

After a full, and anxiety-ridden week at Kirkland Wild, Ashley decided to take a longer spell in the country than usual, and to turn his attention to agriculture. He was aware that he had not spent more than a few days on end at Wyckhamby for months now, and though the farms were faring well enough in his absence, they would surely benefit from a spell of closer management.

In spite of the declining year, he found it impossible not to feel optimistic, especially when the slanting November sunshine gathered enough strength to shed a little warmth over the countryside. One indication of his recent absence was a falling behind in the routine trimming of all the farm hedges. Normally this would have irritated him, and his instructions to Mardle to fit the flail-cutter to one of the tractors would have been curt. But this morning, seeing the hedgerow cobwebs silvered with dewdrops and blackberries still hanging in rich clusters, he decided to stay his hand for another couple of weeks. As he walked the lane towards the nearest of the sugar-beet fields, he noticed a cock pheasant, less than twenty feet in front, pecking the lower blackberries. He stopped to watch the sunlight on its russet back feathers and glinting on its iridescent green head as it pecked one fruit after another with mechanical rhythm. Ashley reached out to pick a few blackberries. The pheasant saw him and froze for a split second before creeping silently but swiftly into the thick undergrowth at the base of the hedge.

The sugar-beet harvest was proceeding smoothly and he was pleased to see that the men had got further through the field than he had dared hope. The culmination of eight months' nursing of this most capricious of crops always filled him with anxiety. Weather was only slightly less critical than with a corn harvest, but there were plenty of other hazards. Sugar-beet was bought by one monopolistic purchaser – the British Sugar Corporation, and payment was based not on yield but on sugar content. That was always an unknown quantity and, since the Corporation did all the analyses in its own laboratories, one was never quite sure how accurate their figures really were. There were swingeing penalties for supplying beets which were too dirty and, a constant threat in chilly Lincolnshire, early frost could freeze and spoil newly-lifted roots, turning them into a stinking liquid mush. But this crop looked promising and so far, reports from the factory at Peterborough had been favourable.

Ashley busied himself for several days about the farm and, within a week, had satisfied himself that his existing business was running as near perfectly as was possible. But ideas of expansion and improved efficiency still attracted him, and he decided to visit Betty Rose – after all, she was his tenant and nearest neighbour – to talk about possible joint ventures. He walked over to Cartwright Farm on a bright afternoon, with the low sun shining on his face. He had phoned Betty in the morning and when he arrived, she already had the tea things set out for him. John, who had moved into a cottage in the village High Street, had gone home early to rest a head cold.

'We don't seem to meet as often as we used to, Betty. I regret that.' He sat in the proffered chair, accepting tea and scrutinising the blue band, painted with white *putti* on the porcelain cup. 'This is Worcester, isn't it?'

'Coalport. It belonged to my mother, who died earlier this year.'

'I'm sorry.'

'Don't be – it was not unexpected.'

'And I'm sorry I couldn't come to your partnership thing.'

'Oh that!' She made a dismissive gesture. 'Just a minor celebration.'

'And how is your partnership doing?'

'Well enough.'

'Gossip has it that you two will be even closer soon.' He sounded arch, expecting a reaction. There wasn't one.

'Village talk, nothing more. The partnership is purely a business arrangement.'

'Is that so?' He felt relieved to hear it, heaven knew why.

'What about you, Ashley? How are all your enterprises?'

'Kirkland Wild? Not quite so good. This downturn that's coming worries me. In the City, they keep talking about a "soft landing", whatever that means. All I know is that PR has taken a nose dive and we are having to work twice as hard to make the same money.'

'Farming's a bit like that. On the scale we do it here, anyway.'

'That is rather what I wanted to talk about. It's going to get harder, in the future, and I think cooperation may become the only way forward.'

'But your business is so huge and ours so small.'

'Even so,' he got up, handed her his cup for a refill and sat down beside her on the sofa. 'I'm sure we ought to be looking at the possibility of some kind of joint venture.' His proximity on the sofa was disturbing. Not unpleasant, quite the reverse, but it made her feel awkward. She couldn't stop herself from looking to see whether the little curl on the nape of his neck was still there. It was.

'What kind of venture did you have in mind?' She could feel her heart beating faster. He looked at her but she turned her eyes away and he could see the pulse in her neck.

'I've been thinking that beef might be a possible one. Quality beef, some of which you could sell through your farm-shop. We could share the cost of buying in calves and make use of some of your old buildings as well as our new shed. You need to do something with your grassland, unless you are going back into sheep.' He chatted about beef cattle, looking into her grey eyes and wanting to squeeze her hand to press home the salient points, but not quite daring to.

She watched the colour of his complexion changing as he warmed to his subject; watched the animation in his eyes and the enthusiasm when he explained about growth rates and carcass conformation. As they talked, the daylight failed and the room turned almost dark. They heard a vehicle driving into the yard and soon the back door opened. John Holman came in, turned on the light and stared at them, dazzled and blinking in the glare.

'Hullo! Feeling any better?' Betty asked. He nodded. 'I expect you'd like some tea.' She jumped up and went to the kitchen to make a fresh pot.

'We were talking about beef,' Ashley said. He found John's yellow-blond hair and pale eyes particularly unappealing. 'A possible joint venture.'

'Why?'

'Well, with hard times coming, I think we should all look at areas of possible cooperation.'

'Ah.'

'Do you disagree?'

'No.' John looked awkward standing with one hand behind his back holding onto his other elbow.

'Good.' There was a silence. 'What *do* you think?'

'About beef? It's a non-starter.'

'Oh?' Ashley felt himself becoming monosyllabic in the presence of this taciturn creature. 'How so?'

'The health lobby. People are becoming vegetarians. Besides, the calf cost always kills it.'

'I see.' Another silence. 'Can you think of any other area where our farms could cooperate?'

'I couldn't discuss anything like that without Betty.'

'No, of course not. But even so, can you think of any likely areas of mutual interest?'

'Not offhand, no.' And that seemed to be that. By the time Betty reappeared, Ashley was finding it difficult to suppress his anger and wanted to leave. Betty walked with him to the lane.

'I don't think your partner approves of me,' he said.

'Oh, I'm sure he does. It's just his manner – he doesn't talk a lot.'

'Are all East Anglians as moody as that?'

'I think quite a lot of the Fen people are.'

'Well, in spite of what he says about beef, Betty, think it over, won't you?'

'Of course I will. We should do some figures.'

'Attagirl!' On a sudden impulse, he put both arms round her, wrapped her in a warm hug and kissed her on the forehead. As quickly, he released her and jogged down the lane waving as he went, although it was too dark for her to see. She had to wait for a full minute while her heart-rate returned to normal before walking back into the house.

'That Doncaster woman phoned,' said John, as she walked into the sitting room, 'just to make sure you're still able to go over tomorrow. I said you'd ring back if not.'

Next morning, after feeding the pigs, Betty drove over to the Rectory in the new – or at least, new to Cartwright – Landrover. She was to get a briefing from Sally who was planning what she felt might be her last trip to Mudando for quite a while. Betty would visit Camilla at Kendale General every day until Sally got home, probably in early December.

'Betty, I *have* to go.' Sally was tearful. 'I simply cannot put this off a moment longer.'

'I know.'

'But if anything should . . . You know, if any—'

'I'll get hold of you. I've got all the numbers.'

'I mean, if you feel that things are, you know, *about* to—'

'Sally, please don't torture yourself. I'll do whatever's necessary. Just try to enjoy your visit and do the best deal you can. Worrying isn't going to do anyone any good.'

Next morning, as she flew over the arid lands of North West Africa, landed at Kano in Nigeria and took her connecting flight to Mudando, Sally thought of little else but that poor, brittle creature in Kendale General. Whenever she closed her own eyes she saw Camilla's glittering with pain, the brows damp with sweat, the hair matted and stuck to her scalp. She willed herself to put these images to the back of her mind and to concentrate on the business in hand.

Simon would be waiting at Mudando airport to meet her, as usual. How she looked forward to seeing him! When he had been staying with them at Wyckhamby, just after getting his degree, he had been no more than a boy, childish, in spite of his glowing academic achievements, and rather spoilt. But over the last couple of years he had matured. Now he was a man, full of laughter, with a wicked twinkle in his eye and a spring in his walk that made him seem almost to lurch as he strode along, but for all that, he had the gravitas and stature of a man.

He had come out onto the tarmac to greet her as she stepped off the plane into the searing heat. 'Sally! Sally!' He embraced her. 'We're all so sorry about Camilla and everything.' Exhausted from her long flight, and from a string of sleepless nights at home, she was quite unable to control her emotions any longer. She burst into tears and wept copiously and noisily onto his ample shoulder. In Europe, this might have been unseemly, but here it was perfectly acceptable and indeed, Simon took it as a rich compliment, even though her tears made the colours run on his beautiful robes. He held her for several minutes while his admiring aides looked on, their faces contorted with sympathetic grimaces.

Later, at the Prince's air-conditioned house, after doffing her damson and cream cotton outfit, showering, resting, and then donning the set of Mudandan Robes that had been laid out for her, Sally strolled through to the building's large central room for an audience.

The Prince rose, kissed both her temples and then motioned her to a chair near his own. 'My dear, dear Mrs Doncaster,' he said, keeping hold of her hand. 'I could hardly believe you wanted to desert us, but then I heard the details of your sad, sad news from Simon here,' he indicated his son, standing behind the throne. 'We are so sorry.'

Once sympathies had been expressed, Sally began to talk to father and son about selling her business. Negotiations would proceed at a gentle pace and could be expected to last for several days. But, since the parties' interests were, by and large, common, the atmosphere would be harmonious throughout. The Prince was interested in acquiring the majority share of Raylon Tropicals and would turn it into a Mudandan firm with Simon at the helm. Sally would keep a minority share-holding in the company and would provide advice from time to time, visiting Mudando about once a year. The price they offered was reasonable, the terms acceptable. Within a week, they had drawn up contracts.

Sally made daily use of the Prince's telephone to keep in contact with Betty who was plotting Camilla's progress. Each day, the message was the same – no change. She spent the afternoons, when the rest of the household slept, by the Prince's swimming pool, accompanied by Simon. Each morning, before breakfast, she borrowed one of the Prince's quieter horses and rode into the bush, with Simon at her side. Each evening, she feasted on local delicacies, with Simon to advise her on which would best suit her Western palate and which might prove challenging. As with every visit she made to Mudando, he was attentive and entertaining.

By the ninth day, the whole business of agreeing to sell her firm was just about buttoned up, but the Prince seemed to be hunting for reasons why she should extend her stay. When she spoke of going home he looked crestfallen and said: 'They'll want to see you up country. Won't you visit them first?'

'Oh Prince!' Sally sighed. 'I knew you'd ask and I *do* want to, but I must get home this time because of Camilla.'

'You will be missed, especially now that your visits will be so far between and few.'

'I know. Oh, I know!' That evening, before going to dine, she decided that twenty-four more hours would be enough and was about to dial the airport to book her flights when she caught sight of a shadow among the draperies at the doorway of her suite.

'Hullo?' She was slightly alarmed, thinking it to be a servant. They were all fascinated by her belongings and by her. Even in these jet-age days, few white people visited Mudando. But it was Simon who stepped out of the shadows.

'How long have you been there?'

'Five minutes.' For once, he was not smiling. 'You are ready to go, aren't you?'

She rested her hand on his folded arms and smiled.

'I must. Tomorrow.'

'So soon?'

'I'll be back.' She gave his upper arm a little squeeze. He sighed. 'Don't be sad.'

He was silent for a while. 'It won't be the same. Not now. You won't have a reason to come.'

'Of course I will! There *is* a contract, you know.'

'Once a year?' He walked over to the window and opened it. The sound of crickets filled the room and a surge of tropical air, laden with the scent of frangipani, cancelled the air conditioning. 'Do the past few days have any meaning?'

'Meaning? Of course they have meaning. I've loved it. And you, Simon, you've been a poppet!'

'A . . . poppet?'

'Utterly!'

'And that's it?' He still wasn't smiling.

'What do you want me to say? You know I love it here, especially when we go up-country. But I can't stay, Simon, much as I want to.'

'And now you've sold the business, we'll hardly see you.'

'Simon! Whatever's the matter?'

'That night at Wyckhamby? Remember that?' His voice harshened with emotion.

'An aberration!' She reached past him to shut the window. The air conditioning began to cool and deodorise the room again. 'You were just an excitable boy and I was over-wrought. It won't happen again.'

'I still want you!'

'Ridiculous!' The discordant edge in her laughter cut him. 'I'm old enough to be your mother!'

'If you don't feel the same for me as I do for you, you shouldn't mock me.' He turned to stare at the window.

'Feel the same? Oh my *God*, Simon, if you only knew what I feel for you.' He turned back to face her. 'But that is just desire.' The hurt on his face alarmed her. 'Oh, my dear boy, that was unfair. I *am* fond of you, deeply fond. But it simply isn't *right*, don't you see?'

'I do not.'

'What would your father say?'

'My father has advised me to come and speak to you.' She stared. 'His fondest hope was that ... Well, it's irrelevant now.' He turned to leave.

She called softly: 'Simon! There is one other little matter.' He halted in the doorway. 'What about Jules? Mudandan morals do run to marital fidelity, do they not?'

'You have no marriage.' He spat the words out in a toneless staccato. 'From all you have said on your visits here, and from what happened to us in England, I have no doubt of that. As far as you are concerned, your husband may as well be dead.'

He walked out of the bedroom.

Chapter Twenty-two

Breakfast at Bridge House was a rather distracted affair of burnt toast and slopped coffee, punctuated by the rustle of newspaper pages and the occasional slurp or crunch. By the time Maggie's *Independent* and Leonard's *Telegraph* arrived in the mornings, they would both have been sated with news from BBC Radio, but their broadsheets were as useful as barricades for each to preserve their personal space as for reading. Maggie usually worked through her paper the wrong way round, checking the radio listings first – she never watched television now – then finding the arts page and the leading articles, turning finally, if there was any time left over, to the front pages.

This morning, just as she was about to skip the Business Section, she noticed a picture of a face that looked familiar. 'Philip Wild,' the caption said, 'seeking refuge in a larger pool.' Surely he'd been at one of Elaine Kirkland's awful parties?

'Good God, Len, just listen to this!' she said, and read aloud: '"Another victim of the current slump in Public Relations is Kirkland Wild, originally one of the brightest of the new stars in this ailing industry. After a disastrous year, Philip Wild, one of its most senior partners, has resigned and will join forces with Sherborne Humphris, it was revealed yesterday, leaving behind a debilitated company with a depleted client list. The other main partner, Ashley Kirkland, is said by some ex-colleagues to have contributed capital rather than talent to the company."' She skimmed the text to find more salient points, '"Yesterday, Mr Kirkland did not deny that he was seeking a buyer for Kirkland Wild, but City analysts say that its worth will be difficult to assess." Oh, listen, Leonard, this is awful!' Maggie read on: ' "In today's uncertain climate, without a solid backing and track record in Public Relations, Kirkland will probably find it less costly to cut his losses – which in KW's case are extensive – wind up his crippled firm and focus on his, presumably more profitable, farming activities." '

As soon as breakfast was over and Leonard had gone off to surgery, she dumped the dirty plates in the sink on top of last night's supper things and went to rummage in her desk for the notes she had scrawled about Betty's garden. They were untidy to look at but their content was professional enough and would serve Betty well. She grabbed her *Independent* and a handful of plant catalogues from the top of the kitchen dresser, threw on her winter coat – a shapeless affair in black and beige dogtooth check – and began to walk over to Cartwright Farm. A sharp overnight frost had lined the margins of the Venn with ice and coated the low-lying grasses of the water meadows with rime.

She met John Holman in the yard, bent over an ancient implement whose function was a mystery to her, and greeted him cheerfully. 'Lovely sharp morning!' He looked up and gave a half-smile. 'What is that contraption?'

'An old horse-hoe. I'm hoping to convert it for the strawberries.'

'I didn't think strawberries and horses had that much in common.' His spanner paused over a rusted stud. 'To pull *through* the strawberry crop.'

'But you haven't got a horse.'

'No.' He pondered for a moment, smiled to himself and then said, 'and it needs a special one for this job – a strawberry roan!'

'Oh ha bloody ha!' Maggie was surprised at the first show of humour she had ever detected in this quiet but, she felt sure, decent man. 'Betty in the house?'

'As far as I know.'

Maggie walked to the back door, opened it and hallooed. Betty's muffled reply emanated from within.

'In the study!' Maggie found her at her desk surrounded by papers and struggling with a calculator. 'Pull up a pew!'

'Most extraordinary thing,' Maggie moved a pile of *Farmers Weeklies* from the carved oak chair beside the desk and sat down, 'but your partner has just cracked a joke!'

'Never! Must be a mistaken identity!'

'Just what I thought. You could have knocked me daan wiv a fevver!'

'Actually, John does have a sense of humour – quite a healthy one. People think he's sullen, but he's not; he's just quiet, and rather shy.'

'Hullo! Do I detect more than a dab of fondness?'

'Not in the way you mean.'

'Oh ah! That's your story.'

Betty began, with the merest hint of agitation, to stack her papers, making room on the desk. 'You're just as bad as the rest!'

'How d'you mean?'

'If I'd taken on a female partner, not a soul would have commented, but because I'm a widow, and the new partner happens to be male, everyone seems hellbent on matchmaking.'

'You can see their point of view.'

'Not from where I am. John is a professional farmer and I rate his ability pretty high. I also rather like him. He was a saint during Jack's illness, I'd have gone under without him. But as for the other thing,' she met Maggie's gaze, 'nothing. Nothing at all.'

'The other thing? What can you possibly mean?'

'Maggie! Stop teasing!'

'Aha! You mean Lorve! Affairs of ze, 'ow you say in Eengleesh, ze 'eart!'

Betty giggled. 'That is positively the worst French accent I have ever heard.' She indicated the space she had cleared on the desk. 'Let's get down to work. Did you bring those catalogues?'

328

'There's something you should read in the paper first, if you haven't seen it already, about your landlord.'

Betty took the *Independent* and, as she scanned the article, John came into the room. 'This is terrible,' she said, absently mouthing the text. 'Poor Ashley!'

'There's not much poor about him,' John said. He read over Betty's shoulder. 'Must be down to his last million.'

'You shouldn't be envious, John,' Betty said, 'it isn't like you.' John said nothing. 'I know what it's like to have a foundering business.'

Oh come on Betty!' Maggie said. 'I love Ashley dearly – he's the most scrumptious thing since they invented Crunchie bars – but he's only losing part of an empire. You were struggling for survival.'

'And no thanks to him, you did survive,' John said.

'But on balance, he's helped more than he's hindered.' The steadfast look on Betty's face, familiar to both John and Maggie, discouraged further discussion.

Later that day, when rainclouds had gathered on a westerly wind, melting the hoarfrost and making the footpaths greasy with mud, Ashley and Andrew met in the Wyckhamby Farms buildings to discuss commodity trading. Since he had shown himself to be competent, and contributed handsome profits to the farm's coffers, Ashley allowed his son full autonomy, but still liked an occasional report, as much to make the boy feel that he was part of the general enterprise as to supervise him.

Independence, once he had got over the frightening part of having responsibilities, suited Andrew. Not only was he trading for Wyckhamby Farms but, unbeknown to Ashley, or to anyone else in the family, he was running a personal account and was earning himself a tidy income. All the security for his private activities came from the farm's capital reserves, so, unless he made a large blunder, he could hardly fail.

After the demise of Kirkland Wild, his father was in a dark mood. 'If there's one thing I find utterly intolerable,' he said, 'it's being underhand.' He looked tired. His beard was growing, after a hasty shave that morning, and his eyes were bloodshot and black-edged. He poured himself a whisky, even though it was mid-afternoon. 'That bloody Wild! Sneaking off in that *creepy* way. And at a time like this!' He waved the decanter at Andrew who shook his head, and poured himself another slug. 'If the bastard had only told me he wanted out, we could have found a replacement, together, and then he could have gone – with good grace.'

'Ah, but that way, he couldn't have taken half the clients with him.'

'My God, Andrew, you *are* learning!' The boy smiled; praise from his father was still at a premium. 'I don't think you began to use your brain until you were about twenty.'

'I didn't even know I had one!'

'Thanks to your trading futures, we've done bloody well on barley, wheat and potatoes. God knows, we'll need that extra dosh this year.'

'How much do you reckon you'll lose on KW?'

'KW? You make it sound like lubricating jelly!' Ashley went quiet for a moment, and then, 'Lose? Oh, I don't know. Three hundred thousand. Maybe even half a million.'

Andrew was shocked. It was a large figure in comparison with their total turnover, and farming wasn't nearly as profitable now as it had been in the late 1970s when Ashley had expanded his business so fast.

'That's a big figure.'

'Could be even more!'

'The firm could end up making a total loss this year, then?'

'I'm sure we will.'

'What are we going to do?'

'Oh don't worry, we're loaded with assets. We can lose for quite a while and survive.' But the ignominy of failure, Ashley thought, hurt more than the financial loss. He reached for the decanter again but changed his mind and walked over to Andrew. 'Enough of this gloom! Come on, show me what you've been doing. Cheer your old father up.'

Andrew put a set of disks into the computer and filled its

screen with the latest records on his trading: they made wholesome reading. After half an hour or so, Ashley was satisfied that all his questions had been answered and that his suggestions had struck the right note with Andrew.

'Seen enough?' Andrew said.

'Absolutely. You seem to know more about the job than I do now.' Andrew preened. He took the disks out of the computer and switched it off. 'One query, though. Weren't you trading in soya beans as well as wheat, barley and potatoes?'

Andrew looked alarmed and then quickly re-composed his features. 'Yes, but only in a small way. These,' he tapped the disks they had just been looking at, 'are the main ones.'

But Ashley had caught that little sideways shift of the eyes and the cleared throat. 'Ought I to look?'

'Not necessary.' The little dry cough again. 'It's just a small thing.'

'Still,' Ashley turned the computer back on, 'I'd just like to glance.' He held his hand out for the disk. Andrew passed it to him.

'Actually, I am out on a slight limb at the moment. With soya, I mean.'

Ashley did not respond but called the appropriate page up on the screen. 'This is your stock held?' He ran a finger down a column of figures.

'Futures, yes.

'And these are the prices you bought at?'

'You know they are.' Andrew's voice had gone quiet and husky.

'But Jesus Christ, man! You bought too dear!' Andrew was silent. 'What's today's spot price? If you sell today, what would you lose?'

'I'm not quite sure.'

'Isn't there a gismo on this thing that will tell you?' Ashley tapped at the keys but kept snarling up the computer's electronic logic. 'Here, you do it.' He stood behind him and called out prices. Andrew fed the information into the computer as he heard it. They waited while the numbers were crunched in the works behind the green screen. Figures began to appear, first in a line, then as columns and finally as totals.

'You're twenty-seven thousand pounds out!' Ashley walked across the room and back again, shouting, 'How could you have been such a cretin?'

'Stay cool, Dad! It's not what you think.'

'Not what I *think*? Are you saying you haven't lost twenty-seven thousand?'

'I haven't sold. I'm waiting on the market.'

'Waiting on the market?' Ashley bellowed. 'Haven't you *seen* the headlines? The Americans have forecast a glut of the stuff. That's why the prices are collapsing.'

'Father, try to calm down!' Andrew was shaking. 'This is why I didn't want you to see. I still want to wait on the market.'

'Until your loss doubles? Oh no, my boy. You sell!'

'Father, please! That would be a panic move.'

Ashley poured another drink, put it down untouched and paced up and down, tripping on the carpet edge once and swearing.

'Do you know what you are doing? I mean, do you *really* know?'

'Nobody in this game really knows. You just build up as much info as you can and then gamble. They're all calculated risks and—'

'What about this soya business? Did you expect the market to fall this much?'

'I knew it would soften, but no, not to this extent. I also know it will firm. Soon.'

'How?'

'Intuition.' Andrew shrugged, but Ashley's look demanded a more detailed explanation. 'I'm sure the US harvest is not half so good as they are letting on. They want to put the wind up Brussels.'

'How the hell do you know that?'

'Weather. Remember that dry, cold spell they had in the Mid-West in May?' Ashley wasn't in the habit of keeping tabs on the weather of the American Mid-West but he was impressed by the boy's apparent knowledge of his commodity.

'No, but apparently you know what you're doing.' Andrew looked relieved. He had another fifty thousand at stake that his father didn't know about. 'But don't screw this one up, for Christ's sake. We can't stand too many losses like that, not on top of what's happened already.'

There was a knock at the door. 'That'll be Betty Rose,' Ashley said. 'You staying?'

'No thanks.' Andrew cleared the figures from the computer screen. 'I'll leave the real farming to you.'

Ashley felt a pang of disappointment. The boy still seemed unable to stir up any interest in the land. He suspected that this flair for commodity trading was based on a love of gambling and that filled him with dread. Living dangerously was not something they could afford to do at present.

Betty came in as Andrew left. 'I'm terribly sorry to be so late,' she greeted him, 'but I was held up at Kendale Hospital, visiting Camilla Doncaster.'

'Come in and get dry, anyway.' He took her wet anorak and hung it over a radiator. 'You're soaking.'

'Not really. It isn't raining all that hard, but the wind is horrible.' She had a leather briefcase with her and as she sat down, she began to undo the clasp to take out a batch of paper covered with neat pen figures and ruled lines.

'You've never done all that by hand?'

'Of course!' She began to lay the sheets out on the desk. 'We can't aspire to a computer yet.'

'Well, I'll get my secretary to run these through ours.'

'What for? They're all done.'

'Yes, but we can change the factors – prices, growth-rates and so on – and then see how that affects profitability.'

'Oh. Oh yes, of course.' She laid out the papers and they began to study the sums she had done. After a while, Ashley leant back in his chair and put his hands behind his head. Betty noticed how tired and drawn he looked. There were tension lines all round his eyes and a frown that she hadn't seen before wrinkled the skin of his forehead. 'I read the piece about Wild in the paper,' she said. 'I really am sorry.'

'What? Oh, *that*! That's nothing. It was more like a hobby than a business, anyway.'

'I know it was more than that.' He looked up from the papers, met her cool gaze and shrugged. A little later she said, 'We do have a slight problem with all this.'

'I'm sure we have several. What in particular?'

'It's John. He's not at all happy about the idea of raising beef.'

'No, he made that clear before.'

'He thinks it runs against the trend.'

'But he is in favour of a joint venture of some sort?'

'I'm not sure. I think he is, but he seems unenthusiastic about this one – and that's not like him. He usually has such an open mind.'

'Does he? I hadn't noticed.'

'Ashley, have you and he had some kind of an altercation?'

'No.'

'Good, because if we are to cooperate, we need him to be fully with us.'

'But do we?'

'Well, of course! What other arrangements could we possibly have?'

'Two-way. You and me.' He looked directly into her eyes. She gazed back.

'I'm sorry, Ashley, I can't operate like that, it's too complicated. I work in partnership with John.'

'I don't mean anything underhand.'

'Perhaps not, but when I threw my lot in with him I meant it to be everything.'

'You make it sound more like a marriage than a business arrangement.' He shrugged again and got up. 'I've bought some calves already, by the way – in my own right, of course, but they're the sort of thing I had in mind for the joint venture. Want to have a look?'

'Of course.' She followed him out to the yard and into a long, low building which smelled of milk and sweet, fresh hay. He switched on the lights revealing a double row of roomy pens. Fifty calves nestling in deep bedding of clean straw began to stir and stand up. The harsh electric light sparkled on their damp noses and made them blink large, wistful eyes.

'Ashley, they're beautiful!' Betty ran an expert eye over them. She looked for weaker ones, for imperfections, but they all seemed equally thrifty. 'From one source, presumably?'

'What makes you say that?'

'They're so . . . uniform.'

'Well done. As it happens, they're all from a pal of mine in Lancashire. He runs a thousand milkers but likes to cross his heifers with beef cattle. He used to rear them himself, but now he's looking for a regular buyer.'

'They're better than anything we could find on the local markets.'

'They're the best.'

'Costly?'

'Obviously, but look at the premiums we could earn on their carcasses.' Betty tried not to wince at the word. It was hard to think of these pretty animals, with their sweeping eyelashes and gleaming coats, as meat on the slab. Ashley didn't notice her reaction and went on, 'We would sell direct, to top end customers. A small output of the very finest quality, perfect for expensive restaurants, smart London butchers, that sort of thing.' He talked on with enthusiasm about potential outlets he knew would be interested, and described new ideas he had been developing on rearing methods.

'Seems as though you could do this on your own easily enough.'

'I could, but you have that spare grassland and your covered yard. You can't really use that for pigs, so, with our combined facilities we could do better.'

'It's quite an undertaking for us. We do have limitations on capital.'

'Apart from the facilities, Betty, I *want* to work with you.'

'Can't think why.' She appeared dismissive but was flattered.

'Can't you?' He put his arm round her waist. 'After your farming performance in the last few years I'd have thought it obvious. You're a good operator. You've got what it takes.'

She took his arm away, holding onto his hand for a moment, noting the long fingers – Jack's hands had been square and calloused – before letting it go, almost with reluctance. 'I'll have to talk to John.'

The following Friday, Ashley drove over to meet the partners of Cartwright Farm. By then he had fed all Betty's figures into his computer and had juggled with as many variable factors as he could, looking at the joint venture's prospects in hard times as well as good. For her part, Betty had measured up her redundant buildings, had walked over her grassland to assess its feeding potential and had revised her cropping programme to accommodate winter forage crops for the maturing cattle. But she had not discussed any of this in much detail with John. He had been so damning last time she and Ashley had mentioned it that she was loath to bring it up again, in spite of the promising figures. Just before Ashley arrived, she provided him with a summary of her proposals.

'It's pretty simple,' she said. 'As long as we go for the premium market we can make it pay – and make it use up otherwise useless buildings and dubious land.'

'Yes, I can see that,' John said, after scanning her papers for a few minutes, 'but it's a pity I didn't see these notes sooner. There's hardly time to study anything.'

'But this is only a preliminary meeting. Nothing gets decided here, except whether to go on with the investigations or not.' John said nothing but continued to read the data. Soon Ashley arrived.

After ten minutes, he and Betty were getting down to details. John had said nothing. Five minutes further into the conference and John's silence began to bug Ashley.

'You're very quiet,' he said. 'What do *you* think?'

'He's always quiet,' Betty said. 'Now, what did you say about daily weight gain?'

'No,' Ashley said. 'I think John should say what's on his mind.' They waited nearly half a minute for John to speak. There was a hostility which Betty couldn't fathom. She realised, now, how wrong it had been not to have insisted that John follow all her preliminary researches so that he was properly briefed. At last he spoke.

'As I said before, beef's going against the trend.'

'That's often the way to succeed,' Ashley said.

'And as often it isn't.' He looked at his hands and then tossed his hair back.

'No, that's not it,' Ashley said, feeling his irritation rising. 'There's something else you don't like about all this.' John kept silent, tossing back the pale forelock a couple more times. 'Come on, man, spit it out!' Ashley wanted to grab the pallid hair and pull it out. Still, John said nothing.

'We must clear the air, John,' Betty appealed, 'if we're to work together.'

At last, after a sigh, John began to speak without looking up. 'It's our relative positions, if you really want to know.'

'What is *that* supposed to mean?' Ashley demanded.

'I think you know.'

'I'm the landlord and you're struggling peasants, is that it?' Ashley's voice was rising. 'You think I'd be unprincipled enough to take advantage of your weaker position?'

'Every man has his price.'

'John, that's not fair, you know—'

'You've got the power, the money, the status. You can do what you like – we can't. We have to struggle to exist. You could lose thousands – hundreds of thousands – without really hurting. We can't afford to lose a single penny. If a joint venture failed you'd merely have wasted your time. We could have lost our livelihood.'

'Betty,' Ashley appealed. 'We've gone through all the paperwork. You know the score – can't you get him to see sense?'

'I've seen the figures,' John continued in a toneless monologue. 'It all looks good in theory but demand could fall. It's a risk we cannot take.'

'Do you agree with that?' Ashley asked Betty.

She thought for a moment before responding. 'Whether I do or not, Ashley, John and I are partners.'

'So you accept his veto?' Betty was silent. Ashley jumped up. 'Well, I've obviously wasted my time. I'll leave the two of you to struggle on in noble poverty while I go to count my millions.' Betty stood up. 'No, don't see me out.' He raised an impatient arm, executed a cross between a farewell wave and an angry gesture, and strode out of the room. Betty felt she had betrayed him. For the first time in their partnership, she also felt angry with John.

'What do you think you're doing?' She was breathing in short gasps.

'It's the only way. I don't trust him. If the chips were down he'd crap on us.'

'That's an outrageous thing to say.'

'Maybe.' Another sigh. 'But it's hard for you to judge. You're besotted with him. Any fool can see that.' He too strode out. Astonished, Betty stood still for several minutes.

Walking back to his cottage in the High Street, the distress John Holman felt was so acute that his chest actually ached. He kicked an abandoned soft drink tin hard enough to dislodge one of its ends, which spun and lay glinting in the gutter. Then, guilty about litter – Wyckhamby was always a finalist in the Best Kept Village Competition – he picked it and the rest of the can up and put them in the litter bin outside the post office and shop before unlocking his own front door. He shucked off his shoes and went straight to the bedroom, taking a second key out of his pocket to unlock the little bureau which stood by the bed. Inside was a camphorwood box which he stroked with his strong, calloused hands before opening. He took out a couple of letters and a bunch of mummified flowers – pinks and Michaelmas daisies – which still bore a trace of clove-like fragrance. These he laid reverently on his bed before lifting out a hardcover notebook. Inside, between notes and dates written in his small, slanting hand, old greetings cards, newspaper cuttings and photographs were pasted to the pages. He opened the book, more or less in the middle. Stuck to the left-hand page was an article from the *Kendale Messenger*, browned at the edges. The headline read, 'Wyckhamby Function Breaks Records,' and the article was topped with a photograph whose caption read, 'Mrs Betty Rose – Supermum Fund-raiser.' He stared at the picture for some minutes before uttering a low moan. Then he put everything back into the box, closed the lid, put the box into the bureau, locked it and pocketed the key.

At the same time, Ashley was sulking in his study. He had particularly wanted this enterprise to get going, partly because of working more closely with Betty but also because he planned to market the beef exclusively through London contacts, since that would give him another legitimate reason for making regular journeys up to town. He could go ahead on his own, of course, but the venture really needed the covered yard at Cartwright for fattening the beasts.

After fuming for a while about the hatefulness of Betty's so-called partner, he began to fish about in the files, gathering together everything to do with Cartwright Farm. He wasn't sure what he was looking for, but he was motivated by a kind of intuition. This beef idea was beginning to drive him. He just had to have access to Betty's covered yard, even if it meant getting his hands on the farm.

He found nothing and began to store everything away. Then he remembered that the lease agreement was in the safe and, just for thoroughness, he decided to get it out and re-read it. Most of the clauses covered stewardship of the land, making the tenant responsible for weed control, woodland preservation, sensible crop rotation and so on. There were items about the landlord's rights to fallen timber, details of sporting rights and a diktat against ploughing the permanent grassland. In spite of his quest, Ashley's attention wandered as he read the turgid legal language. Then he came to the clause on subletting. He read it several times and then phoned his land agent, Hector Enfield.

'If a single tenant takes a partner and farms the rented land as a partnership, who is then the tenant?' Ashley asked. 'The partnership? The original tenant? Or the two of them as individuals?'

'Come again?'

'The fact is, Hector, I've a notion that my tenant is subletting.'

'How? To whom?'

'To her partner. I was blind not to have seen it before.'

Enfield thought for a moment. 'Is there a clause in the agreement forbidding subletting?'

'Yes.'

'Then you may have a case. But Ashley,' Enfield sounded puzzled, 'I thought you were quite happy with the way that woman has sorted herself out. She's a model tenant.'

'Oh, I'm happy with her. It's her partner who bothers me. I'm not necessarily wanting to take any action but I like to be armed with knowledge. Just look through the document, would you? To see whether we've got a case.'

Ashley hung up and rubbed his hands together before pouring a drink. If he could prove a sublet, he would threaten them with notice to quit unless Holman resigned. Then he would give Betty the opportunity of farming in partnership with him. She'd be much better on her own, with him to support her – as and when she needed him. She'd thank him for this, in the long run. And if she didn't play ball with him, well, Vacant Possession on Cartwright Farm would add another couple of hundred thou to his balance sheet and that wouldn't do any harm at all.

Chapter Twenty-three

Ashley was still in his study, gloating over the prospect of forcing Betty to shed her partner when the phone rang. He assumed that Elaine would answer it and began to tidy his desk before going upstairs for a quiet bath. For once, they had enjoyed an evening to themselves and he hoped that this caller, whoever it was, would be brief. But when it was still unanswered after five rings, he lifted the receiver. In the kitchen Elaine, after preparing for a lunch party next day and in the middle of making a roux, hoped he would answer but, after five rings, pulled the pan off the heat and snatched the kitchen phone herself, just in time to hear Ashley's curt, 'Hullo?' To her surprise, the caller was Philip Wild. 'What do you want?' Ashley snapped. At first she thought he was addressing her on the kitchen extension, but soon realised that they had lifted the receiver simultaneously and he could not know that she was listening.

'Ashley!' Wild's voice sounded strange, almost sneering. 'A couple of points.'

'Kirkland Wild has been wound up.' Ashley's tone was bitter. 'I've nothing more to say to you.'

'But I have, to you.'

'Then you should speak through your solicitors.'

'That's really what this is about. You're not planning to sue, are you?'

'Nobody betrays me and gets away with it.' It was bravado. Wild's action had been underhand but Ashley hadn't seen much point in going to law. Legal fees would have been huge and a settlement by no means certain. But it seemed, now, that Wild feared prosecution and was about to make over-tures for an out-of-court settlement.

'I wouldn't, not if I were you.' Hardly a supplicating tone.

'You force me to take action.'

'You see,' Wild paused, 'this may come as a bit of a surprise to you, but I know exactly what you are.'

'I *beg* your pardon?'

'Oh, it doesn't bother me, not in itself. Quite a few of the people in my dinner-party circle are gay, but I'd guess that it bothers you. A lot.'

'What the hell are you talking about?'

'Don't be obtuse, Ashley. I had my suspicions, oh, a year or more ago.' In the kitchen, Elaine's grip tightened on the receiver. She dared not hang up.

'Are you trying to add slander to breach of contract?' Ashley's tone was becoming shrill.

'And I followed you, one lunchtime. Well, several lunch-times, actually. You go to Dorothy's, don't you? And that place in Old Compton Street.'

'Going to those bars doesn't mean one is gay.'

'Mmm, no, but once you came out with a bloke in a leather jacket and earring. He looked decidedly odd.'

'This is *scandalous!*'

'You were holding hands. I was in the snackbar opposite. I saw the pair of you.'

'How dare you make such, such *disgusting* allegations!'

'The snackbar owner – bloke called Fred Balchin – saw you as well. Less than sympathetic, Fred is. To your type, I mean. Naturally, he doesn't know you from Adam, and I wouldn't dream of enlightening him. And, if I hear nothing more from you, you needn't hear another peep from me. Ever. Get my drift?' There was a click followed by the dialling tone.

Ashley sat very still. Numb. Half an hour later, the door opened and Elaine came in. Her face was drained of blood and she staggered slightly.

'Christ, Elaine, are you OK?' He jumped up to support

342

her but instead of letting him, she froze and then shrank back from him.

'Keep away,' she said quietly. 'Just . . . keep away.'

'Good God, darling! You've been out without a coat!' She was wet through and shivering. 'You heard?' he indicated the phone. She nodded. 'How?' She shuddered with an extra spasm of trembling. In anguish, he ran to the bootroom, came back with a dry ski jacket and passed it to her. She put it on her shoulders and went into the kitchen. He followed. She stood with her back to the sink. He walked towards her.

'Keep away!' She picked up one of a pair of porcelain dinner plates which had been set to drain. 'You gave me these for my birthday, when? Five, six years ago? Were you doing it then, I wonder?' She stroked the deep blue and gold leaf pattern round the rim. 'Royal Doulton. Pity they don't make this pattern any more.' She threw the plate onto the floor at her feet but instead of shattering, it bounced, spun and settled upside down. She picked up the other and dropped it so that it hit the first one edgeways on. It chipped its rim but the one already on the ground broke in half. 'Now we don't have a set.'

'You don't *believe* that filth, surely?'

'Why would he invent it?'

Ashley looked at his wife's face and groaned. 'Oh Jesus Christ!' He sat on the floor. 'Oh Jesus, Jesus, Jesus.' He put his head between his knees.

'They say that once a boy has been corrupted, he's queer for life.'

'Elaine!'

'The question is, are you a corrupter or just corrupted?'

'Elaine, stop!'

'Thank God you didn't get Andrew. At least he's still normal.'

'Please stop it.' He sat back against one of the cupboards which lined the kitchen and began to bang his head on the door. 'It was a one . . . off. An . . . adventure, OK? I was distraught over Wild and the bloody mess up there. You don't know, you can't imagine the stress.'

'I can't talk about it. I've got to think.' She stepped over his legs and went out of the kitchen. He was still sitting on the floor when she came into the kitchen twenty minutes later, wearing a red lambswool sweater and navy slacks, carrying a coat over one arm and her overnight case in the other hand. 'I don't know when I'll be back.'

'Where are you going? For Christ's sake, Elaine, it's nearly midnight.' He got up to try to restrain her but she froze him with a look that forbade contact.

'I can't talk. Don't try to reach me.'

'Don't you think you're over-reacting?' he said, but she had left the room before he finished.

She drove towards the Great North Road, stopping just outside Kendale to telephone a small country hotel she knew in Hertfordshire and booked herself a room. They promised to ensure that someone would stay up to let her in. She arrived between one and two in the morning and went straight to bed where she lay rigid for a couple more hours before drifting off to sleep. Rational thinking was beyond her at this stage. Her mind swirled with disjointed images, mostly of Ashley: the look on his face when he realised she had overheard the conversation; Ashley happy, acting the host, treating their guests with his special brand of courteous charm; Ashley watching her unwrap a present; the tender kisses he planted on her head when she fretted about Andrew; Ashley making love to her, gently and with such selflessness. And interspersed with these images, she kept seeing him hand in hand with males – with leering skinheads in leather jackets, with young men of Andrew's age . . . Could he make love to them with the same tenderness, or was it more like some kind of sweaty, animal rutting? What *did* queers do together? Her mind revolted, and she retched, a dry choke. How could she allow a man who had done those things to be with her, enter her. She lay fighting nausea and finally, too exhausted even to think, fell asleep.

After a late breakfast, she drove to Knightsbridge and, at eleven, knocked on Annabel's door.

'Mummy! What a lovely surprise!' Annabel kissed her

mother and then noticed the suitcase. 'Aren't you staying at the flat?'

'No, I decided to give that a miss. I hate being on my own and your father hasn't come up this time.'

'I say, Mum, are you all right?' Annabel had not noticed, at first, the greyness under the eyes but she had picked up the numbness in Elaine's voice.

'Um, not totally. Would it be all right if I dossed down for a day or so?'

'What is it? What's wrong?'

'Nothing, really.' Elaine hesitated. 'I've just had a bit of a row with Dad.'

'But you never row! That's one of the amazing things about you two.'

'There's always a first time.' Elaine wanted to cry but couldn't. All she could do was shake.

Annabel took her by the hands and guided her to the sofa. She was alarmed; this was so out of character. 'Tell me.' Annabel sat close.

'I'm not sure I want to.' The shaking subsided a little. 'I'm not sure I can.'

'Then don't.' Annabel felt helpless.

'Rather sudden, you see. I don't quite know what to do.'

'Is it? No! Can it possibly be another woman?'

'*Definitely* not that!' Elaine laughed, a dry cackle which made the short hairs at the back of Annabel's neck bristle. She hugged her mother who sat stiffly.

'And you definitely don't want to talk about it?'

'No.' Elaine had stopped shaking now, Annabel noticed, but she looked exhausted.

'You can stay as long as you like,' Annabel said, 'and there's no need to doss. Now that Melanie's moved out, there's a spare bed.' She glanced at her watch. 'Christ, I'm late. I've got to get to Berkeley Square.'

'Must you?'

'Mummy, it's *work*! There'll be eight hungry executives waiting for me.'

'Couldn't I come with you? Hand out the hors d'oeuvres

or something?' Annabel thought for a moment. She could do with an extra pair of hands but wasn't sure how well her mother would, as they say, relate to her customers. 'I need something to occupy my mind for the moment. Darling? Please?'

'Oh, all right.' She got her coat out of the cupboard in the hall and fished in the pockets for gloves. 'In fact, my bloody partner's getting so unreliable these days, having a dependable helpmeet will make a nice change.'

The second half of November was unseasonably soft. A gentle westerly breeze kept the temperature above freezing and between occasional showers, the sun shone in a scoured blue sky. The pace on farmland around Wyckhamby slowed as the late-autumn jobs neared completion. An unwary countryman might congratulate himself on a fine, easy season but the fickleness of the English climate was well understood, especially by those who depended on the land for their livelihoods.

At Cartwright Farm, all the winter cereal crops had emerged in their rows, contrasting with the bare ploughland, making the fields look like a patchwork of emerald and chocolate corduroy. Most of the sugar beet was safely piled in the yard, awaiting dispatch to the factory and there was even talk of beginning some of the spring cultivations – normally commenced in February – at Christmastime.

For Betty and John, the only task still outstanding was to finish the potato harvest. Throughout the autumn, the Pick Your Own customers had steadily worked through the potato field and carted off sack after sack of ware. But it had been a much heavier crop than the partners had expected and as a result, there were more potatotes than could easily be sold over the farm gate to locals. By the last week of November, in spite of a string of busy weekends with customers fanning out over the field like ants, there were still almost ten acres unharvested.

'If we don't get them lifted and stored quickly,' Betty said, 'we'll lose most of them to frost.'

'There's plenty of time, if the weather holds,' John replied. But the weather did not hold. The wind turned northeast for a couple of days and then dropped to a barely perceptible current of arctic air which blanketed the whole country with a pall of freezing fog, making the sunless days raw and the nights bitter with black frost. Being outdoors, especially after such a balmy fortnight, became an ordeal and the Pick Your Own customers deserted Cartwright Farm for the comfort of the supermarket.

Since Betty and John lacked mechanical harvesting equipment, lifting the last half-field of potatoes would be difficult, particularly as time was not on their side. All they had was a device which went behind the tractor and scooped the tubers clear of the ground, running them along a short conveyor which riddled out loose soil before depositing them back on the land. From there, they would need to be gathered by hand into baskets, each basket then being lifted and tipped into a trailer, ready for carting into the store. There, the potatoes had to be kept in the dark, to stop them from turning green, protected from frost to which they were vulnerable, but kept cool enough to prevent them from sprouting. John estimated that they had about 150 tonnes to harvest.

'Fifty trailer-loads!' John said. 'I don't think we can do it.'

'Yes, we can,' Betty said, 'if the whole family chips in. Don't forget the girls will be home this weekend. That'll help.'

They worked through the bitter fog, picking potatoes off the ground into plastic baskets so fast that their arms ached and their fingers, in spite of gloves, became chapped and raw. They took it in turns to drive the tractor which pulled the trailer, winning a few minutes in the warm cab while the rest of the little group toiled, bending to pick tubers and straightening to tip their baskets over the high sides of the trailer.

Days went by slowly in a grey agony of aching backs. On 2 December, a thin watery sun glimmered for a couple of hours between midday and early afternoon, but otherwise the weather was dull and raw. Friday came and with it, the

Rose youngsters. They complained but nevertheless bent to their work with a determination which enabled the creeping tractor to go up a couple of gears, travelling along the rows of lifted potatoes at twice the speed. By Sunday evening they were halfway through the crop, but then the weather worsened. The freezing fog cleared away and the weak, easterly airstream escalated to an icy wind which drove frost into the ground.

On Monday morning, in a sunlit landscape covered with sparkling rime, Betty and John walked over the remains of the crop. 'It's only penetrated the soil a couple of inches,' Betty said. The sunshine had lifted her spirits and, in spite of the peril the four remaining acres of potatoes were in, she could not resist a feeling of optimism.

'Could be enough to wipe the lot out,' John grunted. He kicked the ground, breaking off a crust of frozen soil and exposing the yellowish skins of a group of potatoes. 'See how near the surface they are? Those heavy rains nearly washed them out of the ground.' He squatted, teased a tuber out of the solid soil and pressed his thumb into the part that had been nearest to the surface. There was a grey stain just beneath the skin which, under the pressure of his thumb, yielded droplets of juice. 'This has been nipped.'

'Only slightly.'

'Enough to have it rot in the store and spoil the others. I think we should abandon the rest.'

'No!' Betty couldn't bear to give up. Not now.

'Why not? They were a bonus anyway, after such a big harvest. We'd be wasting our time now, to try to get these in. Besides, they could ruin the whole heap.'

'We can make a separate pile with these ones and break them out for selling first. I can use the spoilt ones in the pig feed – a few at a time. They're far too nutritious to waste.'

'If you're sure.' John looked resigned. The conditions they had been working in could have broken anyone's spirit, even that of a toughened Fenman.

'I'm sure,' Betty said. They toiled in the bright air, discarding, at first, as many frosted tubers as they could and hoping that the ones they loaded were all sound. But having to look at each one slowed them down too much and by lunchtime they were back to a frenzy of picking, tipping and carting. Betty lost track of time. All she was conscious of was the pain in her back and arms, the constant cackle of the tractor edging along the row and the rumble of potatoes falling out of her basket. Each night, they phoned the local weather service but it seemed to Betty that they hadn't even bothered to change the recording. The needle was stuck in a groove which promised moderate to severe frost.

On Thursday, Betty slipped on the mounting step of the tractor, caught her hand in the cab-door handle and wrenched her wrist. The pain was slight at first but by mid-morning, her wrist had swollen and she could hardly move her fingers. Using the other hand made matters worse because her injured hand grew numb with cold and ached fiercely. At lunchtime she got John to bind up her wrist with a crêpe bandage. This at least kept her hand warmer and she worked on, refusing John's offer to let her drive the tractor while he picked.

'We've only got about one more day's work,' he said. 'Take it easier.'

'Absolutely not!' And by the end of the next afternoon, with the spotlight on the back of the tractor cab trained on the last row of lifted potatoes, they both stood and, with exhaused bodies but exultant hearts, tipped the last red plastic basket of potatoes into the wooden tractor trailer. With her good hand, Betty flung the empty basket high into the air. 'My God, John, we've done it!' She threw her arms round him and kissed his cheek. 'We've done it! Ouch!' she squeaked as she jarred her hurt wrist, and pulled back. It was too dark for her to see the expression on John's face as he climbed into the tractor cab to take the trailer out of the field.

In the shed, set up as a temporary store, they examined the new pile of potatoes harvested since the sharper frosts. The proportion that had turned black and begun to rot was much smaller than they had feared. Betty had been right to harvest this last part of the crop which would add an extra margin to their vegetable profits.

'I bet there's forty tonnes of salvageable ware here,' Betty said. 'Maybe even fifty.'

'If they keep, we'll make an extra two thousand clear profit. You were right to go for it, Betty. I would have left them in the field.' He gazed at her, making her feel slightly uncomfortable.

'Don't be silly,' she said, looking at the ground. 'I couldn't possibly have got them in without you. Let's go and celebrate. We can have a real Harvest Home now that all the crops are in.' She helped him place straw bales and tarpaulin over the potatoes and then went into the house, leaving him to lock up the buildings and turn off the lights.

Indoors, she hastily lit the sitting-room fire and drew the curtains. She felt sure she had a bottle of white wine hidden away somewhere and rummaged in various cupboards until she found it. She got the corkscrew out of the drawer but could not open the bottle single-handed. The injured wrist ached almost unendurably now that she was thawing out.

John came in after a short while. 'You didn't pick up your post.' He handed her a bundle of envelopes bound with an elastic band.

'Can you get the cork out of that?' She indicated the bottle and then began to open the mail. 'Cheque from Kendale market,' she said, 'and another one from the grain co-op. Goody!' He handed her a glass of Hock. 'Well,' she said, 'aren't you going to propose a toast?'

He shrugged. 'Don't know what to say.'

'How about,' she continued to tear open envelopes as she spoke, ' "Here's to our harvest!" or "all is safely gathered in," or . . .' She stopped speaking and became absorbed in one of the letters she had opened. 'Oh my God!' She sat down quickly and scanned the thick letter paper again. 'Oh no, no! Not again!'

John reached for the letter. He glanced at Hector Enfield's signature and then read the typescript of the Notice To Quit. He read it again, slowly, mouthing the words.

'They can't do that,' she said.

'They say you've sublet. If they can *prove* that, they can chuck us out.'

'But why?'

'You know why. Vacant Possession doubles the value of the farm.' Betty's lower lip trembled. She thought of Jack, poor Jack, killing himself to keep the farm. She thought of the years of skinflinting, of eighteen-hour days, of making do and mending until the whole weariness and dreariness of her existence wore her down. She and John had only just pulled themselves out of that. This potato harvest had been an exceptional strain but until quite recently, she had worked like that day after day, to buy security. And here was this new threat to the tenancy. Was the whole nightmare to start all over again?

'Here, Betty. Have some Liebfraumilch.' John pronounced it 'leebfermilk'.

She took the glass and sipped but the wine tasted sour.

Chapter Twenty-four

Ashley hoped that Elaine would come back quite quickly. He had expected her to telephone next morning, or within a couple of days at the most. When almost a week went by he began to worry. He had several ideas concerning her whereabouts, but was not sure what to do. He could hardly contact friends to ask if they happened to know, offhand, where his wife was. There was no need even to hint, in public, that there might be a rift. Not yet, anyway. He thought several times of phoning Annabel because he suspected that Elaine might be with her, but if she wasn't, a call would have alarmed her and he didn't want that. Furthermore, he was anxious to avoid any enquiries from his daughter because he was not sure whether he could trust himself to give truthful-sounding answers.

A week after her departure, he sat and brooded in his study, gazing at the portrait of Elaine which hung over the fireplace. The artist had persuaded her to sit outdoors, with the wisteria on the house in full bloom behind her. Wearing her deep green evening gown, she stood with the tapered racemes of the flowers all around her, their blue-mauve colouring contrasting with the dress material and with the honey-brick of the house. How clever the artist had been to blend the highlights of her bright brown hair with those bricks – same hue, different texture. Wyckhamby Manor without Elaine was not a concept he could bear to ponder.

Andrew came into the room without knocking. 'Sorry, Dad, I didn't know you were in here.' Ashley looked at his son, wearing baggy chino trousers and a mud-coloured shirt.

He caught the boy's profile and then glanced again at the portrait. He and his mother had the same outline, the small nose and high cheekbones, but Andrew's chin receded a little more, making him look weaker.

'What do you want?'

'I just wanted to tell you that soya prices have shot up. The US harvest *was* much smaller than estimated. If we sold now, we'd recover our position, almost.'

'Then sell, boy! Sell, for goodness sake!' The force of Ashley's instruction took Andrew by surprise.

'OK Dad,' he said, instead of remonstrating, 'when the office opens tomorrow. By the way, where *is* Mum?'

'Mmm? Oh, she's gone off to town for a few days. We had a bit of a tiff.'

'You and Mum? You never "tiff".'

'Nothing serious. She'll be phoning any time now.' They both started when the telephone on his study desk rang. 'This is probably her now.' He lifted the receiver. 'Er, hullo? Darling?' His voice was shaky. Sensing his father's need for privacy, Andrew withdrew.

'Ashley.' Elaine's voice sounded strained. 'I will be home tomorrow evening.'

'Oh, Elaine.' He was almost in tears. 'If only—'

'We have to talk. Be there.' She rang off.

'Yes,' he said to the buzzing receiver. 'Yes, of course.'

Next morning, over breakfast, he said to Andrew. 'Oh, by the way, your mother's coming home tonight.'

'Oh, great!' Andrew's eyes lit up. The boy's pleasure reached out to Ashley. Perhaps this hellish episode would conclude. Soon.

'Have you sold that soya yet?'

'No, Dad. The price is still rising this morning. We can recover all *and* make a modest profit if we sell now.'

'Well, make sure you do!'

'Oh sure, Dad! Straight after breakfast.' They finished the meal in silence. Ashley had little appetite and soon went out to find Mardle and discuss winter jobs on the farm.

After his more leisurely breakfast, Andrew went to the

Wyckhamby Farms buildings where he now had his own small office, and checked his information screen. The soya price was still firming up nicely. If he sold, he calculated, he would make a total profit of between forty and fifty thousand. He decided to raise the stakes. 'We'll hold on for now,' he told the computer screen.

Ashley found it impossible to concentrate on his work during the day. That night, he would have to convince Elaine that he loved her and wanted, desperately, to win her forgiveness. He drove to Kendale and bought a huge bunch of freesias because he knew she loved their scent. He also bought a piece of fillet steak, a pound of fresh asparagus – madly expensive, flown in from California – some imported new potatoes and the very large, very black mushrooms which he knew she adored. He planned to prepare a special dinner. It would be almost like proposing to her again, he told himself.

Back at home, he managed to persuade Andrew to take himself off for the evening and began to prepare the meal. He was a competent, if limited cook. He decided to roast the lump of fillet, in a very hot oven for a short time so that it seared on the outside but kept its delicious juices within. The asparagus they would eat as an appetiser, lightly boiled and dressed with molten butter.

He was peeling the leathery skins off the mature mushrooms when she came quietly into the kitchen. Hearing nothing, but detecting a waft of 'Ysatis', he turned from the sink to see her standing by the kitchen table, cool and well-groomed, taking off her gloves.

'Looks as though you're preparing quite a spread.'

'Oh, well!' he shrugged.

'I hope it's not especially on my account.'

'Well, I thought . . .'

'You thought you could buy me with a smart meal?'

'I just wanted to make a pleasant environment in which to talk.' He opened the refrigerator and took out a crystal jug which clouded over instantly with condensation. 'Want a

Martini? I've got them ready chilled in here.' She shook her head.

'Aren't you drinking anything?' There was consternation in his voice. 'I've got a Pommard for supper and champagne with pudding if you fancy it. Oh yes, and there's something else here.' He opened the door to the scullery and a moment later reappeared with the freesias in a silver ice-bucket. 'I couldn't think what else to put them in. I bought the entire stock.' He set them down on the kitchen table. Their fragrance diffused through the kitchen. 'It's the yellow ones that smell best. Remember that place near Adelaide, where they'd run wild? The scent coming off that hillside! Where was it – Mount Lofty?' He was babbling. To make himself stop, he turned back to the sink and resumed peeling the mushrooms. She did not move but stood, holding her gloves.

'Haven't you anything else to discuss – other than flowers?' He put the paring knife on the draining board, turned slowly and, with an effort, lifted his gaze. Her eyes were brimming but her dignity was still intact. He lowered his eyes again.

'I don't know what to say.'

'There are practical considerations. I have to ask certain questions.'

'Such as?'

'Is it all true? Is it *really* true?' He saw a loophole. He could suggest that the whole thing was a malicious plot hatched up by Wild, but his intuition forbade it. She knew the answer to this question and had merely asked it as a means of getting started on the conversation they both knew they had to have. He sighed.

'It is.'

'And you've done it before? This isn't a "one off"?' She read his silence as an admission. 'How long for?'

He shrugged. 'A long time.'

'Have you had a blood test lately?'

'What for?'

'You've heard of AIDS, I presume.'

'Oh Jesus, Elaine! What sort of a swine do you think I am? Do you really think I would put you at risk?'

'If you were doing this *before* the disease was discovered, we could both be at risk.'

His throat was drying. He cleared it with a nervous little rasp. 'I'm all right, I know I am. I've always been careful. AIDS isn't the only disease you can . . .' He saw the disgust registering on her face. 'But I'll have a test if you want.'

'I think I do need a drink,' Elaine said. He opened the refrigerator. 'No, not in here,' she made a dismissive gesture. 'I'm going into the drawing room.'

'I'll bring it through.'

'Not for me. I'll pour myself a Scotch. And I'm not eating anything, by the way. I couldn't.' She went out. He set his meal preparations on hold, took the Martini jug and a pre-chilled glass out of the fridge and followed her.

The drawing room was cold. He cursed himself for not having laid a fire and now, fussed in and out with kindling and logs, balling up the day's newspaper, still unread, and dropping matches onto the hearthrug. Finally, he got something of a blaze going but the room was too large for the chill to be pierced with much more than a token warmth. Elaine had kept on her coat since her arrival. Now she sat on the edge of a chair and pulled it more closely round her chin.

'Let me get you a Scotch.'

'I said I'd get my own.' She jumped up and walked to the window beneath which stood the small Victorian mahogany trolley carrying several heavy crystal decanters and chunky glasses. She poured herself a tot of whisky – offered nothing to Ashley – and returned to her chair by the fire. She looked at him. He caught her eye yet again but was unable to hold her stare for more than a second or two.

'Don't,' he whispered.

'Don't what?'

'Look at me like that.' She sipped the neat spirit and shuddered slightly, almost retched. He cleared his throat again and waited. Neither wanted to resume the dialogue. He realised that he still held the Martini jug and small cocktail glass in his hands. He poured himself a drink and put the jug on the mantelpiece. All the while, she regarded him with a cool expression. She assumed that he was expecting her to make the running but in fact, he dared not speak for fear of worsening the situation.

'How do you feel about this?' Elaine asked, after another tense silence. It was a conversational question – journalist's interview variety: 'When do you see inflation coming down, Chancellor?'

'How the hell do you think I feel?'

'Guilty? Ashamed? *Filthy*?'

Ashley groaned. 'But Elaine, is it,' he moved nearer to her, 'is it so huge a deal?'

'You've made me feel impure.'

'You? Impossible!'

'What I've kept thinking over these last days is whether you regret it – *really* regret it. Or whether you just regret being caught.'

'How *could* you say—'

'Hear me out, Ashley.' She took another sip. 'You see, it isn't just me you've destroyed, it's also our marriage, our life here.' Her eyes brimmed again but she held her head erect and stared at him, out of focus now. 'Everything, really.'

'But there's nothing *serious* about what I did. It's purely dalliance, satisfying an appetite. There's no love. It's not even infidelity really. I mean, lots of men have the odd tumble outside marriage but still love their wives. I love you, Elaine and . . .' Her look froze him mid-sentence. She stood up. He sensed the ultimatum before she opened her mouth to deliver.

'The deal is this.' Her voice was almost steady now. 'If you are prepared to stop it now – don't dare speak. Not yet!' He had opened his mouth to remonstrate. 'If you are willing, and able, to exclude all others, of either sex,' she swallowed, still feeling revulsion, 'I'll consider staying. If not, it's . . . finished.'

She drained her Scotch and poured another. 'I've been travelling all day. I'm going upstairs to have a bath. Don't attempt to follow me. Stay here in this freezing room. You've got a lot of thinking to do. I'll talk to you in an hour, but don't think you can buy me with cheap promises.' Then she walked up to him, reached out to put a hand on his shoulder but decided not to touch him. At last he looked into her eyes and held her gaze. 'Even if you *do* make a promise, I'll have to decide whether or not you mean it.'

Upstairs, in her bathroom, she began to shake. She had hoped that the week away from him might have softened the impact of the pain she felt, but it was worse. She was not sure she could bear to have him touching her. Every time she thought of him making advances, the image of a leering skinhead got in the way.

Downstairs, Ashley emptied the jugful of Martini into one of the massive crystal tumblers from the trolley and took a long pull. He poked the fire, pulling the burning wood from the outsides of the large grate towards the centre to make a hot core and placed three seasoned ash logs on top. These caught quickly and at last, the chill in the room gave way to warmth. He sat and sipped his drink. The silence irked him and he got up again, took a compact disc of Mozart's Clarinet Quintet from the bookshelf and opened the front of the eighteenth-century commode which housed the hi-fi system.

He forced his mind to think about recent events. What would he do if he lost Elaine? He groaned aloud at the thought. He loved her too much to lose her, but could he change his lifestyle? No more pickups, no more casual encounters? His pulse quickened at the memory of the most recent ones. It wouldn't be easy to resist the temptations. They were absolutely everywhere, when you knew where to look. Could he give it up? *Need* he give it up altogether? An occasional visit to the massage place in Earls Court – what harm would that do? Who would know? *He* would know, that was the tricky part. The decision was clear: celibacy, apart from within his marriage, or divorce.

Next to his glass on the mantelpiece was a photograph of Elaine in a small silver frame. They'd had it enlarged from a slide and framed almost as a joke. She was standing in the rose garden at the end of an afternoon's weeding, her skirt torn, her hair wild after getting snagged among the rose thorns but her face, tanned after weeks of hot weather, was relaxed and she was laughing. He groaned again. The decision had to be made this evening. Now.

He rejected the compact dist from his hi-fi and selected an older vinyl recording of Britten's *War Requiem*. How lucky, he thought, reading the label, for Britten and Peter Pears to have a relationship like that. Were they faithful to each other, he wondered. Would one have minded the other having a bit on the side? He wondered about that too. He loved Elaine. Loved her with a wholesomeness equal to any chaste marriage – more than most, in fact, he suspected. It was just this sex thing. No one with whom Guy Wilson had associated had any call on his affections at all – except Rick, and that was over a long time ago. He found the *Libera me* on the record and stood, gazing into the fire as Peter Pears's voice sang the opening lines of Wilfred Owen's poem *Strange Meeting*.

> 'It seemed that out of battle I escaped
> Down some profound dull tunnel, long
>   since scooped
> Through granites which titanic wars had
>   groined.'

He was never able to listen to this part without weeping and now tears, more bitter than ever before, began to sting his eyes. The baritone soloist took up the poem and Elaine came quietly into the drawing room as he sang:

> 'I am the enemy you killed, my friend.
> I knew you in this dark; for so you frowned
> Yesterday through me as you jabbed and killed.
> I parried but my hands were loath and cold.'

She stood still, listening as tenor, baritone and quiet chorus brought the Mass gently to its conclusion: *Let us sleep now. Requiescat in pace. Amen.* The record ticked half a dozen times before the stylus lifted and the arm swung back to its resting point and stopped. She looked at his face. He stared back, unblinking, even though tears blurred her image.

'Could you change?' she asked, her voice flat and low.

'I could try.'

'That's not an answer.'

'It's the only one I can give.'

'I know. I think I knew that even before I came home.'

'Couldn't we try to . . . Couldn't *I* try—'

'This is the crunch,' Elaine cut in, still speaking in a nearly toneless voice. 'Be sure. Be absolutely sure that we all know where we stand.'

'I am trying to be as honest with you as I know how.'

'Oh, ha ha!' Elaine's laugh was bitter.

'I *could* try. Emotional fidelity you've always had. The other is just biological, but it is a compulsion and I don't know whether I can . . .'

'I know that you can't.' She opened her handbag and took out a pink tissue to dab her eyes. 'It's over.'

'Now, darling, please! Can't we discuss this?'

'No. I'm going.'

'Elaine!' It was a cry. He grabbed her hands and shook them to make his point. 'Look! I *will* make an undertaking. I will, really, I promise!' She looked hard at him. He forced himself to look back, deep into her eyes, to smile. 'Please?' She read the smile. She'd seen him using it on business associates, on guests, on Betty Rose especially. She had even thought he might have fancied Betty Rose at one time. Now she knew he was probably keener on Betty's teenaged son, or that sullen partner of hers. She presumed queers liked blue-eyed blonds just as normal men liked blue-eyed blondes.

'I'm sorry, Ashley. We're finished. I'll be staying with Annabel for now. Don't try to visit. I packed another bag while I was upstairs but someone will have to come for the rest of my stuff. I've already transferred some cash out of our joint account into one of my own. The rest is up to the lawyers, I suppose,' the monotone grated on his ears, 'although I don't really know what the procedure is. I haven't had to do this before.'

She walked out but on the threshold, turned back and said, 'This could make a pretty frightful scandal and that wouldn't do either of us any good. Your secret is safe with me, I give you my word on that. But if you make any attempt whatsoever to contact me, I will let the cat out of the bag. I mean that. Not even a phone call.' She left him, standing in the middle of the room with a crumpled pink tissue in his hand.

He stayed in the drawing room until the log basket was empty and the fire too low to provide any more warmth. Losing Elaine did not seem to hurt – not yet. He simply felt numb about it, although he knew that this was like the first shock after receiving a bad injury. You feel nothing at first, even though you can see the wound, but you know that there will be much pain, soon.

Besides losing a wife, his livelihood was at risk. Elaine had brought more than 1000 acres of land into their marriage and by right, owned about a third of the equity in Wyckhamby Farms. Furthermore, some of the shares were held in trust for Annabel and Andrew. Their trustees were unlikely to interfere but when Elaine sought a divorce and pulled the plug, as she undoubtedly would, he would be left in considerable financial difficulty. But he was hardly ready to give these implications any thought yet. All he could concentrate on was the pain that he knew he would soon be feeling.

Andrew had returned late, and gone straight off to his room after a perfunctory 'Good night!' called through the closed door. So he sat alone in the half-light. Eventually the room grew too cold to bear. He got up, surprised at the stiffness in his knees caused by having sat so still for so long.

He noticed that in his earlier haste to light the fire, a sheet of today's *Financial Times* had slipped behind the sofa. He picked it up and glanced at the headline. 'Glut Hits Oilseed Prices' caught his eye. 'Rumours of a short soya harvest in the US were quashed today as news of a flood of Brazilian product took traders by surprise. The surpluses of oilseeds, particularly sunflower and rapeseed, in the EC helped to drive prices down further, causing unexpectedly heavy losses among traders. Prices dropped to the year's lowest today but the slide is expected to continue.' Thank God we sold when we did, Ashley thought. There as least is one victory snatched from the jaws of defeat. Maybe we should sell more and buy back on the bear market. He made a mental note to discuss it with Andrew next morning.

In bed he could not sleep. He tried to grieve for Elaine but the numbness was still there – a black hole at the pit of his being. Someone he knew had just suffered a terrible loss, and that was awful, but it wasn't him.

In his own room, Andrew was as wakeful as his father. He just didn't understand how it could have happened so quickly. How was he going to break it to Dad, that instead of selling their soya futures, he had hung on, hoping to sell at the peak and make a bigger profit? How was he going to tell him that he didn't dare sell now, because if he did, Wyckhamby Farms would lose more than £100,000 on the deal and, worse still, his personal account – which his father did not even know about – would be in debt to at least that much as well. Andrew thought on these things, turned over in bed, hugged his knees and groaned.

PART FOUR

Winter

Chapter Twenty-five

John Holman, hunched in khaki anorak and tweed cap, walked among the scurrying Christmas shoppers, feeling out of kilter with the festive atmosphere. Decorations might have cheered up the streets of a duller town, but at Kendale, he thought, the festoons of coloured lights and plastic angels rather got in the way, hiding ancient corbels and mullioned windows. A small group of brass instrument players – you could hardly call it a band – had gathered in the little paved yard next to Boots and were playing a medley of Christmas tunes in simple four-part harmony. It was late afternoon on the shortest day of the year, overcast but dry, with the temperature hovering just above freezing point.

John was in some agitation. He gazed into shop windows without noticing their contents, kept glancing at his watch, retraced his steps in the High Street half a dozen times and once, stopped right next to the musicians but stood with his back to them, hands clenched in trouser pockets, oblivious of the sound.

There were two, no three reasons for his distraction. His son Elliot was due to arrive in – he glanced again at his watch – thirty-eight minutes' time on the London train. He longed to be reunited but it was such ages since he had seen him that he felt quite jittery about the whole thing. Now that the boy was nine, he wasn't sure whether he ought to kiss him when they met or just shake hands. He knew he'd want to show his affection but was anxious to do the right thing. The first few seconds of a meeting were so important and it would be awful to embarrass the lad, but cruel to snub him with a cold formal greeting if he wanted a hug.

The second cause for disquiet was Karen, his estranged wife. Her usual custom, on these occasions, was to accompany Elliot to the agreed meeting point, hand him over and, after a hasty exchange, go back the way she had come. The exercise would be carried out in reverse at the end of the boy's stay. These rare encounters were brief enough to avoid any unnecessary dredging up of the past but John still found them painful. This time she had phoned to ask whether she could stay overnight. Taken by surprise, he had failed to think things through, had granted her request and now the prospect of her visit filled him with dread.

Looked at analytically – and he had looked at it analytically about a million times – his marriage to Karen had never been likely to survive. It foundered in its third year, during the high-risk period when the biology had lost its lustre but the relationship had yet to develop the joint habits and customs needed to give it a lasting quality. They met during his postgraduate course in Crop Husbandry at Cambridge, a time when, though academically sharp, he was naive as far as relationships were concerned. Apart from adolescent flirtations, there had been no one before Karen – he had been locked into his studies to the exclusion of everything else – and when he met her, selling confectionery at the Regal Cinema, the impact of her large brown eyes and small upturned nose awoke his sleeping hormones with such abruptness that he was quite unmanned. It ruined the film for him but even now, remembering the title – *Close Encounters of the Third Kind* – made his lips twitch into an ironic smile. He could not wipe away the image of those dark eyes so that while, on the screen, the hero was being drawn irresistibly towards creatures from outer space, John was as forcibly impelled, by animal instinct, to his own alien behind the sweet counter.

The courtship was urgent and brief. In accordance with his Methodist upbringing, he was chaste until their wedding night but youth, physical fitness and true love conquered any problems of inexperience and, at first, they lived in an extended ecstasy.

After a year, frictions, of course, developed. Karen was a town girl, brought up on a council estate near Huntingdon Road. When John took his first job, as an assistant farm manager in the Welsh borders, she loved their little tied cottage but hated the isolation. She took driving lessons but somehow never managed to pass her test, and was trapped in a strange countryside with nothing to do. Resentment set in. John decided to try working for the Ministry of Agriculture, though he disliked the idea of being a civil servant, and they moved east to Sleaford which was, at least, a town and didn't have those brooding hills overshadowing everything. But he was soon bored with the pettiness of his colleagues, hated the routine office work and regretted sacrificing the open-air life.

The marriage deteriorated steadily over the next few months until they reached a point where they both agreed that they needed something to bring them together again. Having a child, they hoped, might do the trick. It didn't. Then, when John came home from the office one morning with a raging toothache, and found Karen in bed with a television repair man while Elliot slept in his pram in the garden, he knew that he must leave. Since then he had met Karen about once a year. They were not technically divorced but their only reason for any contact at all was Elliot. John had no idea what relationships she was having, if any. He knew that the television repair man had returned, sheepishly, to his wife but assumed that there would have been others.

After Karen, he had avoided dalliance with females, considering the whole love thing to be fraught with peril. If he had begun other affairs, perhaps he might have been able to shed the last traces of desire he felt for her but as it was, the recollection of those dark eyes still caused a twitch of the knife in his old wound, even though he had Betty now, to work for; to live for.

Betty was the third reason for his agitation. He had bottled up his feelings for her for so long that she had become an icon. Inviolable, to be revered but not touched. Time after time, he had told himself he must make some sort of declaration to her, and time after time his reticence got in the way. Last New Year's Day he had, at last, made a vow to himself that he would, this very year, bring his love out into the open. She might laugh at him, or be incredulous, but he would have to bear that. Now the year was almost done and he had yet to make his move. It was, after all, quite straightforward. He loved her. She, he was sure, liked him. He would ask her to marry him – it was the obvious move for both of them – and once he had her consent, he would secure a divorce from Karen. Simple! But his mind shrank from the thought, of making that first terrifying move . . .

He glanced at his watch again. The train was due in twenty minutes.

He had already bought a little stack of presents: toys for Elliot, modestly priced items for the Rose youngsters, all of whom would be home for Christmas, and cards for his acquaintances in the village. For Betty, he planned something special. He intended the giving of his present to coincide with the opening up of his heart. (Even now, it skipped several beats at the very thought and made him slightly nauseous.) His plan was to make his move after lunch on Christmas Day. While Gill, Mandy and Jim washed up, as soon as the Queen's broadcast was over, he hoped he would be able to persuade her to go for a walk with him in the twilight of the winter afternoon. There he would give her the brooch and . . . The brooch! He must pick it up, now, before the train came in.

He quickened his pace to the end of the High Street and turned into the oldest part of the town where the streets were narrow and twisted. There were no chainstores or building societies here, just private houses and small boutiques. One of these had the word 'Finzi' in gilt lettering above its bowed front, and specialised in old jewelry. His brooch was still in the window display. It was about eighty years old and depicted a sprig of sapphire flowers, possibly forget-me-nots, set in gold. He knew Betty liked it because, when they had visited Kendale together last spring, she had pointed it out, saying that it reminded her of one her grandmother used to wear on special occasions.

He entered the shop and was greeted by the owner, a heavy-jowled woman wearing a dress the colour of estuary mud. 'The sapphire man!' she said, walking over to the window and reaching for the tray which held the brooch. 'Want another look?'

'More than that, I've come to collect it at last.' John had been paying for the brooch, which cost £950, over the period of almost a year and now offered his final instalment of two fifty-pound notes. 'I'm grateful to you for having been so patient.'

'Not at all,' Mrs Finzi said. 'I only hope she's worth it!'

'You may depend she is.' John took his receipt and, with the small leather box making an obtrusive presence in his pocket, ran to his car and drove to Kendale station. The London train was just pulling in as he arrived.

As the crowd on the platform thinned he saw, against the station lights, the outline of a mother and her small boy walking slowly towards the barrier. Elliot carried a duffelbag but Karen was, with difficulty, dragging an enormous suitcase which ran on small wheels. John strode forward just as Elliot spotted him. 'Dad!' he called and dropped his bag to run up and throw his arms round his father's waist. John stiffened at first but then felt himself relax. He stroked the boy's hair, flaxen in texture and as lemon-blond as his own.

'Hullo, son.' John looked across the platform at Karen. She was showing a few small signs of having edged into her thirties, but the wide eyes and tiny nose were quite unchanged and her figure looked almost as perfect as it had when he had first seen her at the Regal. She walked right up to him, stopped and relinquished her grip on the suitcase which started to creep backwards on its wheels until it came to rest against Elliot's abandoned duffelbag.

'Mind the luggage, Elliot!' she instructed. Her Cambridge accent was almost gone, replaced by the long vowels and hissing consonants of Greater London. Before John had time to speak, she kissed him on both cheeks. He felt them burn with embarrassment and glanced guiltily about him as if the kiss was illicit. It was the first time she had touched him since he had walked out and the contact, though hardly unleashing passion, certainly made him feel uncomfortable. She was wearing cherry-red high-heeled shoes and a navy skirt with matching cotton blouse under a jacket of simulated fur which, had it been real, might once have clothed a Polar bear. She gave his reddened cheek a playful pinch between finger and thumb. 'You look ever so well, John.'

'You too.' He looked at his feet, not quite knowing what should happen next. He indicated the luggage with his chin. 'Big case.'

'I was hopin' I might be able to stay for a bit longer than just the one night. Along with Elliot.'

'I see.' He looked puzzled. 'There isn't that much room. It's only a small cottage.'

'Cottage? Aren't you living at the big house, then?'

'What big house would that be?'

'Your farm.'

'Oh? Oh, I see.' He picked up Elliot's duffelbag and handed it to him. 'It isn't *my* farm. I work it in partnership – we're tenants.' He put his hand on her vast suitcase. 'This handle safe?' She nodded. He picked it up as if it were a small pack of groceries and led the way out to the car park.

'Ooh John! I'd forgotten how strong you are,' Karen exclaimed, in a way which made his neck-hairs stir. He stowed their luggage into the boot of his car while Elliot scrambled, unbidden, into the back seat. Then he held the passenger door open for his estranged wife, noticing that her legs and ankles were as shapely as they had ever been.

In the car, she said, 'Tell us about this farm.'

'You don't really want to know, do you?'

'I do, John, really I do.' She rested her hand on his knee.

He began to talk about their country life: what they grew, what work went with what seasons, what livestock they had. At first he summarised in simple sentences, but love of the land loosened his tongue. He described the feeling of turning out on a cold winter morning, when frozen puddles in the yard cracked underfoot and the breath of the ewes puffed in clouds as they munched through the standing kale crop. He talked of ploughing, reliving the pleasure of scoring clean brown furrows through the stubble, burying weeds and exposing fresh clean earth, ready for the new seed. He talked of rolling tender green barleyfields when the first swallows were gliding low and the hawthorn hedges were turning from grey to emerald; of foxes stalking pheasant chicks; of vast autumn bonfires after hedging and ditching; of Sunday walks over developing crops; of harvest suppers, Easter lambing and gathering holly from the wood to sell at Christmas. Finally, hastily, he summarised his and Betty's ideas for new enterprises. He omitted the bit about being sued for Vacant Possession. That was not Karen's business really.

'It's a hard life but a good one, on the whole,' he concluded.

'What about yer partner – what's she like?'

'Fine.'

'How much of a partner is she?' Karen slid her hand a little way up his thigh.

'Business.' He felt his face turning crimson again. 'Purely a business partner.'

Her hand encountered the hard edge of the box containing the brooch. 'Gracious John,' she giggled, 'you *are* pleased to see me.'

'For goodness sake!' John glanced in the mirror. 'The boy!' But Elliot was dozing.

'All right! It was only a joke.' She withdrew her hand, folded her arms and stared at the road ahead. He glanced at her, profiled in the passing sodium lights, the skin livid in their orange glare but the pouting lips and upturned end of her nose perfect in any colour. She looked at him again. 'What is it, anyway, in yer pocket?'

'Nothing. Just a present.' They drove the rest of the way in silence, the child asleep, John trying to come to terms with his inner agitation and Karen wondering how much John's share in the farm was worth.

He turned off the main road into Wyckhamby and pulled

up outside his cottage. Elliot woke at once and looked out of the window at the street, lit with old-fashioned lamps. 'Cor,' he said, 'isn't it quiet!'

'I'm not sure what to do about the sleeping arrangements,' John said, as they unloaded the car and went into the cottage.

'We'll be all right. Elliot and I can share.'

'Hardly. It's only a single bed.'

'Well,' she looked round the little parlour, noticing the neatly arranged furniture, small television in the corner and large open fireplace, 'he can kip down on that settee.' There was a faint but pungent smell of bonfires in the cottage.

'The fire smokes a bit when the wind is in the northwest,' John said.

'I don't mind. It's quite nice, really.'

He lugged her case upstairs and indicated her room. 'I'll start on supper while you unpack.'

He went back down the narrow staircase and bumped into Elliot who was at the bottom, about to charge upstairs with his head down. 'Steady, son.' He circled the boy with his strong arms and stroked the yellow hair again. 'Shall you mind sleeping on the sofa?' Elliot shook his head and then ran up to help his mother.

John lit the fire and then, before busying himself with the meal preparations, crept back upstairs to his own room. While low voices and sounds of Karen and Elliot moving about were audible from the next room, he unlocked his bureau, took out the camphorwood box and sat on his bed, holding it on his lap as if he were cosseting a pet. Then he took the brooch out of his pocket. The box was slightly scuffed but inside, the sapphires sparkled in the low light of the bedroom. In a pigeonhole in the bureau, he found some small, plain white cards. He took one of these, picked up his old Waterman fountain pen and sat for a few moments, wondering what to write. There was much to communicate. It was so difficult; he was a man of such few words. He thought for a while longer but the harder he tried to come up with something that provided the meaning he wanted to convey, the more elusive the apt phrases seemed to be.

Eventually he wrote: 'To Betty, to mark our next step.' Then he changed Betty to *my partner* and juggled with the words a bit more until the card was covered with smudged writing and crossings out. Satisfied at last, he tore the soiled card into tiny pieces and put them in the waste-paper basket, picked up a new card and, in his neatest handwriting wrote, *'To my dearest partner, in the hopes that our relationship will now take the next step and flourish'* and signed it *'your John.'*

The card just fitted into the lid of the box so he tucked it, face outwards, against the black velvet lining, snapped the box shut and placed it in the bureau, which he locked. With all that concentration, he had not noticed that the room next door had gone quiet.

Downstairs, he found Elliot busy laying the table and Karen at the sink, cleaning Brussels sprouts. 'I peeped into the oven and presumed the stew was for tonight,' she said, 'so I put those potatoes on the draining board in to bake. You're ever so organised, John.'

'You have to be when you live alone.' He stood awkwardly by the sink. 'You shouldn't have to do that, you're a guest.' He took the paring knife from her, noticing that whereas he merely cut the outer leaves off the sprouts, she cut a little crisscross at the base of each one. He had forgotten how careful she could be. 'Saucepan under there,' he indicated the shelf with his chin. She bent, clattered, selected and straightened. He watched. She had taken off the red shoes and replaced them with a pair of flat pumps but she moved with a spring in her step that made her poise much more elegant without the heels. She held up the pan she had chosen and looked at him, widening the huge eyes and raising her eyebrows in query. He nodded approval. Soon the sprouts were boiling on the stove and the meal was almost ready.

Later, replete and enjoying hearthside ease together on the sofa, she said, 'Was you planning to do anything special on Christmas Day?'

With a guilty lurch, he remembered Betty and sat straighter. 'I'll be taking Elliot over to the farm to lunch with Betty and her family.'

'Will they mind if I come?'

'It's Christmas Day we're going, not tomorrow.'

'I know that.'

'Had you thought of staying that long?'

'I can go,' she stared ahead, 'if you want me to.' He looked at her profile. He was undecided.

'We'll see.'

Soon, they made up a bed for Elliot and got him settled. Karen kissed him on the forehead and said, 'Be good and don't fuss. You know where the toilet is?'

'Mum! 'Course I do!' John watched her straightening the sheet and blanket, trying as best she could to tuck it into the upholstery of the sofa to make it more like a proper bed.

'A new experience for him,' she said, turning to John.

'Sleeping on a sofa?'

'No, being a family – *in* a family.'

'I see.' Why did that make him feel such a swine? To hide his face, he bent to kiss the boy good night.

'Dad, will we see the farm tomorrow?'

'Of course you will.' He switched the overhead light off but left a small table lamp on. To Karen he whispered, 'We seem to be in the way now.'

'Well, I'm tired out. I'm going up.'

'You'd better be first in the bathroom,' he said. 'It's downstairs, by the way, through there,' he indicated the kitchen door. While he waited, he read the *Independent*. At last she was finished and came back in, kissing the top of his head before creeping through the living room and upstairs. He heard the latch click on her bedroom door and then went into the steamy bathroom for a brisk toilet before going to his own bed.

For a healthy man living alone and unfulfilled, erotic dreams are inevitable. John's, if they focused at all, were about Betty but more usually they involved abstract beings. He might be swimming in a warm ocean surrounded by lissome shapes or sharing a sunlit riverbank with nymph-like creatures. Once he dreamt he was naked, riding a horse bare-backed behind a naked woman and for weeks afterwards, was unable to shake off the physical sensations he dreamt he had felt. But tonight he was dreaming of Karen. Three times he watched her taking off her fur jacket to reveal full breasts and flat stomach; three times he awoke, startled at his wickedness. Once he got out of bed, unlocked the bureau and touched his camphorwood box for reassurance.

Next door, Karen heard him moving about and crept into his room. She was, of course, wearing the furry jacket. It barely made her decent. 'Can't you sleep either?' She shuddered slightly. 'I'm ever so cold.'

'I'm not surprised. You're practically naked.' She came closer. He felt the simulated fur tickling his cheek. 'Karen, don't! This isn't right.'

'Why not?' She undid two buttons of his pyjama jacket. 'I know you want to.'

'But it isn't *right*.'

'John, we're husband and wife,' and she stopped any further protests he might have made by clamping his mouth with hers.

Early next morning, John lay awake. Sex with Karen had been ten times more wonderful than he remembered and even now, lying sated and warm with her breathing lightly at his side, the very thought of it began to arouse him all over again. His body felt more relaxed than it had for years, but his mind was not relaxed at all. He knew she would ask if she could move in with him and he knew that he wanted to sleep with her a lot more. She was his wife. It was really his duty to have her back. For Elliot's sake, if for no one else's, he should attempt to repair their marriage. Really, he should. But he was in love with Betty. Wanted to be with Betty. Wanted to end his days with Betty. Karen, sooner or later, he knew, would irritate him, would be frustrated at Wyckhamby, would want to go back to London. But the moral aspect was tricky: he knew that divorce was wrong and that troubled him. Ought he not to make at least some attempt at reconciliation before the final abandoning of his first marriage? He groaned quietly and turned over onto his side.

Karen opened her eyes, looked at the outline of John's

muscular back and nestled closer. Still in the afterglow of their lovemaking, she thought of John's body and smiled to herself. He really was the best she had ever had. Big, athletic, but gentle. She loved the colour of his hair – same as Elliot's. Pity he was so quiet and moody, she thought, but supposed that that was caused by living in the country. Certainly, Elliot showed no sign of having inherited it. And this farm, she thought, just how much of it was his? Farmers were supposed to be rich – whoever heard of a poor one? And yet his car was quite old and this cottage, well, it was all right – quite pretty really – but not ever so luxurious. Perhaps he was just careful. Fen people were. A Cambridgeshire childhood had taught her plenty about the natives of that flat landscape. Canny, that's what they were. She rested her fingers on his back and then lightly ran her hand down over his loin and hip. He stirred and turned to face her.

'Oh Karen! What are we going to do?'

She ignored his question and smoothed the hair away from his eyes. 'John,' she kissed his nose, 'how many acres did you say your farm was?'

'Two hundred and five.' That sounded huge. She must find out what farmland cost. John got out of bed and picked up his pyjamas from the floor. 'I have to work. Will you be able to amuse yourself?'

'I suppose so.

'Borrow the car, if you want, I can walk to the farm.' She looked crestfallen. 'Oh, don't tell me, you *still* haven't passed your driving test?'

'I haven't. But it isn't that.' She sat up and gathered the blankets round her, not for modesty but to keep warm. 'I was just hopin' I could see the farm.'

'Of course you can, but I need . . . I need to sort various things out first.' He needed breathing space. 'You'll be all right, won't you? Just for today?'

'Yeah, we'll be all right.' She smiled. 'Don't look so worried love! We can explore the village today, Elliot and me.' She reached out to him, causing the bedclothes to fall away from her shoulders. He noticed her nipples beginning to firm up in the cold of the room and quickly passed her the furry jacket.

'You're distracting me. I *must* go to work.' After throwing on his dressing gown, he kissed her on neck and lips, then crossed the room to the door.

'I'll do you something special for supper tonight,' she said, but he had already bounded downstairs, waking Elliot on the way to the bathroom.

This is literally the icing on the cake, Betty thought as she whisked egg-whites and sugar to the right consistency. Every year she promised to give herself more time to prepare but when the festivities approached, she always seemed to end up with an eleventh-hour panic. Now, with a hundred other calls on her time, instead of a fondant creation worthy of Fortnum & Mason, her Christmas cake was to feature the usual rushed snow scene slapped on top of marzipan that had barely had time to dry. She spread the royal icing with brisk strokes and then dabbed her palette knife up and down on the surface to make little peaks. Real snow scenes didn't look like that, of course, but she had never been able to smooth icing properly, and the hasty knifework covered up the inadequacy. 'Anyway,' she muttered to herself, 'I'd like to see a master confectioner deliver a breech-presented calf.'

She dumped the knife into the sink, rummaged in her cake decoration box and fished out an ancient plaster Santa Claus. As she was lowering him onto the wet icing, the phone rang, making her hand jerk. Santa's feet dug a deep groove in the surface of the snow, revealing a subsoil of marzipan. 'Bother!' she muttered and then shouted, 'Can anyone get that?' before she remembered that she was alone in the house. She wiped her hands and answered it.

'Betty? Ashley.' She froze. How dare he ring? She gripped the receiver but kept silent. 'Betty?' His voice sounded strange. 'I've got a problem and I really would appreciate a favour.'

'You ask *me* for favours?' She was about to hang up but his voice had a panicky edge she had not heard before.

'Is your partner there?'

'No, he's gone home, to be with his wife.'

'His *what*?'

'Turned up yesterday. She's called Karen. There's a little boy too, Elliot. He's eight or nine. No – nine, his birthday was in October, he tells me.' Why am I telling *him*? Why am I talking to him at all?

'Betty, I've got a problem. A bad one.'

'As bad as the one you've given me?' There was an intake of breath.

'That's business.' He mixed a little more pleading into his tone. 'This is personal.'

'There's no difference, in my book. I'm going to hang up—'

'*Don't!*' It was nearly a scream, so loud that it hurt her ear. 'Please don't.' She waited. 'I've got to talk. Can I come and see you? Now?' This voice was unfamiliar. Desperation had raised both pitch and volume and she began to waver, her innate sympathy making her soften.

'What exactly is it about?'

'I'd rather come over and tell you.' He sounded so odd.

'All right.'

'Thank God!'

The Daimler's tyres crunched on the new gravel outside Cartwright Farmhouse within three minutes. He walked in, without knocking or ringing the bell, carrying a half-empty bottle of Glenlivet which he set down on the kitchen table. He looked exhausted, his hair needed washing and his shirt had a dark stain down the front – coffee, Betty thought, or gravy. His face had the expression a little boy might have after receiving punishment for some disgrace or other – hurt, bruised, bewildered.

'Whatever's the matter?' In spite of all he had done to undermine her security at Cartwright Farm, Betty felt a protective urge welling up within her.

'It's Elaine. She's left me. Nearly a week ago.' He sat heavily on one of the chairs at the kitchen table and held his head in his hands. 'She's not coming back.'

'Are you sure?'

He nodded. 'She wants a divorce.'

All Betty could do was stare. This was like saying the Queen had abdicated.

Ashley went on, speaking in flat tones, 'The fact is, I don't want too much tittle-tattle in the village. Word will be out soon enough but I need someone reliable, someone everyone trusts to put the record straight. That's you, Betty.'

'Why me?'

'You're the one they'll believe.'

'This is madness. You try to take away my livelihood and now you're asking me to help you. Why should I?'

He looked up at her. 'Because you're honourable. You'd help a desperate man – I know you would.'

'What am I supposed to make people believe?'

'The truth, of course.'

'But what is the truth?' He looked at his hands and shrugged. She went on, 'It's so . . . so sudden. I mean, Elaine and you. It's – well, it's unthinkable. You're both so happy. What's more, you're part of the structure of this place.'

'We were.'

'But what happened?' He didn't answer but looked directly at her. 'Is it someone else? An affair? You?'

'We never really know, do we, what people are up to?' Ashley continued to look at her with a steady gaze. 'Even our closest, most trusted, have secrets . . . do things we know nothing about.'

'Elaine? *Elaine* had . . . secrets?' He dropped his gaze and shrugged. She could not resist the impulse to put her arms round his shoulders. 'You poor, poor man.'

'The thing is, I don't want her to be incriminated.' And it's *me* he calls honourable, Betty thought.

'But Ashley, I still can't believe it. I mean, where did she—'

'I'm sorry, Betty, I'd really rather not say. Perhaps the less you know . . .'

'Of course. Of course.' She went to the cupboard and got out a couple of glasses. 'We'd better open that bottle.' She took it from his hand and poured a small measure into each. He removed the bottle from her and trebled his portion.

'You shouldn't drive, you know. Not if you drink that much.'

'One more won't hurt.' He swallowed the tot in a single gulp and then shuddered. 'When they ask—'

'—I know what to say.' Betty rehearsed aloud. 'It's nobody's fault really. She's gone and won't be back. It's all very sad but there it is.'

'I *knew* you'd get it right.' He stood up and held her. He needed a shave and a bath but she still thrilled at the contact. There was so little touching and holding in her life these days since Jack's death and with the children all growing up, and she hungered for it. She twiddled the curl behind his ear with her index finger and stroked his neck. Ashley said, 'I want to kiss you.'

'No.' It was too soon, too disorientating.

'Betty, this tenancy thing.' Sensing her body stiffen, he took his arms from her waist and stepped back. 'I'll get them off your back, I promise.' He picked up the bottle but put it down again. She replaced it in his hand.

'Take it. We hardly ever drink.'

'Save it for Christmas,' he said. 'At least *you* can celebrate in company.'

'Oh Ashley, you won't be alone on Christmas Day?'

''Fraid so. Andrew's going to spend it with Annabel.'

'You're welcome to come here.' Betty made hasty mental calculations about adjusting seating arrangements and quantities of extra food she might need. 'There's plenty for everyone.'

'That *is* kind.'

'It'll be family – and the Holman family, too. His wife and child.'

'Ah,' an edge had crept into his voice, 'then I think I'd better decline.'

By Christmas, John's dilemma was so uncomfortable that he even thought of driving away and leaving everyone to their own devices. Every minute spent with Betty had been an agony. She was so full of what a splendid thing it was, his wife turning up like that: how it must be very satisfying for him after all that time alone; how well behaved and intelligent Elliot was; how like his father he was and how pretty Karen was, on and on until he wanted to grab her there and then, smother her with kisses and say, 'It's *you* I want, just you and nobody else!'

To make matters worse, she hinted that she was quite jealous of Karen. That she herself was very fond of him, that she knew exactly what it was like to be lonely, that she had had nobody in her bed since Jack had been killed and that perhaps that had twisted her judgement sometimes. She even hinted – he was quite convinced this was what she meant – that she wished John had made advances, and that such advances might well have been responded to . . . but thank goodness he hadn't, now that Karen had arrived.

Early on Christmas morning, he had gone downstairs in the cottage to light the fire and set out his gifts, mainly for Elliot, in a little pile under the Christmas tree. For Karen, there was a box of soap and a large bar of milk chocolate – that would have to do. When mother and son came sleepily downstairs – Elliot had the spare room now that Karen shared John's bed – he had mugs of tea ready for them. Karen handed him a parcel wrapped in brown paper which he held while Elliot tore the wrappings from an assortment of plastic toys, packets of sweets and a small scale model of a John Deere combine harvester. 'Oh Dad, it's *brill*!'

'Aren't you going to open yours?' Karen asked, prodding John's parcel. He slid a thumbnail under the sellotaped flap and carefully unfolded the paper. It was a rather foxed copy of *The Handley Cross*, by Surtees. 'It's all about huntin' and that.' He leafed through the first few pages. The text looked turgid but the cartoons, he supposed, were quite jolly: '*Mr Jorrocks has a bye day*.' It was the last thing he would have given himself for Christmas.

'It's very fine. Thank you.' She opened her soap and

exclaimed that it was her favourite brand. Then they watched Elliot playing with his toy combine harvester.

'We mustn't be long,' he told them. 'We're due at the farm at noon.'

While Karen and Elliot pottered in the kitchen, he went upstairs to change into his suit. He took the brooch out of the bureau and looked at it. He had decided that he still wanted to give it to Betty in spite of recent events. He had saved and sacrificed to buy it for her and she must have it, even though his plans as far as she was concerned were now gone so horribly awry that he didn't think he could bear it. He opened the box and took the card out, planning to replace it with a simple message of goodwill.

'Dad!' An urgent call from Elliot, downstairs. 'Dad, I can't get this undone!' He put card and box on the bureau and came down to the sitting room. 'Cor, Dad, you look posh!'

Karen came in from the kitchen. 'Ooh, dead suave, I must say,' she retorted, and skipped upstairs to tidy herself before going to Cartwright Farm for Christmas lunch.

She was down in a moment, still in her dressing gown, and threw her arms round John's neck. 'You *darlin'!*' she squealed and kissed him again and again. 'You darlin'! It will, of course it will!'

'What are you talking about?' He was confused.

She held up the white card and read, in her nasal London voice: '"*To my dearest partner, in the hopes that our relationship will take the next step and flourish.*" Oh John, that's ever so nice!' She pinched both his cheeks and kissed his astonished mouth. 'You are a scamp, you know, livin' in this tiny 'ovel of a place and then bein' able to buy a precious thing like this.' She fished the box out of her dressing-gown pocket and snapped open the lid. 'Antique, too. Can I wear it to Cartwright?'

John turned away and looked out of the window. Outside, in the freezing fog, the village street looked like a faded photograph. Was this some kind of divine intervention, reminding him of his moral duty? He supposed it must be. 'If you like,' he said.

Chapter Twenty-six

Lunching with his bank manager in the restaurant of the White Hart at Kendale, Ashley stared gloomily out of the window. The sky was leaden, the ground filthy with mud and the Venn, wider and deeper than upstream at Wyckhamby, was in full spate with brown, turbid waters. If it continued to rise, it might even engulf the lower part of the hotel's gardens. 'Filthy bloody weather,' he muttered. 'Do you realise, Geoffrey – no, I don't suppose you do, not being as they say "of the land" – but it has rained every single day since Christmas?'

'Surely not,' said Geoff Woods who, since the bulk of his larger borrowers were farmers, resented the snub. 'That would be more than two months.'

'Well, it has. Not a day has passed without there being at least a trace of water in my rain gauge.'

'"February fill dyke", don't they say?'

'Possibly.' The aphorism made Ashley cringe. In his experience, folklore never worked except as a means of avoiding hard work or as an excuse for the one truly unforgivable sin in agriculture – untimeliness. All in all, it had been a stressful morning and he regretted having asked Woods to lunch. It was the first time he had ever had to explain why he was, albeit temporarily, somewhat financially embarrassed. The Kirland Wild débâcle had cost him dear, at a time when he needed to plug every drain on his resources. Worse, the net loss on commodity trading, under Andrew's reckless administration, had exceeeded £113,000. Andrew himself was cleaned out. His reserve capital, some of it put aside for him by his grandparents, was also gone.

Once the truth about his trading misdemeanours had been revealed, Ashley had made sure that Andrew compensated the family firm with as much money as he possessed, but he had decided to allow him to keep his new Range Rover, all his clothes and his personal possessions. He had planned, as a kind of symbolic act more reminiscent of Victorian melodrama than of real life, to throw him out of the house and to let him fend for himself, but Andrew had pre-empted him and fled just after the beginning of January. He sold his Range Rover and landed himself a reasonable job with a leading firm of commodity brokers in the City. It just shows, Ashley had told himself, what crap they employ.

Thankfully, the farm itself made a reasonable trading profit and that diluted his total losses, but the biggest problem now was Elaine. Almost a third of the Wyckhamby land belonged to her and she wanted to sell, but the prospect of an outsider acquiring any part of his farm was unthinkable. All those years of effort, of investment in the land: installing drainage systems, bearing down on perennial weed problems, brushing up stewardship year by year so that the soil became more and more fertile – why should someone else benefit from that? He thought of the upland pastures and woods, sodden in rain now but soon to produce their carpets of windflowers, primroses and violets. An ignorant owner might decide to fell the trees to make a little extra money or worse, as some of his neighbours did, use the woodland as a dumping ground for farm refuse. That would be intolerable! He *had* to find a way of buying her out, but even at tenanted values, this would mean raising at least a million pounds, probably more.

Hence his need to talk to the bank about raising extra finance. There would be no problem, of course. His assets were still large compared to his borrowings, so the bank would be happy to advance the money. 'But your gearing is getting a little higher than it should be,' Woods had warned. He was concerned. What had been such a cast-iron business seemed suddenly to have developed rather a lot of cracks.

Now there was a divorce to finance, apparently, and there appeared to be so many other calls on his client's resources.

'No problem, long-term,' Ashley said, tearing his gaze from the sodden scene outside. 'Have some pud.'

'Thank you, no. I have to watch . . . you know,' Woods patted his bulging midriff and glanced enviously at Ashley's flat stomach.

'Well, I might.' Ashley waved for the sweet trolley. He had no intention of eating any of the concoctions on offer, covered as they were with dollops of whipped cream, but the boy who trundled them over was well-knit with slender hips and an impish grin. Ashley happened to glance at Woods as the boy recited his repertoire of sickly desserts, caught the other man's wistful stare and wondered just how many other secret, respectable queers there really were. He decided to be reckless.

'Built for speed, eh?' He cocked an eyebrow and indicated the retreating boy as he wheeled his wares back to the other side of the room.

'I *beg* your parden?' The sharpness of Woods's reaction said it all.

'The trolley – well designed.'

'Oh, I see.'

Ashley enjoyed his bank manager's discomfiture. He had had enough of explaining away his losses. 'Coffee?' he asked brightly.

'Please!'

'By the way, Geoffrey, there is one asset I have which could almost double its value. At a stroke.'

'Really?' Woods pricked up his ears. Words like 'asset' and 'value' were like bells that made Pavlov's dogs salivate.

'Cartwright Farm.'

'What about it?' Woods heard warning bells. Betty and John were customers.

'Vacant Possession there could bang a couple of hundred thou onto my balance sheet. That would help the, ah, gearing, would it not?'

'Indubitably.' Woods wiped his mouth with a napkin. 'But you have two excellent tenants there.'

'Indeed. But,' Ashley leant forward to speak confidentially, 'supposing I told you they were in breach of their contract?'

'How?'

'In forming this partnership, Mrs Rose has sublet.'

'A technicality.' Woods was dismissive.

'Vacant Possession would be worth going for, financially.'

'It would be immoral.'

'Would it?' Ashley leant back again. 'On its own, it's a weak venture. They can't possibly survive the hard times to come, however many clever sidelines they dream up. But as part of Wyckhamby Farms, that extra two hundred acres would really earn its keep.'

'What about the partners?'

'Better to lose face now, while they're still solvent, than to run up a big overdraft and then go phut!'

'I can't really discuss this with you, Ashley, it's unethical,' Woods said, but he knew that there was a lot of truth in what he was hearing.

'Of course it is.' Ashley waved at the waiter again, this time watching Woods watching the boy. 'Have another coffee?'

'No, I really must get back to the bank.'

'What did you say your name was?' Ashley asked the boy.

'Damon, sir.'

'Well, Damon, we'd like the bill if you would be so kind.' He gave the boy a fulsome twinkle. Having anticipated Ashley's request, Damon had the bill on a plate in his other hand, concealed behind his back. He laid it on the table and Ashley ran his eye over the figures before placing his Platinum Card on top.

As they were leaving the restaurant, Ashley said to Woods, 'By the way, about Cartwright Farm. We have actually served notice to quit.' The other man looked startled. 'Just in case we decide to follow it up. We may not need to, but you never know, do you? It's survival of the fittest.'

*

The wet weather lasted well into March, causing the Venn to rise, not only over the hotel gardens, but also over much of the low-lying land in Wyckhamby. Saturated land was impossible to cultivate, so spring planting was held up for weeks, guaranteeing reduced yields. Furthermore, it had been wet for so long that now, even the autumn-sown crops were getting waterlogged roots and beginning to deteriorate.

On the first day of spring at Cartwright Farm, John and Betty, unable to get onto the land, were sitting in the study watching rain beat against the windows. John, not for the first time since Christmas, was quizzing her about the tenancy. 'What were Ashley's exact words?'

'I can't remember. He just said he'd get off our backs.'

'Well, I don't like this not knowing.'

'Look, if Ashley says he won't follow up the notice to quit, he won't. Not unless he's desperate.'

'I think he's playing cat and mouse.'

'Nonsense, John! Don't be such a worryguts!'

But John did worry. On the farm, even in good weather, the keen edge of his satisfaction would have been blunted by the knowledge that their land – the essential raw material of their livelihoods – could be snatched away from them at any moment. Getting stuck into hard work helped to take his mind off the problem but now, with the ground saturated and impossible for spring cultivations, and with all the usual winter tasks long since completed, he was getting into the habit of sitting in the little farm study and brooding.

Going home provided scant relief. By the time he arrived at the cottage, which had always seemed so roomy before but now felt cramped and pokey, a tetchy Karen would be waiting for him. If his meal was not ready she would be defensive; if he was late and it was spoiled, she would attack him for being thoughtless. She was, as he had feared she would be, bored with village life. Quite often, she took the morning bus to Kendale and then she would come home with a new dress, a china ornament for the mantelpiece or a box of expensive, imported chocolates – pointless purchases which soon eroded his meagre savings. He found it hard to be angry with her on these days because at least the trips seemed to make her happier.

Elliot, too, was a worry. At school, he was behind the rest of the class with his reading and writing and his teacher had already contacted Karen to complain about discipline problems. 'I'm not sure what you were used to in London,' she said, 'but here in the country, we still value the old-fashioned methods – the three Rs, as they say – and we do expect good behaviour.' This had puzzled both Karen and John because, at home, Elliot was such a sweet-natured, biddable little boy. In fact, as far as John was concerned, Elliot had been a big compensation for having Karen back. The initial awkwardness he had expected that day, just before Christmas at Kendale station, had never happened. Even though he hardly knew his father – they had spent fewer than half a dozen snatched holidays together in nearly a decade – Elliot had taken to him with an easy familiarity. Their relationship could hardly have been more relaxed if John had come home from work and into his life every day since birth. Elliot loved the country, especially the farm. He wanted to ride in the tractors, naturally, but he also wanted to know about all the farming activities. His favourite spot was the piggery. He spent hours watching the sows with their young. He cried when consignments of porkers went, each Monday, to Kendale market but he accepted that they should go and tucked into roast pork at Sunday lunch with gusto, snapping the crackling with his small, even teeth.

Sex was John's other compensation. Irritating though Karen could be, the embers of their initial fiery passion still glowed. If she was tense and unhappy, stressed by the ennui of rural nothingness, bed would put it right, would bring her to life and remove the shadow of discontent from her face. If she were elated, they would celebrate with sex, going to bed early, leaving Elliot to watch the tiny portable television in the parlour before putting himself to bed. Erotic dreams haunted John no longer but he did find that although he could forget all his anxieties when he was actually making love to Karen, the speed with which they began to return afterwards increased with each passing week. If only the rain would stop, he thought, and then was startled by the sound of knocking on Betty's kitchen door.

'That'll be Maggie,' Betty said, and jumped up to let her in.

'Hullo, you!' Maggie bustled into the kitchen dropping rainwater all about her. In spite of a canary-yellow woolly hat which she pulled off and shook, her hair was saturated and plastered to her forehead. 'Do you mind?' She threw her wet cape onto the kitchen floor and dropped the hat on top.

'Here, let me have those.' Betty picked them up. 'I'll put them by the boiler.'

'It's *pissing* down out there!'

'Come through. John's in the study.' Betty led the way and the three of them squeezed into the little room.

'The fact is,' Maggie said, once she had got her breath, 'I'm adding to my little business.' She had, over the previous summer, revived her garden design consultancy which, though small, had already begun to earn a little pin money. 'I want to make you a business proposition.'

'If it's capital you're after, forget it,' Betty said. 'We're hard up enough as it is.'

'Balls!' Maggie retorted. 'Farmers always say that.' John tried not to feel embarrassed at her language. She caught the disdain on his face and muttered, 'pardon my French, John,' amending herself after a brief moment of consideration, 'no, sod it! Why should a girl have to apologise to a bloke?'

'You don't have to.' John felt his cheeks burning. 'But about being hard up, well, in our case it's true.'

'I'll believe you. But no, listen, this is what I'm after.' She began to tick off points with the forefinger of one hand tapping into the palm of the other as she spoke. 'I want to start actually *doing* some of the designs I'm drawing. Firstly, I'll get more commissions if I can do the contracting, secondly, it will get me out and about and thirdly, I can keep the business going, if things go quiet, with regular mainten-ance jobs – lawn-mowing, edge-trimming, that kind of thing.'

389

'Will you be doing this?' John asked.

'I'm not scared of hard graft, if that's what you mean, but one of the village boys is going to work for me, full-time. As for the rest, well, there's plenty of casual labour knocking about. I'll do the prinking jobs that need special skill. Bobby – it's Bobby Goss, by the way, you know, the shop boy who always used to fall off his bike – he'll operate the equipment, which is where you come in.'

'Ah,' said Betty.

'I've bought a second-hand mini tractor and some digging equipment. Then there's bags of cement, sand, paving stones, that kind of thing.'

'What are you driving at?' John said.

'Well, you two have always been telling me you have a couple of redundant buildings. I wondered whether we could use one of them as a depot. We'd pay, naturally.'

'Don't see why not,' said Betty. 'Do you, John?'

John shook his head. 'In fact,' he said, 'if you wanted to use any of our farm machinery, we could contract it out to you. I could even drive it.'

'Brilliant!' Maggie crowed. They got down to discussing details and agreed a price.

Getting ready to leave, Maggie said, 'I've already got one handy contract for garden maintenance – at the Old Rectory. In fact, I've just come from there.'

'They're having to spend so much time with Camilla,' Betty said, 'that I should think gardening is pretty low on their list of priorities.'

Maggie sighed. She took the half-dried cape from John who had fetched it from the boiler. 'Must be terrible for them all, having to bear something like that. The poor child's bones are as brittle as blackboard chalk, apparently.'

'I know,' Betty said. She still went to the hospital twice a week.

Maggie pulled open the back door. 'Look, it's stopped raining! Perhaps we'll get a spring after all. 'Bye, all!' And she strode, as briskly as her amplitude of figure would allow, down the lane towards the Wyckhamby Farms offices. Since forswearing alcohol, she had taken to munching chocolate bars in times of stress and had slowly but steadily increased her bulk. This was one reason for setting up the contracting service. She wanted to get herself a bit thinner and a bit fitter. As she walked, she felt in the pocket of her cardigan and found a single piece of Callard & Bowser's treacle toffee, wrapped in red foil. Of late, she had been eating toffee instead of chocolate on the understanding that it was harder, took longer to eat and was therefore better for her weight problem. She unwrapped the piece, put it into her mouth and told herself not to bite but to suck.

Ashley was in his office when she arrived. His smile was warm but he seemed to have lost weight since Elaine's abrupt departure and that, thought Maggie, made him look somewhat ascetic, and therefore even more interesting than before. She still found it almost impossible to believe that Elaine had been indulging in sexual peccadilloes under everyone's noses. Still, you never really knew people, even if you thought you did, and Ashley was so noble about it. He never even mentioned it now, although you could tell how much it had hurt him just by looking at the man.

'Maggie, how well you look!' Ashley took a chair, placed it in front of his desk and indicated that she should sit.

'Bollocks, Ashley, I'm as fat as butter and fair puffed after walking less than a mile.' He chuckled at that, turning up the twinkle in his hazel eyes to maximum emission. 'You look bloody marvellous as usual, though.'

'You say the nicest things! I'm beginning to feel a little more like facing the world again.'

'How are you managing at home?'

'There's a housekeeper now. She does for me, up to a point, but obviously the Manor doesn't look as . . . as well as . . .' He seemed unable to finish the sentence. Maggie felt she could cry. She sat, not quite knowing what to say. He went on: 'Have you made any progress with your new business?'

'I'll be up and running as soon as this sodding weather breaks. I've got that Goss boy starting on Monday week.'

'Splendid! And you will be doing maintenance, as well as landscaping?'

'Absolutely!'

'I was wondering whether you might be interested in sort of running things here? The garden, I mean.' Maggie had hoped this was why he had asked to see her. 'Elaine used to do it all,' he went on. 'She used to borrow a farm-hand if she wanted a bit of brawn but the amount of work she did herself was staggering. There's no way I could—'

'My dear Ashley, I know this garden almost as well as I know my own. It will be a pleasure to look after it.'

'What will it cost me?'

'Can't say offhand. Well, yes I can. I probably have a better idea of what's involved than you do – Oh Christ, that sounded appallingly presumptuous, Ashley. I'm so sorry!'

'I'm sure it's true. How much?'

'In round figures, about . . . ooh,' she screwed up her eyes, wondering how far she dared go, 'eight thousand a year?'

'That much?' He looked surprised.

'Six,' she made a hasty correction. 'No more than six.' He still looked pensive. She sighed. She really had no idea of where her true costs might be and wondered why the hell she hadn't suggested that she go away and prepare a carefully calculated quotation. But she needed this work. Badly. 'Five, then,' she said at last. 'Five if we use your mowers.'

Ashley hesitated for no more than a couple of seconds. 'Fine. When can you start?'

'First of April, weather permitting. By the way, your lake needs dredging. That little stream that feeds it is almost choked with silt. We could do that for you and then replant it all with bog primulas and things.'

Ashley held up his hand. 'Woah, steady! We are in a difficult trading situation this year. Absolutely no frills. Anyway,' he glanced at her sharply, 'you couldn't do anything that big. You haven't the tackle.'

'Oh yes, we have.'

'What, diggers? Earth-movers?'

'You'd be surprised at what we can do.'

'Where are you keeping all that equipment?'

'Cartwright Farm.'

'Are you by gosh!' He thought for a moment or two. 'Pretty friendly with those two, are you?'

'I know Betty much better than I do John. He's the silent seething type as far as I can see.'

'I think he's a bit peculiar. Something to hide, perhaps.'

'He's been a godsend to Betty.'

'Are you sure?'

'It's obvious. I even thought they'd get spliced at one stage. They think the world of each other, any fool can see that. Then that tarty wife of his turned up.'

Ashley looked at her intently. 'Maggie, can I take you into my confidence?'

'You can. But what's this all about?'

'I care a great deal for Betty. More perhaps than you've ever realized, any of you.'

'You astound me!'

'Maggie,' his voice took on a quiet, conspiratorial tone. 'While you're up there, with your landscaping plant and all that, would you keep an eye on her for me?'

'How d'you mean?'

'See if you can find anything out about, oh, I don't know, anything. How they operate together, his status in the partnership.'

'His status?'

'Mm. I realise they are partners, but is it fifty-fifty or is he a minority holder? Do they have just the one joint bank account or what. You know the sort of thing.'

Maggie was shocked. 'You want me to spy? On my closest friend?'

'Maggie, Maggie!' He leaned across the desk and put his hands on top of hers. 'It's your closest friend I want to protect. Don't you see?'

Chapter Twenty-seven

'I know it's no comfort, but I'm afraid I can't give you a sensible answer.' The consultant leafed through the papers in front of him for the third time. 'Camilla's living on borrowed time now, really. She's putting up the bravest fight.' He looked up at the couple sitting on the other side of his desk: the woman in an expensive worsted suit and cream silk blouse, her honey-coloured hair faultlessly groomed but the cosmetics on her sun-tanned face tear-streaked; the man absent, distracted. Jules Doncaster did not give the impression of being distressed, in fact he seemed quite relaxed, but the consultant noticed that his fingernails were bitten down to the quick. He addressed himself to the woman. 'You have a courageous daughter, Mrs Doncaster.'

'Stepdaughter,' Sally said, reaching for another tissue from the box on the consultant's desk. 'I told you before.'

'I'm sorry. Please forgive me.'

'You said it might be a couple of months at Christmas. That's why I put off going to Africa for so long.' Sally had resisted increasingly urgent calls from the Prince in Mudando. His newly-acquired business had developed a series of crises, each one more intense until finally, in March, she had been obliged to fly out, not knowing whether Camilla would still be alive when she returned.

'I know. I know.' He put the papers back into their folder. 'But she is quite peaceful now and that must be a relief to everyone.' He got up. Clearly the interview was at an end.

'Peaceful,' Jules said, 'because you've got her so full of junk she can't think straight.' It was the longest speech he had made all afternoon. He looked startled at his own outburst and quickly corrected himself. 'It's for the best, of course. I understand that.' He put the middle finger of his left hand into his mouth but quickly pulled it away again, putting the hand into his trouser pocket.

The consultant showed them out of his office. Slowly, they walked to the car. Sally wondered how long she could bear this waiting. Camilla was so ill now that she could barely see and certainly could not move. Sally presumed she was aware when they were beside her but she wasn't sure.

'I can't take much more,' Sally said. 'Did you *see* her?' Jules unlocked the BMW and they both got in. 'It's as if . . . as if God were playing a sort of cat and mouse game.'

'Don't torture yourself,' Jules said. He did not touch her but stared straight ahead. 'It won't be long now.' She looked at his profile, staring through the windscreen, watched him carefully put his keys into the ignition and turn them. The calmness on his face infuriated her. It increased her own feelings of guilt.

'What *is* it with you? How can you be so, so fucking complacent! Are you dead or what?' He did not react. 'Well?' she screamed. 'Well?' Fresh tears ran along the dried tracks of earlier ones. 'How can I make you come alive again?' He reversed out of their parking place and then drove forwards, continuing to stare ahead. His hand, resting on the gear lever, stirred with a slight tremor which she did not notice. 'God damn you for a cold, heartless bastard.' She knew this accusation was unjust and horribly cruel but his behaviour begged it and she was hurting too much to stop herself. 'God damn you!'

She fished in her handbag, brought out a powder compact and lipstick and pulled down the passenger sun-flap to expose the mirror. 'Jesus Christ,' she muttered at the sight of her face and began a hasty repair job with tissues and lipstick. Once, she glanced at Jules as he drove. His eyes were dry, his demeanour calm but inside he was being torn apart. And she knew it.

'When it's over,' he said, quite calmly after a couple more

miles, 'I'll be going too. For good.' The lipstick smudged on her lower lip. She stopped trying to apply make-up and stared at him. He continued to look straight ahead. 'Better all round. Don't you think?'

They sat in silence for the rest of the journey until he pulled into the drive of the Old Rectory. 'And by the way,' he said, 'you can keep this place. I hate it.'

How I love it when it's like this, Betty thought, watching the first swallows of the year dipping down over the Venn, snapping up the insects which flew among the tiny white flowers of water crowfoot. She was celebrating the completion of all her spring cultivations by walking along the banks of the river towards Wyckhamby Manor, planning to cross at the ford, provided the river had gone down enough not to come over the tops of her wellingtons, and to walk back through the village to John's cottage for a cup of tea. John had suggested that she come any time in the afternoon so that she could linger on her walk if the weather was good, which it was.

'Oh bother!' she muttered aloud, for a figure was approaching on the riverbank upstream. It was too far away to identify but she suspected it might be Bert Mardle heading back to his cottage after visiting the Manor. As they approached each other, she realised, with the usual swirl of mixed feelings, that it was Ashley. He kept stooping as he approached and once, seemed to stagger, almost to fall into the river.

She stared curiously, but as he got nearer, she realised he was picking flowers. When they drew abreast, he handed her a posy of cowslips, marsh marigolds and frail, lilac cuckoo flowers. 'I spotted you from miles away,' he said, 'so I picked you these. Nearly fell in the river getting those May blobs.'

She laughed at the name – it was what the village boys called them. In Sussex they had always been kingcups. Betty took them and looked at him. The worry lines round his eyes seemed to be permanent these days.

'You've lost weight,' she said.

'Healthy living,' he asserted. She doubted that. She suspected that he was skimping his meals and drinking a bit too much.

'How are you coping?'

'Splendidly. Come and see for yourself.'

'I can't, I'm having tea with John and Karen in the village.'

'Funny route to take.'

'I promised myself a wander along the riverbank first.'

'Come up to the Manor, do. You can have a quick cup with me first,' he smiled.

She raised the bouquet of flowers and inhaled the delicate, china-tea fragrance of the cowslips. 'All right, I will. Thank you.'

It was natural to slip an arm into his and understandable that they should take the short cut through the little copse on the slope below the Manor. Primroses studded the woodland margin and, as they walked, she could smell sweet violets, blending with the fragrance of leafmould and young foliage. 'So beautiful here, don't you think? Especially in late April.'

'Your being here is what makes it beautiful.' He halted and turned to her. 'You could make a gasworks beautiful!' He stopped her laugh abruptly with a kiss, fair and square on the mouth.

She knew he was going to and she wanted him to do it. Years of celibacy had made her thirst for human contact – no, for more: for love, sex, the whole damn thing. He held her tightly and probed her mouth deeply with his tongue. He had perfect, very white teeth. After a few moments she pulled away. 'Ashley, this is wrong.'

'Oh no, Betty, this is right. This is the rightest thing possible.' Linking hands, like secondary-school kids on their first date, they walked up to the Manor.

'Come upstairs.'

'Absolutely not!'

'Oh Betty, Betty!' He kissed her again, in the hall. She sensed the strength in his arms and the sweetness of his scent, fresh, slightly musky but exciting. He nuzzled her neck and

397

nipped her ear lobe, making a tingle run like fire from there to the tips of her toes. She had not realised until that point how badly she needed a man. She didn't even think women should have appetites of that sort. She realised, with a shock, that she was wearing ancient underwear and giggled. 'What's the joke?'

'I'm not exactly dressed to kill!'

'Nor me. The answer is simple. Let's not be dressed at all.'

'No, Ashley, really I—' but he had her in his arms again and try as she might, she could not think of a single reason for resisting him, except that she would be very late for tea at the Holmans. He led the way to his bedroom and showed her the bathroom.

'I'm just popping up the corridor for a shower,' he said. She ran a shallow bath and washed before towelling herself vigorously. In the mirror she grinned at the pink image. Not bad for your age, she thought, running flattened palms down her smooth stomach and then turning to see herself sideways on. Your bum's still quite neat she thought, pouting and thrusting her breasts forward. A strong point, her breasts were. Jack had always said so, anyway.

The memory of Jack brought a pang of guilt. *What did she think she was doing?* Should she get dressed and run? She could, even now. But she left her clothes in the bathroom, borrowed a towelling robe from the door and flopped down on the wide, firm bed.

He came in with a skimpy towel round his waist. 'I forgot my dressing gown,' he said, and then noticed she was wearing it. 'Aha! Asserting yourself already!' He took the towel off and wiped himself behind the ears. She could count the number of nude male bodies she had seen in her life on the fingers of one hand. Jack's was quite small and rather hairy, her son Jim's slim and boyish, when she had last seen him naked. Ashley was neither boyish nor hairy. His proportions were balanced, with long, muscular legs, a broad chest which tapered to a tiny waist and pert buttocks. His chest had a sprinkling of fur and there was another line which broadened slightly as it ran from just below his navel.

'Are you circumcised?' she asked.

'Yes, actually.' She had never seen him embarrassed before. 'Why do you ask?'

'No reason. It's just that I've never ...' Now she was embarrassed.

'It makes no difference. Just a notion our family must have had that it was hygienic or something.'

'I'm sorry I brought it up.' She felt awkward. He got onto the bed and untied the sash of her towel robe. She felt her heart beating wildly with a mixture of anticipation, tension and not a little fright. 'Ashley,' she said, in a faint voice.

'Mmm?'

'Be gentle. I'm not really very experienced in—' but he smoothed out her anxieties with gentle, attentive caresses.

For ages afterwards, she lay quietly while he stroked her arms with his fingertips. She had had no idea that sex could be like that. It was as if she had been a musical instrument which he knew how to tune into glorious harmonies and melodies. He was so patient, so energetic and yet so gentle and sympathetic. What a fuddled amateur she must have appeared to him. How clumsy, how inelegant she had felt at first, until she had simply followed his lead and learned to sense his needs.

'Ashley,' she said, at last, 'I don't know what to do.'

'Sshh!' He stroked her hair. 'Sshh,' and then, after a minute or so, 'plenty of time to think about all that. Just relax now.'

'Heavens, I must go!' She sat up and reached for his towel robe. 'It's getting late and I don't want to hurt John's feelings.'

'Ooh no, we mustn't do that, must we.'

'No,' she ignored his sarcasm, 'no, I mustn't. It would be unkind to be too late.'

'I'll give you a lift,' he said, getting out of bed. 'You'll be even later if you try to walk the rest of the way.'

The clock on St James's Church said 6.30 when Ashley's Daimler, now five years old, drew up outside the Holmans' cottage. It had been stuck at 6.30 for at least a decade but still gave Betty a jolt of anxiety until she glanced at the dashboard clock. 'Is that clock right?'

'Three minutes fast,' Ashley said. 'It's almost five.'

'Gosh, I was expected ages ago. No, Ashley, don't!' He was about to kiss her. 'Not here, not yet.' She got out of the car, slammed the door and ran for the front door which was already being opened by Elliot.

'Cor,' he said, when he spotted the Daimler. 'You've got some rich friends, Aunty Betty.'

'Here,' she stooped to kiss his cheek, 'take these and see if you can revive them.' She handed him her posy of wilted wildflowers. 'Break a bit off the bottom of each stem and then put the whole bunch in a big jug of water, right over their heads.' He scampered off to the kitchen, leaving her to make her own way into the small sitting room. It seemed a lot less neat and tidy than when John had been living on his own. A clutter of ornaments had replaced his books on the shelves and in the fireplace stood a large pot Alsatian dog which, like the bull on the window-ledge, had gilt tips to its ears, nose, tail and feet. John came in from the kitchen.

'Sorry, we didn't hear you. We're planting lettuces out the back.'

'Hullo, John.' Why did she feel guilty about the previous couple of hours? What was it to John what she did in her own time? 'I'm sorry I'm a bit late. I walked the long way.'

'You're not late. We agreed any time.'

'I came over by Wyckhamby Manor Copse. It all looks so pretty at this time of year. I do love it when the meadows are full of cuckooflower and the first swallows come.' To her surprise and to his concern, her eyes brimmed.

'You're overworked,' he said, with reproach in his voice, 'First day off in months and you spend it traipsing about the countryside. Here, sit down.' He plumped up a cushion.

Presently, Karen came in, carrying a tray with tea things, followed by Elliot who had a plate of sandwiches in one hand and a packet of bought cakes in the other. 'Ooh, 'ello Mrs Rose,' Karen said. Betty wished she'd use her Christian name. ''Ere, Elliot, set them down on the little table.' Elliot did so, with exaggerated care.

'Looks nice,' Betty said.

'I made a sponge cake but it come out of the oven all hard an' flat. I 'ad to throw it away.'

'Oh, I'm useless at sponges,' Betty said. 'Mine are *leaden*. What I usually do is make a good, rich fruit cake. It doesn't matter how solid they get, as long as they're cooked through.'

'Mmm. I've tried them too. I never know when they're done. I plunge a knife into 'em that many times they're nearly sliced *before* they come out the oven!' She gave a little shriek. 'John gets ever so cross. Says I waste food.'

They settled down to afternoon tea. Afterwards, Elliot brought the revived flowers in so that Betty could help him identify them. 'You can press them between blotting paper,' she said. 'It preserves their colours. I've still got some I pressed when I was your age.'

John said, 'I nearly forgot to tell you. Geoffrey Woods – you know, at the bank – phoned yesterday. He wants us to go in and talk to him.'

'Really?' In spite of their having survived recent crises, Betty still stiffened at the mention of the name. 'What does he want?'

'He didn't say, but I told him we'd go on Monday afternoon. Is that all right for you?'

'Mmm, after I've been to see Camilla.'

'That's what I thought.'

Geoffrey Woods was solicitous when they arrived at the Shires Bank two days later. He fussed about, organising chairs for them, looking into his secretary's office to order cups of tea and finally, sitting at his desk and opening the large brown folder that lay before him. 'This is your file,' he said. 'And what an example to all business people it is.' They smiled. Such compliments were a little embarrassing.

'We had a couple of bountiful years,' Betty said.

'Exactly! Now, what I'd like to know is, how are things this year?'

'It's been less easy,' admitted John.

'But we're fine,' said Betty.

'Are you sure?' Three wet months after Christmas had spoilt some of the winter crops, especially those on low-lying land, and had made spring sowings catchy and late. Even the most efficient farmers had lost growing time and were predicting reduced yields. 'A lot of farmers are forecasting a poor wheat crop,' Woods commented.

'Indeed, and so are we. But we're less dependent than some on a single commodity.'

'Glad to hear it.' There was a short silence. The man seemed hesitant. 'How about your tenancy?'

'Tenancy?'

'Everything all right there? No problems or anything?' John and Betty looked at one another. 'You see, your tenancy is really your only substantial asset. It is the security for your borrowing here.'

'We realise that,' John said, 'but our trading position is healthy enough.'

'Indeed, indeed,' said Woods, 'but I, well, I heard a little rumour.'

'Oh?' Betty knew what was coming.

'That there was some problem over the tenancy.' The partners sat in silence. 'That you had been served with a notice to quit.'

'That's true. Before Christmas – but that was a formality.'

'What's the problem?'

'Technically, our partnership may constitute a subletting,' Betty said, 'but our landlord—'

'He banks here, doesn't he, Kirkland?' John interrupted.

'I'm not really at liberty to say.'

'I bet he does, the—'

'John!' Betty was anxious to keep this civil.

'The fact is,' Woods said, 'that you have had notice to quit. In writing.'

'Ashley Kirkland has also informed me,' Betty said, 'that he has no intention of taking the matter any further.'

'In writing?'

'No,' Betty said, 'but Ashley, as I'm sure you will be the first to agree, is a man of his word.' She looked at Woods, whose eyes dropped before her direct gaze.

'Of course.' He shuffled the papers in their file for a few moments. 'However, I think you should know that the bank is a little, er, disquieted about the notice. We won't need to take any action now, but I must remind you that your overdraft arrangement allows us to demand repayment at any time.'

'Yes, we understand that,' John said.

'And if we felt that your tenancy might become forfeit, we would have little choice but to foreclose.' He shut the file, and they stood up. Showing them to the door, he said, 'Meanwhile, we press on with our work. Goodness knows, no one deserves success more than you two.'

'Thanks,' Betty said.

'Tell me,' Woods continued, 'those self-pick raspberries. Are they going to be available this season?'

'Of course.'

'Capital, capital! Margaret and I picked fourteen pounds of them last year and froze the lot. Delicious!' He opened the door for them. 'My secretary will show you out.' He watched them being escorted from the outer office and then shut his door.

He returned to his desk and leafed through the file again. This was a sad case. They had worked so incredibly hard and had managed to drag a run-down business back into prosperity, against all odds. But could he really support them now? Geoffrey Woods knew, and they did not, how Ashley's finances were looking and, whatever he might have said, Ashley was bound, if things got any worse for him, to want to maximise his capital. Furthermore, it might be more prudent, from the bank's point of view, to support Ashley's bigger and, in the long run, more viable business than theirs. In the hard times to come, with the removal of farm support prices, they were unlikely to be able to survive anyway. It might even be best if the bank brought things to a head by foreclosing *before* the tenancy was actually lost. That would mean that when the fight came, if fight there was, the partners at Cartwright would have no weapons. They might even settle out of court for a sum to cover their borrowings and quit peacefully. Now that would be a good solution all round: good for the Shires Bank, good for Ashley – one of this branch's largest customers – and really, taking all things into consideration, good for the partners, even though they wouldn't thank him for it. Not at first anyway. He was moving to his decision to foreclose, but to let them get this year's harvest in first. He had first charge on all assets so that would eliminate the risk of any bad debts as far as the bank was concerned. The rest of the creditors could divide what was left among themselves.

On the way home, John was despondent. 'He's up to something.'

'I don't think so. As long as Ashley keeps his word, we'll be fine.'

'I don't think he will keep his word. I think they are plotting something. When the time is ripe they'll pounce, you mark my words.'

'John, stop. You're talking out of spite.'

'You think so?'

'I know so. Now come on. All we've got to do is show them we can perform.'

'But that's just it. *Can* we perform after this wet spring? We're bound to take a tumble in profits. No, what worries me is that Ashley sees a downturn in his own fortunes. If that is so, he could bide his time and then quietly inform the bank that he intends, after all, to follow up his suit to evict us. Then all the bank needs to do is wait until we've got the harvest in and then go for us. We'd be cleaned out.'

'This is pure conjecture,' Betty said. 'It could happen but I know it won't. Ashley will keep his word – of that you can be sure!'

He dropped her at the end of Cartwright Lane, drove into the village and quietly entered the cottage. Karen had been to Kendale. 'Why didn't you say you were taking the bus into town?' he asked, with exasperation in his voice. 'We could have brought you back.'

'I don't like that jeep thing. It smells and it's filthy.' She was sitting surrounded by the spoils of yet another spending spree. A vast box of Dairy Milk chocolates rested on her lap and at her feet various carrier bags lay with their contents: an electric food-chopper, a summer dress with matching cotton jacket, white sling-back shoes and a lavish coffee table book on container gardening among them. John took in the scene with growing disquiet. Elliot came in carrying an expensive photograph album.

'Look, Dad. It's for pressed flowers. Aunty Betty says you'll show me where the best ones grow.'

John stroked the boy's blond thatch. 'Mum should have stood you a haircut while you were in town, son.' Then he looked at Karen. 'How much have you spent?'

'Oh, don't be so stingy. You farmers are all the same, everyone says so.'

'Have you any idea how many farming bankruptcies there were last year?'

'Come off it, John. No one ever heard of a poor farmer.'

He decided it was, at last, time to give her chapter and verse. After all, she had spent all of his savings and was now running up debts. Heaven knew how she had managed to get a credit card, but she had.

'I've spent the afternoon at the bank.' He spared no details about his financial position, ran through the history of Cartwright Farm and pointed out to her that she had spent more in four months than he had in two years. She listened, her eyes growing wider and wider. When he had finished, she picked up a chocolate then put it back, carefully, into its crinkly paper holder, burst into tears and ran upstairs to the main bedroom. She did not come down all evening.

Eventually, for the first time since she had arrived, he decided to sleep alone and tried to settle on the sitting-room sofa. But his body was too long and it was impossible to get comfortable. Finally, he crept up to the second bedroom where Elliot lay, pulled the covers back and gently moved the sleeping child over to make room before slipping in beside him and lying with his nose resting in the sweet-smelling hair at the back of his son's neck.

Next morning he arose at dawn, went directly over to Cartwright Farm and worked hard all day, rolling the cereal crops. At dusk, when he'd been driving without a break for fourteen hours, Betty drove up in the Landrover.

'Isn't it time you went home to your family?'

'Maybe.'

'Not maybe, definitely! What's brought all this work on? We're not behind or anything.'

'Worry, I suppose.'

'Well, stop worrying! Worry kills, and I want you to be here running this joint with me in a couple of decades.'

'Ha ha. Some hopes.'

'Oh we will, don't worry. But for now, you should be with your wife and that delightful little boy of yours.' She saw the tender smile cross his face and thought what a lovely father he must be. 'There can't be many days of the Easter holidays left. Why not go on a long walk with him tomorrow? He's mad about nature.'

'I know.' Stopping the tractor to relieve himself earlier that day, John had spotted a moorhen's nest, concealed among the reeds at the edge of one of the farm ponds. Showing it to Elliot and watching his face light up would make an exquisite highlight to the ramble. In spite of the short time he had lived in Wyckhamby, the boy already knew more about the countryside than most of his village contemporaries. At this rate, he'd make a fine steward of the land when he reached manhood, but would he have Cartwright Farm to take over? He rather doubted it. And would Jim or Mandy Rose be his farming partners? He doubted that too.

'Well?' Betty chipped into his thoughts. 'I can finish this rolling tomorrow.'

'All right.'

'That's more like it! We can leave the tractor here. I'll run you up to the village in the Landrover.' He locked the tractor cab, handed her the key and jumped up beside her in the other vehicle.

On the way she said, 'I wanted to tell you something, about the bank and all this tenancy business.'

'What of it?'

'Well, there's no need to worry about it, that's all.'

'You've already said that.'

'No, I mean I *know* that there'll be no question of being threatened by Ashley.' She pulled up outside his cottage.

'How can you, or either of us possibly know that?'

'Well,' she made a conscious effort to get the words out, 'we're having an affair, you see.' He stared at her for a moment and then was gone. Used to his taciturn ways, Betty simply drove home, glad that he had told him and hoping that she had eased his anxiety.

John stood for a full two minutes on the doorstep. He had known all along, really, but had just hoped that she had merely been attracted, infatuated perhaps. He hated the idea of anyone, anyone at all having to do with Betty. But Kirkland? It was more than he could stand. He couldn't put his finger on it but he just knew that the man was bad news.

Then he noticed that none of the lights was on in the cottage. He unlocked the door and walked in. The sitting room was in such disarray that at first he thought a burglar had been in. Then he realised that Karen hadn't cleaned up. He called, 'Karen! Elliot!' He ran upstairs but no one was there so he ran down again. In the kitchen he found a note on the table, held down by the milk jug.

Dear John,

Things haven't been quite as happy as I hoped and I know you'll agree it was for the best that Elliot and me should go back to London.

I hope you're farming worries sort themselves out. Elliot is crying buckets while I write this. I've told him he can come to you're home for holidays I hope that is all right and he can.

I don't know where I'll be staying but I'll write you again when I do. I'm sorry John.

Yours truly, Karen.

John went back upstairs, more slowly this time, and switched the light on in the little bedroom. The photograph album was open on the unmade bed, with a wilted cowslip lying on a piece of white blotting paper beside it. The stem of the flower had stained the paper with its greenish sap. He walked into the main bedroom and saw that the wardrobe door was open, and a heap of coat-hangers was thrown on the bed. He went to get out his camphorwood box. The little jewel case was on top of the bureau. He picked it up and opened it. Inside, the card was still there, but the brooch was not.

Chapter Twenty-eight

'No! No! No! NO! It cannot, can*not* be true.' Sally stared across the consulting-room desk at Leonard Bates. 'It must not be true, don't you see?' Anticipating a storm of tears, Leonard pushed a box of tissues towards her.

'Why not? You've years to go yet before you are beyond childbearing age. It's not dangerous or anything.'

'But I'm not supposed to be *able* to. Certainly not with Jules, anyway.'

'Ah.' Leonard wasn't sure what to say next. 'Do you mean that your husband is . . .'

'Sterile? He might as well be.'

'I see.'

'No you don't, Leonard. You don't even see the half of it.' Sally undid the gold clasp of her crocodile-skin handbag and scrabbled inside for a small looking glass and lipstick. Leonard watched as she pursed her lips to the image in the mirror. 'Christ, now I've smudged my face.'

'Wouldn't you rather do that in the loo?' Leonard was conscious of a waiting room full of patients. Outside, the May sunshine aggravated his frustration at being stuck indoors.

'Christ, Leonard, can't you let a girl compose herself for a moment? I've got to think.'

'You could terminate.'

Sally put her lipstick away and thought for a moment. 'No, I couldn't.' She closed her handbag. 'Heaven knows I wish I could, but with Camilla and everything . . . it would feel like, like murder.' Her eyes brimmed, smudging mascara. 'Oh *sod* it!' She took several tissues out of the box.

'Sally, I want to help you.'

'You can't, Leonard. I've got to deal with this on my own.'

'On the physical side, I mean. We need to take care of Mother while Baby develops.'

'Jesus, Leonard, it's a foetus!' Anger dried the tears. 'You can save the "while Baby develops" style for your more cretinous patients, but don't use it on me!'

'I'm sorry.' Leonard smiled, embarrassed. 'But you will need to attend clinics and so on. I'll give you a diet sheet and some literature to take home.'

'Clinics?' The thought of waiting for hours with groups of young mothers appalled her. 'Can't I come privately?'

'Not advisable,' Leonard said. 'Maternity is the one thing we do quite well in the Health Service.'

'But I have so little time!'

'Really? I thought you sold your business.'

'I have, but I still do a lot of consultancy, particularly for the Mudandan government.'

'Well, there'll be big responsibilities for both you and your hus—er, Jules, to consider.' It was difficult for Leonard not to slip into his routine procedure for expectant mothers. Most of his pregnant patients were half Sally's age and enjoyed a tenth or less of her income. They tended to be inarticulate and docile in their responses.

'He's going to leave me. Did you know that?'

'Sorry?' Leonard put his head forward to hear more clearly.

'When, you know, when Camilla ...' She took another handful of tissues. 'Soon, anyway.'

Leonard wasn't sure what she was going on about. 'I'd like to see you again.' He stood up. 'On Monday.'

'That's it, is it?'

'Sally, I'm sorry but I have a room full of people out there, all with problems.' He showed her out and dealt with another twenty-three patients before walking through the garden to Bridge House for a cup of coffee before going on his rounds.

He expected to find Maggie in the garden and strolled around, enjoying the scene – so different from her drunken days – of well-kept borders and neat lawns. In spite of her new commitment to designing, building and maintaining other people's gardens, her own was a shining, weedless example. He searched for her, peeping behind hedges, into arbours and through trellises but, to his surprise, the garden was empty.

Approaching the kitchen, he heard voices and saw, through the window, that she was engaged in conversation with John Holman. Not wanting to get involved, he peeped in at the window, shouted 'Hullo!' and then wandered off to begin his rounds without coffee.

In the kitchen, Maggie and John were poring over a number of old horticultural books, of which Maggie had an extensive and growing library. She was taking notes while he sought out the references.

'I think you've hit on a pretty hot idea,' she said, leafing through a 1921 edition of Thomas Rivers's catalogue. 'There's quite a trend in reviving these old varieties.' John wanted to convert some of the grassland at Cartwright Farm into a fruit orchard. His idea was to build up a collection of old-fashioned plums, apples and pears and use these as stocks from which to raise young trees to sell to city people who were moving into the country and renovating old farmhouses and gardens. Authenticity was what they were after – a rare commodity in the sanitised countryside of the 1980s – and if they could get it they would pay for it. Many of these merchant bankers, barristers and company directors, wealthy after having had their tax burdens halved and their city properties trebled in value by a hot economy, had quaint ideas of what country living should be like. Some wanted to act out their fantasies by milking goats or making their own cider, others preferred riding to hounds in winter and hosting garden fêtes in the summer, as if they were latterday squires.

'If we get the orchard planted up,' John said, 'I thought we could take budwood from the trees to make young stock to sell. We could also keep the orchard grassed over and graze it with geese to keep it cropped, keep it fertile and catch the Christmas market. What do you think?'

'Sounds bang on to me.' Maggie, who was liking John

more and more these days despite his reputation for dourness, had never seen him so animated. It had been such rotten luck for him, having his wife bugger off like that and then seeing Betty get attached to Ashley Kirkland. She felt sure he and Betty would have made a good match. Still, Betty was sitting pretty now. God knew, she deserved someone as good as Ashley, but people seldom got what they deserved, not in real life, and she wouldn't be sure that Betty was really safe until she and Ashley were married and his new bride was safely ensconced at the Manor. Would there be dinner parties up there again, she wondered, and then decided that there would be. Ashley would want that. She wondered where Elaine might be, but soon cleared her from her mind. How anyone could betray such a sweet man was quite beyond her.

She dragged her attention back to John and answered his question. 'What? Oh, this nursery closed down some time ago,' she said, indicating the catalogue, 'but I know plenty of sources of all these old varieties.' They discussed the project in detail but her mind kept harking back to Ashley.

'You seem to have switched off,' John said, at length.

'Sorry, dear boy, but I'm getting a bit tired. Look, take as many of these books and things home as you want. That way, you can run through the details with Betty.' Maggie did not miss the brief furrowing of the brow and read the shadows passing in his pale blue eyes. 'Will you need your landlord's permission for this orchard?' She knew that he would, but couldn't think how else to bring the subject of Ashley and Betty into the conversation.

'Of course, but that shouldn't pose a problem. Not now.'

'No, I suppose not.' She decided to press a little more. 'You've had rather a shitty deal in all this, haven't you?'

'How d'you mean?'

'Well, first your wife . . . and then Betty and Ashley getting together.'

'Those two events are unrelated.' He quickly gathered up the papers ready to leave.

'Not for you they're not.' He blushed and looked at the floor. 'You must admit, dear lad, there's a horrid irony.'

'Not really.'

'But you *do* care for her.'

He shook his head. 'She's my business partner. I worry about her, naturally. I don't want her to get hurt.'

'But it's wonderful for Betty. She couldn't do better than to end up with Ashley, but you, on the other hand, could lose out – on the partnership, I mean. She could hardly be your partner *and* your landlord's wife.'

'That is not what worries me.' John's colour had deepened almost to crimson, 'And she could, anyway. We have a formal, binding partnership agreement to run Cartwright Farm as *our* farm: fifty-fifty. The only thing that could stop that would be our going bust or losing the tenancy. Who she's married to is quite immaterial.'

'I see.'

'Now, let me ask you something.' His voice was quiet and controlled but Maggie could read anger in the veins pulsing at his temples and the tremor in his hands.

'Fire away.'

'Why do *you* think so much of Kirkland?'

'Same reason everybody else does. He's your all-round good egg.'

'Really?'

'He's kind and honourable, a gentleman – and before you come over all liberal and sneer at the term, I do *not* mean in the sense of "upper crust" at all, but in the sense that he thinks mainly of others, that he has courtesy and good manners and that he is loyal.' She added to herself that he was also about the most dishy male she had ever come across and for that reason or perhaps because he had some kind of magic about him, he was almost impossible not to like. 'Don't you agree?'

'I do not.'

'For Gawdsake, why not?'

'Various things.' John put the books down on the table again. 'The tenancy at Cartwright, for instance.' He described how Ashley had tried to edge the Roses out before Jack had been killed and how their recent Christmas had been ruined by his serving them with notice to quit and how, even now, they were unsure of their position.

'But surely, after the latest developments, that's all behind you,' Maggie said.

'There's a problem with me too. He has never taken to me, never accepted my position or recognised what I've done to help Betty. He's always trying to undermine me.'

'Phaugh – sheer imagination on your part!'

'He also keeps prying into our affairs. He's desperate to find out exactly what the nature of our partnership is. Now if he wanted to prove that Betty had broken her tenancy contract by compounding with me, he would need to know exactly what kind of contract we have. Do you see? If he has, as you suggest, decided to let the matter drop, why is he still trying to find out details like that?'

'Curiosity?'

'Oh, come *on*, Maggie! There must be more to it than that.'

'Concern for Betty. Obviously he loves her.' John coloured again. How easily he blushes, Maggie thought.

'Maggie, I don't want you to think I'm just being envious or resentful but there's another possible motive. You see, I'm pretty sure his finances are getting strained. His London business folded and that cost him a bomb but I think he's lost more than we know about.'

'Ridiculous notion!'

'Maybe. But look at the signs.'

'What signs?'

'Well, his car hasn't been changed for a while. There are a couple of his labourers' cottages for sale in the village. Why would he sell those if he didn't have to?'

'Surplus to requirements. Nothing more.'

'Then there's the expense of the divorce.'

'But Elaine was in the wrong, so surely he won't have to pay out for that?'

'He will if she owns any of the estate. Besides, *was* Elaine in the wrong?'

Maggie stared at him. In the last few minutes, he had said

more words than she had heard him utter since Christmas. 'My God, John, what are you saying?'

'Think about it. *He* was always away, not Elaine. The village gossips would soon spot a frequent visitor to the Manor. There would surely have been tittle-tattle if Elaine had been up to anything. It's much easier to avoid detection in a large city than in the country, everyone knows that.' Maggie stared, goggled, even. 'You realise what it means. If the divorce is his fault, he will be paying out a fortune, not to mention all the professional charges. So you see, he could be in for quite a bit of financial bother. That's why he wants Vacant Possession on our farm.'

'But what about Betty? They're devoted.'

'But *are* they?' John narrowed his eyes. 'This is what really worries me. I hope to God I'm wrong, but I think he may just be using this infatuation Betty has on him to undermine our position.'

'Oh really! Now you've gone too far. You're just bitter, that's all.' Over the preceding minutes Maggie had watched his bile increasing and the words becoming more staccato. His accent had thickened too, taking on flat, East Anglian tones. Now he'd finished, his mouth was clamped shut, down at the corners, lips compressed and drained of colour. He was taking short, rapid breaths, expelling air through dilated nostrils in audible puffs. 'My God, John, this has been eating you up. You *do* love her.' He stayed silent. 'You may not say anything but you can't fool me.'

'Got to go,' he muttered and picked up the bundle of books and papers. Maggie also rose and opened the door for him

'John,' she placed a hand on the books he was carrying. 'I won't breathe a word to a soul. You can depend on that.'

'Thanks,' he muttered, *sotto voce*.

'Oh, and you're wrong – about Ashley, I mean. Quite, quite wrong.'

'You think so?'

'I've known him for years and I've a lot to thank him for.'

415

John shrugged, walked out of the house and strode down the garden with his strange, lurching gait.

Maggie wanted some fresh air. She decided to skip lunch, went to the potting shed, found a hoe and began to weed the kitchen garden. She laboured for a couple of hours but became frustrated with the fiddly work of cutting weeds out from between the plants. When she had decapitated several vegetable seedlings, she dropped the tool down between the rows of peas and French beans and strode off along the banks of the Venn for what she decided would be a good, enervating walk. As she walked, rapidly enough to make her breathless, the resentment she had felt all afternoon about John Holman's accusations began to subside. She could understand his emotions, especially now that Ashley and Betty were together, but for him to try to vilify Ashley like that was unforgivable – quite unforgivable. But it set her thinking. She began to look back at, and to analyse conversations she had had with Ashley over the past years. He had an enigmatic side to his nature, there was no denying that, but to suggest underhandness? No, Ashley could never be underhand. Look at that incident when he set the whole place on fire at harvest. He'd published an apology, for God's sake, and made big donations to local funds, *and* planted lots of trees about the village to make up for the ones he'd burnt.

As for his being short of money, that was a laughable concept. After all, he had so much property, so much land. And not just here, either. He owned buildings in London and another farm, vast by all accounts, in Australia. And above all, he was seriously dishy. Not, she told herself, that that had anything to do with it. Still, Betty was a lucky cow. Maggie felt guilty at once for even thinking of Betty as being a cow. God knew, she had had enough trial and tribulation for one lifetime. Good luck to her. She deserved Ashley. Good God she did! Maggie accelerated·her stride even more. Overhead the sun shone among the fleecy white clouds but the gentle breeze from the west was stiffening into a wind which prevented her from feeling uncomfortably hot.

Perfect striding weather, Maggie told herself, and decided

to follow the towpath of the river all the way downstream to the next bridge, and then to return on the opposite side. It would mean a round trip of more than eight miles, but it would do her good. The furthest she had walked in years was no more than a couple of miles but she was strong, she told herself, and the exercise would help her to shed some of her bulk. When she got to the last bend in the river before the main road which crossed it just outside Saxford, she wasn't so sure. By then her legs ached and the sky was clouding over. She wished she had planned this walk more carefully and been less ambitious. She had brought no weatherproof clothing with her and felt quite thirsty but had no money. Anyway, it was miles to the nearest shop.

When she came to the bridge, she rested on the parapet for a while until a thirty-five tonne petrol tanker roared over it at terrifying speed, the huge wheels passing within a couple of feet of her. If she had staggered at that point, she could have been smeared along the road like jam on a scone. That made her shake and she scurried down to the path on the opposite side of the river, deciding to walk a little before finding somewhere to sit down.

Then it began to rain. 'Sod the bloody weather,' she muttered, and pulled her cardigan more closely round her shoulders. 'Better keep going.' She trudged. The rain was gentle and once it had got started, the wind had dropped, making it feel warmer. The path was less frequently used on this side of the river and occasionally disappeared altogether. A couple of times, she found herself plodding through arable crops – one of field beans, just coming into flower and smelling sweet, the other a large field of oilseed rape, so yellow it almost hurt her eyes and stinking of musk. Hundreds of small black pollen beetles came out of the rape and for a mile she was scratching, fidgeting as they found access to the insides of her clothes and irritated her skin. The rain began to come down in larger drops, and more disconcertingly, daylight began to fail. She had no idea how long she had been out but knew that it had been late afternoon when she started. Her wristwatch was still on the draining board in the kitchen at Bridge House.

By the time she approached Wyckhamby again, it was practically dark. Every inch of her was soaked and her cardigan had become a shapeless object pulled nearly to the ground by the weight of water. She was at the brink of despair when she rounded the bend in the river and saw a light in the distance. She assumed that this was Bridge House – Leonard would be worried sick – but as she neared the village she realised that it came from Wyckhamby Farms buildings.

The nearer she got to the farmyard, the more impossible seemed the half-mile further from there to Bridge House. The warm orange glow from the office window drew her moth-like, and before thinking any more about it she had crossed the yard and was trying the handle of its outer door. It opened quietly and she entered the building but, hearing Ashley's voice behind the door to his private office, decided to listen for a moment to find out who he was talking to. If it was someone she knew, she would not mind interrupting. If it was a stranger, she'd just stay in the vestibule, warm up a little and then creep off home. Soon, she realised he was speaking on the telephone to someone called Heck or Hector but it was difficult, through the thick door, to hear his precise words.

'The fact is, Heck,' she thought she heard him say, 'I'm a bit strapped for cash just at the immediate moment.' There was a pause while Heck answered, then, 'No, I'm perfectly serious. You know the reasons, or you can deduce them . . . No, really, I would find it very difficult to find that much even in the medium term . . . Well, *you* may think it peanuts but it's a lot of dosh. Times are hard for farmers now, you know that.' Maggie looked down and saw the puddle of rainwater widening at her feet as she listened. She hoped it wasn't running under the door. Then she heard something that made her attention click back to Ashley, and she strained to make out the words. 'Cartwright? I know we could but I don't think it's on . . . No, I don't care about that prick of a

418

partner of hers but I'm not sure about her . . . Mmm . . . Mmm. Do I? Well, perhaps I am.' He began to talk about Betty casually, in terms which shocked her, then she heard him say, 'In bed? Bloody fantastic. Talk about a merry widow. You ought to try it some time! It's that sex-starved it might go even for you!' Then he laughed, the silly, high-pitched schoolboy kind of laugh she'd heard men do in pubs when they boasted about their achievements. Maggie burst into the room, her ample breast heaving with rage. Ashley stared at her for several seconds and then said, 'Why Maggie, how wet you are!' He muttered an apology into the phone mouthpiece and hung up. Maggie stood breathing heavily, a fresh pool of rainwater forming beneath her. Ashley jumped up. 'What *has* happened to you? Here, let me sort you out.' He went to take off her cardigan.

'Don't!' Her vehemence surprised him.

'All right.' She took it off unaided, dropped it onto the floor and shivered. He opened the door to his wood-burning stove, put the contents of the waste-paper basket into it and struck a match. 'We'll soon have you warm.' He got some sticks out of a box in the corner and added these to the flaming papers. The room warmed up quickly and Maggie's clothes began to steam.

'I heard it. What you said. I heard it all.' But Ashley smiled at her and she felt doubt beginning to replace her anger.

'What did I say?'

'You know very well. About Betty.'

'What about Betty?'

'Filthy things. About her being good in bed. A merry widow.' She was pretty sure that was what he'd said. Now Ashley began to look angry.

'What do you think you're saying?'

'I heard you! On the phone. It's pointless trying to deny it.' Could she have misheard? He was showing no hint of embarrassment and that was disconcerting.

'Have you been on the bottle again? Hitting the juice a bit, is that it?'

'How *dare* you?'

'Well, once a piss artist always a piss artist, isn't that what they say?'

'But I *heard* you, I'm sure I did.'

'I don't believe this. You creep into my building, like a burglar, you half-hear a fragment of telephone conversation and then you jump to some crazy conclusion and start slagging me off while you drip rainwater onto my Afghan rug.' Maggie's self-doubt grew as his tirade gathered strength. 'You insult me, you insult the woman I love. Just how much of a fucking nutcase are you?'

'I . . .' she gulped. Could she have imagined it? It was raining hard outside, the drumming water had made it hard to hear very distinctly, and she was deeply fatigued. But the tone of voice, the words – could that have been imagined?

'Well?' He was glaring at her, looking directly into her eyes.

She gulped and swallowed again. 'I . . . I don't know. I thought I heard. I'm sorry. Oh God, Ashley, I'm so sorry.' She began to sway and felt she might faint. He was up in a flash. He set a chair by the stove, ran out to the vestibule and found a couple of anoraks, one for her shoulders, the other for her lap. He got out a decanter, offered it and then shook his head.

'Jesus, I'm sorry,' he said. 'How tactless of me. Let me boil a kettle.'

'No, don't bother. I'll go in a minute, soon as I'm warm.' The moment she'd spoken, Maggie regretted it, realising how profound her thirst was.

'You don't mind if I do?' He poured himself a stiffish tot and added soda from a siphon. 'It was unforgivable, what I said just now.' She opened her eyes, surprised. 'About you drinking again. I'm sorry.'

'It's all right, really.'

'How long have you been off it now?'

'I can't remember. A couple of years. More.'

'Good for you, Maggie.' He smiled again, crinkling the corners of his eyes, the hazel irises twinkling in the light of the flames from the open stove. 'Good for you.' She felt herself relax. She was still soaked through but her wet clothes were at least warm now. 'And I must say, you look a lot fitter than you did.'

'Oh bollocks, Ashley. I'm overweight and you know it.'

'But your new business is going well?'

'Like a bomb. I'm taking another man on next week. Full-time.'

'Splendid!' He drained his glass, picked up the decanter and poured himself another slug. 'Plenty of design jobs coming in?'

'Well, not like last time, obviously, but I'm sticking to local customers these days. I don't want to go traipsing around the country. Not now.'

'Pity that first design business of yours folded. Still, I suppose you lost rather more than just a business. Poor old Leonard certainly did. That wonderful wine collection!' He was still smiling while he spoke but now Maggie realised that the glitter in his eyes was cold anger and that he was playing with her. She felt like a hunted animal, in danger but too exhausted to move. He mimed a drinking action, a quick rotation, back and forth, of his right wrist, hand cupped as if round a glass and winked at her. Then he lifted his real glass and drank. She realised he was trying to humiliate her but he had underestimated her pluck. He was seeking out raw spots to chafe but the result was that her anger rekindled and she re-entered the fight.

'Cheers!' she said. 'How much do *you* get through in a day?'

Ashley laughed. 'Lots. But *I* call the tune. I can stop or start whenever I want.'

'That's what I thought too.'

His smile evaporated. 'I have never let alcohol ruin *my* livelihood. You, I seem to recall, chucked away your one big chance – that Science Park commission – because of just that.'

'Not so! I lost it because of a slanderous statement. I was actually on the wagon when whoever it was betrayed me. It was the betrayal that made me want to drink.' She was trembling but not with cold.

'Betrayal!' Ashly sneered. 'Who could possibly have betrayed you?'

'That's all over now. You've no need to make me feel shitty about the past, I can do that quite well unaided.' She forced her stiff limbs into action and, with considerable effort, stood up. She wasn't sure how far she could walk. 'And I *did* hear what you said on the phone.'

'Did you really?' The sneer was the first unattractive expression she had ever seen on his face. 'What did I say?'

'I'm leaving.' She had to get out but her head was reeling and she found it difficult to stay on her feet. Somehow, she had to find the strength to get away from here.

'Come on, Maggie, what did I say? Think. Perhaps a drink will clear your head.' He poured whisky into a clean glass and added soda. 'It's a beautiful malt.' He took a pull from his own glass, swallowed and sighed. 'Aah! Smooth as silk.' He walked over and put the glass into her shaking hand. The bouquet of Glenlivet caressed her tired olfactory sensors and the pang of craving which suddenly wracked her body was stronger than any sexual desire. Perhaps one stiff slug would give her the strength she needed to walk the last half-mile home. She raised the glass to her mouth, sniffed again and paused. 'Just one won't hurt you, Mags,' Ashley said, kindness returning to his voice. An image of that odious university professor swam into her vision. How could he, how could they have known that she had a reputation for the bottle? And then it dawned on her. After all those years of wondering, it was so obvious! The only possible source of that slander had to be the man she had always thought of as a benefactor, the man who had laughed raucously to a mate on the phone about fucking her closest friend and the man who now stood with her at the brink of the abyss, knowing that one sip could be fatal. If Ashley had suddenly sprouted horns and a tail she would not have been more surprised. She straightened herself up and raised the glass in salutation.

'Cheers, Ashley,' she said, 'you've earned this,' and she shot the whisky into those glittering hazel eyes, threw the crystal glass onto the stone floor and ran, or rather, hobbled out into the night.

Outside in the yard it was pitch dark and the rain drove into her face, blinding her and shocking the breath out of her body. She had no idea where she was going but stumbled in what she hoped was the direction of Bridge House. All her muscles ached but anger gave her the strength she needed. She blundered into an open half-door and hurt her knee. After that, she felt her way more carefully, eventually coming out from between two buildings and discovering a kind of wooden rail. As she felt her way along this, the walkway narrowed and the concrete underfoot, slick with rain falling onto slimy algae, gave no purchase for her tired feet. She slipped, and felt her legs giving way. She clutched at the rail for support. It snapped and as she fell she realised that the stench of cattle manure had been getting progressively stronger. Before her body hit the surface, her brain registered the awful fact that she was falling into the Wyckhamby Farms slurry lagoon. Even at that moment, she might have uttered a wry guffaw about landing in the shit again but before her lips could form a smile, the filthy, viscous liquid had closed over her head.

Chapter Twenty-nine

Ashley woke abruptly, startled by the telephone. He spent most of his evenings alone nowadays, dozing in front of television, an abandoned supper tray on the little Victorian ebonised table beside him. It was Leonard Bates, apologetic but anxious. 'Sorry to ring so late, but I don't suppose you've got Maggie with you?'

'Lord, no!' He was still sluggish. 'She left hours ago.'

'So she *was* with you.'

Ashley's mind became more alert as he remembered the scene with her earlier that evening. 'Ye-es. Hasn't she come home?' He assumed she would be sitting somewhere alone, sulking.

'Obviously not. Was she,' Leonard paused for a second, 'all right, when she left you?' The fear of a return to the bottle, though faint now, was always there.

'Perfectly.' Ashley had no intention of incriminating himself. 'She's probably chewing the fat with a crony somewhere.'

'At this hour?'

Ashley looked at his watch. It was almost one in the morning. 'Good Lord, is it that late?'

'Well, sorry to have bothered you. Good night.' Leonard rang off and Ashley went upstairs to bed, wondering what repercussions his recent scene with Maggie would have. He wished he had not said those *stupid* things about Betty to Hector Enfield. Men out on a shoot together might talk like that, discussing women and the pheasants they were slaughtering in the same breath, as if both were legitimate prey. At the Kendale Fatstock Dinner, where females were forbidden, the same men would giggle about the sexual favours – mostly fictitious – that certain local women would grant. Usually, this all-male talk revolted Ashley, but sometimes he felt needful of the schoolboy comradeship. Enfield would know perfectly well that what he had said about Betty was just talk, and that neither would contemplate for an instant that Enfield should so much as make a pass at her. But Maggie would read more into the remarks than there really was and the matter could get back to Betty. He did not want to hurt Betty. He looked at himself in his bathroom mirror and groaned. How he wished those awful remarks unsaid!

Maggie was still missing early next morning. Leonard, accompanied by a policeman, arrived at the Wyckhamby Farms buildings at seven, just as Ashley was entering his office. 'We saw you leave your house,' he said, following Ashley into the building, 'and assumed you'd be on your way up here.'

'As you see,' Ashley unlocked his office door and held it open for them both. 'Do sit down.'

'Ashley,' Leonard's face was lined with stress, 'have you any idea where Maggie went after she visited you?'

'None at all. I assumed she'd have gone home.'

'Excuse me, sir,' the policeman said, 'what time did the lady leave?'

'Couldn't say. About nine, I suppose. Nine or half past. It was dark, anyway.'

'Must have been later, then.'

'Maybe. It was raining hard.'

'What sort of mood was she in?' Leonard asked. 'Was she agitated or upset about anything?'

'Why should she be?' Ashley put on a slightly bemused smile.

'That's what I want to find out. Why did she call, by the way?'

'Oh, you know,' Ashley flipped a hand, 'routine stuff, about the garden.'

'May we have a look round the buildings, sir?' The policeman was anxious not to waste time.

'By all means, if you think it'll do any good.' Ashley gestured towards the door, 'Help yourselves.'

'Thank you, sir.' The policeman stood up and replaced his cap. He looked less human but more efficient in it than out of it, Ashley thought.

Half an hour later, the same policeman knocked and put his head round Ashley's office door.

'Sorry to trouble you again, Mr Kirkland, but could you come out for a moment?' Ashley sighed, saved the work on his computer and followed the policeman outside. He was led along the narrow walkway between the buildings to the slurry lagoon. 'Mind your step, sir,' the constable said as Ashley's leather soles, in spite of their studs, slipped on the mossy concrete. Leonard, pale of face, was standing by the edge of the lagoon.

'What are we supposed to be looking at?' Ashley asked and then spotted the broken wooden rail, one half of which had swung like a tiller, out over the surface of the slurry. There were streaks on the slimy concrete next to the rail but after all the rain, the surface of the slurry lagoon was inscrutable.

'I'll have to contact my sergeant, sir. The policeman looked out over the lagoon. 'Is there any way this can by emptied?'

'We take slurry out from time to time, and spread it on the grassland as fertiliser, but *emptying* it? That would be quite an undertaking.'

'But you could do it?'

'Oh, we could do it. The big question is, where do we put the slurry? We can't spread it all on our grass. We haven't enough, and the arable crops are too advanced now – it would spoil them.'

'What about spreading it on your neighbour's land?'

'Not easy.'

'We do need to empty the, the . . .' he struggled to find the right word for this expanse of filth, 'pond, sir.'

'I'll do what I can.' Ashley started back for the office. 'Want to come with me, Len?'

While Leonard sat in the same chair that Ashley had put out for Maggie the night before, Ashley called up Mardle on the radio phone and instructed him to gather the workforce from the various parts of the farm where they were doing fieldwork, to hitch muck-spreaders to their tractors and begin the task of removing 40,000 gallons of slurry from the lagoon and spreading it as widely as possible over his land. He picked up the other phone and dialled Betty Rose's number.

'Ah, Betty, we have a serious problem. Maggie Bates has gone missing. Fact is, we have to drain the slurry lagoon . . . What? . . . Oh, that's very decent. I've got Len Bates here.' He looked up at Leonard. 'She's coming over at once.'

Betty arrived within minutes and greeted both men. She turned to Leonard and said, 'I'm sure she's all right. I bet there'll be a simple explanation.'

'Wish I shared your optimism,' Leonard said. Nearly an hour passed before the first spreader came, sucked up a load of slurry and departed. More police arrived: Sergeant Snell from Kendale and a Detective Constable whose name escaped everyone. By mid-morning, three tankers were pumping up the stinking liquid. Ashley had telephoned a contractor who promised to bring more slurry-transporting tackle along at midday. By lunchtime, the level had dropped noticeably.

By mid-afternoon, the lagoon was nearly empty. The stench of fermented cow manure – a sweet-sharp stink, reminiscent of rotting corpses – had invaded the whole area. The grassland had become dark with slurry spread so thickly that Ashley feared it might kill off some of the sward. Two tankers were transporting it to Cartwright Farm where Betty had allowed them to spread it over her grass. Gobs of the stuff were spread along the road and up Cartwright Lane, which was getting badly churned up by the extra traffic of ribbed tractor tyres.

For Leonard, the waiting was almost unbearable. His emotions ran from misery at the prospect of having lost his wife to rage at her carelessness. She was such a bungler, so

427

uncouth at times and so loud and embarrassing but God, how he wanted her back!

The depth of slurry in the lagoon reduced more rapidly as the last loads pulled away until there was no more than a thin layer of the stuff, littered with chunks of more solid debris, across the concrete bottom of the pool. Of Maggie there was no sign.

'It's hopeful, Leonard,' Betty said. 'I told you. I'm sure she's all right.' She and Ashley had been watching the emptying process for much of the day, trying to find ways of comforting Leonard and preparing for the awful moment when the body might be dicovered.

'Now we've got it empty, we might as well clean it out,' Ashley told Bert Mardle, who connected up the high-pressure hose and began to squirt the bottom with a jet of pure water. Now that a clean area was developing, Sergeant Snell climbed down behind the hose into the base of the lagoon followed by Ashley and the Constable, and began to scrutinise the rubbish on the bottom in the hopes of finding a clue. He took the hose from Bert Mardle and played its forceful jet on one of the larger lumps. A colour began to appear under the force of the water and the lump was soon recognisable as fabric.

'Anyone need a spare anorak?' he laughed, as the water washed away the layer of excrement to reveal pale-blue nylon. Then his hand froze. 'Hang on, what's this?' He handed the hose back to Mardle and squatted to touch the cloth. Carefully he turned it over. The material had become stiff, almost unrecognisable as a garment, but part of a sleeve and the hood were quite visible. He turned the hood slightly, so that the late-afternoon sun could shine into the opening. He didn't expect to find a skull inside – police work was seldom that exciting – so he wasn't especially disappointed to find the hood empty. Just the same, he endeavoured to turn the stiffened fabric inside out and, when his hand slipped and shook the whole anorak open, the bone fragments inside still failed to convince him that these were human remains. It wasn't until he found the piece of jawbone, complete with teeth, two of which had amalgam fillings, that the truth sank in.

Sergeant Snell instructed his Detective Constable to contact headquarters at Kendale and then he looked at the little pile of human remains. Caustic action of the slurry had digested most of the body and would have dissolved it all, had it not been partly protected by the nylon. It was impossible to recognise anything about it except that it was human. It could have been any age and either sex. He couldn't even tell when the body had got into the lagoon but suspected that it would have been there for years, rather than months.

'We'll know more when forensic have had a go at this,' he told Ashley. 'We mustn't move anything here now until it's all been checked over.'

'No, of course not.' Ashley's attention was caught for a moment by something glinting in the sunlight on the bottom of the lagoon. He was about to investigate when the Constable standing beside him, walked over to pick it up.

'Hello, what's this?' He held it up to the light. Ashley could see that it was a large signet ring. He let out an audible gasp of dismay and then glanced round, recovering himself almost instantly, and found himself staring straight into Betty's eyes as she stood on the concrete edge six feet above him. Her eyebrows were slightly raised in question. He glanced quickly away and addressed the policeman.

'Well, what is it?' (He knew what it was.)

'A ring. Gold, probably.'

'Really? Let me look.' He reached a hand out and took it. 'Well I'm damned!' He let out a delighted laugh and said again, 'Well, I'm damned!' He tossed it into the air and caught it with a flourish. 'I thought I'd never see this again. Lost it years ago, in the milking parlour. Yes,' he warmed to the reminiscence, 'it slipped off my finger, just as I was putting a milk cluster on one of the cows. Must have got washed down the drain and into the lagoon. Well, well, I *am* glad you found it.'

Up on the edge of the lagoon, Betty was puzzled. This reaction seemed genuine enough but the look of pain that had first crossed Ashley's face had a louder ring of truth. That ring, she knew, had sad connections as far as he was concerned, but it wasn't anything he was likely to talk about. That much was obvious. It occurred to her that Elaine might have given it to him. That might explain his first reaction, but why would he want to suppress that? She suspected that there was something undeclared. She felt sympathy well up for him and was wondering whether to climb down to be with him when a cry from Leonard made her start and turn round. A figure was walking with a staggering gait, like a drunk, towards them. It looked like something made out of soil. The limbs and clothes were encrusted with dried cowshit. The eyes gleamed unnaturally out of a shell of flaking ordure and the hair, stiffened with manure, stuck out at all angles.

'Maggie!' Leonard cried. 'Oh, thank God you're alive!' But the figure shuffled to a halt at this and stared. It swayed a little and walked forward again. Leonard rushed up and hugged his wife, in spite of the filth that covered every inch of her. She gazed at him with wild eyes that showed no sign of recognition.

'Hello,' she murmured. 'Hell'va party!' She giggled, retched and sat down on the concrete rather heavily.

'Betty, go and ring for an ambulance,' Leonard said, and got down on his knees beside Maggie.

'She wasn't drunk at all,' Betty told John, later in the week when they were having coffee in the kitchen at Cartwright. 'It seems that she'd taken it into her head to go for a long walk.'

'I know, it was after I'd been to see her.' John felt guilty about that.

'She got soaked through in the rain coming back, must have seen a light in Ashley's office windows and gone in. Ashley says she stayed for a chat, got dry and then went on home. He offered her a lift, apparently, but she refused. You know how stubborn she can be. Anyway, she must have lost her bearings in the dark and fallen into that awful slurry lagoon.

'What I'd like to know is how she got out.'

'She must have worked her way across to the opposite side – there's a more sloping edge there – and then crawled out and crept under a tarpaulin in the barn. She'd have been physically exhausted, and ill from the toxic fumes of the slurry. She slept, or was unconscious, for nearly twenty hours. When she came to, she had a raging temperature and couldn't remember a thing.'

'Amnesia?'

'Just a temporary thing, I gather. Poor old Maggie.'

'What about the body?'

'Oh, that's all in this morning's *Kendale Messenger*. Here!' She picked up the newspaper and showed him. 'Youth or a young man apparently. Been there between three and five years.'

'Poor sod. What on earth was he doing there?'

'Nobody knows. Could have been a young runaway, the police say, or a vagrant looking for somewhere to kip down.' She got up. 'I must do the pigs. Could you lock up for me this evening, John, I've got to be out.' She was going over to Wyckhamby Manor but shrank from the idea of telling him. She knew that her relationship with Ashley upset him.

Later, as she walked across the parish, she reflected on how forgiving the countryside could be. Less than a week before, the whole area stank of slurry. Every acre of grassland in the parish had carried a blackish scum where the contents of the lagoon had been spread, and all the farm lanes had been clotted with dung and cut into deep ruts by the extra traffic. But another twenty-four hours of rain had washed the evil-smelling liquid into the ground, transforming pollutant into soil nutrient which, after a couple of warm days, gave the meadows a fresh, spring-like verdure. The lanes would take a little longer to repair but the mud was beginning to firm and could soon be disc-harrowed and rolled flat. They had been lucky that none of the slurry had found its way into the Venn. Had it done so, the damage to waterlife would have been extensive, but coming to the bridge, Betty saw that the stream was as clear and sweet as usual and that the trout, many of which she was sure she knew as individuals, were hanging just below the surface, waiting to snap up falling insects. The speckles on their backs varied in size from fish to fish and one or two were darker than the rest. She wondered how they managed to keep so still in the current, their heads facing upstream, tails moving lazily as their bodies made constant adjustments to changes in the flow of the river.

Anticipation of Ashley's embraces put an extra spring into her stride. After years of sleeping by herself at Cartwright Farm, she had, since that afternoon with him, become more acutely conscious of her solitary state. Ashley could put an end to loneliness – there was no doubt about that – but, if their relationship was to last, several matters needed clearing up. His divorce from Elaine would be through before long, she knew that. She had no doubt, either, that he would want to marry her. That was implicit in their relationship and there had been no need for either of them to mention it. But that would be in the future and there was a meantime to worry about. So far, few suspected that her relationship with him had transcended from the platonic. Her frequent visits to his house were easily explained – she was, after all, his tenant – but sooner or later, the shrewder of the Wyckhamby gossips would sniff out the hot news of their liaison. That bothered her, but not nearly so much as the moral question. Technically, her relationship with him was adulterous, and that hurt her conscience.

Then there was John. She had grown deeply fond of John, particularly in the previous year before his wife had appeared. His body had always been appealing to her, especially the long, powerful arms and fair complexion, and she felt safe and comfortable in his presence. She knew that the closer she got to Ashley, the more vulnerable he would be. No doubt, if they married, Ashley would expect to absorb Cartwright into Wyckhamby Farms and pay John off, but she was not prepared to countenance that. That wasn't the idea of their getting together at all and as far as Betty was concerned, she had every intention of continuing her business in partnership with John, as before.

She crossed the river, peeping through the front gate of Bridge House into Maggie's garden as she passed. It had never looked so lovely but she wondered how soon neglect would begin to show. Maggie, it seemed, was going to take a long time to recover. Certainly, this amnesia was perplexing and Betty wondered whether she *had* slipped back into drunkness. How else could she have blundered into the buildings and fallen into the lagoon?

All the time she had been walking, a cuckoo had been calling from one of the ancient ash-trees lining the road but as she neared, it uttered a hoarse, bubbling chuckle and flew off towards the spinney below the Manor House. She climbed over the stile into Ashley's water meadow, retracing the steps of that Saturday afternoon when he had come towards her along the riverbank, stooping every few moments to pick wild flowers. The cowslips were gone to seed now and the river margin plants approaching their climax. A fish jumped in the shallows and the loud splash startled her, but her thoughts soon drifted back to Ashley and to the puzzle that had been chafing the back of her mind since the accident: his reaction over the signet ring. What was it about that ring that had dismayed him, and why had he amended his emotion from sorrow to joy?

He greeted her from the garden, took her arm and walked her down to the lake. 'Your lawns want cutting,' she said.

'Don't I know it. I've lost my garden contractor for the moment.'

'Maggie? She has deputies, surely?'

'They haven't deputised yet, for some reason.' They strolled into the wood behind the lake and in the cool shade of a high rhododendron which was shedding its last faded red blooms, he took her in his arms and kissed her, probing her mouth with his tongue and sending tingles down to her toes. Betty pulled away, at length.

'Ashley, don't. Not out here, someone might see us.'

He laughed. 'We've nothing to hide, have we?'

'No, of course not,' Betty wanted to walk again, 'but I'm not sure I'm ready for people to know about us. Not really, not yet.'

'That's daft. Besides, some know already.'

'Who?' Betty looked startled.

'Maggie Bates, poor drunken woman.' He slid his eyes away from hers. 'I bet your partner's got a shrewd idea too.'

'Oh, they're almost family. But I don't want it to be general knowledge.' She began to walk.

'Where are you going?' He caught her arm and pulled her to a stop before encircling her waist. 'Do you remember when we loitered here at that dinner party? The nightingales?'

'Oh yes! I wonder if they'll sing again.'

'I wanted you so badly then.'

'Ashley! Are you sure?'

'I want you now!' He kissed her again, and put his hand under her buttocks, lifting her upwards and pulling her to him. She could feel the heat of his body through her cotton dress and her pulse began to race.

'Oughtn't we to go in?' Her voice was husky with desire but unease grew in concert with her arousal.

Later, as they lay side by side in his bedroom, Betty luxuriated in the afterglow of sex while the cuckoo called incessantly outside.

'If that bird doesn't soon stop, I'll shoot the bloody thing,' Ashley said. He got off the bed. 'Fancy a drink?'

'Not for me, but don't let me stop you.' She watched him go over to the dressing table and pick up a small decanter. 'Fourteen-year-old malt. You sure you don't want any?' She shook her head and watched him pour a generous measure into a small crystal tumbler that stood beside the decanter, and then sip. He sat on the dressing-table stool and smiled at her. 'You wouldn't have done *that* a few weeks ago!'

'Done what?'

'Just lain there, starkers like that.' Immediately she sat up and reached for his towelling robe. 'No, darling, don't. Oh blast, now I've made you feel self-conscious!'

She sat, his robe around her shoulders, and gazed at him. 'I could never be tired of looking at your body,' she said.

He blushed a little and fiddled with his glass. Absently, with his left hand, he picked a cuff link out of his open stud-box, looked at it, replaced it and then took out a heavy ring. Watching him closely, she detected the shadow that passed over his face, just as she had seen in the slurry lagoon but more fleetingly this time. He enclosed the ring in his hand, caught her gaze and smiled.

'Is that *the* ring?'

'Yes. Wasn't it a lucky find?'

'No, I don't think it was.'

'What do you mean?' His voice developed an edge. He was suddenly embarrassed at being naked and took the second dressing gown, a thin mid-blue cotton one with a yellow paisley design, from the the back of the door and put it on, tying the sash firmly.

'Ashley! I saw your face.'

'What *do* you mean?'

'Oh, you crowed with delight at the discovery but that was after your initial reaction. I know it upset you.'

'Oh, did it?' He sipped his malt whisky and cocked his head at her. 'And I suppose you know why?' There was almost a sneer in his voice.

'I've got a fair idea.' He looked startled, guilty. It dawned on her – it *was* about Elaine! The ring upset him because of her, but he had hidden his emotions because he, *and not Elaine*, had been at fault. The more Betty thought about this, the more obvious it became. She had never really believed that Elaine had done anything wrong.

'Well?' He was brusque. She hadn't quite worked it all out, not yet. Why, for instance, was it a man's ring? Could it have been a gift to him from some woman?

'May I see it?'

'If you must.' He tossed it over and she caught it, surprised at its weight. It was obviously very old, the gold untouched by its years in the cattle manure but before that, chafed and scored with wear, the initials all but gone from the flat part.

'Well?' he said.

Betty sighed. She wished she hadn't brought this up, but knew that it had to be faced.

'Elaine wasn't unfaithful. You were.' He dropped his gaze. 'This ring is connected to your actions, not hers.' But who, she wondered, could have given him such an odd present? Clearly, he could never have worn it, not in front of his wife. Perhaps it was an old heirloom that he had given to his mistress and she had tossed it back at the end of the affair. But it was too big for a woman to wear. In fact it was too big for a man with slender hands and anyway, how did it get into the lagoon?

'Nonsense!' His words cut into her thoughts. 'That ring belonged to my great-grandfather, Thomas Kirkland. If you look, you'll see the initials.'

'It's worn smooth.'

'Tilt it to the light.' She did, and could just trace the outline of a copperplate T and the bottom portion of a K. If it had been his, he must have given it to someone.

'An incongruous present for a lady.'

'Quite so.' He finished his drink and held his hand out for the ring. She weighed it again in her hand before passing it back. If his mistress had not worn it on her finger, how else would she have kept it near her? On a gold chain, perhaps, as a pendant?

'A pendant,' she said aloud. 'It was worn as a pendant.' His reaction surprised her. He seemed to shrink. He put the ring back into the stud-box, closed the lid and sighed.

'So you *do* know.' His voice had sunk to a whisper. 'You must have known all along, ever since that night when he came to the Manor and you answered the door to him.'

He came! What night? Betty thought hard, trying to remember anything that might have been significant. Gradually, the recollection of that rainy March evening focused. The boy! He had the ring on a leather thong round his neck, the forefinger crooked through it. She remembered Ashley's angry words at the door, his coming back inside with rain on his shoulders. He had quizzed her about the incident several times afterwards, as if the boy was bothering him somehow. She stared at him. She hadn't known but she did now. And now that she did know, so much of Ashley's enigmatic side was explained.

'I do know.' She looked at her lover. His face was lined, now, and his eyes almost black in the darkening room. She watched him pour another drink. He held the decanter out to her but she shook her head. She was dumb, not from shock but because she didn't know what to say next. There was more, she knew that. But she also knew that unless she picked her words with care, he would clam up. She had to know all, and he had to shed all.

Then realisation hit her. The body in the lagoon! It had to be the boy. 'Oh my God!' She jumped up. 'Oh my God, Ashley! What have you done?'

'It was so wet.' He was speaking in a low monotone. 'He must have lost his way. Fallen in. Too weak to get out. Maggie got out, tough old bird, but not Rick. I had to send him away . . . had to, you see. Elaine would never have . . . never have . . .' He made a dry, retching sound. Betty could not bear to see his pain. She walked over to him and held his shoulders.

'Shh! Sshh! Calm down,' she murmured in a soft, cooing voice. It was like comforting Jim after an asthma attack. She relinquished her hold, sat on the edge of the bed and faced him. 'I must have chapter and verse.'

'Of what?'

'You. The way you are.' She shivered and got up to close the window and draw the curtains before sitting on the bed facing him. 'I dare bet you've never confided in anyone.'

'About what?'

'Ashley, there simply isn't time for you to evade the issue. This is crucial. If we are to be together, I must know all about that . . . that side of your life.' In response, he emptied the decanter and drained his glass in a single gulp. Betty pressed him. 'Get drunk if you must, but if you still want me, I must know. Everything.' In response, he got up and walked out of the room.

Betty went into the adjoining bathroom, washed herself and began to get dressed. She had to get out, to think. If he was prepared to communicate they might be able to save this relationship – if she really wanted to save it. The idea of sex between males was distasteful, but nothing about Ashley revolted her and when she thought of his tender caresses she suppressed a little whimper of distress. When he was dressed she began to pull the bedclothes into some sort of order. He came in, carrying another bottle of Scotch, a bottle of Sancerre and a wine glass.

'Oh,' she said, 'what's this?'

'I needed another bottle and thought you might appreciate a glass of something halfway decent.' His eyes were herring-red, now, his cheeks haggard and his breath whisky-laden.

'Are you sure you want to drink any more?'

'It's the only way I can get it out.' He resumed his place at the dressing table and indicated that she should sit on the bed. He filled the decanter, with exaggerated care, from the bottle and poured the remainder into his glass. He took a deep draught, grimaced and then began: 'What you really want to know, I presume, is firstly, whether I had anything to do with this boy's demise and secondly, whether my . . . my . . .' he pursed his lips, straining to come up with a suitable term, '*thing* with him was just a one-off aberration or whether I am a genuine, dyed-in-the-wool' – he spat the words as if they were insects in his mouth – 'gay, queer, woofter, poofter, shirt-lifter, friend of Dorothy's or whatever you want to call it. The answer to the first question is no. I was unkind to turn him away but I am not culpable.' He looked at Betty, sighed and said with some effort, 'The answer to the second question is, I'm afraid, yes. Now you know, you can piss off home if you want and leave me alone.'

'I want to stay. But I must know about it – all of it.'

'There's nothing more to tell.'

'Nothing? When it's ruined your marriage, destroyed your happiness?' She reached out and took his hands in hers. 'How did it start? Did some man interfere with you when you were little?'

438

His short laugh was mirthless, bitter. 'It doesn't happen like that. It's different for different people. For me it began at my prep school, when I was twelve. Naturally, boys herded together experiment with each other. For most it was a passing phase but for one or two of us, the play became more serious. I got very attached to a classmate. Went home with him for half the holidays and he came to the farm for the other half. We did eveything together, in every race we were neck and neck, and when we took the Common Entrance Exam at the same time, our scores were almost identical. In fact, if we had not sat at opposite sides of the exam room, they might have suspected us of cheating. But we went on to separate public schools – each of us to our fathers' *Alma Mater*. I didn't see him for a whole school year and I grieved for him – so much so that my parents allowed me to spend the summer holdays at his home. By then we were both almost fifteen and had more or less passed through puberty. On our first day together, his parents had to go out to dinner. We had the house to ourselves and our thoughts turned simultaneously to sex. But whereas before, we had merely played, this time without thought or hesitation we made love as adults. We knew the world would frown on what we were doing but we knew that for us it was right, and *clean* and beautiful.' He stopped.

'You haven't given me any wine,' Betty said. He opened the bottle and poured her a glass. 'Thanks.' She sipped. 'And then?'

'Back at school I pined for him. My work began to fall back and I was deeply unhappy. I was also sexually frustrated. You have no idea what strength the sex urge has in a fifteen-year-old boy. Sports are supposed to take the edge off it but the fitter I got the stronger the drive got. Showering with the other boys after games was an unbearable torment, and one which sharpened over the years as their bodies developed. Gradually, I became aware that there were one or two who were as I was. In the most secret of places, we would meet and give each other relief from our sexual tensions.' He paused, picked up his glass and put it down

439

again. He was drunk, now, but still capable of coherent thought and speech.

'Go on.'

'It gets pretty sordid.' She waited. He continued. 'When I was nineteen, on a trip to Cambridge, I got picked up in a public lavatory by an academic who took me back to his rooms. That began a pattern of behaviour which has persisted. Whenever I was frustrated, I would loiter, get picked up and taken back to bachelor flats, or for rides in cars if my partners were married.'

'You said "has persisted".' Betty felt her revulsion rising. 'Do you mean that you still do that?'

Ashley looked at her, grey-faced, shaky-handed and said, after a long pause, 'I'm the one that does the picking up. It tends to be that way when you are in your forties.' Betty expected a chill in her feelings for him but she still wanted to touch him, even though the things he had confessed were repellent.

'And Elaine found out? After all that time?' By his silence she assumed that she had. It seemed impossible that they could have been married for so long without her having suspected. 'What about us? You must love women too?'

'Hardly anyone is exclusively either way,' he said. 'It's a matter of degree, though few have the courage to admit to it.' Betty nodded. She had never wanted to have sex with another woman but certainly she felt more drawn to some than to others.

'But you *loved* Elaine. How could you do that?'

'An animal thing,' he shrugged. 'Depraved, yes. Repulsive to normal people. But harmless.'

'Except to your marriage.'

'It needn't have been. There's no love in it, no real infidelity. Rick, the poor dead boy in the lagoon, he was the only one I ever actually fell . . .' He was unable to finish.

Betty sipped her Sancerre, warmed to room temperature now and tasting sharp on her tongue. It was a lot to absorb. She was sorry for him, having had to live a lie, but the hub of his story was dark and sinister. Whatever relationship he had above board, the temptation to go on with these furtive practices would always be there, and she doubted whether he would be able to stop.

'You've been brave, and truthful,' she said, taking hold of his hands again. 'That must have taken a lot of effort.'

'I've never told anyone what I've told you.' She believed him.

'I need time to think all this over,' she felt her eyes stinging with unshed tears. 'But I think we may have to . . . to stop.'

'Betty! *No!*'

'I must have time to think.' She picked up her things and got ready to leave. He tried to speak but couldn't. He went into the bathroom to wash his face in cold water. When he came back into the bedroom she said, 'You have to tell the police – about the boy, I mean, that he came to see you that night. He must have relatives who don't know what happened to him.'

Ashley shook his head. 'He was a runaway. I tried to find out about his background but he vowed never to tell me. He'd been in London for two years when I met him, working as a rent boy. There are hundreds of runaways who never get traced.'

'You still have to tell the police.' Betty's voice had become businesslike. 'You won't incriminate yourself by doing that but you must tell them.'

'Yes. But Betty—'

'I need a breathing space. I have to think.'

'Of course.' He held the door open for her.

As she walked downstairs she said: 'It seems to me that your unhappiness is rooted in your deceit. Lots of homosexuals lead happy lives in the open. Had you ever thought of, what do they call it, coming out?'

'In Wyckhamby?' His laugh was bitter.

'Maybe you should think about it. The hardest person to admit these things to is, perhaps, yourself.'

'Why are you saying this to me?'

'Because I . . .' she hesitated. The statement should have

been, 'Because I love you' but the words wouldn't come out. 'Because I hate to see anyone in torment'.

They went downstairs and he opened the back door for her. She turned to him before leaving. His eyes were barely visible in the darkness but the neat ears were outlined by the light from the hall and she reached to stroke the small curls of hair that nestled behind them. She was about to say that she still wanted him, but then remembered that she was standing on the same doorstep as the poor runaway who had drowned in the lagoon. She would walk home, she always did. She kissed him and left, the tears cold on her cheeks in the freshening easterly wind.

Chapter Thirty

The little congregation followed the coffin out of St James's Church and gathered round the pile of yellowish subsoil that bordered Camilla Doncaster's new grave. Yesterday, the weathermen had said, was the coldest July day since 1887, but the keening easterly wind had dropped overnight and now a thin rain more suited to October than to midsummer settled onto the ripening crops, soaking into the ears of wheat and barley and causing their stems to collapse with the extra weight of the water. If the wet spell was brief, no serious damage would be done to the cereals but the rapeseed crop was at its most vulnerable. The acreage, in Linconshire, of this member of the cabbage family had increased, year on year, for more than a decade, thanks to a generous subsidy from the taxpayers of the European Community. Nearly half the weight of the seed consisted of vegetable oil which was used to make margarine and cooking oil by crushing firms who would formerly have used palm oil from the African colonies, and, in a truly free market, would use more soya bean oil from the United States. The rape crop was cut down at this time of year and left to ripen in swaths before being picked up and threshed by combine harvesters. Rain on the brittle, semi-ripe pods caused them to crack open and spill their seeds onto the ground. If the damp weather lasted for more than a day or two, the seed might even sprout in the unthreshed rapestraw and the crop could be ruined. It was an uncomfortable time for growers.

Rain made the worshippers uncomfortable too, dribbling

down necks, making shoulders clammy, causing sleeves to stick to wrists.

'Stay near me, Betty,' Sally whispered. The two women stood side by side, next to the vicar. Jules stood apart, among the other mourners who included the Rose youngsters – Mandy had come back from France where she was staying with a family in the Touraine – John Holman and one or two villagers. Camilla had been ill for so long that she had few friends of her own age when she died. The vicar, accustomed to funeral weather, smoothed the polythene bag that he used to protect his praybook from the wet, so that he could read the words of the burial service through the plastic film. Betty sought Sally's hand and held it, feeling a responsive squeeze.

'Are you able to stand up this long?' Betty whispered. Sally's grip tightened slightly in response and she nodded without taking her eyes off the coffin which was about to be lowered into the wet earth. She was large with pregnancy and her features were puffed with oedema. Soon, the vicar was reading the final Collect: 'We meekly beseech Thee, O Father, to rise up from the death of sin unto the life of righteousness.' Betty thought of Camilla and wondered how well God could have loved her, making her suffer so much and for so long. Was it really the sins of the rest of us that caused this blight on the lives of the chosen ones? What was the basis for God's choice anyway? Didn't His loving and loved subjects deserve an explanation? With a start, she realised that the vicar had read the grace and that the service was over.

There was to be no gathering after the funeral. The death had been dreaded at first, then accepted as inevitable and finally, as the young girl's fight for survival brought her extra weeks of agony, longed for. The grief was gone. All that anyone felt was relief and Sally's mind was more preoccupied, now, with her pregnancy and with Jules's imminent departure. 'Come to the Rectory,' she whispered to Betty. 'I've got to talk.'

'But Jules, isn't he going?'

'Gone!' Sally indicated her husband who was walking

slowly out of the churchyard. The two women watched him glance back towards the rest of the funeral party and then, without a wave, get into his car and drive away.

'Oh Sally!' Betty looked at her. She was dry-eyed in faultless maquillage and black silk, a flowing dress specially made to disguise her bulging front and glamorise without offending the tenor of the occasion.

'It was planned. It's better this way, really.' She was cool, poised and when she shook hands with, and thanked the vicar, gracious – regal, even. Betty also shook hands with him, recoiling slightly, as always, from his limp grip, and walked with Sally through the wicket gate into the Old Rectory garden. Drops of water from the trees pattered onto the midnight-blue straw hat as she passed under them and she hoped the colour wouldn't run.

In the house, Sally took a bottle of Frascati out of the huge double-doored fridge-freezer in the kitchen and found two long-stemmed glasses. She drew the cork, filled them both and handed one to Betty.

'I'm beginning the next chapter,' she said, 'of my life.' She raised her glass and drank. 'We've been grieving for Camilla for years. It's over now, thank God. With Jules, it was all over some time ago.' Her eyes filled for a moment but she overruled the emotion. 'I'm going out to Africa, to Mudando, did you know?'

'You seem to do that all the time.'

'Possibly for good.'

'But what about—'

'This?' She patted her bulging middle. 'Made in Mudando. When I told Jules, he thought I meant that I'd had an affair with an expatriate – a galloping anthropologist or something,' she laughed, a little too loud. 'But this is the genuine native article. Do you remember when I told you about Simon?'

'That was years ago. You said it was just an indiscretion.'

'So it was, that time. But now it's serious.' Betty looked shocked. 'And you can take that disapproving expression off your face. It was Simon who initiated it this time, with, I might add, full approval of his royal father.'

'Isn't there a big age difference?'

'Fifteen years isn't that enormous.' The real age difference was nearer twenty years, but she and Simon weren't into measuring.

'What about the cultural differences?'

'What about them? I know all about that, do you? You ought to come out and meet the family. If you did, you'd see that they can be rather more civilised than people around here might think.'

Betty felt envious of Sally's ability to face difficulties and to make big decisions with such apparent ease. Her own life, in contrast, seemed riddled with dilemma and yet, almost every decision she made now threw up a set of awkward conequences.

Ashley's confessions in May had shaken their relationship almost to destruction. She was still strongly attracted to him – even now, the thought of his embraces quickened her pulse – but since he had bared his soul to her, she knew that a marriage would be unsafe. That secret side to his life would, she was sure, re-emerge once the ardour of their nuptial state had cooled, and she did not think she would be able to tolerate that. Shortly after his confession, she had returned to tell him that she would not share his bed until she had been able to think things through. She was still thinking

The police had investigated the death of the boy but had not been able to trace any relatives, and had assumed that he had been just another missing vagrant.

Ashley had been made aware of the likely costs of his divorce, which were far, far higher than his gloomiest expectations, and worse, Elaine's solicitors were pressing for an early settlement. His bank manager, also concerned about the divorce, had asked him to reduce his borrowings by a significant amount as soon as possible.

'And how the hell am I expected to do that?' Ashley had asked, angrily. He had decided that, among all this uncertainty, he had to get Betty to clear the air. He had asked her to come over 'to discuss the future'.

At first, Betty had demurred. 'I'm not ready yet, Ashley. I need more time.'

But he had insisted: 'Time is something neither of us have much of!'

She had gone and within minutes of arriving, he had sat her down in the elegant drawing room of Wyckhamby Manor and proposed, or at least, made a proposition. 'I have to confess, Betty, that I am facing certain financial difficulties.'

'I know.'

'How can you possibly?'

'The number of cottages you have for sale, the age of your car, the fact that you are doing your own labouring at times.'

'How observant you are,' he said, not without sarcasm. 'Can you imagine why?'

'Your London venture folding, the commodity trading losses you told me about and of course, we all know what's happening to farm incomes.'

'Very astute, but you've missed a major point.' He began to pace. 'My divorce. Elaine is not being exactly greedy but she wants what's rightfully hers.' He paused. 'Don't you want to know what that amounts to?'

'It isn't really my business, Ashley.'

'Oh, but it is. She owns a third of my patch, you see, and she wants to sell out. Her share has been valued at more than a million!' He sat beside her on the sofa and held her hand. 'Oh Betty, Betty, it's all such a mess.' He stroked her fingers and said, 'The bank is threatening to foreclose on me. I have to liquidate more assets but I think I've worked out a way to put things right.' He sat up straighter. 'You asked what I'm proposing. Well, I'm proposing to you.'

'I beg your pardon?'

'It's like this. We could get married. We both want to anyway. You'd move in here, of course, and then I could sell off Cartwright Farm. With Vacant Possession it should make, what, nearly half a million? I've thought about Mandy and Gill, and your boy. There's plenty of room for him, and for the girls whenever they want to visit. It's the perfect solution, don't you see?'

'What about John?'

'Oh, we could pay him off. He's well qualified, he'll find another job.' He turned to her. 'What do you say?'

'Ashley, I'm sorry but I cannot marry you.'

He stood up and began pacing again. 'Why not?'

'Not because of your sexual orientation – that I can live with. I'm afraid you would be unable to abstain from occasional dalliances outside our relationship; even that, I might have been able to tolerate. But your unwillingness to be open about it even to yourself – that I *cannot* go along with. It would destroy us just as it has destroyed your marriage to Elaine.'

Ashley walked to the window and stood with his back to her, peering through the gathering gloom at his unkempt garden. He sighed and then rested his forehead on the cool glass.

'Well then,' he said. 'That's that.'

'I'm sorry, Ashley.' She felt guilty, as if it were all her fault.

'There are a couple of things I think you should know.' He turned round. 'I happen to know that if we do not come to some amicable agreement about the future of Cartwright Farm, the bank will foreclose on you. Once you've got your harvest in, that is.'

'You're just trying to scare me.'

'Really?'

'Ashley, it won't help anyone if you're bitter.'

'The other thing is that whether or not I choose to, your notice to quit the farm is bound to be followed up.'

Betty paled. 'You wouldn't. Not after all we've been to one another.'

'I no longer have any choice in the matter. I am running out of resources.'

'I could change your mind, simply by threatening to inform people about you.' She was alarmed by the terrified look that came over his face. 'But I won't.' He looked searchingly at her, feeling uneasy in the candour of her wide,

448

grey eyes but holding her gaze. 'I won't ever do anything to hurt you.'

'Oh, *Christ* what a mess!' He stepped forward and held her. She kept her arms by her sides.

'But I will fight you for Cartwright Farm, Ashley. I'm sorry for the plight you are in, sorrier than you could possibly know. But I will not lose my farm either to you or to the bank.' And she walked out of the room, pausing at the door to say, 'Come out of the closet! It's your only route to emotional survival. If you do, and the village ostracises you, I promise that I will stay loyal to you, regardless of what happens to Cartwright.'

Back at home, she found John in the grainstore, spraying the surfaces with insecticide in preparation for harvest. 'Isn't it a bit early for that?'

'Not really. Elliot is coming tomorrow, remember, and I want to spend some time with him before harvest begins.'

'Of course.' Betty was glad the little boy was coming for the summer holidays. He loved farm life so much and adored his father. 'That'll be nice for both of you.' He heard her sigh, turned and read the distress on her face.

'You look ever so tired.'

'Oh, *thank* you!'

'Oh no, I didn't mean ...' He was mortified at his tactlessness.

She put her hand on his sleeve. 'I know, John,' she said kindly. But as it happens, I am rather. The fact is, we need to talk. We've got a problem.'

'You've been over at Kirkland's, haven't you?'

'Yes.'

'And this is about us?' She nodded. 'He wants to steal the bread from our mouths. Again!'

'Let's go inside.'

'No. I've got to finish this first, otherwise the chemical will be wasted.' He resumed spraying and Betty left to make some tea. He was done in less than half an hour and joined her in the kitchen.

'John, I've got quite a bit to tell you. Will you promise to

449

keep quiet until I've given you the facts? We can discuss it all when you know everything that I do.' He nodded. Betty began to speak in dispirited tones that filled him with foreboding. He paled and clenched his fists as she described Ashley's seduction, that spring afternoon when she had been on her way to his cottage. When she explained how strongly she was attracted to him, he felt so miserable and so furious at the same time that he had to resist a powerful impulse to leap up and smash things. He could not bear to think of anyone touching her, taking advantage of her good nature, taking from her at all. Betty was a giver, that was why he loved her so much. Kirkland, he knew, did nothing but take.

As she gave chapter and verse of Ashley's financial problems he could restrain himself no longer.

'I *told* you he was in trouble.'

'John, please! You did promise.' He stayed silent while she explained how shortage of cash was forcing Ashley to endanger their farm and finally, she mentioned his marriage proposal and that she had turned him down. She had managed to tell him everything without breaking Ashley's confidence. John's relief that she had turned the creep down was clouded with incomprehension.

'Is that the whole story?'

'Pretty well.'

'It doesn't add up.'

'Oh?'

'You turned him down.'

'Do you think I would betray you?'

'Never.' John blushed with shame for even thinking that she could do such a thing. 'But it still doesn't add up. He's keeping something from you. There has to be something else; there's something still unsaid.'

Betty was shaken by his adroit guesswork. She hated deceiving him. 'Yes,' she said. 'There is more.'

'I knew it.'

'But I can't tell you about that. I promised.'

John sighed. He knew that her word was not likely to be

broken. 'He always has the upper hand. If only we could put the pressure on him for a change.'

'That would be sinking rather to his level, don't you think?'

'I only want to get him off our backs so that we can live.' He looked hard at Betty. Seldom had he seen her so low. His heart almost burst for love of her but he had bottled it up for so long now that he felt he might never be able to speak of his true feelings. 'You need a rest. I ought to get home and leave you in peace.'

'John, couldn't you stay a little? I feel rather . . .' She broke down.

He leapt up, knocking his chair over in his awkwardness, and fussed about tearing off pieces of kitchen paper and standing by her, wringing his hands while she blew her nose and tried to stop weeping.

'I'll stay as long as you like.' It didn't seem right to put his arms around her, so he stood with a bunch of absorbent paper, to hand out as needed.

When the storm had passed and she was able to speak again she said: 'You *are* my partner, and if I speak to you in confidence, do you swear that what I tell you will go no further?'

'I do.'

'Well then,' and she told him everything she knew about Ashley.

His eyes widened and his excitement grew. 'Don't you see,' he said, as soon as she had finished, 'that's our trump card!'

'What d'you mean?'

'We just tell that blasted *fairy* that if he wants us to keep quiet, he'd better leave us alone and make damn sure we keep the tenancy.'

'John!' Betty was shocked. 'Do you want to sink to the level of a blackmailer?'

'We're sunk if we don't.'

'No! I will *not* allow it.' Her vehemence took him aback. 'Don't you understand? I told you this in confidence.'

'It's our only hope.'

'No, it isn't. Something else will turn up.'

'Oh, ah?' John was growing angry. 'You'd rather stick to a principle than keep your livelihood?'

'I must!'

'How *pathetic!*' He stormed out of the house and went home.

Maggie took until the end of the summer to recover from the prolonged bout of pneumonia that followed her accident. At first, she had suffered total amnesia and could not even recognise Leonard, but her memory had returned until she could recall most things up to her long walk, and everything since she had regained consciousness, between clean white sheets in the cottage hospital. Of her scene with Ashley and subsequent plunge in the slurry, she could remember nothing.

'One thing I just don't get,' she told Betty when she was convalescing, 'is why Ashley Kirkland is being so bloody to me. I mean – look at his garden. What a bloody tip! And yet, we were supposed to maintain it for him this summer.'

'Ashley's in one of his enigmatic moods these days, I'm afraid,' Betty said, reluctant to air her own problems.

'You can say that again. When Bobby Goss went to get the mowers out, Ashley told him to clear off and that in future he'd mow his own bloody lawns.'

'Just a misunderstanding, I expect. You mustn't upset yourself about it.'

'But it's so frustrating having this blank in my mind. It was like that sometimes when I went on a piss-up. Do you suppose I might have insulted him or something, without knowing it?'

'Surely not!'

'The other mystery is what the hell I was doing there in the first place. I mean, I presume I'd gone to his office about something to do with the garden but – at night? In the rain? It doesn't make sense.'

'It'll come back to you.'

'I wish it would.' Maggie sighed, shifting uncomfortably in

her chair. 'Six weeks since the accident and I'm still as weak as a kitten!'

Another six weeks later and Maggie was back at work. Harvest was over, the days were drawing in and the chimneys in the village fed woodsmoke into the evening air. But still Ashley had not approached her, and still she had not remembered.

Relations between Betty and John had never been more strained. He resented her for not using her knowledge about Ashley to put on pressure; she was afraid that he would lose patience and talk. Every morning they expected bad news in the mail, either from the bank or from Ashley's land agent. But none came and the tension mounted with each passing day. November began with a sharp frost which heralded a long cold spell. Still no news. 'The swine's playing with us,' John said.

'Who, Ashley or the bank manager?'

'Take your pick. They're both swine as far as I'm concerned.'

Sally Ray – she had shed the name Doncaster shortly after Jules's departure – had her baby in early November at Kendale Hospital. The obstetricians and paediatricians concealed their surprise at the colour of its skin but were impressed with the mother's fitness, for her age, and the ease of her confinement. She flew out to Mudando, with her tiny new daughter, as soon as she was fit to travel.

The whole royal entourage stood on the tarmac apron of the little airport under the cruel glare of the African sun, waiting to meet their newest citizens. Simon gazed at his child with ecstatic eyes and escorted the mother with exaggerated care, as if she were an invalid, into the waiting air-conditioned limousine. They resumed their life where they had left off on her last visit. The difference was that now, since Sally planned to be with Simon for the foreseeable future, there was no urgency about anything.

Back at Wyckhamby, the 'For Sale' sign outside the Old Rectory gates attracted a great many gawpers who had long wanted to see for themselves the fabled luxury the 'new gentry' were rumoured to have installed. It also added to the number of serious buyers who drove the price up to unrealistic levels by outbidding each other.

Betty and John still had not heard, either from bank or from land agent. Neither of them had spoken to Ashley, who seemed to spend most of his time in his farm office or in his study at the Manor. Rarely, he travelled to London for an overnight stay but he had been obliged to cut down the workforce at Wyckhamby and the farm now demanded almost every minute of his time.

On the last Friday of November, John had come in, tired and irritable from struggling with the sugar-beet harvester which had broken down twice and had become blocked several times with dead weeds in the conveyors – a result of the wet spring and subsequent difficulty with weed control. 'I've had enough,' he told Betty. 'This suspense is driving me insane. If we don't hear anything next week, I'm blowing Kirkland's gaff.'

'If you do, it will be the end of our partnership.'

'Well, that's probably ending anyway.' He went home to fume alone, in his cottage. But when, next Sunday, he came as usual for lunch, he was carrying a *News of the World*. 'Just read that!' He slapped the paper down on the draining board where Betty was peeling parsnips. She wiped her hands and picked up the paper. 'Gay Farmer Exposed in Club,' it said. 'Millionaire farmer Ashton Kirkwall, of Wyckhamby in Lincolnshire, was arrested with two other men, for gross indecency in a gay Soho club earlier this week.' She put the paper down, not wanting to read the rest.

Early next week, a stringer who worked on the *Kendale Gazette* faxed a copy of the report on the discovery of the boy's body to the *News of the World*. Soon, the village was crawling with reporters and stories about missing rent boys began to circulate. There was speculation about the possibility of homosexual orgies having been organised at the Manor, about child abuse and about the laxness of the local police in failing to uncover vice.

Elaine was tracked down and questioned by reporters. She sent Ashley a postcard which read: '*It was bound to happen, but I'm sorry it has.*' Reporters also tackled Andrew and asked, over a bottle of Dom Perignon, in the snug of his favourite wine bar, if his father had ever molested him when he was a boy. 'Not that I remember,' he said, 'but I will not be having anything more to do with him. I have no father, not now.'

Village people began to shun Ashley. Someone slashed the tyres on one of his expensive tractors while the driver was taking a lunch break and someone else scratched the word POOF into the paintwork of his Daimler when it was parked outside the Mardles' cottage. In the past, he had never received anything but respect or affection in the village, but now he was confronted either by abusive gestures or cold indifference. People he'd known for years crossed the street to avoid him and, on the one occasion since the news broke that he'd gone into the saloon bar of the Heron, it had emptied within seconds. He had muttered an embarrassed apology to the landlord and fled.

He would have been even more deeply affected by the locals' attitudes, had he not been so preoccupied with financial problems. He had cut costs to the bone at the farm and was trying to sell his flat in Hampstead, but the bank still wanted him to halve his overdraft and he did not know where to raise the cash.

The deepest resentment he felt was entirely misplaced. Not realising that the press interest had originated from the *News of the World* stringer, he had assumed that Betty had been the source, betraying his confidence out of spite. He did not even realise that the mortifying incident at the Rough Trade Club, in Berwick Street, had been reported at all, much less that it had been given a paragraph in a national Sunday newspaper.

All he had done was to stand at the back of the tiny auditorium, where men in raincoats watched boys dancing in the nude, and felt the thigh of the man just behind him. He had shown no resistance but a deep voice had muttered, 'OK, sunbeam, that's enough, You're nicked!' He and a couple of others had than been arrested but, after an interminable wait at Vine Street police station, had been charged and let out on bail. There would be a magistrate's court, at which he would plead guilty, a fine and, he assumed, minimal local publicity miles from Wyckhamby. He had considered his secret still to be safe, but he might just as well have confessed on television, he thought, now that Betty had virtually shopped him.

For her part, Betty was frantic to contact him. She knew how hurt he would be and was appalled that he might think her responsible for his exposure. She just *had* to reassure him but, try as she might, she could not reach him. She rang but almost always got the engaged tone and assumed, rightly, that he had left the phone off the hook. She visited the Manor several times but he wasn't there. She spotted his Range Rover at the edge of one of his fields but as soon as he saw her approaching, he drove off. Finally, more than a week after the story had broken, she saw him outside the Mardles' cottage as she was driving past and stopped to accost him. 'Ashley, I must talk to you.' He gave her a look of such loathing and contempt that she flinched.

'I have nothing to say to you. My legal advisers will be dealing with you from now on.' And he strode into the cottage, leaving her on the grass verge. That evening she made one final effort to phone him but each time she dialled the 'number unobtainable' tone was all she could hear. She called the operator who checked and told her that the number she was dialling had been changed and that the new one was ex-directory.

The letters she and John had been dreading both arrived in the same post the following Tuesday. The bank informed them, in cold terms, that it required them to fund their overdraft. A land agent's document – not from Enfield, oddly enough – instructed Betty that as she was in breach of her tenancy contract, she would be required to vacate Cartwright Farm by Lady Day the following year. 'We've got four months to get out,' she said to John when he arrived at the farm after taking a consignment of porkers to Kendale market. He turned pale and sat down rather heavily on a kitchen chair and read both the letters.

'We're done for.' He sighed and slumped forward, resting his cheek on the table and hiding his face with his arms. 'We'll have to start winding up straight away,' his voice sounded muffled. 'If they make us quit halfway through the growing season, they'll have to compensate us for crops in the ground.'

'Quit? We're not quitting.'

'We'll have to. We're done for this time, well and truly.'

'You may think so,' Betty's eyes blazed, 'but I'm not going down without a fight.'

'You? What do you think you can do?'

'Find another bank, for a start.'

He sat up to explain that no bank, however irresponsible, would lend them a penny in their present predicament. But catching sight of her face, burning with defiance, he kept quiet.

Chapter Thirty-one

At the bank, Geoffrey Woods was apologetic but firm. They no longer had adequate security and therefore the overdraft facility was withdrawn. 'You do realise that until we have liquidated our stocks, we can't possibly pay you,' Betty said.

'Naturally,' Woods replied, 'and I don't want you to have to rush into liquidation, either. We could put a receiver in but I would prefer to trust you two to do the right thing.'

Their solicitor was pessimistic. 'I see little chance of the High Court finding for you,' he said. 'Your legal costs could be crippling.' He advised them to quit without a fight but to request maximum compensation for loss of crops and add to that a figure for the disturbance.

'Settle out of court, you mean?' Betty asked.

'By all means. If they made a counter offer of half the amount we demand, it would be a good settlement and I'd advise you to take it.' John was bitter about that but willing to act on the lawyer's advice. Betty was not.

'No. We'll go to the High Court. We've nothing to lose.'

'Apart from a great deal of money,' the solicitor said. 'You could be bankrupted.'

'We'll go to court,' she decided, and initiated several weeks of frenzied activity. With the bank pressing, time was not on their side and they needed a decision before spring work could begin in early March.

Ashley reacted to the partners' plight with wry amusement. John did not realise that the bank was leaning as heavily on Wyckhamby Farms as on the Cartwright partners and assumed that this final bid to evict them was motivated by spite. Betty, however, appreciated his situation and would still have talked to him if only he would allow her to.

As soon as he heard about the bank's foreclosure – Woods had tipped him a very unofficial wink – Ashley had rung Hector Enfield to set the eviction into motion. Enfield had sounded terse and uneasy.

'Is anything wrong, Hec?'

'I don't like what you're doing.'

'Neither do I, old boy, but needs must.'

'And I'm not sure I want to act for you any more.'

'What?' Ashley affected disbelief but he had recognised the tone in Enfield's voice. It was one he had already heard from several of his close associates.

'I think you know why.' Formerly, Ashley might have remonstrated, but he had been quick to learn what all repressed minorities know instinctively: that it is easier to take the insults than try to fight them.

'Yes, I know why.'

'I think it was a mistake to make it legal,' Enfield said. 'Centuries ago they used to hang queers.'

'And small children for pinching spoons. You've made your point,' Ashley replied. 'Land agents are two a penny. I'll find another in five minutes.'

The Cartwright partners spent a bleak Christmas, poring over legal papers and making endless calculations. Elliot stayed with them and all the Rose children came home. Gill, well into her medical training, could only stay for a couple of days but Mandy and Jim were both down from university for the Christmas vacation and had much longer. The young did all the work they could to make the occasion festive but Betty and John could not clear their problems from their minds.

Heavy snow was forecast for the day of the hearing, 4 January, and Betty's heart sank. 'If they have to cancel the court, I don't think I'll be able to bear waiting any longer.'

'It's only a forecast. Weathermen are often wrong.' John said, trying to comfort her. But early on the afternoon of

3 January, the sky darkened and snow began to fall. By dusk several inches had accumulated and it seemed to be snowing harder then before. To save him from having to trudge to the village in the blizzard, Betty suggested that John should spend the night at Cartwright Farm, and went to turn on the radiator in the guest room. She put out an old dressing gown of Jack's and found a new toothbrush for John in the bathroom cupboard.

Neither slept. Betty lay worrying about what she would do if they lost their case. The money they would owe would come to such a huge sum that she was unable to imagine it as a real figure. When they had sold off every asset and settled with the bank, there might be enough to pay about a tenth of the sum. As for the rest, well, they'd have to find some way of working that off. But working as what? What could they do that would win them more than a pittance? She lay, wide-eyed, almost feverish with guilt for dragging John into this hell. Poor dear, gentle John. If she had not been so stubborn, they might have been able to salvage a little capital out of the liquidation, perhaps even enough to finance them while they each started another career. That would have been more sensible than trying to cling to this hopeless venture.

In the unfamiliar guest-room bed, John was equally restless. He knew that he would never have had the guts to go through with this the way Betty had insisted. Now he wondered if he shouldn't have been firmer and insisted they wound up. After all, he was equal partner and had equal say. But Betty? When her grey eyes – lovely, warm, compassionate eyes that they could be – took on that look of zeal, there was no stopping her. And when she focused them on him, all he wanted to do was support her, protect her and help her to make sure that she achieved her impossible goals.

Since Karen had left, his love for Betty had increased to an ache he could hardly bear. His camphorwood box of Betty memorabilia was now so full he had to press hard on the lid to shut it. But still his reticence ruled him and he shrank from making any sort of advance.

When she took up with Ashley, he was tortured. When the

news broke that he was a queer, John wanted to kill him, not for being a homo – presumably he couldn't help that – but for deceiving his beloved Betty and fouling his own relationship with her.

Next morning, they discovered that the temperature had lifted half a degree, not enough to turn the snow into rain, but enough to prevent it from accumulating on the roads. They drove to Kendale through a filth of slush and grime and waited, with dry mouths and queasy stomachs, for the hearing to begin.

Six thousand miles away, the Prince of Mudando was sitting in his bedroom and thinking how well everything had turned out. He had a new grandchild and that was fine – even though she was only a girl – but far more importantly, his son, the apple of his eye, the reason for his living, had, at last, taken the bride of his choice. Just why Simon was so much in love, not only with a white woman but with a white woman so much older than himself, had long baffled the Prince. Not that he disapproved: Sally was one of the finest women to have entered his country, that was certain. Intelligent, beautiful, dignified ... had he not longed for her embraces himself? But he was so much older than she, and anyway, it wouldn't have been right to have taken on another wife while his first two were still with him. Like Simon, he admired Sally for her business sense and her intelligence, but the race business worried him. Would it be polluting the line somehow, bringing in the white blood? Judging by the bawling little creature Sally had brought with her from England, probably not. That baby was tougher and prettier than anything he'd seen in Mudando, and he knew babies all right. Didn't he have hundreds of them held out for a touch and a blessing on royal walkabouts?

In another chamber, at the cooler end of the palace, Sally and Simon lay side by side, naked under their mosquito net, her slender white legs making a contrast with his smooth purple-black limbs. She rested her hand on his chest, marvelling at the smoothness of his skin and then ran it slowly down, feeling the outline of his nipple, which hardened under her touch, over his flat belly and down to the wiry brush.

'Sally,' Simon said, his voice as smooth and honey-like as his skin. 'You'll get me all steamed up again.' In response, she dabbled her fingers in his frizzled pubic hair and watched his penis lift its head like a lazy snake. 'I warned you!' They both laughed.

'It must be time to get up.' The room was beginning to darken.

'It is. My father wants to talk to us.'

'Oh?'

'About his plans.' They dressed. Simon wore his robes but Sally opted for a simple sheath of white poplin with a sky-blue silk foulard at the neck. The Prince welcomed them to his private drawing room room with a friendly nod and the three of them relaxed on comfortable sofas.

'How have you settled in?' the Prince asked.

'It's not a question of settling in,' Sally said. 'I've been coming for so long that I feel as much at home here as anywhere.'

'Now you do, but in time, you may feel the call of your native home.'

'I might.' Sally looked at Simon and took his hand.

'My son feels it too,' The Prince continued. 'After his education in England, he feels he belongs there.'

'Naturally,' she stroked his hand as she spoke, 'but we can visit whenever we want.'

'Indeed,' the Prince went on, 'it is important for us to have strong trading links with Britain. Now that you and, er, *Simon* are together,' he was using the Anglicised form of his son's name in deference to her, 'you could make a fine team, serving our interests in Europe.'

'Makes a lot of sense,' Sally said. 'Don't you agree, Si?'

'In fact,' Simon said, 'this is really my idea. I've been nagging Father for years about having a proper British headquarters – an office, probably in London, with residential quarters as well, so we have somewhere more civilised to stay than those horrible hotels in Park Lane.'

'There is another reason for this.' The Prince shivered slightly and pulled his robes around him: 'A less pleasant one.' Sally thought, suddenly, how old he was beginning to look. 'I have been slipping a certain amount of our capital – private moneys, not state funds – into England, as an eventuality.' He looked almost coy. 'In case of a coup.'

'Here?' Sally laughed. 'This is the last place I'd expect anything like that to happen! Your people adore you. You've led them into the present century without losing any of their traditions.'

'Apart from female circumcision,' Simon chipped in. 'He banned that.' Sally cuffed him and crossed her legs.

'Yes, most of my people love me,' the Prince said, 'but not all. Besides, we live in times of rapid change. I think, or rather, Simon thinks it would be prudent for us to have a bolt-hole.' He blinked at them, slightly ashamed at having to admit to feelings of insecurity. 'Just in case.'

The most surprising thing about the High Court hearing was how quickly it was over. Betty and John had been warned that it might take days and that with each hour, the costs would increase. But in fact, it was all over comfortably within the day. All that happened, in essence, was that the judge had spotted a technicality overlooked by all the other legal experts and had simply thrown the case out. The tenancy was safe for three generations, according to the 1976 Act. Jack had been first tenant, succeeded by Betty. The partnership, as long as it included Betty, was no different from a third succession and was therefore able to be upheld by law.

The main part of the hearing was over very quickly. The rest of the time was spent by the legal people haggling over costs. The partners were awarded costs but that, according to their counsel, wasn't enough. He pressed for an award from Ashley for breaking what he called the 'Quiet Enjoyment' clause of the tenancy contract. And he got it – a further ten thousand pounds on top of all their costs. John and Betty left the court immune from further molesting by Ashley and not a penny out of pocket.

They should have been elated but Betty regretted the whole affair. 'Country living shouldn't be like this,' she said. 'I wish it hadn't happened. A good tenant needs a good landlord.'

'You think Ashley was good?' John looked scornful.

'Maybe not, but now he will always be hostile. We need someone who will cooperate.' She still harboured a desire to rekindle her friendship with Ashley – a forlorn hope, she knew, but she longed to tell him that it was not she who had exposed his secret.

Security of tenure was only half their problem. Now they had to sort out how to finance their future. Geoffrey Woods had slipped out of the bank to be at the hearing, and now came trotting up to congratulate them.

'I can't tell you how pleased I am for you both,' he said, his face creased with an embarrassed smile. 'Obviously, we will have to review your situation but, unofficially, I can assure you that there will be no problem, now, with the overdraft.' He left with the partners staring at each other.

'Our first task,' John said, looking at the retreating figure, 'is to get ourselves fixed up with another bank.'

'Hear hear,' said Betty.

She elected to drive home, guiding the car gingerly through the slush which was hardening now as the evening temperature dropped to freezing. Having John beside her was comforting, and as they were emerging from the Kendale suburbs she said, 'You might as well stay a second night.'

'Thanks, but I ought to get home, especially if it freezes. I need to turn off the water to prevent a burst.' Her disappointment was sharp. She had looked forward to his presence, quiet, reassuring and comforting, for a whole evening. Besides, there was a lot to discuss.

'I've got a casserole and Jim promised to do the vegetables. We could stop at your cottage and check everything first if you liked and then you could come on to the house.'

'No, it's OK, really.'

'Suit yourself,' she said, trying to keep her voice bright. 'I'll drop you off, anyway.'

Both partners spent their evening alone, John huddled near his smoking fire and Betty listening to Radio 4 in the sitting room, Jim having slipped off to the Heron to sink a couple of pints with his friends as soon as they had eaten.

Early next morning, as Betty was coming back from her first checking over of the pigs, the phone rang. 'This is Galahad Stamp,' a nasal female voice whined. 'I have Mr Marden-Thomas for you.'

'Thank you,' said Betty, wondering why a smart estate agents' firm like Galahad Stamp would want to speak with her. She heard a click followed by a tired Sloane drawl.

'Ear, yah! Marden-Thomas hyar. Am I speaking to Mr Ho'man?'

'No, I'm his partner, Betty Rose.'

'Ear.' This seemed to perplex him for a moment. 'Is that E. Raise?'

'Yes.'

'And you are a partner, not just a wife?'

'I hold fifty per cent of the equity in the firm, I manage half of the enterprises and I do all the marketing of our products – when I can fit it in between coffee mornings and Mothers' Union – does that qualify?'

'Ear! I'm *aw*fully sorry. I didn't mean to be peartronising!' He paused for a moment. 'Feact is, I've got some news that will be of some considerable concern to you.'

'Oh?'

'Ears. My client, Mr Earshly Kirkland has instructed us that the whole of the Wyckhamby Estate is to be sold, either at auction or by private treaty.'

'I can hardly believe it.'

'Near. It is quite a surprise. But the point is, the farms may well be divided into lots. As tenants, you would be in quite an, um, eadvantageous position to buy.'

Betty laughed out loud. 'Mr Thomas, we are hardly in a position to buy land. We can barely keep our heads above water as it is.'

'I see. Well, I thought you should know. May I leave you to discuss it with Mr, um, Ho'man?'

'Yes, I'll discuss it with Mr Holman. If we win the pools, we'll let you know.'

John already knew. On his way back from Kendale, where he had been to collect a set of oil-filters and gaskets for the tractor which was having its annual overhaul, he had spotted two men setting up a noticeboard at the western end of Ashley's fields. Curious, he had stopped and watched for long enough to see that it was a 'For Sale' sign which detailed: *An important Gentleman's Estate comprising a fine 18th Century Manor House, numerous outbuildings, cottages and prime agricultural land in excess of 3,000 acres, most with Vacant Possession &c.*' He drove on to Cartwright, bursting with the news.

'Looks like we're going to have a new landlord. It seems that Kirkland really is in Queer Street now. Oh ha ha! I made a joke.'

'Don't, John.' Betty could hardly bear to think about the pain Ashley must be suffering. 'He can't help what he is and he doesn't deserve to lose everything.' She thought, not without a pang of sexual hunger, of his tender, considerate lovemaking. Even now, she wondered whether he would listen to her if she went to the Manor. She wanted to bring him comfort but knew that any approach would meet with rebuttal. He was done with her and probably done with village society.

'Not exactly losing everything. He should come out quite well off.'

'That depends on his debts. He's had a run of awful luck.'

John was just about to say, 'A man reaps what he sows,' but read compassion in Betty's voice and kept quiet. He hated to see Betty tortured like this, even if her feelings were entirely misplaced, and he wasn't about to make it worse for her. 'The question is,' he said, changing tack, 'what sort of landlord are we likely to get?'

Within a day or two, strange vehicles were cruising up and down Wyckhamby High Street and stopping by various field gates. John and Betty were able to get a clear idea of who the likely buyers were, because each of them wanted to visit

Cartwright Farm and to ask questions about local cropping and animal husbandry. Betty resented the intrusions but bore with them because she knew that her landlord had every right to sell and therefore to allow strangers to probe, to dig out soil samples and to quiz her. John, on the other hand, became morose and uncooperative, telling visiting agents that they'd have to ask the owner if they wanted information.

It was clear, after a while, that there were a couple of front runners, the hottest prospect of which was a land agent rumoured to be working for a financial institution called 'Rural General Pensions'. 'May I speak to you in complete and absolute confidence?' the agent – one of a clone wearing Harris tweed and cavalry twill – said to Betty. 'My clients are keen to buy but prefer to farm their new acquisitions in partnership. Agricultural tenancies are a thing of the past now, and yours would be problematic.' Betty's heart sank. All that nightmare of insecurity looked set for a reprise. 'We'd offer a handsome figure for you to quit.'

'I see.'

'But I'm not sure we'd be in a position to offer a partnership. Our clients tend to team up with – and please don't think I'm being in the least insulting or patronising here – but they tend to team up with more modern farm businesses. We do not consider arable units of less than one thousand acres to be commercially viable. Now, the rest of the Wyckhamby Estate could be immensely profitable. Your two hundred acres of poorish land, on the other hand,' he sucked in his breath and shook his head, 'well, frankly, I can't imagine how you've been able to survive this long.'

'But we have.'

'Maybe. But with Common Agricultural Policy reforms just round the corner, I don't think you have a snowflake's of surviving the future. Not a snowflake's.'

'And if we want to stay?'

'We can't do a lot about that. But you'll have unsympathetic landlords. At worst, our clients might ask us to apply pressure; at best they'll leave you alone and step in when economic events have overtaken you.'

'I see.'

'This conversation hasn't taken place, by the way.' He got up to leave. 'I would appreciate your confidence. I merely contacted you in your own interests. Good day to you.' And with that he was gone, leaving Betty to brood for the rest of the afternoon.

Later, when John came back in from the yard, his hands black from working at the innards of the tractor, she replayed the conversation and poured out her fears.

'You know,' he said, 'I'd never have expected it to come from you but I think, at last, you are beginning to realise that we can hardly survive here on this little farm, even with a sympathetic landlord, let alone one hellbent on finishing us off. Times are going to get really hard. The nineties could even see an exodus from the land with mass bankruptcies and of course, small farmers will be the first to go.'

'And we know what will happen to their farms,' Betty said. 'They'll be swallowed up by huge agribusinesses, ruining the land and destroying life in the villages. It's an intolerable thought. *We're* the ones who care for the countryside, people like us who live on the land.' She clenched her fists in frustration, whitening the knuckles. 'I cannot see all that lost without a struggle.'

'Haven't you struggled enough?' He met her gaze and felt his innards lurch. How he loved her when she was like this, but how he hated to see her tearing herself apart. 'Well, haven't you?'

'John, is there any way at all that we could buy this place for ourselves?'

'Don't you think I've wracked my brains on the thing? No, there isn't. No way at all.'

They heard a vehicle in the yard. It was Maggie Bates, coming to store a couple of terracotta urns she had acquired for a client. She banged on the kitchen door and peered in. 'Wotcher! Any chance of a hand with these pots? I can't get them out of the car on my own.' John jumped up to help her.

'Come and have a cuppa, when you're done,' Betty said. Within a couple of minutes, they had stowed the urns in the barn and returned to the kitchen. Betty had set out cups and saucers, taken a heavy fruit cake out of its tin and put it on a plate. John shook his head but Maggie accepted a generous slice and munched at it greedily, holding the whole piece in her paw and ignoring the side plate and dessert knife Betty had put out for her.

'Mmm, scrummy!' she said, scattering crumbs down her chin. When she had washed the cake down with a slurp of tea she said, 'Now, you two, what's the misery for? I thought everything had worked out just fine for you.' They told her as much as they could about their predicament without breaking the agent's confidence.

'Why don't you hock yourselves to the eyeballs and buy the bloody place yourselves?' Maggie asked.

'We've looked into all that,' John said. 'The sums just don't add up. We'd have to borrow so much that our earnings wouldn't even cover interest charges, let alone provide something to live on.'

'You'd have to do what big businesses do when they're skint. Strip a few assets.'

'It's no good even talking about it, Maggie. It's not on,' Betty said. 'There'd be no assets to strip.'

'Well, bugger me!' Maggie cried. 'I never thought I'd see *you* ready to throw in the towel, Betty Rose!'

'But this time we're in a jam even we can't get out of,' she replied.

Maggie fixed her with an arch expression. 'And what is the most profitable crop of all, these days?'

'Whatever it is, we're growing it,' John said. 'We've diversified ourselves to the fullest extent. Besides, these sidelines only bring in pin money. We'd need a hefty pile of dosh.'

'You don't follow me,' Maggie said, growing slightly breathless in her excitement. 'The rich farmers, these days, are the ones who are selling off building plots. If you bought Cartwright, you could flog a barn or two to developers.'

'No!' Betty said. 'That would bring strangers into our back garden. I'd rather lose the farm than have that.'

'But that's brilliant,' John exclaimed. 'That's the answer! *If*
we could get planning consent.'

'I said no!' Betty retorted.

'Not a barn,' John said, 'but the bottom field.' Betty
pursed her lips. She disliked the idea of ruining farmland but
she was desperate to find a way out of the trap they were in.
'We could propose a small development,' John went on, 'no
more than about four good houses and a few starter homes.
It needn't take up more space than an acre.'

'It'd spoil the entrance to the village,' Betty objected. The
idea went against all her instincts.

'Balls!' Maggie scoffed. 'It's within the curtilage and would
add to, not detract from. We could landscape it a bit – tart it
up with trees and so on. Villages have to move with the
times.'

'We'd never get permission.'

'We'd never know if we didn't try!' John's eyes had lit up
more brightly than Betty had seen in months. 'I can't believe
we didn't think of this ourselves. Maggie, you're brilliant.'

'Got any more of that cake?' Maggie said. 'It just hits the
spot!'

By the end of January, they had commissioned an architect
to draw up outline plans for a discreet development of
dwellings on the edge of the village. The architect was
dubious about their chances but was happy to accept a fee
for doing his best anyway. Maggie helped to amend the
drawings so that the layout of the houses would blend more
comfortably with the landscape, and she drew up a set of
plans for furnishing a larger green space around the houses
with trees and shrubs. The whole package was now with the
Kendale and District Planning Department.

'All we have to do now, is convince the bank to lend us
the money,' John said. They had met two of the other
Kendale bank managers but were not convinced that either
would be any more reliable than Woods. At length, in spite
of the distance, they had made an appointment to meet the
area manager of McCrae's Bank at Market Lenton.

'In a nutshell,' said Mr Salmon, a man of rufous colouring

and rubicund complexion, 'you want us to bridge you so that you can buy your farm, intending to fund your purchase by re-selling part of the land for development, yah?' The partners nodded in unison. 'What happens if you don't get planning consent?'

'We then liquidate, sell the farm, refund our loan and find another job,' Betty said. This was shit or bust. 'As we would be buying at tenanted value and selling with Vacant Possession, we should make a comfortable gain.'

'But,' said Salmon, 'if you do get consent and you go on farming, aren't you still going to need a lot of financing? Your borrowings are already pretty high.'

'We know,' John reddened. 'But we think we can survive.'

'It rather depends on what we make on the development land,' Betty pointed out. 'Prices are so buoyant now, we hope we might be able to reduce our indebtedness considerably.'

'Any more land coming your way?' They both shook their heads. Salmon looked up from their file on his desk. 'You are hardly of a size to be profitable,' he muttered and circled a figure on their papers with his pencil. Then he closed their file. 'This is a marginal thing,' he said. 'I see no problem in bridging your purchase, although that will be terribly expensive for you.'

'And you'll take on our current overdraft?'

'For the time being, yes.'

'Thank you.' Betty heaved a sigh of relief mixed with anxiety.

'But I don't think your forecasts are accurate for your farm profits,' Salmon went on. 'They seem to me to be rather optimistic, and I don't believe you can live on as little say you say you do.'

'The figures are there,' John's colour deepened. 'Those are actuals, not forecasts.'

'Of course.' His incredulity was obvious. He assumed, wrongly, that much of their trading would be in cash without books. It was the only way these piddling farmers could manage.

'You can bid for your farm,' he said. 'We'll back you on that to a top price of three hundred thousand. But I cannot promise security in the long run, and I doubt whether we'd be in a position to provide much of an overdraft once you've got your land. I must make that clear now, to avoid any misunderstandings in the future.'

'I see.' John looked at Betty.

'And I would advise you, as firmly as I can, to consider liquidation, after you've purchased. You stand to make a considerable gain that way, especially if you get your planning permission. Good heavens,' he said, rubbing his pink hands together and warming to his theme, 'with the profit you're likely to make, you could abandon peasant farming altogether and start a property development business!'

Chapter Thirty-two

Ashley disliked everything about Marden-Thomas, in spite of his good looks. Tall, sandy-haired and blue-eyed with clean, pinkish complexion, he was the type who always got the lead in the school play, but was inclined to bully his juniors – and get away with it – and was, on the quiet, less than honest. He seemed to be light on brains, too, but since he was a partner with Galahad Stamp, Ashley assumed that he must be endowed with a generous helping of low cunning. The proof of the pudding . . . he thought, eyeing the man's shiny brown leather brogues, his heavy twill trousers and tweed Norfolk jacket. The bottom line was all that mattered, now that he was finished with Wyckhamby.

As long as he got out with enough capital left over, after paying everything off, he didn't really care. He was tired, dog-tired. He'd lost weight from eating a skimpy diet, he slept badly and all the while, his debts grew steadily as the interest charges clocked up with each passing day.

He glanced out of his office window, watched a handful of snowflakes whirl against the grey sky and thought what an irony for St Valentine's Day to come at the most miserable time of year. He was not only loveless but also sexually frustrated, stuck in this village where few people would speak to him and where he felt unable to look anyone in the eye. With the farm now cut to a skeleton staff and demanding his daily labour, he had little chance of going adventuring in London. Before, he had been unable to comprehend loneliness but now, busy as he was, he had never felt so isolated.

'I think you'll be able to sell without having to go to

auction,' Marden-Thomas said. 'We already have an interesting line-up of possibles.'

'Such as?' The Sloane drawl set Ashley's teeth on edge.

'Several of your neighbours are putting in for le—and which abuts their farms. There's near need to divide the estate up, to suit them, but their offers will help to push up the overall price.'

'I don't want to delay too long,' Ashley said. 'I've already sacked my manager in Australia and need to get out there before the end of March. I'd love it if everything here was tidied up by then.'

'Theart's quite a tall order. It's a big property to sell.'

'Well, do your best.'

'Our hottest prospect is probably Rural General. They are buying more and more farms with Vacant Possession these days and farming them with employed managers. Their people have been over all your leand twice, but don't be surprised if we don't hear from them for a little while now. Their usual tactic is to make it look as though they've cooled orff – helps to avoid pushing the price up – but if they *do* come in, they usually buy through nominees.'

'So we don't know who has purchased until it's happened?'

'Exeactleah. Does theart worry you?'

'Not in the least. There is one thing, though.' He hesitated and then; 'The one tenanted farm, Cartwright?'

'Ears?'

'Any sign of the tenants going for it?'

'Doubtful.' Marden-Thomas shook his head, making sandy waves of hair tumble over his forehead. 'They lack the fineahncial oomph. I don't rate them at all as buyers.'

'Good.' Ashley felt relieved. 'I'm especially keen that they shouldn't buy.'

'Really? Why's that?'

'Oh,' Ashley avoided his agent's blue-eyed gaze, 'private reasons.' If I've got to go, he thought, I'm damned if they should be allowed to stay. He would never forgive Betty for her betrayal, never!

'Well, I don't think you need worry on that score. They'd never get the finance.'

Marden-Thomas left Ashley to his work and drove to London, keen to get back to the city before the weather got any worse. The red light on his dashboard warned him that the outside temperature was below freezing, in spite of it being midday, and as he cruised down the A1, the snowfall became thicker.

At Cartwright Farm, Betty looked out over the whitening landscape and sighed. Snow was a nuisance on the roads, she knew that well enough, but she loved the soft mantle it laid over the countryside. Beneath its protective blanket, winter cereal plants were safe from damage and, when it melted, the extra water would soak slowly into the ground, building up reserves for next season's growth. Trees on the horizon made dark silhouettes against the brightening background, each species showing up its special characteristics more clearly than usual. Limes, near the village, bristled with young branches along their lower trunks but the three mighty oaks, standing in a group atop one of the hills above Ashley's land were clean-limbed with craggy, gnarled upper branches. The hedgerow ashes pointed grey fingers to the sky but along the Venn, different species of willow, many with ancient, cracked trunks, dropped reddish or parchment-coloured twigs down to the surface of the water. 'I can't bear to think we might lose all this,' she said, turning to John who was on his hands and knees on the sitting room floor, poring over a series of farm plans. She looked back out of the window and watched a fieldfare pecking the remains of a half-rotten Bramley apple she had put out. The snow made its markings more distinct but the average person, she supposed, would still think it was just a thrush. 'What would we do?'

'Steady!' John said from the floor. 'It's not over yet.' The 'we' had made his heart skip a beat. Did she mean 'we' together or 'we' going our separate ways? He looked up and saw her straight back, shoulders and head silhouetted in the light from the window. Her hair was short and disciplined but there was a wispy zone at the top of her neck which made her look, he thought, less robust; more vulnerable. He wanted to kiss the neck and smooth the back hairs. For him, losing Cartwright Farm would be a painful blow but one he could get over. For Betty it would be as bad as bereavement. She might take years to get over it: perhaps she never would. Yet, however sanguine he tried to make their figures look, it was seeming less and less likely that they would be able to stay. They had to buy the land, they had to raise working capital to continue to farm and the earnings they expected to make simply would not cover their costs.

'If only we were able to purchase at an absolute knock-down price . . .' Betty said, not for the first time.

'If!'

'But we can try. We can put in a low bid and see what happens.'

'The only thing is, I wish we could do that without anyone knowing that it's us bidding.'

'Why the secrecy?'

'Can't say really.' He sat back on his haunches, then kicked out his legs to get more comfortable and pushed back his fair hair. He always wore it quite long and when he had first come to Wyckhamby, Betty had wanted to tell him to get a haircut but now, she couldn't think of him looking any other way. Karen had made him wear it shorter but once she had gone again, the hair grew and Betty was glad about that. 'For one thing,' John continued, 'offering a silly price is embarrassing, somehow. For another, Kirkland might want to wreck our purchase. Out of spite.'

'Oh John, really! How many times do I have to tell you? He simply isn't like that. You don't know him the way I do.'

'Don't I? It could have been me he tried to seduce, not you.'

'Stop it!' She folded her arms and glared at him, not angry but feigning anger, like a mother admonishing her child. 'But I agree about the nominee idea. It's more comfortable to do it under a cloak of anonymity.'

'So what do you think we should bid?'

'How low dare we go? Fourteen hundred an acre?'

'Oh no,' he shook his head, 'that's only a whisker below market value. We should drop to at least twelve.'

'If the first offer is turned down, we haven't queered our pitch at all, have we?'

'Of course not. We can start at whatever level we like.'

'Let's make it a round thousand then.'

'That'd work out at less than a quarter of a million for the lot!' He shook his head. 'No, that *is* ridiculous.'

'Mmm.' Betty's eyes were gleaming. 'Two hundred and six thousand, yes, that *is* a bit mean. Tell you what, let's offer two hundred and ten thousand. Can't say fairer than that.'

'Dream on!' John muttered, but they went into the study all the same and, while John looked over her shoulder she telephoned the solicitor and arranged for her to draw up an offer and to act as nominee.

Next morning, Ashley received a phone call from Marden-Thomas. 'I think our friends Rural and General have acted more quickly than we expected. An offer has come through Greenwoods, the Kendale solicitors – nominees, obviously – but not for the whole estate.'

'Well?' Ashley was eager for a result.

'It's not to be taken seriously but they have bid two hundred and ten for the tenanted farm. It's probably just testing water. Neahturally I intend to turn it down, but need your approval to do so.'

'Hold on.' Ashley thought quickly. 'A financial institution as big as Rural General would hardly be interested in owning just a little peasant holding like Cartwright. 'As you say, they're obviously trying to fly a kite with this one, but why don't we call their bluff? If we let them have Cartwright for that pittance, they will be far more committed to purchasing the rest and *then* we could play hard to get, and squeeze the price of the main estate up to a more realistic level. You could even let them suspect that I am desperate to sell at this stage.'

'It's a gamble. I'm not sure it's wise.'

'I am,' said Ashley. 'Go for it!'

'It's against my advice. I've a reputation to consider.'

Ashley thought, don't drivel to me about reputation, you Sloane twat. Look what happened to mine! 'Don't worry about that,' he said aloud. 'You're acting under your client's instructions.'

'But it still—'

'Just do it!' Ashley shouted, and then moderated his tone. 'Please?'

On the morning of 20 February, the kitchen phone at Cartwright Farm made both partners jump. They knew their offer would be turned down but nevertheless, like lottery ticket holders before a draw, had spent the last two days tense with anticipation. Betty answered it.

'Betty, darling, it's me. You'll never guess but I'm here, in London.'

'Sally?'

'Yes! Simon's here too. We want to come to Wyckhamby before we go back but we're not staying long, not this time. It's too cold!' She paused, and Betty wasn't sure what to say. 'Can we come tomorrow?'

'Of course.'

'And, my dear, I know it's rude to ask, but can we scrounge a bed? We've nowhere else to go!' The Old Rectory was already sold and the new occupants, a merchant banker and his horsey wife, were due to move in next month.

'If you like.' Betty's heart sank. She wasn't sure she could handle social graces, not with all this on her mind.

'We'll be ever so good, honest!'

'You'll have to take us as you find us. We're not grand, as you know.'

'Oh, we don't mind! We'll take you out to a posh dinner, how's that? You can ask Ashley Kirkland, if you like. Make a foursome!'

'I don't think so.' Betty laughed at the idea. 'Quite a lot has gone on since your departure.'

'How mysterious you make it sound. Tell me more.'

'You'll find out when you come tomorrow. Give yourselves plenty of time, the roads will probably be quite bad.' Betty extracted an expected arrival time from her and bustled off to air the guest room and review her food stocks while John mooned about the house or shuffled papers in the study. The trouble with snow was that it tended to enforce idleness on a farm.

Betty was shaking the duvet when she heard the phone ring again. John answered and she stood still, hardly breathing so that she could hear his voice, muffled through the closed door.

'Yes,' he said. 'It is . . . Really? . . . Thank you.' His voice sounded flat. She ran down, taking the stairs two at a time.

'Well?' He was standing by the telephone, his face crimson.

'They've accepted our offer. Two hundred and ten, subject to contract.'

'My Lord, John!' Betty began to sway and sat down. 'It's ours. The farm is ours.' She put her arms round him and squeezed. 'It's *ours*.'

'Steady, love,' he said, his cheeks burning. 'This is only a little hurdle, remember. On its own, this is useless. Now we need the planning permission. It's that, or we sell.'

'But for that little! Couldn't we hang on anyway? I'm sure we could.'

'Betty! You're not being realistic.'

'No, I suppose not.' She felt all the elation evaporating. 'But . . . but being so *close*.' She was afraid she might cry. She dabbed her eyes with her apron, went out of the room and threw herself into more housework. Later, calmer, she poked her head round the study door and said to John, 'I'm sick of being stuffed up in this damned house. I'm going to a tramp through the snow. Want to come?'

'OK.' They rugged themselves up with scarves, anoraks and wellingtons and walked off, down Cartwright Lane. The snow had all but stopped and the sky was clearing, promising a sharp frost. They moved so briskly that they were soon breathless, with glowing toes and ruddy faces. After nearly a mile, they slowed their pace and decided to walk back, passing through the village so that John could go to his small cottage. But when they got to the High Street he said, 'I'll walk you back to Cartwright.'

'Oh, there's no need.'

'I don't like to see you go off alone.'

'Ridiculous,' she laughed. 'You're more alone than I. At least I've got Jim for the vacs. And the girls come home from time to time. Gill wants to get married, to a houseman at St Thomas's, did you know? Ridiculous concept! I told her she's far too young, but I'm dying to meet him. He sounds just right for her.'

'I'm not totally alone,' John said. 'Elliot comes for a day or two every holidays.'

'How you must miss him.'

'Karen has had official custody since the divorce came through, but sometimes I don't think she's that interested in him.'

'Have you spoken to her about it?' He looked awkward. 'You haven't, have you?'

He shook his head. 'I hardly like to.'

'You know, John,' she took his hand in hers and swung his arm as they walked, 'I'm fond of you, very fond indeed. But you have one big fault.'

'Only one?'

'You're terribly bad at coming out and saying what you need to say.' She glanced at his face and saw the discomfort. 'Oh, I shouldn't have spoken. Sorry, sorry!' They took a few more paces and she said, 'No, I'm not sorry. It's true. You're far too reticent about things like that.'

'My business.' His tone was clear. She was overstepping bounds. They walked on in silence.

'Elliot adores coming here,' she said, after an interval, 'and he's quite potty about you. Our children never had the relationship with Jack that he has with you. You don't know how lucky you are.'

'I miss him so much.' Betty was surprised to hear the catch in John's voice. She linked her arm through his again and gave it a little squeeze.

'Then why don't you ask Karen if he can spend more time here? If she's indifferent, she'll probably be relieved.' John was silent.

They arrived back at Cartwright Farm feeling better for the exercise but grateful to get into the warm. As they were removing their togs, the phone rang. 'Let it ring,' John said, but Betty answered it before she had taken off her anorak.

'Oh Maggie, hullo!'

'I've been trying you for ages,' Maggie said. 'Where the hell have you been on an afternoon like this?'

'Out for a walk.'

'Good God, what a notion!'

'We both feel miles better for it.'

'Ah,' her voice dropped a semitone. 'I hate to temper your joy but I went to the planning meeting at Kendale this morning.'

'Oh.'

'I'm terribly sorry, Betty, but the proposal was turned down.'

Betty sat down and undid her anorak. 'Did they say why?'

'Not regarded as in-fill in accordance with the structure plan or some such crap.'

'I see.'

'The usual chairman couldn't get in because of the snow so that bloody colonel chaired the meeting. He's a real "build nothing anywhere" type. Prick of the first water!'

'Well, thanks for letting me know, anyway.' How am I going to tell John, she wondered. Then she remembered that Sally and Simon were coming tomorrow. How on earth was she going to be able to put a brave face on all that?

The irony was more than she could bear. They had won the farm but now would lose it. She heard John come into the kitchen. He knew. She erupted into bitter tears. He stood wringing his hands, not knowing what to do. His own eyes filled, not with self-pity, but with the pain she was suffering. He passed her three sheets of kitchen paper and then stood behind her, massaging her shoulders.

'Don't cry, Betty,' he said in a soft voice. 'Please don't cry.'

Sally and Simon arrived next day, in time for lunch. Betty,

subdued and fatigued, had asked John to stay and support her. He had readily agreed.

'Darlings!' Sally cried. 'It's so *cold!*' She was wearing a voluminous, cream-coloured mink coat, matching hat and furlined boots. Betty had expected the baby as well but apparently it was in Mudando with a wetnurse.

'How was your journey?'

'A doddle, wasn't it, Simon? The motorways are all fine, it's just your funny old lane that was nasty. We nearly got stuck there.' She dropped her coat onto the sofa. 'But Betty, we saw the For Sale notices. Such developments! What's going on?' Betty furnished her with details.

'What – Ashley Kirkland, gay? And *broke?*'

'Oh, I don't think he's exactly broke,' John said, 'but he is having to make adjustments.'

'He probably wants to get away from here, too,' Betty said. 'Start a new life.' Those very words made her eyes sting. 'Speaking of which . . .' her eyes filled and she couldn't trust her voice. John took over.

'She's a little upset,' he said, 'because we're on the way out too.'

'You? How could you? This farm is your life!'

'We don't have that much choice.' John explained their predicament.

'My dears, what beastly luck,' Sally said later, as she toyed with the lasagne that Betty had made for lunch and tried to sip her Rheinpfalz without grimacing at its taste. Throughout the visit, although neither Betty nor John meant it to, the subject of their plight kept cropping up. Betty had no idea what she or John would do now. She wasn't yet ready to face the future and certainly did not want to talk about it. She wondered whether she would be able to work with John. What lay ahead was forbidding enough on its own but, she realised, a future without John was a grim prospect and she pushed her mind away from it.

By the time Sally and her new husband had gone, the acuteness of her disappointment had blunted and she realised that they had been a useful diversion. But the reality of their situation haunted them day and night, sapping their energy and preventing them from being able to concentrate on their daily jobs.

'Have you thought about what you want to do yet?' she asked John a few days later, as melting snow turned their lane into a slushy mess.

'A manager's job, I dare say,' he said. 'But I won't start looking for a while. I'm keeping the cottage for the time being anyway.'

'Oh good,' she said, relieved that his departure would not be too soon.

'Anyway, we've still got to get this place sold, and until it is, we have to work as normal.'

'That's going to be the worst part.' Her voice would keep catching and her eyes stinging. 'Farming as though we were to be here for ever, but having no future – no future at all.'

QUANTAS Flight 217 on 20 March was half an hour into its journey from Singapore to Perth when Ashley first clapped his eyes on the cabin steward. The crew had changed at Singapore but by then he was so tired he had hardly taken note of anything and had sat, midway between dozing and wakefulness, his feet swollen from the altitude and his temples throbbing from the steady intake of whisky. It had been a silly extravagance to fly first class but he was glad of the elbow room. Almost all the passengers had disembarked at Singapore but he had decided to stay put while the Malay cleaners tidied up the aircraft around him. Few had got back on board, so on this last leg to Australia each first-class passenger had a member of cabin staff to himself.

More wakeful now, Ashley sat up and found himself looking at the steward as he worked his way backwards, pulling the drinks trolley down the aisle. The trolley came abreast and the steward turned.

'Fancy a drink?' Ashley gazed at the sunny smile, even teeth and sapphire eyes and felt his stomach lurch. He stared for several seconds 'Sir?' The smile widened.

'Oh, er, Scotch please.' He couldn't stop his gaze from

wandering over the steward's frame as he leant over the trolley to scoop up some ice from the chromium bucket. The steward turned with the drink and met his gaze.

'Here we are, mate.' The accent was at odds with his looks – a harsh, roughened sound from the body of an angel.

Ashley refused dinner, the fifth meal he had been offered in twenty hours and dozed. Gradually the other passengers put out their reading lights and Ashley alone was left, wakeful but dopey from fatigue and whisky. He closed his eyes.

'The name's Clive, by the way,' said a voice in his ear. He opened his eyes. The steward had sat down in the seat beside him.

'Ashley,' said Ashley, holding out a hand. Clive kept hold of the hand, traced the callouses in the palm, then turned it over and ran his fingernails over the back.

'G'day, Ashley,' Clive said. 'Nice hands. You a golfer?'

'No, a farmer.'

'In England?'

'Until recently. But I've got a place in Western Australia – Jackson's Creek, out beyond Bunbury. D'you know it?'

'Nope. I'm from Sydney.'

'How old are you, Clive?'

'Twenty-eight, why?'

'Oh, nothing. I just wondered, that's all.' Ashley made no attempt to get his hand back. 'Want to come down and have a look at Casuarina – that's my place?'

'That's pretty civil, Ashley. I'd love to.'

'Then meet me at the airport, after I've come through Immigration.'

'Thanks, I will.' A call button pinged and Clive got up to see to his passenger. 'Too right I will!'

At exactly the same time as Ashley was making his descent into Perth, Betty and John were on their way to London. It was ages since either of them had been out of the country and the unfamiliar landscape surrounding the A1 – greening now, for tomorrow was the first day of spring – added to the mysterious circumstances of their trip. First, a letter had arrived from a firm of London solicitors. They had been asked to come to a meeting at Grosvenor House, on Thursday 20 March at 11 a.m; in the event of their agreeing to come, their expenses would be paid, including overnight accommodation at the hotel.

John had forgotten how exhilarating it could be, driving in London, and once he had got over the initial fright, he set about it with dash and an assertiveness that impressed Betty. At the hotel they both felt decidedly scruffy in such opulent surroundings.

The meeting, they were told, was in a private room. Everyone else was there already and they were escorted to the door. Betty knocked timidly and walked in, followed by John. The first person she saw was Sally, who leapt to her feet and said: 'There you are! How lovely to see you both,' and she embraced and kissed each of them. Simon then intoduced his solicitor, a secretary and a man whose name and function went straight out of her head.

The solicitor, called Evelyn Venables as far as Betty could remember, or was it Venison, said, 'My clients, as you may have gathered, are the Principality of Mudando, represented here by the Prince's son, His Excellency Simon—'

'Oh, come on, Evelyn,' Simon chipped in. 'Let's keep this as informal as possible.' Betty noticed that he was wearing a Cambridge tie. 'The gist of why we asked you both here is this: for various reasons, my father and I have been wanting to acquire property in Britian. We flew here last month, as you know, and by the time we had come up to visit you at Wyckhamby, we had selected and purchased a small piece of your London Docklands. But after staying with you, we were fired with the idea that my father, if he should ever want to come to live in Britian, might be happier on a country estate than in London. He would have plenty of room, a nice garden, a place for his horses and so on. What we have done, therefore, is to acquire the whole of the Wyckhamby Estate, except, of course, for Cartwright Farm, of which you were former tenants and are now owner-occupiers. When we stayed with you, you explained that you would be obliged to sell again because of lack of finance and because the farm would be too small to generate enough income to pay interest.'

'Oh, *I* get it,' John said. 'You want to buy from us to restore the estate to its former size.'

'Wrong, John,' Sally responded immediately. 'We have neither the expertise nor the inclination to farm any of the Wyckhamby Estate. All we would want to keep in hand is the Manor House and about fifty acres surrounding it.'

'Then why are we here?' Betty asked.

'We've asked you up here,' Venables explained, 'to offer you the tenancy of all the farmland and buildings. The Principality has acquired some neighbouring land, too, so it'll be close on three and a half thousand acres in all. Now we've a fair idea that if you are being obliged to sell your own farm, you're obviously short of cash and are therefore unlikely to be able to raise enough working capital to manage such a big operation as the Wyckhamby Estate.'

'You're quite right,' Betty said. 'It's way out of our league.'

'But we don't want you for your money,' Simon said. 'Money's not a problem.'

'The fact is,' Sally said, 'I've seen how you two have survived all this time on that tiny farm of yours.'

'We know you both have all the expertise you need to run Wyckhamby; that you have good local knowledge and, above all, that you are likely to . . .' Simon hesitated, trying to find the right words. 'To care for – no, to *love* the land. We will advance the necessary working capital which you can pay back as part of the rent over, what, twenty years? Your farm profits should cover that comfortably, and give you a pretty decent lifestyle.'

'This may sound silly,' Betty said, 'but we don't want to lose Cartwright.'

'Darling, you don't need to,' Sally said. 'You've got to have somewhere to live, so you might just as well keep title to Cartwright and pay off that loan out of profits, too. You could afford it, your business will be large enough. Or, alternatively, we could buy Cartwright and rent it back to you with the rest.'

'No,' Betty said. 'If we can own it we will.'

'That's just the kind of tenacity that has made us offer you the lease on the estate,' Simon said.

'Look, this is all too much for me to absorb,' Betty said. 'I need time to think it all through, we both do.'

'Of course,' Venables said. 'That is why we arranged accommodation for you here. We do not expect an immediate answer, not even in principle.' Betty and John looked at each other for a few seconds.

'Oh, we don't need time to decide whether to accept or not, do we, John?' Betty said. John, silent and red of face, simply shook his head. 'We just need time to work out exactly how to adjust.'

'Then you do accept, in principle?' All faces were turned to Betty.

'You bet your sweet arse we do!' she said, and then clapped a hand in front of her mouth. 'Ladies and gentlemen, what *have* I said, I *do* beg your pardon.' And everyone laughed.

A year and a day after that meeting, on the spring equinox, the dining room of Wyckhamby Manor was ringing with the cheerful voices of a dozen diners. Sally looked down the long table at her young husband and smiled. On his right, Maggie Bates was fingering her glass, which contained fizzy water, and telling him what a lot of balls it was to suggest that his lake should be doubled in size, and that all it needed was a bloody good dredging. She obviously liked him and he her.

Betty, looking more beautiful than John had ever imagined she could in a simple cream sheath with a huge amethyst pendant on her breast, was listening while Leonard told her about the things she would see when she went on holiday to Kenya next month. On her right, the ambassador of a small African nation listened attentively and added a political contribution or two of his own.

Peregrine and Vanessa, the new people from the Old Rectory, were telling anyone who'd listen how much they had enjoyed the previous weekend at Elaine Kirkland's and her daughter Annabel's new place, La Bastide Anglaise. It was *the* newest, *the* grandest and by miles *the* most expensive of the recent spate of Country House hotels to have opened anywhere in Britain. 'Right in the Yorkshire Dales, yah? *The* most fabulous views – seriously pretty – and the food, my dears! Not much change from a hundred quid a head, yah? Serious money but what a cellar! Serious stuff!'

John sat next to the ambassador's wife. 'Where do you farm?' she asked.

Here,' he said. 'All round here. With my partner.' He indicated Betty, now smiling, now listening and thought how excellently her new wealth suited her, but how wonderfully she had kept her feet on the ground. This morning she'd been up to her waist in baby pigs.

'Your wife is most beautiful woman,' said the ambassador's wife, following John's gaze.

'Oh no, she's not my wife.' He reddened. 'We're business partners.'

'All the same, you very much in love, I think,' the ambassador's wife winked at him. 'You have wife too?'

'I'm divorced.'

'Ah tch! tch!' She clucked in sympathy. 'Children?'

'A son. Elliot. He's eleven.' The ambassador's wife noticed John's eyes go tender. 'He lives with me now, in the village,'

'I think you lovely father,' she said, took a mouthful of lamb and chewed it, smacking her lips. 'You make lovely husband too, no?' She gave him another lascivious wink.

'What a wonderful evening,' Betty said, as John drove her home in the new farm Range Rover. 'Maggie's so rude to Simon, but he loves it!'

'You looked . . . *heavenly!*' She had never heard him say anything of the kind before. She felt there was more.

'John?'

'Mmm?'

'Now that Elliot's with you for good and we're on an even keel, as it were . . .'

'Mmm?'

'What I'm getting at is, well, would you like to move in

with me? You and Elliot, I mean. There's plenty of room at Cartwright.'

There was a silence which lasted the rest of the way home, then: 'Wouldn't really be right, Betty. People might talk.' John switched off the engine and turned to look at her. 'You know, they might think that we . . . you know.' She couldn't see his face but could almost feel the heat of his burning cheeks.

'That's rather what I had in mind.' She sensed him stiffen. The atmosphere between them was almost palpable. 'After a wedding, of course.' He turned his head towards her and, holding his hot cheeks in her hand she kissed the tension away. 'You do care for me a bit, don't you? Don't you?'

In the lane, just behind the Range Rover, a barn owl flew on silent white wings, hunting for voles among the budding cowslips.

THE END

Careby, Lincolnshire 1993